"Through sharply imagined scenes and deft dialogue, with prose so colorful and precise it borders on poetry, Duberstein skillfully conjures a man who finds himself through loss. In this picaresque page turner, *The Hospice Singer* grabs your attention and will not let you go."

—Dale Rosengarten, author of *Grass Roots* and *A Portion of the People*

"Getting inside Ian's head so thoroughly, entertaining us with a delightful cast of characters, and consistently derailing expectations and cliches, Larry Duberstein tells this story with wit, originality, and great heart. *The Hospice Singer* once again rewards us with the Duberstein touch of sweet, sad surprise."

—Joan Baum, book critic for Connecticut's NPR station WSHU

"This is a nuanced and intimate portrait of a man paddling through the swamp of a late midlife crisis. *The Hospice Singer* finds Larry Duberstein at the top of his game as he masterfully explores the tragedy behind all human comedy—and vice-versa."

—Marc Schuster, author of *Tired of California* and *The Grievers*

THE
HOSPICE SINGER

A novel

LARRY DUBERSTEIN

3

Also by Larry Duberstein

NOVELS

The Marriage Hearse
Carnovsky's Retreat
Postcards From Pinsk
The Alibi Breakfast
The Handsome Sailor
The Mt. Monadnock Blues
The Day the Bozarts Died
The Twoweeks
Five Bullets

STORIES

Nobody's Jaw
Eccentric Circles

THE
HOSPICE SINGER

A novel

LARRY DUBERSTEIN

Rootstock Publishing
Montpelier, VT

First Printing: May 2022

The Hospice Singer, Copyright © 2022 Larry Duberstein

Release Date: May 3, 2022

Hardcover ISBN: 978-1-57869-085-5
Softcover ISBN: 978-1-57869-084-8
eBook ISBN: 2021923405

Library of Congress Control Number: 2022900434

Published by Rootstock Publishing
an imprint of Multicultural Media, Inc.
27 Main Street, Suite 6
Montpelier, VT 05602 USA

www.rootstockpublishing.com

info@rootstockpublishing.com

Book design by Eddie Vincent, ENC Graphic Services
(ed.vincent@encirclepub.com)

Cover design by Jamie Kirby

Cover art by Kim Cunningham: "March, Troy NH," linoleum block print, 12" x 12", ©2002

Author photo credit: Chris Justice

For permissions or to schedule an author interview, contact the author at
brimstonecorner@yahoo.com.

Printed in the USA

Part One

How Can I Keep From Singing

NOTHING SHOCKED THEM. Their very reason for being in this stranger's house precluded shock or even surprise, given the range of extremes they had all witnessed.

Last month they sang for Ada Crouch, her palimpsest-textured face the same color as the off-white pillowcase behind it and so motionless through the entire hour that her son in ushering them out felt obliged to give assurance his mother had greatly enjoyed the music when all they truly wondered was whether she was in fact still among the living.

And maybe wondered, just slightly, whether the son, named Sonny, was entirely sane. Ian was not the only one to whom the thought of Norman Bates and his dear old mum had occurred. But none of it had come close to shocking them.

Ian's wife Polly felt the whole enterprise was at root so inherently shocking that, forced into posing as "the bringers of eternal peace," they were likewise forced to present a false composure. Euphemism was a clue: to call dying "a phase of life" might be true literally, but it was false emotionally. And Polly, a doctor of the mind with three diplomas on her office wall, knew what she was talking about.

Tonight, however, Ian would have confessed to shock. No version of horror was too horrible, not when horror was what they bargained for.

It was the opposite of horror that knocked him back, the apparent health and unquestionable beauty of the client. When a young, buoyant creature greeted them at the front door, bringing them into a warm room with tribal rugs on the floor and colorful paintings on every wall, when she brought out a tray of pastries and a silver coffee service, he assumed this must be the sister. They often got a sister. Later on they would all agree that this felt more like walking into a book group than a hospice sing.

Then Karin asked her, "Are you alone in the house tonight?" and her answer ("Yes, but then I generally am") made clear she was not the sister, not a friend. She was, somehow, the client. Noticing their reaction, she added with a tiny wry smile, "I suppose I should have had someone wheel me out in my pajamas."

Not bedridden, not in pajamas, Anita Richardson was dressed in standard northern New England fashion, blue jeans and a checked flannel shirt. Each of these garments, the shirt with top button undone and the jeans fitting nicely, contributed to the picture of a lovely, healthy woman. Lovely was one of his mother's words. Ian could hear her assessment: Doesn't she have a lovely figure! Both words, lovely and figure, comprising her generation's nomenclature for what the world now called bodies. Good *bodies*, if not something more specific.

Ian placed himself halfway between generations. Having come through the late 1960s, he was not about to pretend he did not notice. On the other hand, best not to dwell on her *body* when they had come here to sing her to the grave. He was processing all this when the young woman directed her next remark at him, particularly, her eyes almost commandeering his. "I know what you're thinking and if it's any help, it seems strange to me too."

He was sure she had chosen his face at random, the way when speaking to a group you did tend to settle your eyes on a single target for your remarks. Still, it felt personal and he struggled to maintain the distance she had so quickly closed. He was blushing as he turned toward Karin for guidance, expecting her to take the handoff, but Karin left him stranded while the client continued to smile at him expectantly.

"It's just that"—he paused, still getting no help, singled out, stuck saying it—"you look a lot healthier than any of us do."

And with this Ian had broken two cardinal rules at a blow. He had related to the client Outside the Group and he had broached the unspoken: *We are not here to administer the last rites.* But hadn't she been the one who broached it? In any case, she was still speaking directly to Ian as she went on. "You feel you were lured here under false pretenses, right? That I was in the mood for a free concert."

"No," he said too hastily, forgetting himself to the point where he was simply making conversation. As he would learn, Anita Richardson had the knack of making that happen. "But honestly? I thought you must be your sister. *Her* sister, I should say. When you came to the door looking so—"

"I am definitely not my sister," she said, with a markedly different tone, as though "sister" was a dirty word. Something behind that. "And appearances notwithstanding, the medical establishment assures me there will be no miracles. So I do hope you'll sing."

They never chatted about prognoses, about what lay ahead. Never. What they discussed, provided a client was even fit for discussion and inclined to engage in it, was the weather or the music. What they had done in their working lives. With men, there might be some sports nonsense. Requests were not unusual, and over the years they had extemporized a few numbers—"singing beyond the songbook," Karin called it. More typically they just listened, in a quiet inward way. If Ian saw a smile or a peaceful expression, he imagined the client was recalling a moment from the past, from a time when death was impossible rather than imminent. If a client spoke, it was usually to praise the singing or say thank you.

Everything settled into place when the singing began and from there it went smoothly. Asked if she wished to hear anything in particular, Ms. Richardson demurred wordlessly with a dreamy negative shake of the head indicating that the singers knew best. Ian had the impression she was making an effort to accommodate them, tamping down the display of energy that had upset their expectations. But she did not know their rules of engagement and would unknowingly create another issue as they were leaving. The others were already outside stamping their feet in the snow when Anita Richardson touched Ian's arm lightly and spoke to him: "You know my name but I didn't hear yours."

Of course she didn't. Policy dictated as much. Yet here she was asking, waiting for Ian to add to his dossier of violations. "Well no," he said. "There was only one of you. Five of us."

"Still. You must have one."

"A name?" He hesitated, but there was no escaping it. "Yes. I'm Ian Nelson."

"Well then, goodnight, Ian, and thank you all again so much." Thanking them all, though only Ian was close enough to hear it. "People do steer clear if they know your goose is cooked. Your presence, your being present, was more helpful than you can know."

As the door closed over her face, Ian could still see it, some sort of hologram effect. Pretty was such an indefinable word, 90 percent subjective. One man's meat and all that. For him, in Ms. Richardson's case, it resided in the way her green eyes turned merry and liquid when charged by her smile. Well, it was in the features themselves, the eyes and the lips, but the smile was what advanced it beyond the subjective.

Now as he braced for discipline—the knives would come out in what Karin's husband Philip termed the "post-game huddle"—Ian could only hope the thickening snow might cut short tonight's hash-up. But all he got was one quick jab from Harv ("Glad you could join us") before the talk became general. The truth was they all felt the occasion had been unique, perhaps enough so to justify some lapses. Never had they come away from a sing with the consensus that the client buttressed *them*, not the other way around. Karin confessed she had flashed on an image of this client abruptly turning the tables and singing for them.

"I can tell you that is one strong woman. You know, over the phone she told me she felt just fine—except for the headaches. When the headaches come, she collapses in agony. When they don't come, she bakes."

"She sure does," said Ted Curtin. "Great cookies. You have to schedule an encore, Karin. The cookies and the *brownies*."

There might be an encore, there might not. Sometimes one sing was enough for the client; they found no benefit in it. Even if a second concert was requested it might not come to pass, as between every tonight and every tomorrow lay the unexploded ordnance called death. Their people had the one thing in common, that they would all die soon.

Carter Hodge was the outlier. Given two months to live when hospice came to claim him, Carter lasted two years, long enough to break the mold and become a friend. One night he interrupted their serenade (Carter's word for it, rendered with his characteristic twinkle) to joke about being billed for their services—they had already serenaded him half a dozen times. When he did prove mortal, Karin discovered he had arranged for "payment in full" by leaving the Angel Band five thousand dollars in his will. "For gas money," it said.

The snow tapered and the wind settled, leaving behind a dome of crisp December air. Had it continued whipping in his face Ian might not have ventured downtown for his ritual decompression ramble along the River-walk. The walking and the alternate hush and rush of the water navigating between the granite-block retaining walls could provide a baffle between the emotions of a sing and the reliably comfortable moment when he rejoined Polly at home. The contrast was just so intense: he and Polly dishing up some Cherry Garcia ice cream and teeing up a Netflick while the client, Ian could not un-know, would have lapsed back into discomfort and fear. If those emotions were unusually well concealed by tonight's client, it didn't mean they weren't there. She was either brave or putting up a brave front. Either way, good on her for managing it.

Faux lantern fixtures along the bridge picked out highlights on the water and on the thin crusts of ice that had formed at the turnings. Ian stopped halfway across the bridge for some time—he could not have said how long, five minutes or twenty-five—as he felt a sort of torpor taking him over. Normally these night walks cleared his head but tonight, though he had been energized leaving the sing on Brierly (fleeing the scene, really, after bungling so many of the protocols), that surge had flagged before he reached the downtown. Drained and weary though it was barely eight o'clock, he was reminded of how he felt in the days before he discovered the "problem" he had begun to notice in his chest was that he needed triple bypass surgery.

"How was it?" said Polly, uncharacteristically. She was usually hands-off, almost the way she would be with one of her therapy patients. *Let them tell what they choose to tell.*

"It was a good night. Everyone in sync."

"And the customer?"

"Very appreciative. The snow stopped, so I walked to the river afterwards. Funny thing is, I suddenly felt so tired I could have fallen asleep standing up on the Ruggles Bridge."

"The cold air can do that. But you know, this business—it is something big to absorb. You sing your songs and maybe you go for a walk or a beer, but at some point your brain must remind you that your audience is back there dying."

"Not only do I never forget that, Harv is always there to remind me. One of his riffs: we're with the band, it was a great gig, and hey, if no one was dying we'd be out of work."

"Cute."

"That's Harv. But humor is welcome. A walk to the water is too. Washed clean, you know."

"Chilly tonight, I imagine. The water."

"No worries, I didn't stay in for long."

She had checked in. Maybe his low energy showed, like Tinker Bell's light fading. Not that she asked about the music or the client, Polly never did that. Less typically, this time Ian did not get around to telling her.

Much of the snow had melted by Saturday and the sun was blinding as they drove to Mill Street Eats for their standard weekend breakfast—the spinach omelet for Polly, bacon and eggs for Ian. "Heart healthy victuals," he grinned. Polly had stopped reminding him the opposite was true.

In the afternoon she went up for her Saturday nap and Ian took Fred a few miles down the railroad trail. He drew a dirty look from a couple of joggers trying to shame him into leashing poor Fred, who hated the leash and who would never do her business where anyone might step in it. She was a dog, but she was twice as fastidious as any human.

They came back up Liberty Ave. and continued through the wrought iron portal to Watchman Park and the pond. Ian enjoyed seeing the oldsters (possibly his age or younger) guide their remote-controlled iceboats, adding body English and eccentric dance moves to the quiet work their fingers were doing. Though these men had no doubt noticed Ian and Fred, there had never been an exchange of pleasantries. They never spoke a word to one another either, though clearly (winter or in the summer, when their iceboats were traded in for miniature yachts) it was a little club whose members enjoyed being together.

At the southern boundary of the park, where Fred liked to pee on a particular white oak tree (designated the Squirrel Oak on account of the daily episodes of the long-running serial Dog Trees Rodent), Ian realized they were just above Brierly, one block from the house where they sang a couple of nights ago. Brierly and the streets it crossed made up a neighborhood known as Below the Park. For some reason, humble Blaine named its neighborhoods the way Manhattan did; Ian and Polly lived at the outer edge of Park Entry.

The houses on Brierly, Longleaf, and Catamount had been built between 1900 and 1925: wood frame, steeply pitched, gable dormered, tightly clapboarded structures with a quarter acre in front and half an acre behind. He knew that bedded beneath the snow in back, most of those houses had small productive gardens. The client's house was one of the simpler ones, almost a cottage, and seeing it now by daylight Ian associated it with the houses in Saroyan's California, with their message of the simple values, family and community, that were said to be receding from American life.

North American life, he heard Jack Sutcliffe's voice chime in, correcting that detail of his daydream. The rest he could correct for himself; he knew his gloss was impressionistic and sentimental. Just as a dying woman lived behind the handsome front door at 85 Brierly, each of the other doors closed over all manner of conflict, stress, and grief. The only harmony created by the white clapboards and milled window trim was visual. Even in Saroyan's human comedy there was tragedy lurking behind the façade.

Glioblastoma. Karin was the one who knew that night—by now, of course, they all knew. There had been no signs of ill health, just a routine checkup and one day later a phone call placing Anita Richardson on Death Row. Ian certainly knew the drill. You went about your business—eating your vegetables, saying your prayers, being kind to all—and yet there occurred a tiny tug in your chest, a sensation of something blossoming in there, and hours later they were cracking you open on the operating slab.

Polly was still upstairs when he and Fred got back to the house, so Ian went to the small office they shared (a converted pantry off the kitchen that they called Googleville) and Googled "glioblastoma." He spelled it wrong, naturally, but the Google knew what he meant and spewed forth a plethora of articles, some with only a paragraph to offer, others containing pages dense with data. An hour later, he was ready to pose as an expert on the subject.

Five of them crowded into Karin's Outback and rode over to Barlow to meet the Warring Sisters. Karin ran it down for them on the way: the younger sister wanted the sing, the older sister opposed it, the middle sister, the one who lay dying, had not registered a vote. "I'm not sure how the deadlock was broken," said Karin, "but here we go."

They were met at the front door by the older sister, who informed them they would not be allowed inside the house. "Off to a flying start!" said Bill Crichton, as they huddled back in the car with the heat going.

"Start?" said Ted. "It seems we are finished, no?"

"Let me try the young one on her cell," said Bill. "She might not even know we're here."

"The 'young one' does have a cell," said Karin, "but she is over fifty. You make her sound like she might be into Katy Perry."

"Tony Bennett, then? The gateway to Lady Gaga?"

"No. Here's what we're going to do, people," said Karin. "We'll stand right below that window and sing. Outdoors, like carolers. Call us cool."

"Call us cold," offered Ian. "It's eighteen degrees."

"Look," said Karin. "The gatekeeper there is not our client. I think we owe it to the client to give it a shot."

So, standing below the soft-lit window in a light stinging snow and, having been apprised that Celia Kingsbury loved the classic hymns, they launched into "The Old Rugged Cross" before noticing that the window sash had just been raised a few inches. They were set to do "How Great Thou

Art" when the door opened and a thin gray-haired woman in a thick gray sweater leaned out to motion them in. "The coast is clear," she said. "Edith has gone up to bed."

Ian's first thought was that this was a job for Polly. Here was a tricky family dynamic indeed. He thought of Lear's three daughters and was trying to recall their names as they shook off their coats in a vestibule. He came up with two (this benign one was the Cordelia, gatekeeper Edith was the Goneril) and was still chasing after the third daughter's name when Karin led them inside. They went in single file, as always, and with the goal of *making ourselves small* if anyone could figure out how that was accomplished. Naturally there were jokes whenever Hank Hinckley, all three hundred pounds of him, was with the group.

In what looked like a makeshift sickroom off the kitchen, they formed their semi-circle at the foot of a bed that seemed, at first, to be occupied only by a pile of quilts. Bill's nose had returned from deep purple to its normal shade of pink and his opening bass line, *Oh Lord my God*, was sufficiently resonant to make an empty water glass tremble and cue the four-part harmony. When the lead came back to Bill and he ended with his voice-of-God notes from an undiscovered octave, a woman's face emerged from the pile of quilts and spoke. "Bless you, you wonderful people. I so hope my sister didn't—"

Here she broke off, falling into a rattle of deep coughing that left the Cordelia to complete her sentence. "She hopes you can excuse Edith's inhospitality. Edie wants to do right, she is just a bit overprotective."

"Edie believes," said Celia, her coughing spell for the moment resolved, "one's final days should be empty. *Quiet* is her word, empty is my translation. Thank you so much for filling in this particular night for me."

She wept softly through "Softly and Tenderly" and having no voice or strength by the end of their program, blew them a kiss, her stringy arm emerging to make a motion like that of a child waving away a blown soap bubble. The Cordelia stepped outdoors with more thanks and an apology. "I meant to bake something for you, but the day got away from me."

"No problem at all," said Karin, though it was a problem, such that they made a pit stop at the Barlow General Store for a gigantic bag of corn chips and five candy bars. The car was warm, the mood was breezy, and they sang "Over the Rainbow" on the drive back to Blaine.

Polly had been surprised to learn that the aftermath was usually this way, lighthearted and comradely. She expected that witnessing death up close would leave them downcast. But Poll did not sing. She did not grasp the way singing, making music under any circumstances, uplifted those who made it. Devout atheists could be moved to tears by a song they barely registered was about belief, just as they could rise and clap, their hearts made full, by a song in praise of Jesus the Son of God.

Polly didn't dance either. She liked to say that she expressed herself in words.

Tonight's sing provided more than the usual jolt, partly by giving them three amusing characters to discuss and partly because it had started so badly and ended so well. Plus, they agreed they had been of some small value to Celia Kingsbury. It appeared as if hearing those familiar melodic hymns from behind her shuttered eyes, she might well be picturing the bright green pastures of Heaven as she drifted in and out of a peaceable sleep.

They were going back to the young woman on Brierly—The Blastoma, as Harv, who classified them by ailment, called her. Because they had sung for Lear's daughters a week earlier, Ian and Harv were dropped from the starting lineup. There were eighteen singers in all and juggling the Angel Band roster was an art Karin likened to coaching a basketball team, you could only play five at a time.

Then when Ward Longstreet came down with a cold, Ian was asked if he would mind coming off the bench last minute. Knowing him for a constant walker, as an enticement Karin offered to let him walk over ("It's in your neighborhood") and meet them at the site. Ian was fine with that, though he needed no persuading and no special concessions. He was mildly intrigued by the pretty client—he could admit as much to himself, at least—and curious to see if she still looked so untouched by her tragic condition.

Getting places early was deeply ingrained in Ian Nelson. His parents regularly attended a nine o'clock church service and he'd learned early on that quarter of nine was "shaving it close." If you planned on being literally punctual, Ian's father preached, you risked being late. This was his approach to everything. He spoke in terms of *margins* as the key to success. In tennis, his sport, going for the lines meant going for a spot three feet inside the line.

Ian arrived well within the margin, content to wait, enjoying the sting of the chill night air on his face. Unfortunately, The Blastoma must have been at the window because she spotted him and, opening the door, leaned out to accuse him. "Lurking!"

"Sorry," he said awkwardly, as though he really had been lurking.

"Me too, I meant to put on pajamas," she said with a grin, "so you wouldn't think I was my sister." She surprised him by remembering that brief exchange. After all, wasn't it her brain that was supposedly compromised? Amazing she could be so sharp mentally and so fit physically on the verge of death. Life is funny, he thought, and so is death.

"Please come in from the cold. I have coffee ready."

"I'm fine," said Ian. "I should wait for the others."

Anita Richardson did not know the drill and Ian was constrained from explaining that they always arrived as a group, went inside as a group. (*We do not discuss the process, lest it be seen as a process.*)

"That's silly," she said. "It's freezing."

He found himself trapped, forced to choose between two further violations of protocol, going inside solo or elaborating his reason for demurring. Then it got worse. "All right then," she said, "if you won't come in, I'll come out."

She leaned back, grabbed a green parka and a green watch cap, and walked out to join him at the mailbox. As they stood there making conversation, Ian felt like a small boy fearing the wrath of the school principal after a spit-balling incident. *I am a grown man in my sixties*, he told himself in an attempt to quell this childish anxiety, but it kept bumping up against reality: *Karin will shoot me for this.*

What had they spoken about? What had they said in the five or six minutes they had stood together in the cold, Anita lively and lighthearted, Ian unable to match her mood for worrying. Worrying about the young lady to begin with, compromising her health just to be hospitable. Worrying about Karin's swift astringent justice.

When Ian joined the Angel Band, Harv had cued him: "If you bust protocol, she will bust your chops. Our wonderful, selfless jefe does not always bring the Kumbaya." Ian was a big boy and could handle criticism from others, Karin included. He was his own severest critic, though, and hated to violate his own deeply held moral code—son of a pastor, that was always there. And making himself the story at a hospice sing constituted a clear enough violation.

Right now, walking slowly home, he set all that aside and worked at reconstructing the conversation, calling up her breezy remarks throughout which death was nothing more than a stray, glancing detail. When she brought it up ("My condition, in case you wondered . . .") Ian did not cop to having Googled it. Instead, he feigned ignorance, asked the expected questions. Those questions were necessarily grim, but Anita could not respond to a single one without making him smile.

Had she undergone radiation? "No. They did promise me an extra month or two on Earth in exchange for losing my hair. I chose the hair."

Ian might have said "great choice" had they been two people bantering normally (he had already noticed that her hair was full and wavy, undiminished) but given the context he restrained himself and asked about chemotherapy.

"I voted no on chemo too. With apologies to the poet, I decided I would rather just go gently into that good night."

She had even stopped taking the prescribed drug, a busload of prednisone. "It made my head look like Charlie Brown's. But get this. Ibuprofen was the one drug that did help with the headaches, so they warned me off it on grounds it would be bad for the stomach lining. I was like, are you kidding? We are worried about the long-term effects on my stomach lining?"

It was impressive that Anita could find humor in her fatal condition, but he felt he was on shaky ground laughing along with her. Soon there would be Karin approaching like a chill wind from the east. Right and wrong notwithstanding, it could not look good if they drove up and the headlights caught him joking around with the client. What was the new word? *Optics.* The optics would be bad.

"Hadn't you better get back inside where it's warm?" he said finally.

"I've been inside all day. Really, Ian, this air feels lovely."

His name again. A better brain than most, blastema notwithstanding. Freshly made acquaintances, book titles, film titles—they were all instantly elusive to him now, and his was a brain supposedly intact. Meanwhile, Anita was off and running about her KPS ("Karnovsky Performance Score, for the very few who don't know") and the further medical follies that came with it. For, a week ago, they had emailed her a printout pegging her KPS at sixty. No elaboration, no words of comfort, just the devastating number. Ian went on pretending to be "one of the very few" unaware of what such a number signified.

"It was like 'bad job, girl, old death gaining on you now!' Then yesterday I get another email casually correcting a clerical error. It seems I actually racked up a seventy. I felt so much better I almost didn't mind that they fucked up so egregiously."

Egregiously, no less. After apologizing to Dylan Thomas. Besides being full of life in the grip of death, Anita Richardson was also full of words and thoughts. What a waste, he could not help lamenting, that the world would soon be losing her.

He had a dream that night in which the Angel Band appeared at the foot of his bed and began singing a song he had urged them, so far unsuccessfully, to take on. Someone had put a beautiful melody to Tennyson's poem "Crossing the Bar"—*Let there be no moaning at the bar / When I put out to sea*—and the resulting song was gorgeous, stately, and above all apt, yet no one else voted to add it to the set list.

Which did not prevent them from singing it to him in the dream, the one he woke from just before five a.m. Polly stirred and kept sleeping but Fred was quick to take advantage. Awake, Ian was fair game. Fred could lie as still as a fur tree (her fur, their joke) until Ian emerged and reached for his water glass. Then it was game on, with Fred pacing, leaning, sighing—whatever it took to flush Ian out and get her day going. He took her out to the backyard to pee, then doled out the dry kibble she craved as if it was sirloin. This was all routine.

Getting back in bed at this point was not routine for Ian, it was rare.

He did not always welcome Polly's interpretations, her certainty, as though dreams were never subjective, but he was eager to hear what she made of this one. He made the tea and brought it to her in bed, offered to pay her hourly rate.

"OK, were you in the band? In other words, were you singing to yourself?"

"How could I have been?"

"Ian, it was a dream. You could have been all five singers. There could have been fourteen monkeys in the choir. It was a dream."

"You know, I'm not sure the singers even had faces. Or faces I took in."

"The voices, then? It does matter whether you were both the listener and the singer."

"Lay out the possibilities for me."

"Let's wait on that. I'm pretty sure you're going to have this dream again. Pay closer attention next time. See if you are with the group."

"How can I decide to pay attention if I am inside a dream? Give me a hint, Poll. I really don't get it."

"Here's what I will say. These sings have started to be more about you than about the people you sing to."

"In a bad way?"

"I didn't say that. Good? Bad?" Polly extended her arms, palms faceup, and seesawed them up and down to indicate a balance. Ian knew she would offer no more on the subject.

Jack Sutcliffe did not welcome Fred as a visitor to his winter paradise. Granted the fish were underneath the ice sheet but according to Jack "they always know who is on the roof." Ian brought the dog anyway and left her in the car with a promise to hit the Dinsmore Falls Diner for a big second breakfast on the drive home. Fred loved their home fries.

Jack set up camp about a hundred yards out on Hollow Lake. Every December, he pulled his shanty over the thick ice, assembled the grill, bored holes for his tip-ups, and planted the Belfast flag. All of it, Jack included, would remain in place until instinct (informed by generations of experience, his own and that of his forebears) told him ice-out was imminent. Jack could read the ice the same way he could read the rivers in spring; he knew the secret mutterings of water in all its forms.

When Jack was surly—today, for example—he was given to complaint, though he never would have allowed anyone to call it that. He did make complaint palatable by dressing it out with humor. To Ian's meaningless boilerplate how-are-you, Jack shook his head: "Diminished."

"As in what? Shorter? Thinner?"

"Thinner, doubtful. Shorter, yes. After the age of fifty we all start getting shorter."

"I guess that means I'm diminished too."

"You? Hell, they took a little piece of your heart, didn't they?" Jack was spooning grounds into the boiling water for his cowboy coffee. "That's old Janis Joplin, you know."

"Not exactly—" Ian began, with regard to his heart, not to old Janis. His heart, though it had been "attacked," was still all there. Jack was on a roll, though, and cut him off.

"They take your height and your heart and that's not all by a long shot. They keep chipping away. Running, gone. Walking, on its way. This contraption they gave me isn't for walking, it's for leaning. Hey, soon enough they'll take away leaning too."

"You aren't by any chance having trouble adjusting to turning eighty, are you?"

"They told me I had to swim and damned if I didn't do it. In that exercise puddle over in Dexterville."

"You went to a gym?"

"Call that a gym? Ian Nelson, I know a gymnasium when I see one. That joint, the so-called Movement Center? It's just a bunch of old folks trying to keep moving. *Yoga* classes! Safe to assume you're having coffee?"

"If you call that coffee."

"So far they haven't taken taste away. I still like to eat, still like a good cup of coffee. Bastards did take away orgasm, though."

"They did?"

Ian had to smile at the unlikely swerve Jack's tirade had taken. In the first twenty-five years of their friendship, he had never heard a mumbling word from Jack Sutcliffe on the subject of sex. He had thought it might be banned outright in the north of Ireland! Then there had been an admission, a reference to a certain lady in Willow Falls who was "not exactly a prostitute" and who Jack visited now and then. Only a friend, was Vanessa.

"I saw that look," said Jack. "What's this old man doing talking about orgasm."

"No—"

"Oh yes, I saw the look. But damn it, orgasm is good and I miss it."

"Did they take it away . . . recently?"

"That's okay, laddie. It's okay for a youngster to be curious about such matters. Do your research, by all means. What are you up to now, sixty?"

"Sixty-six," said Ian. "Hardly a youngster."

"When you get to eighty, sixty-six will feel like childhood play to you. Hell, you still have running and walking *and* orgasm, don't you?"

"Well—"

"Uh-huh. I share and tell, and you don't."

"I was getting to it. Yes, to taste and orgasm, but I never did run or pay a visit to a movement center. Never went in for exercise in the modern sense."

"I hated that damned pool, laddie. I will swim in the sea, every chance. Or here in the lake. But push myself back and forth in that chlorinated concrete swamp? They can keep that one."

"My doc used it as a threat. He said if I promised to walk a minimum of two miles a day, he wouldn't sentence me to the pool."

"Pool feels okay after you're out. Might even feel a benefit afterward. No such delay—deferred gratification, is it?—with taste or orgasm. That's in the now, as they say. Living in the Now."

"That is what they said fifty years ago, Jack. Hippies?"

"Those hippies were fortunate I didn't shoot them. Out here all summer, skinny-dipping and more. But did I hate them or was I envious? I knew just enough to wonder."

"And?"

"And it's time to check the tips, see if I have something to taste at suppertime."

Jack's protestations notwithstanding, he was a stubborn, sturdy old Celt, capable of "doing for himself" for many more years. Driving away from the

Hollow, Ian felt sure that whenever Jack's time did come, he would not be inviting the Angel Band over for cowboy coffee or gentle melodies. Jack would go out on his own terms and those would include a heavy dose of unnecessary suffering. Probably he would refuse the morphine and just grouse about the pain.

Although there was a sing in Union Mills, this time Ian was riding the pine for real. Winter was the busiest time, though, with plenty of opportunities, so one rarely minded missing the cut. Ian and Polly had become stay-at-homes since the weather turned, seeing few friends, never dining out, and he suggested they scout out the new brewpub on Washington. The early buzz was good.

Polly had to stay late at her office, though, keying in session notes that had been piling up in her chicken scratches for a month. She could only translate her own written notes if the memory of writing was reasonably fresh. Like groceries, she would say, they had a definite shelf life.

So he watched the news, fed himself a packet of Trader Joe's ribs he found in the freezer, walked Fred, read his way forty pages into a book about the Spanish Civil War, then got up to walk Fred again. Supposedly Watchman Park had become a bit sketchy at night. In Blaine that meant drugs and if there was crime it would be robbery to acquire funds for buying. You read about it in the paper, though. Ian had not heard of anyone having a problem firsthand.

Though it was true, he mused as they circled the pond, that no one else he knew frequented the park at night. Maybe, he remarked to Fred, we will be the first to have a tale to tell. But they came through the park unscathed and as they were exiting at the Brierly end, Ian wondered about Anita Richardson. A couple more weeks had passed. If they walked past her house, would he be able to tell? If the lights were on, would that prove she was still alive? Pretty much everyone in the Angel Band checked the obituaries to see where their recent clients stood. Was it so different to check a house?

Jack Sutcliffe had said it, no harm in being curious. The only harm here was in getting caught again. He didn't see her at first, then he did; she was standing on the front stoop wrapped in a blanket. "Hey there," she said, "did you come to sing me a solo?"

"I'm not good enough to sing solo," he managed. "I need the group to drown me out."

"Ah, modesty. One of the seven deadly virtues."

"I guess you're feeling okay? Out in the cold again?"

"Clear night, so many stars. I get tired of sitting still inside. But who's your friend? Aren't you going to introduce me?"

"Sorry. Anita, this is Fred. Fred, this is Anita."

She was already greeting Fred at ground level, enveloping the dog in her blanket and swaddling her. "She's very sweet, isn't she? Fred, though?"

"It's short for Fred."

"I should have guessed. Well, Fred just whispered to me that she would like a treat, so we'll go in, just for a minute. Come along if you like."

The "minute" made it hard to say no, though the easy way she got him talking made it highly unlikely the stay would be that brief. The infractions just kept on coming. But then, he reasoned, if they were called to lift Anita's spirits by singing, how did it make sense refusing to talk to her?

"Here's a question," she said, "if you don't mind. And you may."

They were at a small table in the corner of the kitchen, Anita sipping water, Ian the tumbler of scotch she insisted would do him good. "This is not about me, it's about you, or your group, and it might sound dumb. But I've wondered if you go to the funerals. I mean, once you lose a customer, do you just cross them off the list?"

How to say that their "customers" were rarely people they got to know, or that going to dozens of funerals was not really a healthy way of life. Though Jack had told him about a fellow in Boston who went to all the Catholic services because there was always plentiful food and drink on offer afterwards.

"We have all been to a few of those. These days they call them celebrations of life, or memorials. Funeral sounds too funereal."

"Do you follow up in some way? With the families?"

"There was one family where I did the exact opposite of following up. Four brothers, and the youngest died in his forties. I liked those guys, but for some reason I avoided them after he died. Saw Ralphie at Lufler's one day—the hardware store?—and I dodged over an aisle so he wouldn't see me. I honestly don't know why. You confront the dying, how hard can it be to say hello to the living?"

Why was he telling her this? This was an incident about which he felt distinctly ashamed. He had never mentioned it to a soul. Something about Anita Richardson put him off his guard. They were well past the proposed minute by now, soon enough they would be past the half hour.

"I do have another question, one I would love to ask all of you. Really, it's more of an essay test: of all the concerts you have given, which was the hardest. And why. Five hundred words or less."

"Mine was the kid," Ian blurted out, and this too he had never spoken about, not even to Polly. "A ten-year-old child."

"Oh dear, it would be a child," she said, drawing a breath and letting it back out. "I never thought of that."

"I nearly died once. Very nearly. I was fifty-seven at the time, though, and had enjoyed a fair portion of my life. I used to joke that it would be my contribution to the average age of death. We can't all get to ninety, you know, not if we want to maintain the average. But here was this skinny little kid—"

"You wonder about God," she said. Ian thought she definitely had grounds to wonder if her "contribution" to maintaining the average was roughly half a life.

"He was a musical prodigy, an accomplished cellist. He enjoyed our singing, at least he said he did, but he couldn't help offering a little critique after each song. About pacing, or tone. About the soprano coming in a shade flat. Always with this cute shrug of apology, like maybe he was helping us out?"

"I should not have asked," said Anita.

"No, I probably shouldn't have answered," he said, miming the zip-your-lips gesture. Ian had cried at that boy's bedside and Karin had reprimanded him later: "It's not about *you*."

"You said you nearly died." Ian was standing now, time to leave, but Fred, curled at Anita's feet, did not budge and neither did Anita. "Of what?

If you will forgive one more thoroughly impolite question."

"Heart," he said, patting it. "I'm fine now. Better off than the Tin Man." This, a regular riff between Ian and Doc Wiggins, was his standard line for blunting sympathy.

"So you know."

"The fear? Yes. I had pretty good odds, though. I had a decent prognosis. Not that I believed it. Doctors, you know. But I did believe it *might* be the truth. Not like it was—"

"Curtains?"

Ian just breathed. Shook his head in wonder at where the talk had gone, and in admiration of her incredible *sangfroid*, though he was never entirely confident he knew what the word meant.

"Well, for your sake and mine, I am glad you beat the rap." She laughed as, sensing his discomfort, she ruffled Fred's feathers and finally rose to let the minute, which had lasted an hour, expire. He thanked her for the scotch, wished her a peaceful night, and bowed himself out.

Two minutes later they were going back through the park and four minutes later Fred was paying respects to her favorite tree. Ian had often wondered how long it might be before Fred, left to her own devices, unlocked her nose from the base of that tree. An hour seemed distinctly possible. A day? The rest of her life? What was time to a dog?

He wished Fred could speak just a little English, enough to address a few basic topics. She knew she chased the squirrels up this particular tree but did she know why she did that? Did she know it was now eight o'clock the same way she always knew it was four o'clock, time for her kibble? Ian had read that someone taught a chimpanzee a language dubbed "jerkish," two hundred words or so that the chimp could understand. Did Fred's linguistic mastery match or exceed that number? She could easily know that many words without being able to speak any of them.

In the end it took a crescendo, starting with soft suggestions and ending with shouts, to pry Fred's nose loose from the tree roots and continue their loop back to the house.

"You were gone a long time," said Polly, who must have come home earlier than projected. Work had been keeping her lately. She was pleased, though, not at all critical. Five miles a day was Ian's prescription—"More miles equals more years" was the formula supplied by cardiologist and oddsmaker supreme Deepak Salim—and she guessed he had hit his mark tonight.

He was about to explain that they had "run into someone" on their ramble, except that was not exactly the case. Poll would picture an open-air conversation with a fellow dogwalker in the park, not cozy crumpets beside Anita Richardson's hearth. Hesitating over exactly how best to characterize the occasion cost him the chance to reference it at all and he stopped at a shrug. "Were we? Fred got herself glued to that tree. You know, the infamous Squirrel Oak."

"She must have used superglue," is all Polly said, this time with a slight edge. She had extra-sensory perception, must have extra-sensed something fishy in his testimony. But Ian knew enough not to go into it any further and let her have the last word.

A note came to the house, which turned out to be an invitation. Anita Richardson was inviting them over—Ian, Polly, and Fred—for drinks. ("Would Fred be okay with just water?") She was normalizing. Which was both good and not so good.

"This is one of your sings?" said Polly. "But one who somehow knows the dog?"

"She was a stranger before we sang. By chance we've chatted since then," said Ian, inadvertently clouding the details. "I have no idea how she knew my last name."

"Or Fred's first name."

"Fred was with me. When we chatted," he said, squirming internally as the mild dishonesty deepened. There was always more to tell, yet he kept not telling it.

"So you'll go?"

"For a drink? I will if you will. Though"—trying for lightness—"I don't know about Fred. A lousy pan of water?"

"I can't speak for Fred but I have to be in Binghamton all week for that conference. Or am I silly to think you'd remember?"

"Poll, I proofread your talk. I filled the freezer with all-natural no-nonsense burritos. I remember. I just didn't put the dates together."

"I wonder if you'll learn to cook when I die. My guess is no, you'll just remarry. Whatever's easiest, right?"

"Easiest is to keep you going. If that's okay with you."

"This woman with the drinks, what is she dying of?"

"Some sort of brain tumor."

"It seems odd she is socializing. That doesn't happen, does it?"

"Well, there was Carter. Usually, no. But she's young, that's the saddest part. I guess she wants a little company."

"The company of strangers? Or not. It's your company she wants, since I really am a complete stranger to her. Best you go."

"Karin would shoot me. Better I make up an excuse. The dog ate the invitation?"

"Even if you didn't suffer from pathological honesty"—a lightning bolt of irony to have this come at a moment when Ian was at best splitting hairs—"you couldn't lie to a dying woman."

"Who better? It makes sense to give any comfort one can to the dying."

"I say don't lie, don't tell Karin, just go. See if you can figure out what she wants. Why she invited you."

"Us. She invited us."

"Be as obtuse as you like, Ian, so long as you solve the mystery. Be subtle, though. Don't burst in saying Why me?"

"I promise not to burst in. Or be obtuse. If I go."

Why him? Anita was not responding to the question specifically—he hadn't asked it—but she was providing an answer. "You were all so kind that night. Well, of course you were. But the others seemed different, like they were there in a professional capacity—this is not a complaint, please understand that—professionals doing a job at my house, the way a plumber would, you know? Whereas you seemed to see me as a person, right away."

"I get credit for that? Not being a plumber?"

"You'd be surprised how thoroughly we become not-a-person. Become a problem, something awkward, casework. Your life changes. It ends, really, the minute the medicos say it is going to end soon."

"Except that the woman we sang to that night looked more likely to go skiing in Utah next week than to chemotherapy."

"You didn't see that same woman the day after."

"Headaches?"

"Is it called a headache when they bury a hatchet in your brain?"

"You can laugh about it."

"Didn't you? With your heart operation?"

"Hardly. With me it was all fear and trembling."

"But why should we keep from laughing?"

"I didn't say we shouldn't. Those who can, should. We do a nice song, by the way, 'How Can I keep From Singing.'"

"Sing it."

"Now?"

"No. After I'm dead."

Embarrassed to be singing solo, Ian sang badly. It was a difficult melody, plus his part was in the harmony block. That poor kid, the miniature music critic, would have scorched the performance. He stopped after the first chorus and waited for the phony praise. Instead, Anita was silent for a moment before changing the subject.

"I hope you all know how grateful I am—for the singing. Honestly, I'd never heard of such a thing. But what I'd really love is to have you tell me stories."

"Lullabies and stories? Back to a happy childhood?"

Anita gave him a why-not sort of shrug.

"That was a bad joke," he said. "My wife is the shrink in the family."

"Is she. That's great, you get free therapy."

"Doesn't work that way. Inside a marriage, I am told, the therapist lacks distance and objectivity. I'd have to pay the going rate to someone else."

"I guess it's cheaper to stay sane. Her name is Polly—the Internet told me that. It's a name I have always liked."

"The Internet knows all."

"No secrets anymore."

"Fortunately, we have no secrets. Polly and I."

In fact, he and Poll had joked that if Edward Snowden spied on them, all he would find were family photos, dinner arrangements, and "work product" of no interest to anyone. Now, though, Ian realized he did have a secret of sorts from Polly. A harmless one, more of an oversight compounded by delay and now by the awkwardness that spun off delay.

"I've overstayed," he said, rising to leave, resolving not to visit again without Polly. "It sure doesn't appear to be the case, but you must have to husband your energy."

"Husband it. That's such an odd term. I mean, does anyone ever wife their energy? But it's fine, Ian, you can go if you are feeling tired. As long as you promise to come back and tell me stories."

Oy, he thought. His only Jewish word. Or was it Yiddish? "I'm very bad at that sort of thing," he said. "Ask my kids."

"What I'd like," she said, breezing past his disclaimer, "would be a serial, with episodes. Even with your wonderful singing, I could kick the bucket a minute after you leave. With a serial, I'd have to stick around for the next installment."

She was game, this young woman, brave beyond any reckoning. And so alone. Someone other than Ian should be here keeping her company, caring for her. Where were those people, where were the friends, parents, siblings, cousins? Where was the boyfriend or the girlfriend?

He didn't ask. Leaving was difficult enough when everything they said led to something more they wished to say.

"You could tell me about your other concerts. They must all be fascinating and that would make a sort of chapter story."

"I'm afraid we have to uphold client confidentiality."

"Is that what we are? Clients? I'll waive that, so you are free to tell me about me, anyway. I'd love to hear what you all said about me afterwards."

"You mean how healthy you seemed."

"No, I mean the gossip, the lowdown. You can't all be nice, can you?"

There was a slight awkwardness to not hugging at the door. Everyone in Blaine, everyone in the surrounding Copper River villages—Greater Blaine—hugged all the time. People hugged hello even if a minute later it would be time to hug goodbye. They hugged in front of the post office, in front of the diner, in the bookshops. But this woman was a client. She was ill. She was also a pretty woman half his age.

Fred solved the moment for him. Fred served as distraction, transition, and resolution, as they each in turn hugged Fred instead of one another. Then Ian was outside with the door closing slowly behind him. He exhaled the tension, inhaled the chill. The cold air was clear yet somehow visible against the streetlights' cast. Proud of herself for having mediated, pent up from an hour's patience, Fred bolted in and out of the roadside snow, barking and snapping at the snowdust as she raised it.

Clarifying matters with Polly was the first order of business. The lack of clarity had been trolling Ian's conscience and it needn't. But Polly, uncharacteristically pressing the point, did not make it easy. "Did you go?" she said. She had not yet taken her coat off or taken her little suitcase upstairs.

Ian blanked on it. Go where? Then he remembered Polly urging him to accept Anita's invitation, leaving for her conference, leaving his decision in the wind. She never pushed him about the sings, was in fact slightly dismissive of them. And then there was her style of never asking, waiting for whatever account was offered, in all interpersonal matters. Now this: "To see the lady who was wanting company."

Ian was mindful the phrase was his. He had rendered it blandly, though, and it was coming back on a blade edged with sarcasm. Still, it provided an avenue. "I did. I took your advice and I went over for a bit. I couldn't even tell you what we talked about—nothing, really. Despite her diagnosis, she just acts like a normal, friendly person."

"Friendly, to be sure, given the invitation."

This, from Polly, was tantamount to jealousy. They were in their sixties and neither had been jealous in decades. Jealousy was pegged as Polly's least favorite emotion; apparently, she had taken an oath against it as an overly rational teenager. There had not been a hint of it during the year that Ian and Louise Gold were paired on a dozen nighttime home visits. No doubt it helped that Louise was fifty to Ian's forty, and that in an unkind moment Polly said Louise had "the face of a camel." Still, the propinquity.

Wasn't propinquity generally what did it?

"I guess she thinks of us as friends. We sang there twice and then we did bump into one another in between."

"She bumps? I thought she was on her deathbed."

"Some days are better than others, I guess. The thing is killing her a bit slower than the doctors predicted, I gather."

"You guess? You gather? How did she put it?"

"Gee, Poll, I don't know. They gave her two months to live and it's been three or four. Something like that."

"Good. Then you might have the chance to sing to her again."

Here it was, the precise moment to wash the whole thing clean. To reveal that Anita had asked him to come back and tell her *stories*. It sounded incriminating and it also sounded silly, and both aspects factored into his hesitancy. Meanwhile, Polly slashed again and stole the moment. "Or maybe she'll send *us* another visiting card, more drinks and snacks and such all."

"Come on, Poll, what is this?"

"Right. What is this. Won't she want company again next week? Won't you feel a duty to be helpful again? And *friendly*?"

"That's the thing," he said, bracing himself, finding a way. "This is pretty strange and I honestly don't know how to handle it. I am definitely open to your professional advice. She wants people to—instead of singing?—tell her stories."

"People?"

"Well, the choir, I guess. The Angel Band."

"Ian, you are blushing so ferociously I am afraid your head might burst open."

She was laughing, though. Taking her foot off the gas, letting him off the hook she had hung him on. Maybe it had never been jealousy, just her sense that he was not forthcoming. Or again, some therapist's chess game she was trying out, amusing herself. Though she did conclude the matter by saying "There's something here that doesn't feel right," she said it matter-of-factly. He was released from the inquisition and simultaneously released from the iron heel of conscience. However he chose to "handle"

Anita's unusual request, there was clarity now; no secrets between them, Ian and Polly.

How does one tell a story? Ian began by trying to describe the house.

"I guess you could say it was straight out of Norman Rockwell, a postcard of New England. Fields, stone walls bordered by big oak trees, a huge old barn, paint flaking off a million white clapboards—"

"I knew you were lying."

"Lying?"

"When you said you were not good at storytelling. But don't let me interrupt."

Most people are vain, but the Angel Band's clients rarely had the luxury of vanity. They wore what was comfortable, if there was any comfort to be found. Robes were standard issue—easy on and easy off, loose-fitting, and reasonably effective at concealing the depredations of disease. No one even tried looking as good as Anita Richardson did today and she might not even have tried. The blue jeans and light blue cardigan sweater were just clothes, all she had to do was put them on. She looked great because she was great looking. Even her hair, brown at night, tilting toward auburn in the daylight, seemed careless, loosely gathered into a simple clip.

On the other hand, Ian could admit he *had* tried. Had chosen the blue-and-white striped shirt, had checked twice in the mirror before leaving the house. No big deal, just not what he would normally do. So he wanted to look his best. Why not? Clearly Anita liked something about him and as a former high school guidance counselor, not to mention a former high school student, Ian knew that we all try to live up to such liking when we sense it. Certainly at sixteen; also, apparently, at sixty-six.

"A tiny Irish girl let us in. She looked about twelve years old, freckles and pimples jumbled together. Behind her on the couch, in a sea of pillows, lay a white-haired Black woman. Now, I know this area, I have known the few Black families that have come through our schools, so I shouldn't have been surprised. She saw that I was, though, that we were. I imagine she had been seeing surprise like it for a long time.

"'Oh yes,' she said. 'I know we are few around the Copper River villages,

but we do exist. I have been here fifty-one years and do you know what? I
have always been the same color.'

"That this was a proud, gracious, highly educated lady did not surprise
me at all."

Ian could hardly have been surprised, not after knowing Ella Morehouse,
a woman as proud and gracious and high-degreed as anyone and who,
though negligibly Black, did identify as such. A quadroon? he had said,
showing off his Faulkner. "Something like that," she had smiled. "A tint
sufficient to keep the two of us under the radar in Blaine. They can't
conceive of it." That was Ella, convinced that no one at the school suspected
the affair simply because all-white Blaine sported all-white imaginations.

"What did surprise me a little," he went on, "was that with all her
dignity and all her pain, this lady had such a great sense of humor. 'Do
you suppose,' she said to us, 'they turn everyone white at the pearly gates?
Because they will not keep me out, I *will* be crossing over soon, and I'll be
stepping lively. No need to carry me across.'

"Ward dared to make a joke about it, how if she changed her mind he
would be happy to carry her. Told her she would be easy freight, probably
weighed less than a hundred pounds. And she came right back with a
million-dollar grin. 'Honey, you should have seen me back in my heyday,
you would be hitting the gym to tote me.'

"We always do spirituals, it sort of comes with the territory, you know,
so I could only hope she didn't feel we were stereotyping when we trotted
out 'Nobody Knows the Trouble I've Seen.' We had barely started it when
Mrs. Sterling interrupted. Raised a hand to stop us—"

"Mrs. Sterling."

"I shouldn't have said a name."

"I shouldn't have barged in. Sorry."

"She stopped us and said was there any chance we could do 'Deep
Purple' for her. We couldn't, not as a group. We didn't know it. But then
she cued it for us—*When the deep purple falls, over sleepy garden walls*,
and one of us—no names—did know it, picked it up from there, and for
a minute they sang together. Which was kind of thrilling. Made everyone
happy. And it made me wish I'd known her, had her for a friend. She had

a very interesting life, though we only learned some of the details a few months later."

"Say it," Anita prompted. "From the obituary."

"Both her daughters were lawyers. Both of them in L.A., a far cry from Blaine. One was civil liberties, the other corporate—that alone was a little interesting. She and her husband, who died a few years earlier, were both well-known poets. Not that I knew of them."

"What a lovely story. Even if you gave it a few Hollywood touches."

"Nothing of the sort. I could never make anything up."

"Right. As if such a sterling character was really named Sterling."

"Yes, please, let's say I made that up. I would not be forgiven for saying her real name."

"I'm sure you would be forgiven."

"I would not be forgiven."

"Not forgiven by the Sterlings? Or by your wife?"

"Oh, not Polly. She thinks most of our rules are silly."

"I'm sorry she couldn't come with you today. I hope she doesn't mind your coming?"

"Not at all," he said, too quickly and perhaps with slight inaccuracy. How slight he was not sure. "Poll's not the jealous type."

"Oh, I never dreamed she would be jealous. Just that she might not wish to spare you."

"She's still at work, will be for a while yet. We'll have plenty of time to do our thing later. Cap off an early night by falling asleep in our recliners, halfway through a boring video."

"Do you really have matching recliners?"

Ian smiled and shook his head: no recliners. Anita cocked her head as if to say, See, you did make something up!—or so he interpreted the gesture. He was still flushed from his latest dumb mistake, implying Polly might have reason to be jealous. Implying, in effect, that there was something going on here. It was kind of Anita not to have laughed out loud at him.

When he left a short time later, there was no hug, though she did brush his shoulder lightly as she thanked him and again urged him to "bring Polly next time."

Next time. The phrase followed him home. He should not have allowed the phrase or the expectation behind it to hang there unaddressed. Should have told her flat out that there should be no next time, that there were *complications*—that was the best way to put it—which could not be ignored. As usual, the right thing to say came to him after the right moment for saying it had passed.

The late afternoon sky was almost bright, a frivolous snow floating down through it in large wet flakes. When they pasted his face, Ian thought of how entering the icy ocean might feel to those crazies who dove into the South Boston surf every December. Brave? Adventurous? Masochistic?

Words that were said, words that went unsaid—so many pitfalls to avoid. Unpacking "next time" was an unsaid he should have said, Mrs. Sterling's name was a said he should never have. The worst, though, was reassuring her that Polly was not the jealous type. It was just a poor way of putting it, a misguided attempt to dismiss Anita's more general concern, that blew up in his face. He was still regretting it, still blushing, twenty minutes later at his own front door.

Maybe someday science would find a way for words to be redacted retroactively, or added retroactively when called for. You could revise a term paper to make it sound smarter, why shouldn't you be able to do the same with conversations? He could erase the misguided mention of jealousy and let "Polly won't mind" do the job. Could replace his silent seeming acquiescence with "I'm afraid I've already stretched the Angel Band rules too far" when the prospect of a next time was broached. It was so obvious in retrospect.

Later on, he could only wonder what to say or unsay now, as Polly got right after it. It was a soft opening ("She is quite pretty, your client? You did say that?") but he could tell the third degree was coming, could hear the storm approaching.

"Did I?"

"She isn't?"

"I suppose she is. Or was."

"Was? Did she die in your arms while you were drinking your drinks?"

Ian shook his head, both for lack of a good response and out of bewilderment that Poll was doing this. But she was. "It's interesting that you are so attracted to her. When you think about it."

Ian had tried not to think about it and did not do so now. "She seems an admirable human being," he said.

"Admirable and attractive are not the same thing, Ian. You know what I mean."

"You can't mean attracted like sexually attracted?"

"It's not a crime, you know. Finding someone attractive."

"You make it sound like one."

"That's just the guilt factor at work."

With Poll there was always "the guilt factor at work." Her world turned on the axis of guilt. All good deeds stemmed from it, we all bear it, The Guilt. Catholics and Jews almost institutionally, everyone else willy-nilly. He'd once challenged her by asking if Vladimir Putin bore The Guilt and all she gave him back was Putin's own Cheshire cat smile. Not about to let one exception compromise an ironbound truth.

Maybe this was just one of her games, see if she could get him to confess to . . . *something*. The Guilt, the confession, the absolution? Ian looked at her, a gaze of affection, and shrugged his I'm-innocent shrug.

"Remember 'Love Story'?" she said. "The movie."

"Never saw it. Everyone said it was junk food. Kitschy."

"I saw it with Steve Harper."

Steve. The famous first love. Was this a new game, trying to make *him* jealous? Of course it was a so-called date movie and she was "dating" Steve at the time. "You liked it?"

"Of course not. Point is, the girl is a) beautiful and b) dying."

"I sort of know the plot."

"We laughed our heads off for an hour, then at the end I cried."

"You? Did Steve Harper cry?"

"I think so. It was dark and he would have tried to stifle it, but I could tell."

"You can always tell, Poll."

"You're still missing the point. Same story: the girl dies, the boy cries."

"Me, you mean? Hey, maybe I will. Maybe I should."

"Oh, you should. It's a very moving situation—love and death. It's a classic."

She was pushing it too far and there was a trace of frost in his voice when he responded: "After that one, I believe you expect me to announce it's time to walk the dog."

She grinned and pushed a soft fist against his belly. Game over. "I'm surprised you lasted this long," she said. "Dress warmly now."

Fred loved the large blowing flakes. She bounced around, yipping and nipping at them. Moving targets were fun. And maybe they reminded her of the tiny biscuits Ian tossed her, that she was so adept at catching, though she didn't seem to mind the way the snow bits disappeared on contact and had no crunch, no flavor. The new snow was collecting by now and called to mind a line of poetry about waking to an undisturbed "uncompacted London snow." The poet's name escaped him, the vivid image stayed, of God's pure bedding lying pristine at daybreak.

Back at the house, he checked the day's phone log and saw there were two messages from Jack Sutcliffe. The first was simply *Call me*, the second (no doubt in response to Ian's not having called him) surrendered the information: the medicos had taken away coffee. "He wants me to drink that herbal tea—instead of *coffee!*" He added that he did get a sizable trout that morning and if Ian should happen to find himself in the neighborhood tomorrow, Jack would fry it up for lunch and brew some coffee to wash it down.

"He's lonesome," said Polly.

Probably he was. Empathizing, Ian poured himself a generous tumbler of whiskey and shrugged again when Polly shot him the look. "Before they take it away," he explained, going on to extrapolate Jack's awareness of diminishing pleasures. She softened the look accordingly—Ian was just being a naughty boy—and he absorbed this gentle blow along with the amber.

The Lady in Question

BRINGING POLLY ALONG would solve it. She would like Anita, possibly take over Ian's function of providing a little company. Anita did seem to prefer the company of strangers, or at least she seemed fine with the fact that old friends had steered clear. Possibly she did not wish to be seen by those who had known her at her best as helpless or wasting away.

Though this particular cancer was not a wasting strain, as Ian would witness with startling specificity when he agreed to do her a quick favor. Anita had asked if he would mind picking up the new Colum McCann novel from the library and dropping it by that day. The other hospice people were coming—"the ones who hum but don't sing"—and they always wore her out with their lovely ministrations. She planned on lying down and reading the rest of the day.

The book was out on loan from the library so he went to look for it at the Old Toad Bookshop. There it was, for the low low price of sixteen bucks. For a paperback! The price of books was one of those things that served to remind him of his age. Ian still had some of his college textbooks, Plato for $1.25, Reinhold Niebuhr for $1.95. He would have to borrow this one back to get his money's worth.

Hospice was already on scene when he rang the bell. They answered, two ladies, one quite large and one as small as a child. Ian handed the book to the large one, letting her know Anita would be expecting it. "Anita is also expecting you," came Anita's voice from somewhere offstage. "Stay. They'll be done with me in a few minutes."

The small one grinned like a sadistic prison guard, as if to suggest they would never be done with her. A few minutes? Hah. What if they were paid by the hour?

This was unfair and likely untrue. Everyone had the highest regard for the job hospice did and the way they did it. Good hires, good training. Ian agreed to stay, though the ladies laughed when he offered to help. Turned out they were about to bathe their client, hardly a job for which the gentleman was suited.

Anita resisted. She assured them she had showered that morning and was quite clean, but this was something (Bathe Patient?) they were required to check off their list. Ian sat on the couch and tried to read his way into the novel, only to find himself reading the same page over and over as the jolly voices from down the hall kept distracting him. The dreaded bath sounded like a party. But it would culminate in a brief indelible image, a snapshot imprinted on Ian's mind, when the ladies walked Anita down the hall—frog-marched her, a guard on either side, as in fairness they had no doubt seen clients slip and fall—with a blanket-sized towel wrapped around her. The towel had caught, curled, and come to rest in the small of Anita's back, such that the entire bottom half of her was exposed. A perfectly shaped backside perched atop perfectly shaped legs.

Ian looked away quickly, the procession detoured into a room off the hall, and soon he could hear Anita's next protest ("I can dress myself, really I can, I have already done so once today") as they nevertheless went about crossing Dress Patient Warmly off the list. The image remained. It had not been static, not St. Gaudens' statue of Diana, it had been a moving image, the buttocks rounding and shifting, as smooth and fetching as the marble Diana yet distinctly alive.

The arresting aspect, he labored to convince himself, was not her beauty or any erotic appeal, it was that the process of dying had made no inroads on her body. Wasting away? Hardly. In the not-so-distant, less technologically enriched past, a doctor would have had no idea this woman was ill, much less terminal. No one would have given her that consideration. Her headaches would have been dismissed as female complaints, or neurasthenia.

When Anita reappeared, fully clothed and rolling her eyes as the dedicated ladies set about washing the kitchen floor (which she informed them she had washed yesterday), Ian found the strength to leave. It had been nearly an hour, surely she could understand. She apologized, thanked him for the book, tried thrusting money for it at him, said to come back soon, bring Polly.

She knew it too, the solution was to bring Polly. The problem was that Polly would not come. Did Anita also know that? The situation was already tricky and now Ian was beset by this fresh dilemma: seeing Anita in her jeans or corduroy trousers, would he not too vividly recall seeing her without those trousers, the buttocks and calves at work? She might or might not know why he was blushing as he started to leave.

"And Fred. Do bring Fred too," she urged in the doorway. Her next-door neighbor, an elderly man, waved hello with his snow shovel. Something of a perfectionist, he had been shoveling her walkway with the goal of removing all traces of white. "He's eighty-five," she whispered. "I feel terrible that he does this, but I can't seem to stop him."

"You can't seem to stop anyone from doing for you. Might as well give up trying."

"I hate it. This whole situation is just so damn—"

"Frustrating?"

"Frustrating. Embarrassing. Humiliating. I hate being helpless a lot more than I will hate being dead."

"How about this: I promise I won't do anything for you."

"Too late, you just did."

"Nothing else, then. Nothing in the future."

"Except tell me stories," she reminded him.

Polly was clear: the "situation" was strictly one for Ian to manage, not one where she should interfere. And though she expected he would continue his "good works," she was not particularly kind in characterizing his motivation as tantamount to an adolescent crush.

"Come on, Poll. Adolescent crush?"

"I was pretty sure you would prefer that to midlife crisis."

"I'm one heart attack past midlife and half a century past adolescence. What I'd prefer is for you to call it what it is."

"A good deed? Fine, that's what we'll call it."

Sometimes Ian feared she could peer right inside his brain and scroll through a readout of his thoughts. To call him immature or adolescent was not far off, for that snapshot, that inadvertent invasion of Anita Richardson's privacy, did catch on the edges of his consciousness like a branch that could not quite work its way downstream. And each time the clip of that moment re-ran, he expected Polly to know it and nail him on it.

Ian Nelson was nearly as upright as his reputation would have it. There were times he wondered if he was repressed, had suppressed his natural reactions. He did not disapprove of other men with their loose talk about women, he just did not process life the same way. Or not consciously. A young woman passing by, a stranger Ian would hardly notice, was often a source of leering interest to Harv, who would never even speak to the woman. It wasn't only that Ian failed to see the point of it, he simply didn't have the same reaction.

His actual love life (as he called it, setting aside the word sex) had never been problematic or complicated, so it was possible for him to feel normal or to feel that both ways of seeing were normal. If he was abnormal, or warped in some way, he could wonder if it had to do with religion, even though he no longer believed in God or an afterlife or any of it. But he had at one time considered the ministry and he carried himself with a ministerial rectitude of which, the whole world had by now become aware, actual ministers so often proved unworthy. Pastors played around, deacons leered, priests abused.

And Ian the Righteous had cheated. Once. His moral compass was rarely tested by such magnetic fields as Ella Morehouse, but working so closely with Ella made it difficult, as did her own matter-of-factness about what could be "harmlessly" enjoyed by two willing adults. She made it sound downright unnatural to deny the attraction or worse, to admit it yet deny themselves the enjoyment of acting on it. Nor did it help that, unlike Louise Gold, Ella did not have "a face like a camel." She had a face that drew you in, electric blue eyes set against the slightly toasted skin.

Despite Ella's race-based disclaimer that they were invisible to their purblind white colleagues, Ian constantly feared their connection must show at the school. He wasn't sure about the law, or the rules, beyond the obvious—it had to be unacceptable, had to put his job at risk. And Polly, all-seeing Poll, might have known the whole time, though she never said a word about it. Not even the hint of an accusation. Not until Ella Morehouse had moved back to California, frankly to Ian's relief. One month later, out of the clear blue sky, confirming his sense of her omniscience, Polly said, "You miss her, don't you?"

"Everyone does," he said, just barely managing to dissemble, blushing brightly. "She was very well liked at the school."

At that moment and for some time thereafter, Ian had trouble differentiating between his wife's insights and his own conscience, in the end concluding they were the same thing, at least with regard to Ella. In the fifteen years since then, he had given Polly no occasion to X-ray his brain, and his conscience had given him no occasion to sink into guilt.

Until now. He could claim he felt an obligation to go, Polly could second the motion, and still the going left him feeling guilty. Not just toward Poll, but also toward the Angel Band, by visiting a client on his own and then compounding it by telling her tales about the sings. Betraying the cone of silence: *What happens at a sing stays at the sing.*

And he knew—Anita must know—that whatever interesting moments he may have tried to describe, every protagonist in his stories was now deceased. Surely this fell somewhere on the spectrum between depressing and devastating, yet she insisted she enjoyed hearing these accounts, and Ian, who did honestly feel he had no imagination of that sort, could not conjure up any other "stories" to tell.

At the least he would not slip up again on names. Yet even there, tonight, when he identified a client as "a dear lady in her late nineties," he wondered at once if that was already too specific. Barbara Baum's obituary ran barely four months ago, and Anita could have seen it. How many women of that age had died in the *Blaine Sentinel* lately?

"Not surprising she was ready for hospice," said Anita. "At ninety-something."

"This one was pretty last minute," he said.

"Has that happened? Have you sung to a dead person—by accident, of course."

"No!" he said, mortified that she said the word they always euphemized, though she had spoken it cheerily. Recovering, taking up her upbeat tone, he cited Harv, albeit not by name: "One of the men likes to say that in show business, you always try to leave 'em laughing."

"Well if they're laughing, I guess they can't be dead," she said, not exactly laughing herself, but unaccountably lighthearted.

He went ahead with it, relating how Mrs. Baum had come back to life ("risen from the crypt" was Harv's coarser wording that night) the instant they started "In the Garden." *We come to the garden alone*, they'd sung, and the dear lady of ninety-seven sat bolt upright and came in right on time, if faintly, with *when the dew is still on the roses*. Then sank right back down, disappearing into a white duvet that rose over her like a snowcapped mountain range.

"She died that night, didn't she."

"I didn't say that."

"Do you deny it?"

"That she died that night? Yes, I deny it. Anyway, her dying—or not dying—wasn't the ending of the story. Her smile was the ending."

"You didn't say anything about a smile."

"I was going to. She gave us a little smile as she lay back down. As if to say, this was just what I'd hoped it would be and now I will rest a while."

"Fair enough. That's a nice ending to a very nice story."

Anita had worked for the state arts council in Maine. Before that she had taught school. She painted—some of the work on the walls was hers—and she read voraciously. It made sense that she liked hearing stories. It just did not make sense that she liked hearing his fumbling attempts at conveying such grim tales.

Ian once read Thomas Mann's claim that humor was the salt in a story, as necessary as the salt in a good soup. If one thing was certain, it was that Ian had no idea how to make a story funny, much less a story about a hospice sing. That was a trick leagues beyond him. Yet Anita praised his "wit" and asked for more of it. "No one set a limit of one story per visit, you know. You could do another, if you have time."

Ian had plenty of time, that was part of the problem. He hated how much he liked being there when there were so many constraints about being there at all. Polly, Karin, age, station . . . Above all the situation itself, whose complexities he did not even wish to examine closely. Because the temptation to stay longer, the source of his inertia, was that he knew he would feel his world deflating, flattening out and losing color once he left Anita's house. The pleasure he took from her company was different from the other small pleasures in his week and it was the nature of this difference that he preferred not to place under a microscope.

Sometimes he felt he and Anita were acting out a story he might be telling to her, had it happened in the past. In his Tales From the Hospice Sings, this would be one about the client who preferred stories to songs. Then he tripped over it again: in each of his "stories" the clients were alive, in reality they all were dead. Anita's Tale would have the same grim ending.

As he left this time, as he extricated himself from what was in fact was a hug, he realized it would be grim for him too. He would be losing this, whatever it was, and he would miss it terribly. Polly was right: the girl dies, the boy cries.

Polly had turned on the outside light. This was something she never did—turn it on or, if it was on, turn it off. Hanging his coat up in the vestibule, Ian braced himself. He was convinced Polly had access to all his foolish ruminations. She would declare he was in too deep; the potential for damage was expanding; it was time to stop.

Instead of this lecture, he got a note. She had gone to the movies with Kate Marcus. She would be home around ten.

He would rather have had the lecture. Because they had decided to see this film, the one playing over in Holdenborough, together, later in the week. On a sort of date, even if the film about a Canadian woman struggling with Alzheimer's sounded a bit rough. Ward and Nance had told them it was a must-see and they had joked about that: was it a must because it was such a good movie or because their crowd needed to become educated on this awful curse that would be "coming soon to a house near you!"

Now she had gone with Kate. Without him. Had she forgotten? He opened a bottle of beer and heated the leftover Chinese, spicy chicken with cashews. He enjoyed it, even as he conjured up the aroma of popcorn, the taste of Raisinets. Ian liked to say—maybe he did have a tiny bit of wit?—that the Raisinets were always good in Holdenborough.

Polly had left both of last night's fortune cookies on the table, unopened: "One for you and one for Fred." Though she checked her horoscope every day in the paper, Polly was a nonbeliever in fortune cookies. He had raised the possibility that she was afraid to believe, knowing that fortune cookies held the potential of putting shrinks out of business.

But which cookie contained Ian's future and which was Fred's? Was he to "expect an unexpected visitor" or "be understanding and forgiving tonight"? The only one needing forgiveness was Ian himself, so he elected to expect the visitor. The Nine O'Clock News was declaring itself in loud, overly dramatized headlines when he slipped into sleep on the couch, still expecting.

Rehearsals were the most fun. The Unitarian Universalist (or Yew Yew Church, as everyone called it) did not require the small donation Karin made each time, too small to cover the cost of heating that cavernous hall to seventy degrees on a winter's night. Nevertheless, it would be seventy on the dot when they walked in. The coffee urn would have brewed half a gallon of East Coast Roast, and Meg's Downtown Donuts would have supplied two dozen—mostly glazed, a few jelly, and a Boston Kreme for Harv.

Tonight the feeling was different. Faces that usually glowed on the strength of coffee and communality looked tense. The singing was flattened down by this tension, and Philip was uncharacteristically impatient around some new material. Karin, who normally coddled her singers, was a scold. And Ian was certain it was all about him. His transgressions had congested the very air and his impulse was to clear it by explaining himself. All he needed was an explanation to offer.

Clues kept coming up. Phil mentioned "some irregularities" he would be addressing at the close of rehearsal. Then, in announcing two new songs, Karin made it known they were dropping one, "Hard Times Come Again No More." Other than "Crossing the Bar" (which was never adopted in the first place), "Hard Times" was the only song Ian had aggressively sponsored. One of those gorgeous Stephen Foster melodies, it also gave rise to the complex harmonies they invariably nailed. It was always a "hit" when they did it, and now it was being discarded in favor of a *Beatles* tune!

Final clue, Ian's name was nowhere to be seen on the March roster, though there were three sings scheduled and one of them was a "second coming" (Harv's coinage) at a house in Holdenborough where Ian had participated the first time. *Roster continuity*, one of Karin's Ten Commandments, was being set aside. There were many singers to be accommodated, Ian was okay with exclusion—until he saw the Holdenborough house on the whiteboard. Then it did feel pointed.

Toward the end the atmosphere lightened, the music improved. Ian could even concede that Phil's arrangement of "Hey Jude" was working, it was good, and it did seem to wash some fresh colors into the enterprise. Still, he was braced for the discipline, prepared for Phil to address his *irregularities*. He was ready to get slammed—he deserved it—except Phil forgot to slam him. Maybe he was so pleased with the last go-through of his Beatles fantasia that he chose not to roil the becalmed waters. Let it be, let it be?

Looks were exchanged. Everyone remembered the mention of irregularities and the intent to address them—surely gossip would be harvested from this and flow for weeks—yet no one broached it. They cleaned up the kitchen, pushed the thermostat back to forty-five, turned out the lights, and left.

Ian and Ward Longstreet walked away together. Both traveled to the church on foot and both headed home in the direction of the park, so they usually left together. They would rehash the rehearsal as they walked, occasionally detouring downtown to catch up more generally over pints at The Draught House. This time Ian suspected Ward was on assignment, that the task of delivering the rebuke had fallen to him.

"Nothing of the sort," said Ward, denying the charge. "You take me for a loyal foot soldier carrying out orders? But I will tell you how it *looks*, if you like."

"How it looks?"

If it *looked* at all, then Ian's visits to 85 Brierly had not gone unnoticed. That was bad enough. Exactly who did the noticing was not clarified. Keeping it general, Ward laughed when asked if humble Blaine had recently installed CCTV on every street corner.

"No one is gathering evidence. It's just the buzz."

"So what are they buzzing about?"

"Well, that depends on who you ask."

"Okay, give me a generous sampling. Of this buzzing."

"It's not like that, really it isn't. But let's see. Stephanie's take has gotten some traction. Theory being the lady in question reminds you of your first love—long ago, long before Polly—loved, lost, and forever preserved inside your heart. The distant past rekindled, your faded youth recalled . . ."

"Cry me a river of clichés."

"Not me, bud, Stephanie. Who, by the way, will deny categorically that she reads those romance novels."

"What's your take, Ward?"

"None of my business is my take. Though I did get a chuckle hearing how Polly hit you with the *Love Story* riff. That was rich."

"Wait. You heard that? How could anyone hear that?"

"From Nance, who got it from Polly. Women tell each other that stuff."

"And it spreads like a virus? So by tomorrow I'll be the village fool?"

"Tomorrow?" Ward grinned.

Ian bent down and clumped some snow, underhanded the snowball at Ward's knees. Laughing, Ward held out his hands in a don't-shoot-the messenger pose.

"Don't let it get to you," he said. "You've been doing what we are all supposedly doing, no? Take a sad song and make it better?"

"Can you believe that? The Beatles?"

Now they were branching off, Ian onto Spring Road, Ward onto Longleaf. Intent on letting it go, letting it be, Ian tried to Zen himself down, reduce himself to a random mammal making breath clouds in the stilly air. Tried forgetting (or if he couldn't forget then making light of) Ward's parting riposte as he backpedaled away, extending a crooner's palm and singing, *Remember to let her under your skin. / Then you'll begin . . . making it better.*

If the resolve was to stop, *full stop*, it did not help that he missed seeing her. He had managed to discard Polly's nonsense about an adolescent crush in favor of a much simpler explanation: their visits were fun. They had provided, in all innocence, some of his most enjoyable hours in recent memory. And despite what anyone might imagine, they were harmless.

All the charges that might be levelled against him were in play. Yes, he and Polly were happy yet naturally a bit stale together—Ian playing the part of Ian, Poll playing Poll. Yes, retirement weighed on him. Retirement had swept away purpose, swept away the annual influx of troubled students coming to him for advice, needing him. Who needed him now? Just Fred.

And in some way, possibly, this star-crossed young woman.

He was willing to consider the charge of sexual attraction. Anomalies might occur in literature (he thought of the dwarf and the giantess in Carson McCullers' novel) or in Hollywood, where silver-haired leading men reliably captured young beauties. In real life? All he had was Phil Hammond at fifty-five and Amy Something at around thirty-five. Phil was Phil, though—a player—and their age gap aside, those two had an awful lot in common. Between hiking, boating, birding, cooking, traveling, reading, and the opera, Phil and Amy were more of a match than a mismatch. They were the exception to prove the rule. Ian did not see himself as the exception to any rule.

Weeks went by and the worst Ian did was to slip past her house one night when Fred seemed to be pulling him that way. Seeing the upstairs lights on at nine p.m., he concluded she was all right, she was still there, and he was able to leave it at that.

It was the next night that he and Polly saw the Alzheimer's movie after all. It turned out Polly and Kate Marcus had seen a different film, not this one about the stricken woman fading out, the husband devoted yet cranky, the season moving steadily into bleak Canadian midwinter. Ward was right, it was well done, a quiet understated punch in the gut. But it was just quiet enough to leave room for his mind to wander and it kept wandering to Anita Richardson.

Here was Polly, elbow to elbow with him, believing him fully present. Here were two realistically written, wonderfully acted characters. And there was Anita, who had no business being in the equation, yet was. An odd, antiquated word came to him: forsaken. He had forsaken Anita. It was odd and antiquated, it was melodramatic and wholly inapplicable. How could you forsake someone you were morally obliged to avoid? Accordingly, he had resolved to avoid her. Had made it clear there could be no more visits, no more storytelling.

Or had he made it clear? Ian knew he had said it quite firmly to himself in her presence. He was less certain he had spoken it aloud. If he had not, then she had reason feel slighted. In the dark theater, pawing unhappily toward the bottom of the popcorn box, Ian was becoming convinced he had not found the courage—or the words, at any rate—to prepare her and so had hurt her inadvertently instead of doing what little he could to boost her spirits. Even if her lights were on last night, she might be a lot worse off by now. For a hospice patient, three weeks was a long time.

The film ended, the room emptied out, and soon afterward the town did too—a weeknight in the country—and they drove away in a considered silence. It always took them a few minutes to break through the darkened silence a film enforced. This one went on longer than usual, halfway home before anyone spoke. Was the subject matter so grim, the woman's condition so irrevocable, that the equally silent landscape (moonlit snowfields, snowcapped stone walls, pine branches sagging under snowy imposts) could speak for both of them? Or had Polly infiltrated his vagrant, inappropriate thoughts?

While Ian was considering this, considering The Guilt (guilt that encompassed both his incomplete presence with Polly and his complete absence from Anita), it seemed that Polly had been considering the plight of the woman in the movie. For when she did finally speak, as they slowed for the one blinking orange light between Holdenborough and the outskirts of Blaine, it was to say, "If that happens to me, I don't want to go through it."

"Meaning what? I should drown you in the tub?"

Ian was giddy with relief. The silence had proved golden, the turn toward euthanasia downright jolly versus the threat of her clairvoyance.

"When I tell our children they look vaguely familiar? When I put the ham on the outside and the bread on the inside? Yes, absolutely. If you are anywhere within range, drown me."

"I wouldn't be able to do it," he said.

"Too weak?"

"I can think of other interpretations. Such as, I wouldn't want to lose you?"

"But the Alzheimer's scenario presumes you have already lost me. More to the point, *I* have lost me. It's hard to say who suffered more in that film, the wife or the husband."

"Next time I'm going back to the Raisinets," he said. "There's something wrong with their popcorn machine. You end up with all these un-popped pebbles at the bottom. It's not much fun when you always expect to sheer off a piece of tooth."

"Someone sued for that, you know. For millions. It was probably in Hollywood, where your smile is worth money."

"Did they win?"

"No idea. We can Google it when we get home."

"If we remember."

Every day they vowed to Google something, more often than not they forgot what it was before getting around to it. But here was the very thing. The way they played their parts—he was Ian, she was Polly—but was it not benign? Wasn't it good knowing one another so well, growing old together? He knew she would soon be at the stove heating water for tea. Knew they would both remember the intent to Google, both forget what it was they intended to find out. She had not been reading his mind. They were okay.

Ian formulated a plan. He would go once more to Brierly, once only. Maybe even tell one more story, just be sure to declare out loud that this would have to be the last one. Rules and Regs, the hammer come down. He would make an apology for not coming sooner and make an excuse for having come this time. Put it on Fred. Say they were close by and Fred insisted on saying hello.

Not say that both of them, he and Fred, just wanted to see her smile.

He had finally talked Jack into accepting a cell phone into his life. Grudgingly. "I'll never make a call on that thing," Jack vowed. "Walking down the street talking on the telephone? And I swear to you I will never *twit* if I live to the 22nd century AD."

"Understood."

It was not a smart phone, just a ten-buck burner, thirty cents to make a short call. Alone as he was out on the lake, the old boy needed "a little outreach capability, for safety." The phrase amused Jack—outreach capability, my ass—and safety never came into sight as a consideration with him. Would the device keep him from going through the ice? He was predictably impatient when Ian demonstrated how to make a call.

One day later the phone saved his life. Jack didn't go through the ice, he fell on top of it and could not get himself up. It was some sort of miracle that he had actually placed the phone in his vest pocket, nestled in with the bait packs and hooks.

Jack was already back in his tiny ice palace by the time Ian heard what happened. Nor had Jack been his source. Too proud to admit he had fallen and way too proud to admit the phone had kept him from freezing to death, the old sailor was maintaining radio silence. But Ian and Polly had bumped into the Reifsnyders at Market Basket and Rick was one of the EMTs who went out on the call.

"Your pal tried refusing to go to the hospital. Broken wrist, probable concussion, tries to tell us he's just fine. Could have handled it easily if the ice wasn't so damned *slippery.*"

"So he kept his sense of humor."

"The hell you say. He was dead serious. In the end, we had to lie to him. Told him we were required by law to bring him in for tests."

"Can you do that?"

"Lie? Sure. What choice did we have?"

"Leave him there to freeze?"

"Teach him a lesson? I don't think so, scout. Would you have?"

"Ian," said Polly, "would have moved out to the lake to tend him personally before telling a white lie."

"Good for Ian," said Lena Reifsnyder. "The last honest man!"

Later that night, Polly apologized, hoping what she'd said had not sounded mean. She fully expected he would go out to Hollow Lake in the morning, and she approved.

"I'll start out by reading him the riot act."

"Don't do that," she said. "He's embarrassed that the phone he resisted like the devil ended up saving his life. So naturally he couldn't call you, couldn't face you."

"He'll face me tomorrow."

"Make it soft, Ian. Make it a joke if you can, maybe bring him a kid's plastic toy phone, you know?"

"He is at fault and I am charged with fixing it?"

"Yes."

Poll was keeping it simple and Ian was content to stick with their old line—Polly as judge, jury, and executioner. Not by force alone, more by knowing how best to wrangle people. All these years it had been her wisdom versus his impulses.

"Speaking of your fix-it skills, how is your other charity case these days?"

"I guess I know who you mean."

"Oh, you know who I mean. Have you been to see her?"

"I have not."

"Then you should see to that too."

"Take her a toy telephone?"

"Take her flowers and candy—if she is still alive. Do you even know that much? You should at least make sure of that."

"I should and I shouldn't."

Ian waited. Polly might sort it out on her own and she might not. She might rest her case where it stood, having just frozen him with a curveball on the outside corner. He waited, she outwaited him. "Karin," he said finally, making sure to specify the *shouldn't* for her. "You know. The Rules of Engagement."

Ian woke in solid darkness, nearly stepping on Fred as he made his way to the window. The snow was tapering off, fine crystals faintly etched against the streetlight, but a fresh ton had fallen and Blaine was already smothered. The front yards were full to capacity, as people kept throwing new snow from their driveways. City trucks had started taking loads to the river.

At six o'clock he called Jack, who, of course, did not answer. Ian could picture him trying to figure out *how* to answer, since their lesson had only covered calling out. He could also imagine Jack ignoring the phone, or losing it.

It was still dark when the plows came through. By then Ian had read the paper—his delivery guy was like the old Pony Express, unstoppable—and skimmed the *Times* on the Internet. He had fried his two eggs, drained his two cups of coffee, and cleared off both cars by the time Polly was up. "I can see you're going out there," she said. "I'll stay home, at least for the morning. I can get some work done here."

She was right; he was going. If the Spring Road was plowed, the main roads should be fine. By half past seven he was at Meg's, looking at proof Blaine was still a working-class town: she had baked three hundred doughnuts and tradesmen had decimated the bins. The snowplow guys seemed to favor powdered sugar. Ian let Meg make the selection. Whatever she chose to bag, he was pretty sure Jack would be better pleased by half a dozen doughnuts than by a toy telephone.

As it happened, Jack wasn't pleased by anything. If he was glad to see Ian at all it was because shoveling snow around his bob house and tips was ineffective with one arm in a sling. For a minute, he even pretended he wouldn't eat the doughnuts. As Ian pushed the snow around, he concentrated on remembering a better Jack Sutcliffe, the decorated Navy man, the brusque but kind high school principal. A savvy, interesting man. Ian's go-to source on the natural world and all things rural. Jack was a repository of all the knowledge Ian lacked.

Had that earned him the right to be a pain in the ass?

The driving was slow both ways, so the visit consumed the entire morning. Back home, he made a fresh pot of coffee and got after his own mess, snowblowing the driveway, shoveling the walks, and raking the flat roof over the vestibule where ice dams inevitably formed. Before coming to Blaine, Ian had never heard of roof rakes or ice dams. Never needed a snowblower or dreamed that mice liked to eat the wires of snowblowers so as to disable them just before a big storm.

But the snow gave him a pretext. Whether or not Polly meant what she said, she had said it. She had given him license, just as the snow gave him a pretext. All he lacked was the doctor's okay, because shoveling snow was on the ixnay list. This was the one Deepak Salim edict Ian had needed to ignore. But knowing he would be ignoring it for a third time today, he grabbed a short nap on the couch before heading over to 85 Brierly.

He had forgotten that the octogenarian neighbor might shovel Anita out, or that she could make a phone call and pay someone to shovel. People did that. These alternative solutions only occurred to him as he made his way through the untouched paths of Watchman Park and he was not sorry to see that neither had come to pass. He was needed, albeit the snow looked awfully benign. It had blown up against Anita's front door in an undulating wave that called to mind a children's book illustration, where the implication was a fastness, coziness.

The octogenarian may have gone off to Miami, for his own walkway also lay buried. Ian kicked his way to Anita's front door and pushed the buzzer. She was there instantly, as though she had been waiting for someone else to arrive—she could not have been expecting him, but Ian was mainly relieved to see her looking the way she had looked four weeks ago. No miracle cure, no call for an ambulance either.

"I won't come in," he said, brandishing the shovel he had carried through the park. "I'll just liberate you."

"A liberated woman, how nice. But you will come in, actually, and I hope you'll be quick about it. The snow is already coming in."

This was true, the built-up wave had collapsed, and she danced back to avoid being capsized. He noticed she was wearing cloth slippers. "In a bit, maybe. Let me get after this snow while there's still a little light."

They argued about it. There were hours of light still, she didn't need to go anywhere, why didn't he liberate Mrs. Ahern instead. Mr. Ahern was not in Miami, he was in Oregon. What about the little Aherns, why can't they help their mother? The only little Ahern was also in Oregon ("You see the connection") where they don't even have snow shovels, since it only ever rains.

"Besides, I was looking forward to doing my own clearing, later on. Maybe even in the dark!"

"Obviously you should do no such thing," he said, but this seemed to amuse her, so he added, "I mean it."

When she laughed, he expected her to throw it back at him—he was the one with the bloody heart attack—but she said, "Oh, I know you mean it. That's why it's funny. Coddling me so soon after promising to make me a liberated woman."

He cut a path from the gate to the front stoop, then cleared the mouth of the driveway even though she had no car. Emergency vehicles might need access. Then he went next door and made a more rudimentary path, one shovel blade wide. His heart was still ticking but by then his back was acting up. Mrs. Ahern appeared at a window with her hands clasped in gratitude, Anita in her doorway soon after, waving a bottle of scotch.

"I really shouldn't," he said, stomping snow off his boots in the small vestibule.

"You say that a lot, you know. Should and shouldn't are big with you, aren't they?"

Ian could hardly deny the charge. Almost told her that he once considered the cloth, told her instead that he was surprised she drank scotch.

"I don't drink anything now and I never drank scotch. But I did inherit my dad's liquor supplies. Whatever you prefer, chances are I have it in stock."

"They were—are?—drinkers?"

"They were sociable. And part of a drinking generation."

"Not the '60s?" said Ian, thinking they could be around his age. "Drugs?"

"Dad did say he regretted never trying LSD."

"Why didn't he?"

"It wasn't him. Only the sense of missing out—that was him."

They had lapsed again, into easy conviviality. There was nothing he could do to stop it from happening. In the next half hour he would learn that her father had taught in a community college, her mother had sold real estate part time, they were barely retirement age when they died the same year, three years ago. "Hell of a thing. And then you got walloped with this other bad news."

"Actually, the worst news happened in between times. After they died and before I did."

"Which you haven't, of course." She sent him a side-eye look that said Be Serious. "But what's the story there? What could possibly be worse news?"

"I might tell that story—after you tell yours."

He did have a story, he had come up with one that had nothing to do with hospice sings. It was only after he began—"So this fellow Stan was sick and dying"—that Ian realized it ended in death anyway.

"I love the upbeat beginning," said Anita.

He told how Doris left Stan for a funeral director of all things, ran off with the ghoul to Jacksonville, got a quickie divorce. In Stan's mind they were still a pair—high school sweethearts, thirty years of love in the bank, why waste all that? Above all, why waste the money? The government would get it if he was single, she would get it if they were married.

Doris agreed to remarry Stan. She was all in. Dug out her old wedding dress, invited the old gang, and they did it: the big white tent, the salmon-or-chicken caterer, and the non-denominational officiant who duly pronounced them man and wife. Stan's dream, that their big love be rekindled and that they be together to the end, was looking good. He was happy.

"There were still a few guests hovering around the free bar," said Ian, "when the Uber came to take her to the airport."

"No."

"Afraid so. Right back to the Floridian undertaker."

"Wow. That's rough. Though I guess it does make a good story."

"Which makes it your turn now. Time for your story."

"You know what, Ian. I am super tired. Doris and Stan took something out of me—or maybe it was the scotch."

"I had the scotch. You had the chamomile tea."

This was a first, Anita backing up, hastening his exit instead of protesting it. He could see she was genuinely tired, could understand her condition might work that way. Still, the change felt contextual; she did not want to tell the tale that could be worse than having both your parents die and then learning you would soon be following them.

"I'll tell it next time," she said. "Maybe."

"Maybe? Why wouldn't you tell it?"

Mistake. Taking up the *maybe* when he should have taken up the *next time*. He should have gone straight into the paragraph he had rehearsed, about there being no next time.

"Because I'm afraid if I do tell it, you'll wind up hating me. And I really don't want that."

Ian almost blurted it out: how could I hate you when I . . . . He nearly made the error. It would have been meaningless, just a natural flow of words, the turn a conversation might take, and he canvassed his mind for a more accurate way of reassuring her. How could I hate someone I admire so much? Hate someone whose company I enjoy so much?

In the end he did all right: "Hate you? I'm the guy who shoveled your walkway."

"And thank you very much for that. But then, you haven't heard the story."

"You didn't kill someone? It's not a tale of murder, is it?"

"No, not murder. It's a tale of betrayal. Of evil."

She offered this without a trace of humor, without that grain of lightness that heretofore had not left her for one second. She even looked different: flat, sad, vulnerable. And yes, exhausted. He found himself going to her and when she rose, holding her. Chastely. Briefly. This too was meaningless, a Copper River hug, standardized sociable farewell.

It did stay with him long enough to push him past his own house and keep him walking, stopping only long enough to grab Fred from inside. Polly wasn't home yet anyway and there was something seductive in the cold shroud hovering above the blanched landscape. He thought of it as snow fog.

His emotions were settling. The brief embrace—though embrace was too big a word for ten seconds of insignificant human contact—left him wondering exactly why and how it had happened. It was meaningless, except for the fact that he had guarded against it up to now and maybe Anita had done the same. Gradually, he convinced himself that she must have made it happen. As brave as ever, she had at the same time, paradoxically, made herself newly vulnerable. By some invisible female means—body language? tone of voice?—she had dialed their connection up a notch even as he intended to dial it down.

Polly had cautioned him, touted him onto the possibility his "friend"—so robust, so brave—was a fraud of some sort. She conceded it could be a benign fraud. Her friend Sandra Hopkins gave her social psych students the same assignment each fall: find a way, by fair means or foul, to observe a death closely and then write a five-page paper on the varied reactions to dying. Possibly Ian's friend was enrolled in a such a course. When Ian pointed out that Anita had been accepted by hospice, Polly pointed out that a sociology professor at Blaine State could easily have useful contacts within the health care establishment. If Anita seemed healthy, maybe she *was* healthy and he was a pawn in her game, easily led.

Was it possible? A term paper for Sociology 101? Ian thought of the classic film where Marlene Dietrich bewitches a pathetic old man with nothing more than an exposed leg. Was Ian the pathetic old man here? Was Anita's shapely bottom the exposed leg?

But Polly pushed it too far. When she asked if he was sure his "ministrations" were not being filmed or recorded, wasn't she just trying to scare him, maybe wring a confession from him? The longer he walked through the corridors of snow—talking to himself, considering the charges—the less likely Polly's hypothetical scenario sounded. After hearing her voice for the first mile, he spent the next stretch listening to Anita's, and he simply was not hearing a performance.

Important fact: Polly did not know the lady in question and he did. This was a central lesson from his long career in guidance, that a person's sincerity was best judged face to face. Ian had fielded hundreds of teenagers with an inborn genius for concocting excuses, but bullshit always reeked of bullshit. When they were sitting in your office, across the desk from you, the truth was hard to hide.

In the end, five miles and ten frozen toes later, he resolved to set it all aside. Polly's shenanigans, Anita's evasions—none of it was making him happy. That was one of his favorite strategies, *Try and think of something that makes you happy*, and counselling himself to do so now, he came up with quite a list. His back had survived the shoveling and so had his heart, he was in the middle of a good book by Colum McCann, there was Cherry Garcia ice cream in the freezer, and their daughter Carrie, who they hadn't seen since last May, was coming home next week. The list could go on, but that was enough to clear his head.

Jack fell again and this time he did call Ian. The wellsprings of embarrassment had shifted, apparently, when it was either call Ian once or call 911 twice inside a fortnight. "No medicos," he said, dictating his terms from, presumably, a supine posture while breathing ice fog. "Just come and hoist me up."

Had Jack somehow been in touch with Anita Richardson? They spat out the same word, medicos, with the same bravado, as though to puff themselves up by shearing a bit of respect off the stout medical profession.

It grew into a two-day affair, all told. Fetching him out at the lake, organizing him (mind and body) for the trip to the hospital, the long wait there. Dredging up Jack's sister Ruthie, every bit as headstrong as Jack—you state it, she resists it—then rounding up a vast raft of devices Jack would never deploy: walkers and grabbers and grab bars, thermal this and thermal that.

Jack assented to all procedures and accoutrements in order to escape their clutches, the medicos. He had no intention of doing anything they told him. He had already forgotten what they called the *precipitating event*, had erased both falls from memory, erased any consideration that falling was possible. "Why would I fall?" he said, as though such things were altogether voluntary.

Ian vowed he would try not to grow stupid as he aged. He vowed to try living the myth, which he articulated for Jack Sutcliffe: "What about the bit where with age comes wisdom?"

Carrie rarely came home, though she never failed to clarify that Blaine was not really *home*, not where she had lived as a child. The Spring Street house was not even their first house in Blaine, not the one she returned to from her freshman year in college. While all this was true, reiterating it each time she came east was not necessary. But Carrie was born thorny.

She always came prepared to treat her father as elderly (though not prepared to acknowledge his wisdom) simply because of the heart event. Which was years in the rearview mirror. Ian had shown her the printouts, underlined the words *no further need for remediation*, all of it. "I am supposed to walk a lot. I walk a lot. Ask Fred if you won't take my word for it."

They walked a lot together that week, talked more easily than they could while sitting down. Carrie was living in Colorado now, Boulder, after some years in Salt Lake City, where she had worked at the university named after Brigham Young. Who, she argued, was not necessarily insane. Even Joseph Smith might have been sane, just a good old American charlatan and a talented one at that. But Young was a bold pioneer with, incidentally, a terrific name. "Much easier for a Brigham Young to be charismatic than a Joe Smith," said Carrie, confirming that she had kept her sense of humor out west.

Except on the subject of children. She did not want any. Her parents could not order grandchildren like French fries, no matter how much they *deserved* them. And what sense would it make to "breed" with the boyfriend Warren, when he was past fifty and would be pushing seventy when the putative little Heather or Harrison was still in high school? She was not a cookie cutter woman and they needed to swear off being cookie cutter parents.

"We cook together, we explore around in his camper, we like books and movies and music, we have friends. Why isn't that a life?"

They had heard these sentences before. Polly knew it all professionally and Ian knew it as bedrock liberal thinking. Men without kids were not stigmatized, why should women be? He summoned for himself the example of Ted Curtin, Ted who liked children, or so he said before adding "but you'd have to be crazy to want one in the house for eighteen years." Ted was neither crazy nor, more to the point, unhappy. He was simply childless, or as he preferred to put it, child-free.

"It's fine," Ian said. "Really. We understand."

"Understanding is good," said Carrie, "but wouldn't I love to see acceptance."

"We accept," said Ian, drawing her close as they looked down from the Stony Top ledges. All you saw from up here was forest, as if no civilization had encroached, which was strange with more than a dozen towns within thirty miles of where they stood. With roads and fields, houses and even shopping plazas. How was it that all you saw was trees?

"You are disappointed," she said, "which is different from acceptance."

His daughter's presence had taken him up completely, especially since Polly was still going to the office every day. This was fine, he was delighted having her home and equally delighted that planning out the days with Carrie displaced any decisions he needed to make regarding Anita. His "ministry," as Polly was now calling it, was placed on hold. It snowed just once that week, an inch of light fluffy snow, so he didn't even suffer a pang over not being there to help. In fact, he grew aware of how short a time he had known Anita Richardson, a single season, bracketed as it was by a snowstorm the night of the first Brierly sing and today's minimal snowfall. He had tricked himself into taking the whole episode too seriously. With a little distance and Carrie for a distraction, he had been given space to get some perspective.

Or so he thought. On Sunday morning Carrie got into her rental, ready to leave for the airport. In the turnaround, he and Fred patted the hood of the car as though it were a horse about to be ridden deeper into the adventuresome west. They followed her vapor trail down Spring Street for a quarter mile. Fifteen minutes later, walking through Watchman Park, they felt the magnet tug of 85 Brierly. The hiatus had changed nothing; it was just a hiatus.

A few days before, Polly had baited him. "Why not take Carrie to meet your new friend? They must be about the same age, no? They might have a lot in common."

"Who is this?" Carrie asked, as neutrally as she could manage. She knew her parents' nuances, their tones and strophes (Polly mischievous and challenging, Ian recalcitrant and reliably dodging conflict) and could always sense a tension in the air. "Who are we talking about?"

It was a terrible idea, Ian knew that much. Why was it, though? Maybe Carrie and Anita really would hit it off—Carrie relieved of the Blaine boredom stealing over her progressively, Anita with a fresh contact and lots of fresh western topics. The Grand Canyon, the Grand Tetons, the Rio Grande River. With all that grandeur, what harm could it do?

Yet he was set on avoiding it. "Why not?" was what he said to them. "We'll see how the rest of the week goes."

Then, of course, it did go. It went and so did Carrie.

Ian was back in the starting lineup for a tough one in Hoyt Village. This town was nothing more than a crossroads now, a pretty corner where three rivers conjoined, the Black River and the Christian River flowing into the Copper River. The mill buildings that had made it a thriving village and a hub of sorts remained only as monuments to the bygone age of brick and textiles. Perhaps that made it appropriate for tonight's "vigil sing," the closest they could come to rowing some poor soul directly across the River Jordan.

They made the softest possible entrance—shoes off in the vestibule, barely breathing themselves—and sang their quietest repertoire. They reduced "I Still Have Joy" to a duet, Faith and Ward, and then Faith did "Softly and Tenderly" solo. Ian could not take his eyes off the thin strand of tears, a continuous trickle from one of Mrs. Parenteau's eyes. The water was simply escaping from her and he thought how much she must love the husband she was losing. Then, absurdly, he thought of the drip from the washing machine last week. Of cranking the hose connection tighter and tighter, praying it would not let go and flood the laundry room. It did not do that; neither did it stop dripping.

For some reason, unstated, they skipped the huddle, went straight to the van and for a while rode in silence. Ian guessed the silence replaced anything they might have said about Bill Parenteau, or his wife, or the sing. This one was best left behind. When the talk did begin, it was kept light. Ian was party to that, contributing a recommendation of *Longmire*—first season only, mind—when they did the seen-anything-good-lately part.

They were nearly back to Blaine when he learned that an upcoming sing at 85 Brierly had been cancelled. The client had a bad week, one that in fact required hospitalization. Ian could only hope that darkness concealed the extent to which this casually delivered news jolted him. The *client*. He suppressed the urge to gather details, let the conversation breeze on. To the others, this cancellation was a one-sentence item of business, a chyron, that gave way instantly to Faith's distaste for the new dental assistant at Dr. Spector's office.

Outside the Food Co-op, where they had parked the cars, they said their goodnights and pulled out the same way they would file in at a sing, one by one. The market closed at seven in the winter so that a few minutes later Ian's Honda was the only car in the lot. It would be a good deal later before he sorted out how to handle the morning, how to bring Polly in on it. Because there was no getting around it, he would have to offer help. This was an emergency, things had taken a turn.

When he finally pulled out of the lot, he saw it was not yet eight o'clock. It had been so dark for so long that it never occurred to him he could take action tonight, right now. At least find out how dire her situation was. Unsure now whether to head for the hospital or the house, he decided to swing by Brierly because it was closest. Prepared for either her presence or her absence, Ian was in no way prepared to find an envelope taped to the door with his name on it, or for the note inside:

> *If I am still at Blaine Central when you read this, please come say hello?*
>
> *Thanks, A.*

He read it three times but it was just as direct each time. He was being summoned. Not to her deathbed—her tone was far too lively to believe that was possible—simply to her bedside. Harmlessly, innocently, though he doubted Polly would see it that way. She would see incrimination in the mere fact of it: why Ian? Still, he could not conceal the note from her, or destroy it. *Destroying evidence*, what was more incriminating than that, the coverup always worse than the crime . . . .

But he did destroy it. He proved willing to parse morality this one time, in favor of a less provocative characterization. Frankly, he gave it some spin. Ms. Richardson had declined, been hospitalized, but was encouraging visitors. He would report this to Polly in the morning and suggest they go together to the hospital. The plan was flawed (what if they walked in and Anita beamed at him and said, Oh good, you got my note!) but for now it was the best he could manage.

He would try to go in first, let Anita know he had brought along a surprise guest, and mention it was best to keep the note private. They would have picked up some flowers and Polly would come in to present them. Anita was sick enough to be at Blaine Central and she would look that much worse for the pale green walls, the harsh fluorescent lighting. Poll would finally get it. She would kick in. It would be all right.

Waking at three a.m. meant Ian could either remain in bed for three hours and call it rest or get up in the dark and start the coffee. This was a Hobson's Choice he often faced. One choice he did not have was sinking back into sleep; he was as apt to grow wings and fly. For a moment he closed his eyes and wondered if Hobson always offered two choices and only two, or could he accommodate multiple choice? Then it was to hell with Hobson—who was he anyway, other than someone to blame in the dark night of the soul.

Ian had been strapped with the good man image, Ian Nelson a man beyond moral reproach. This went back so far he did not remember where and why it started. He must have welcomed it, though, or at least accepted it. Interestingly, he had learned that denying it only tended to reinforce the charge: ah, not only is he pure, he is humble!

Once before in his life (Ella, of course) it became obvious what a sham this label was. Pure? Not exactly. Nor were his good deeds at 85 Brierly all that pure, not when Ian was anticipating his own suffering, his own loss, not only Anita's. Yes, it was about the vibrant life Anita might be losing; it was also about his own tiny life shrinking even further.

He kept going over it but the whole mental mess would not budge. He debated: would he be sound asleep now if he had not stopped by her house after the sing? Not seen the note. Was ignorance bliss? They were supposed to sing and go home. The others did it—Ward and Faith, Phil and Karin— they sang and went home. He had to pick at the scab.

Clawing after excuses, he sought refuge where he could find it, St.

Augustine! St. Augustine had faltered and he was a saint. Jimmy Carter was a good man, the most moral president anyone could remember, yet famously he lusted in his heart. Martin Luther King lusted for real. The best among us are sinners. Are any of us as good as we set out to be?

So many people only pretend to be good. They even pretend to themselves. In her work as a therapist Polly was always dredging up the inner self, working to unearth it from the caves of self-deception. Ian was not laboring under any such delusions, not tonight. His inner self was leaping about like a fish on the hook.

Maybe he should not have retired. Maybe he ought to un-retire. Every time he ran into Marta Proxmire at Meg's or Market Basket she would ask if he was ready to come back to work, joking he would always have "the right of return." Ian was pretty sure she meant it. He had been good at his job and they had tried three different people since he left. Not having to work left him too much room for these self-confounding episodes. He had been at sea, looking for causes, asking for trouble. Those insights all came from Polly—hospice was a cause, the Richardson woman was trouble—but Ian could not dismiss them out of hand. Not tonight.

Polly would approve. She was still working, believed in still working. In fact, she seemed to be working longer hours than ever, sixty-five was just a number, blah blah. But it was not just a number to Ian, not when he craved a nap at odd moments through the day and knew he would succumb if he did not get himself outdoors right away. Fred was always there as an excuse; Fred kept him awake. According to Polly, inactivity was what made you tired. He hadn't been so sleepy when he was still at the high school, had he?

But he had. Weary of saying the same things over and over, and often just plain weary, he had dialed up his coffee consumption, doubled it the last few years in harness, even though the common room coffee was terrible. No flavor and negligible caffeine. Every week he thought about bringing in better beans from East Coast Roast, making the coffee more effective if nothing else.

Instead, he retired. At the time, retirement had made sense. Tonight, nothing did.

Blaine Central Hospital was less than two miles from the house. Had Polly agreed to accompany him, Ian would have driven there, so in that sense he was glad she hadn't. It was too nice a day, too generous a sun: sun glistening on the salted blacktop, buttered onto red brick sidewalls, glaring off the acres of hospital plate-glass.

Polly almost did come. Said she was tempted to see "Wonder Woman" in the flesh. More sorely tempted by the chance to catch up at home, create order at her desk, do something about the accumulated calls and emails. "I'm almost at the point where you just ignore them all and start fresh, even if it costs me a few friends." Polly could be so convincing.

She convinced him to call before going, check on visiting hours, check on whether Wonder Woman was in fact still alive. When he called, a pleasant voice asked if he was a relative and, when he was not one, the pleasant voice regretted that she could not discuss the patient's condition.

"You amaze me," said Polly. "Why not just say yes, I am her beloved Cousin Johnny. I mean *really*, Ian."

Going up in the elevator, he had no hard information beyond the inference he took from their willingness to provide a room number. If Anita was dead or in a coma, they would not have directed him to Room 312. Nonetheless, he advanced with trepidation, picturing her stricken, her face lopsided and livid. Halfway down the polished corridor, he stopped, remembering he had meant to bring flowers. Flowers, a book, *something*. He almost rerouted back down to the gift shop where they sold such things, but a nurse was advancing on him, asking if he needed help, and he could only say he was looking for Room 312. When she said "Follow me," he went forth flowerless.

He knocked lightly before pushing through the door and there she was, barely ten feet away and very much herself. Not lopsided, not wan. But she did not react at first, or speak. She regarded him blankly, as though he was not only unimportant to her, he was apparently unrecognizable! Ian had just begun to absorb the severity of this rejection when she lifted a palm to shade the sunlight and her face changed, burst open—the smile spreading, the sea-green eyes igniting—and she exclaimed his name. He was her savior after all.

"I think they are going to let me out of here today," she said. "Any chance of a lift home?"

Not her savior, merely her chauffeur?

"Is that why you left the note?"

"Oh, my, I forgot about that note," she laughed. "It feels like I've been in here for years. There's something about a hospital."

"Something? Or everything. The food. The noise and the bad lighting that make sleep impossible. The excellent odds of contagion."

"That's all true, but everyone who works here has been wonderful."

"Yes, that was all true for me too. The people. But what happened? To bring you here."

"A series of little lightning strikes in my head. The Blob acting up, leaning on my brain. They attacked him with some atomic-strength version of ibuprofen, I forget the syllables. And made a plan to irradiate me next week."

"That's good. You finally signed on for radiation."

"I didn't sign anything. I just told them I'd do it so they would let me out of here."

She lied to the medicos. Lied casually, without hesitation. Couldn't she just as easily have told the truth? Wasn't it her choice, to radiate or not to radiate? She was not a prisoner. It almost seemed she was proud of lying, amused by her ability to trick the medicos. But who was he to judge her? Maybe she simply found it easier, lacked the energy for some sort of principled stand. Did he truly believe that Heaven and hell were in a constant tug of war for the soul of mankind and that lying was a victory for the devil?

On one level, he did. It was ingrained, his father's voice never quite silent. Still, every time he heard that voice ("Good is as close to God as you can get") he could hear his own voice responding, "If it's the alphabet we are going by, Dog is God spelled backwards." Why not fight absurdity with absurdity? He had never said such a thing in his father's presence, though, never talked back to his father. Even now he was treading lightly as he broached it with Anita.

"You lied?"

"Well, *sure*," she said with absolute simplicity. Lying as the obvious thing to do. This complete absence of conscience impressed him in a way, it was of a piece with her devil-may-care courage. Seizures, blackouts, death, *phooey*. It also seemed related, hard to say how, to a corresponding absence of vanity, her hair in disarray, her hospital johnnie stained with carrot juice or orange juice, no matter. Or did she have such a lifelong trust in her physical beauty that vanity was rendered moot?

"There can be very good reasons why people don't always want to tell the truth. If you close that door, I'll give you one really good example. I'll tell you why I left that note."

"Besides arranging a ride home?"

"I wasn't thinking that far ahead. I was thinking back, to the story I didn't want to share? And I decided if you showed up here, I would do it."

"You called it a confession. Said you had a confession to make."

"Yes. Unless you object to being appointed my confessor, I will confess my sins to you."

Ian almost made a terrible joke about deathbed conversions, last minute absolution. He wanted to say the right thing, had no idea what the right thing might be. "Why me?" he said, because it came the easiest. It was not, at least, patently the *wrong* thing to say.

The door swung open and a nurse came in. She checked some readouts on the screen in such a perfunctory fashion that Ian suspected her real goal was to open the door he had closed. She patted Anita on the forehead, said "Feeling much better, are we?" and left. Ian went over and closed the door behind her. Anita took a sip of what looked like cold tea and said, "Why you? Because you have a nice face. Because you are a nice man. I saw it right away when your group came to my house that first night— yours was the face I saw. And I remember thinking, he is someone who might not hate me."

Ian held his tongue, determined to show her only the facial neutrality of a high school counsellor. But seconds later her blurted confession would put him to the test.

"I slept with my brother-in-law," she said. "My sister's husband. My niece's father."

Ian didn't know which was more stunning, that she would do such a thing—betray her sister, commit virtual incest—or that she was conveying this shameful secret to *him*.

"I knew you would be shocked."

"I just don't know what to say."

"The confessor could just listen—like a Catholic priest? Or he could ask why. That would be natural. He could demand to know how in the world I could have allowed it to happen. He could ask if it was a crazy reaction to my parents' dying, or to finding out that I was."

"Maybe it was both?"

"It was neither, but thank you for asking." Exposing herself this way had made Anita brittle and defensive. She sounded altogether different to him. "This happened after both my parents were gone and before I knew about The Blob. Although that cheery news flash came soon enough on the heels of my great sin that it surely felt like God's punishment for what I did."

"I don't believe He works that way, Anita. Doesn't it seem like He punishes a lot of the best people and spares many of the worst?"

"That presumes we can know which is which. It must get tricky at times, no? Don't you suppose God must have a hung jury now and then?" She had gone from defensive to aggressive, and all the while somehow blithe, keeping him off balance.

"What did she say? Your sister. When you confessed to her?"

"I confessed to you, Ian. Richard is the one who confessed to Sally. He's a Quaker and Quakers are upstanding people who are obliged to tattle on themselves."

"Wait. You would have kept something that big a secret from her? Let it just sit there, between the two of you?"

"Absolutely. Because it wasn't important and there was no good to come of airing it. I figured if I kept it to myself I would be the only victim. Tell Sally and everyone becomes a victim, you see. They are a family, they are, or were, RichardSallyKennyLindsay. I thought the family would be better off if we both kept our mouths shut."

"But Richard is a Quaker."

Ian could hardly believe they were having this discussion, much less that he was on first name terms with Richard. How did that happen? Richard might not even exist, this could all be a tall story. Anita liked stories. "Yes," she said. "Apparently he laid out the whole scenario. How we found ourselves left alone, drank too much, fumbled around for half an hour, somehow it happened, barely remembered it the next day. And Sally had the cow."

"Understandably."

"Really? Lives torn asunder, to use a high-falutin' term, for something so brief and trivial and accidental? I knew they would be, though. I know Sally."

"Infidelity isn't usually considered trivial," Ian could not stop himself from saying. "Not by the one who feels betrayed."

"Fair enough. I knew you would have to judge me harshly."

"That wasn't a judgment—"

"Of course it was. Why not admit it? You are appalled and you are right to be appalled. You're sorry you ever met me."

"That's a silly thing to say," said Ian, but as he watched her eyes cloud over until the color in them disappeared, watched her shaking with the effort to restrain tears that kept squeezing out regardless, he did wonder if this could be manipulation. Polly never did that. She never cried about anything. He didn't really believe her when she said she cried at *Love Story*, back in the day. Before Polly, though, there had been Myra, for whom tears were an essential part of her toolkit, a sharp instrument, whether for affixing blame or summoning sympathy. Myra had schooled him in the nuclear option: *I cry therefore you must restore me to happiness.*

And he did feel a need to fix this, simply because repair was his default impulse, not to mention his basic training. *Take a sad song and make it better*? The Beatles were not off base there. Besides, this young woman was in the hospital and facing death. Why *not* fix it, if that was possible? What would it cost him to provide such absolution as he could? But it was clear that any words would ring hollow at this point. In a relationship you began to fix it physically, with your arms, your hands, so this was trickier. To hug Anita now, Ian would have to slide right onto her bed.

He did reach for her hand, sort of a compromise, supportive yet distanced.

She grasped his hand and squeezed it, with a caveat: "Careful now, I am a confirmed sinner."

"Is sin contagious? A germ that can spread?"

"Sinning could be. I did it once, I could do it again."

Now this—the very suggestion, rendered with a sprinkle of false innocence—did feel manipulative to Ian. Unless she was just being kind, returning a kindness by bolstering an old guy's ego. "I don't think so," he said in his most ministerial tone. "Certainly not with me."

"Why not? Just because you are proper and reserved and happily married?"

"And old. Don't forget that one. Richard was young, at least."

This was absurd. He had no idea how old "Richard" was. He had let her turn this into a kind of sideways flirtation, had made him feel complicitous. It was not clear whose hand was withdrawn first but each had retreated to a neutral corner, as it were.

"I'm older than you think," she laughed. "By the way."

This was meant to disarm and re-direct, and it did both. Ian guessed she was thirty-two, she "confessed" to thirty-nine. "I'll never see forty, but I can always say I saw thirty-nine."

"You'll make it," said Ian, disarmed, redirected. "When is your birthday?"

"December. Two days before bloody Christmas. You get the short end that way, and you can't even blame them for skimping on the presents. Sally knew enough to be born in March. Nothing else ever happens in March."

So you paid her back by seducing her husband! The thought was pure reflex, though Anita was the one who had led them back to Sister Sally. In any case, where did the word *seducing* come from, and who said Anita did any seducing that was done. Richard was the boy; boys were the ones who pushed for sex. The ones who took advantage if they could.

Mercifully, the nurse returned, same one who had patted Anita's head. She beckoned Ian out to the corridor: "You are a good dad, but we will need a bit of privacy now, if that's all right."

She blushed when he told her he was not her father, left her fumbling through her mental catalogue for an acceptable alternative (he was sure he saw "uncle" flash through) before electing to go general and avoid risk. "A very nice man, then. Still, if you would?"

Friend. He should have told her what he was, not what he was not. Or told her nothing, let it go, what the hell. Strangely, it was his brief exchange with the nurse, not Anita's extraordinary revelation, that occupied him during his exile to the hallway. That and the enlarged color photographs—river rocks visible through sun-minced water, a white picket fence bowed by hard-pushed snow—which enlivened the drab pastel walls.

"We're all decent now," said the nurse, as she emerged from Room 312 to re-admit him. Still working to withhold or, failing that, disguise judgment, Ian found himself turning to the sister. Who was born in March, when nothing else happens. Who was as unknown a commodity to him as Richard.

"What does Sally say now? Has she been to see you here?"

"Here? In the hospital?"

"I guess I meant in Blaine. Since your diagnosis. Since she's had a chance to forgive you."

"Sally forgive me? She said I was never to darken her doorway again and she meant it. My nine-year-old niece Lindsay got to hear me described in language you would not believe. I was the intended target but Lindsay was collateral damage, a victim of very unfriendly fire. Oh, and she also got to watch her father cower in a corner."

"You can't tell me the cancer hasn't softened her."

"I can tell you it absolutely wouldn't, if she knew."

"Seriously? Your sister doesn't know you're—"

"Dying. Dying is a word, Ian."

"You have to tell her."

"You say I do. You don't know Sal. She poisoned the whole well, everyone we know. It was the same circle of friends: poker games, potlucks, softball. Sal made sure everyone knew I was the she-devil."

"Even so, all that was before the diagnosis."

"I'm not like that, Ian. Hey folks, I'm really sick so it's just fine to like me again? Uh-uh. I moved away and it's like the country song says, from now on, all my friends are gonna' be strangers. Merle Haggard, right? I only know doctors and nurses and social workers."

Even in a small town, or a small intimate city like Blaine, there are people you never meet. To Ian, Anita Richardson seemed like one of those people, their paths had not crossed. At the same time, she seemed firmly rooted in that house on Brierly—been there forever, must know dozens of people—when in fact she'd barely had time to unpack before learning she had months to live.

"Tell me, is she Sally Richardson? Or Mrs. Richard Something? Or—"

"No, Ian."

"Just tell me her name."

"You can't fix this. I don't even want it fixed."

"No, you want to be hated."

"I *deserve* to be hated."

"Let he who is without sin cast the first stone," he said, going Biblical. "That one tends to thin the herd pretty thoroughly."

He was following his professional bent—empathetic, supportive, consoling—though his deeper instincts were mixed. Her own *sister*? She had done something *unseemly*. The word, his mother's, was still firmly lodged in Ian's moral vocabulary.

"You are a nice man," she said, repeating the same bland compliment both she and the nurse had already hung on him. "But it's not like I expected you to be my ride home, even before you knew the extent to which I am *not* nice. I was more thinking, if they kidnap you in an ambulance, they might be legally obligated to take you back home in one."

After thirty years in the Copper River region, Ian could still taste the air, so different from the Boston air or, God forbid, Manhattan. This was a point of pride throughout the region, much trumpeted and universally embraced. The blackflies were a nice curse to have, since they only thrived where the water was clean and the air unsullied. The true believers were unmoved by the news that they had plenty of blackflies way up north, where the pulp and paper mills sullied the air relentlessly.

He was happy tasting it now. More than ready to escape the hospital and the dicey moral issues he had faced in there, he felt a swoop of emotion he interpreted as freedom. Free to come to the hospital and free to leave it. He recalled with perfect clarity the moment he walked out of Beth Israel after they bypassed his heart. The best air was the air outside a hospital.

Uncertain about so many things, Ian was certain that Sally Shumway would have to be told her sister was dying, and fairly certain he was the one charged with the telling. He would not ask Anita's blessing, he would simply do it. It was even possible that in (finally) providing Sally's full name, and adding that she was "still in Portland, last I knew," Anita was secretly hoping he would undertake the mission.

He would try to enlist Polly, *deploy* her. Here was a thorny psychological problem to solve, a challenge that her professional side would find hard to resist. Poll might be the one equipped to bring the sister around. I'm human, Anita had pleaded. Why not expect Sally to be human too?

Nice Guys Finish Last

"I WOULD LOVE it if you came," he said, as he let Polly know about the task at hand. First things first. He was slated to go back to Blaine Central at noon and drive Anita home.

"That's all right," she said, with what looked like restrained amusement.

Polly had a gift for subliminal messaging and Ian had an unfortunate gift for receiving those messages. Her unspoken suggestions came like notes slipped under the door and Ian had trouble twisting free of them, trouble hanging on to his own perspective. Even if he sometimes felt trapped, he did not like seeing them as traps. Poll was free to say or think whatever she wanted; it was on him if her perspective overwhelmed his own. Then too, he knew he would come around—an hour later, a day later—to seeing that she was right.

He was going through such mental gyrations while Polly was getting organized to go out. Their embrace when she left was perfunctory, glancing. It left Ian feeling dismissed, though it was Polly driving away.

Spring was still weeks away, yet another snowstorm forecast for the weekend, but the squirrels and the forsythia each disputed the calendar, the former by going crazy, the latter by going into bud. He decided to join them in getting ahead of the curve. Took a cup of coffee and the radio out to the garage and began untangling the tomato towers, sorting the partial bags of last year's potting soil, compost, and mulch, scouring a mouse nest from the engine casing of the mower. It was always a pleasant chore, a welcoming, to begin addressing the disorder that always mounted through the long winter.

Except he kept hearing the subliminal messages, the radio failing to drown them out. *You don't know who she really is*, Polly said subliminally. That Anita was a dying woman was merely *possible*, she said. *She has you wrapped around her little finger, hasn't she?* For an hour, these loud unspoken charges trailed him around each dusty, cobwebbed corner of the garage.

It was hard to deny that Anita was untrustworthy when she had just copped not only to "sin," but to gross deception. Lying to her sister for supposedly noble reasons, lying to him out of petty convenience. Maybe (as Polly implied, subliminally) everything about her was a lie. For all he knew, there was no Sister Sally. No Richard.

Not all of Polly's suspicions or doubts had gone unspoken. Ian's "little friend" might simply be a woman ditched by her husband. If she seemed so hardy, perhaps she was suffering migraine headaches and not this famous glioblastoma. She might be mentally ill, and a clever manipulator. Polly had seen all these behaviors clinically, in all manner of disguise.

Ian was startled when a tan and white mouse, cow colored, sprang from the motor housing and he saw six tiny pink babies nestled like spoons still inside. Certain the damned thing would never start, he rolled it outside to give it a try, and it started on the second pull. But he had been fooled before; it might not start so readily once the grass began growing.

He tried to stay focused on Anita, his own sense of her, how she seemed in person. Reminded himself again that Polly was shooting in the dark, had never met the woman. True, Anita was comfortable with setting truth aside, but her condition had to be real, and serious. No hospital would keep you five days for a migraine headache. They booted mothers the day after a complicated birth. They had sent Ian packing forty-eight hours after open heart surgery.

He had not told Polly about his decision to locate "the sister," make her aware of Anita's situation. Introducing it this morning would have blown up the conversation as decisively as a gas leak blowing up a tarpaper shack. He knew Polly would resist. Knew that weighing against her reflexive professional interest in the matter would be her professional reluctance to take direct action in a situation where the client had not invited it. Such an intervention was (he could hear her say it) *contraindicated*. The argument he would make was simple: you could hardly make the situation worse, while you stood a reasonable chance of making it better. Didn't that make it *indicated*?

He would frame it as a pleasant day for them, a healing outing. They could watch for early signs of spring here and there along the way. Stop for a nice lunch—he had researched some options on the Google. Maybe stop to hike one of the railroad trails, he had researched those as well. Ian would make the presentation after dinner tonight. Right now he had to get cleaned up and get over to Blaine Central.

Noon, when Anita was scheduled for release, turned out to mean half past two. Increasingly restless in the lobby—oddly, since he had nowhere else to be—Ian slipped away, strolled to East Coast Roast ("A lot smaller than Starbucks and only slightly better") and took a coffee to the Riverwalk. There was slush on all the benches, and orange cones cordoned along the riverbank served as a warning the ice was no longer reliable.

Ian had always been charmed by those Dutch paintings, people routinely traveling on ice skates, canals and rivers serving as winter roadways. It looked so different from skating on ponds and he had always wanted to try it with the kids, maybe skate down the river to Grandville, but he had been too cautious. What if one of them went through here and the other there? What if he went through? He found himself reminiscing about that time, the sledding and skating years, which were also the years the four of them would take short, tame off-season trips to Cape Cod beach towns. Such a long time ago! The kids were approaching middle age and the Cape, already overcrowded and expensive then, was five times more so now.

A yellow lab wandered down to browse the river's edge, pawing at the brittle ice before he settled for peeing on the base of a granite lamppost. The dog's owner, a young woman with a rolling suitcase, looked up and apologized with her eyes. Ian waved off the apology. He might have launched into friendly patter about Fred's similar proclivities had she not been moving so quickly. Not everyone has nowhere to be.

It was an hour later when they brought Anita down in a wheelchair, clearly under protest. Emerging from the elevator, she rolled her eyes and sprang to her feet defiantly to show she could. "Maybe it's a rule they have," he said as she rolled her eyes again. *Rules.* He saw she had nothing with her, just a book and a jacket she was refusing to put on because she could see through the plate glass that the day was sunny. Told him not to fetch the car, she could walk through the parking lot, though she did sit back down when he ignored her and went to fetch it. There was something off-kilter in her eyes—were they crossed slightly?—and her cheeks had none of their usual color. It could be the lighting. In this closed, fluorescent universe, even the Black orderly who wheeled her looked pale. Ian *felt* pale.

But she still looked that way at the Brierly house and her breathing was audible, raspy. As though to deny or disguise all this, Anita called out a jaunty hello to Mr. Whatsit, who was in his yard picking up a few advertising tabloids that someone must have parachuted in from the curb. There were some in Anita's yard as well, but she left them there and so did Ian, eager to bundle her inside.

"Maybe they should have kept you a bit longer," he said.

"No. They were sick of me, and I was sick of them."

"But you *are* sick. And *they* are the hospital."

"Right. As in, Get me outta here."

This was her last burst of brashness before she subsided ("Would you mind fixing us some tea?") and collapsed onto the couch.

"You are going to need help here," he said.

"I'll be fine. One good night's sleep, you know. After however many days without any sleep at all."

"You'll need groceries. If you give me a list—"

"You are a glutton for punishment. Seriously, I'll shop tomorrow. I'll be fine."

He had never seen her bedroom. Abandoned in haste a week ago, the bed was a pile of wrinkled sails, a shipwrecked mess, but she would not stand for his making it. "I'm just going to crawl in and go to sleep. I can straighten things out when I wake up."

He complied, by this time concerned with boundaries, crossing them. Clearly, though, she would need help.

"If you don't mind one more favor," she said, "you could crack a window for me."

"It's about fifty degrees in here, Anita. If you're feeling warm, you may have a fever."

"They took my temp less than an hour ago. Honestly, I am just craving a little fresh air after serving my time in that lovely airless prison."

He opened the window a few inches. As he came back past the bed she reached out and snared his hand, squeezed it, thanked him "for everything." Almost immediately he felt her grip loosen as her eyes fell shut. As a test, he closed the window and waited. Getting no response, concluding she was already asleep, he raised the sash again. It was her window after all, her life.

He went downstairs, punched the thermostat up to seventy, and showed himself out. This time, passing through, he gathered up the flyers from her yard.

This was a slump; he was in a slump and life was a long season. At worst, he was depressed. Not enough to do and nothing that felt important. His work had felt important. Reading two newspapers—encountering the same stories in slightly different typefaces—while drinking two cups of coffee did not. It might be as simple as that.

For many of his friends, the solution was also simple. They had hobbies. The very word sounded unimportant to him, though he saw how dedicated people could be, how they poured themselves into woodworking, pottery, dominoes, or bridge. Philip was growing roses. Ted Curtin was growing weed in his cellar with a setup that looked like a botanical lab.

Ian did walk a lot, if that counted. Most days he logged the prescribed five miles. Maybe it counted if you called it hiking instead of walking. But those other hobbies yielded something solid, a product of some sort, Lillian's pottery or Ted's artisanal pot. Ward turning out those whimsical birdhouses, sooner or later everyone got one for Christmas.

Ian had friends. *They* had friends, he and Poll, and that gave him something to do, coffee or beers or dinner parties that were invariably pleasant. Still, if there were no dinner parties, no cups of coffee to catch up with former colleagues, he would not mind. He could appreciate the way such occasions helped pass the time, he just didn't miss them when a lull occurred.

"I know depression when I see it," said Polly, "and you're not depressed. You are just paddling through the swamp of a midlife crisis."

She was not really listening to him, not paying attention. Hardly bothered to look up from the newspaper as she skimmed quickly through before rushing off to work. It was the crown of her head speaking; she might as well be Alexa spitting out generic answers.

"Is that the best my therapist has to offer? Shrinky-dink boilerplate?"

"Would you rather have me say"—looking up now—"that you are bored to death and grasping at straws in the form of this stricken beauty?"

"That's a bit cruel, isn't it?"

"You did not hear me, Ian. That was what I *didn't* say. What I did say is that you haven't enough to do. Plus, it's March."

This was kinder. An old joke revisited, the grand jury dismissing charges.

"I forgot about The Marchies."

What he remembered, though, was that The Marchies mounted their annual attack on Polly, not him. She would feel *lifeless*, that was how she put it, and that was exactly how he would describe his current state. He had been up and about barely an hour and could easily have taken himself right back to bed.

"It doesn't feel like midlife," he said, "it feels much closer to the end."

"Hardly," she said, still kindly. She was not reprising her suspicion that all the time he spent with the dying, one downer after another, carried the obvious risk of emotional contagion. "You're only sixty-six."

"Death can come at any age."

Her raised eyebrow asked, silently, whether he was referencing his heart surgery or his oh-so-youthful "stricken beauty." She stayed with kindness, though, and laughed. "Well yes it can," she said, "just don't forget The Concert."

The Concert was a nugget that had helped pull him past his compromised heart, past the grinding anxiety of a year in which he did not trust his heart to continue beating. They were driving back from Boston at midnight after a gorgeous Mahler symphony when it struck him that such a moment was worth as much whether you encountered it in high school or at your retirement party—or post-op, with a dicey heart. A life is composed of such elements and while they occur in arbitrary order, they all go into the same personal trove. This had become a useful metaphor, *The Concert*.

"I remember The Concert," he said as Polly, her remedial work completed, ducked into the half-bath to check her hair and brush any toast crumbs off her sweater. Ian wasn't sure she heard him. Still, she had placed them on the same page, spoken their private language, The Marchies and The Concert. They were okay.

He watched through the kitchen window as she eased the car through the turnaround. It was possible he had tried The Concert metaphor on Anita— had he?—even though he knew it could have a fortune cookie ring to it. While homilies might help with a bad mood, they were hardly a cure for cancer. Some problems did not have solutions.

Checking the calendar of days, he saw a void, square after square of whitespace with nothing penciled in, not even a bloody dentist appointment. Fortunately, he did have something to do—getting some supplies and groceries into Anita's house—and for this he was grateful. Most people hated such chores, Ian welcomed them. Unlike a *hobby*, this would not help in the long run. It would not backfill the sinkhole left by retirement or empty nest syndrome, or a compromised heart, or encroaching old age. It would, however, fill the morning hours on a cold blank Thursday in March.

The hospital had drained something from her, either that or whatever had sent her to the hospital in the first place. She admitted as much: "I feel like I'm *listing* or something. Do I look crooked?"

"Not from here," he said, though she did look, if not crooked, indefinably distorted.

"It's like I'm trying to duck away from my own brain. Or from The Blob, I guess."

"Out out damned Blob," he offered, enlisting Shakespeare in the cause.

When she tried foisting a credit card on him, he pointed out that he had scant chance of passing for an Anita. Then, when he came back with the groceries, a couple of bags for sixty bucks, she was ready with her checkbook. "Too much trouble," he said. "Let's just consider it a present."

"No way. If anything, I owe you a present. I'll get you a shirt."

"I can always use a shirt," he said. "Hey, I'm using one now."

"That's what I always got my dad. He was hopeless. There never was a nail or a hook he could walk past without snagging his sleeve and ripping it."

Ian flashed on one of Polly's indictments, the father figure. ("Didn't you say both her parents were gone? Why wouldn't she need a parent's love at a time like this?") Poll had a basket full of indictments, to go with her drawer full of hypotheticals. Of course she did, she was a therapist, for whom notions like the father figure were as much the *lingua franca* as batting averages were to a baseball buff.

Watching Anita stow away the groceries, Ian tried to get a handle on what had changed in her. She appeared fragile, certainly, though anyone returning from time served in a hospital bed would be fragile, need some time to recover from recovery. Her spirit was undiminished. Even with a rare admission that she might have some limitations (her health, she said with a smile, was "somewhat compromised") the surface insouciance was present. Hearing it now, when finally she did seem vulnerable, he realized she had nearly bluffed him into believing in her immortality.

"I'm going," he said. "You need to rest."

"But I'm hungry. I was thinking pancakes—and then I can rest. Do you like pancakes? Fred must like them."

Why not be sensible and simply leave? Tell her Fred loved anything that could be described as food but right now she needed to visit a certain tree in Watchman Park. The tree would have been a perfect exit line. Instead, he found himself offering to make the pancakes. That way, at least, she would save energy.

"I want to use energy, not save it," she said, shaking buckwheat flour into a large, brown-speckled bowl. "In the hospital, where the food was probably inedible—I can't be sure because I never felt like eating—I gave some thought to my last meal. You know, a condemned prisoner's last request?"

"I've heard meatloaf is a popular choice," he said.

"Is it? Where exactly does one go to hear something like that?"

Ian blanked on it. Shrugged. Had he made it up? Read it? Maybe in the book about Dick and Perry, or the one about Gary Something, who they executed in Utah. Anita had lost weight in the hospital, she must have. Maybe that was the difference he was seeing.

"I was leaning toward Thai food, a nice pad Thai and a glass of white wine."

"Hopefully, it won't come to that," he said.

"Why? Because I might die on a Monday and Taste of Thailand is closed on Mondays? The other thing I wondered about was sex. Do they grant a prisoner's last request for sex?"

"You weren't a prisoner," he reminded her. He was on notice about the strange digression and the slippery slope that came with it. Aware that she wasn't listing physically, she was listing mentally. "You were a patient."

"Still, doesn't it seem only human to grant last wishes? Why stop at food?"

"Next thing you'll be putting in for a farewell trip to Disney World."

"The mind does go to funny places when you are waiting to die in a hospital. But you're the reason I came up with this, Ian. It was what you said about how every concert, first to the last, was an equally valid part of your life. Your hospice concerts are a perfect proof of it. So why wouldn't your last sex be just as important as your first?"

"As important, maybe. As possible, maybe not so much."

It was starting to look like an epidemic, everyone lamenting the loss of sex. Jack Sutcliffe, Anita Richardson—and Ian, who last night in bed had tried to recall the last time he and Polly had sex. Assigned the blame, in part, to the excessive clothing one wore to bed during the cold months. But it seemed that everyone he knew was having less sex, while everyone on TV was having more.

Meanwhile, he was wary of what she might say next. The Blob pressing on this poor girl's brain, likely source of any listing or lopsidedness she was experiencing, was also the likely source of this iffy digression. He remembered a film about Chinese agents taking over someone's brain and dictating bizarre speech and behavior. Remembered hoping it was apocryphal.

"Anyway," she said, "it was only a vagrant thought. I'm not advertising for volunteers or anything."

"I'm sure you wouldn't have to advertise," he said, meaning well, of course, trying for standardized reassurance yet instantly fearing the remark could be taken as flirtation. At least he had not blurted out something worse, that maybe her dalliance with the brother-in-law, Richard, *was* her last sex, in which case it could serve as its own punishment. Fragments of the Old Testament lingered in Ian.

"You are kind to say that. And don't worry, I won't ask you to volunteer. I know you are happily married."

So was Richard, he refrained from pointing out. Married.

"Not to mention old enough to be your father," he did point out.

"That's silly. That's like all the other reasons people who consider having sex, just don't. I'll bet that statistically more don't than do."

"Just do it? Is that the philosophy? Is that what happened with—"

"With Richard? A good question, because that is exactly how it happened. To the extent I was reasoning at all, I reasoned this is happening, why not let it happen. Instead of *bad idea!*"

It was a good idea for Ian to leave her now, a good idea for Anita to get some rest, and both these notions were established with no further discussion of final requests from prisoners or patients. The pancakes were dry, needed too much maple syrup, and were left half eaten, though Fred differed and took hers plain.

The takeaway from that exchange at Brierly—*why not* versus *bad idea*—also applied to Ian's impulse to contact Sally Shumway, the aggrieved, unknowing sister. Not challenge her (Lady, your sister is dying!), simply let her know. Surely, she should know.

He asked for Polly's vote. Her participation, too, but if nothing else her knowing vote on why-not versus bad-idea. The thing she did, the shrinkish nod, could be taken for assent, or corroboration, when all she was really doing was moving her head slightly. For once, Ian chose to push. To ask until she answered.

"We've been over this," she said.

"We sort of have. But I don't remember your saying you agreed or disagreed."

"It's enough to know we went over it."

"It's not enough for me, Poll. I really want your input. I trust you on stuff like this."

With a scrunch of her eyes and compression of her lips, she told him he was fishing for approval and would do what he wanted with or without it. "Look. I can't tell you what to do with this woman or her sister. I can only tell you that it seems you have become obsessed with a situation that objectively has very little to do with you. To borrow a phrase from my old mentor Karl Schine, you have disappeared down into it."

"I see."

"Do you?"

He did not, of course. How could he see over the rim of the deep hole she had dropped him into? Polly could be stubborn, and never more so than when standing by the received doctrines of her profession. All he wanted was the human spin, the human impact. And he could not cease believing that their many misunderstandings might have been prevented if Polly had come to meet Anita Richardson and invested a fragment of her abundant humanity.

He was on his own, Polly even phrased it that way. Ian knew it translated to disapproval. She meant to stop him and usually it worked; usually it did not matter enough to spark resistance. Did it matter enough this time?

He decided to shelve it, remembering that for a change he actually had things to do. For a few hours that morning he would be helping Jack Sutcliffe move back from the lake and for a few hours in the evening there would be his first sing in over a month. His first get-together with the Angel Band since the snow had begun turning to mud.

Ian was particularly glad of the sing, ready to be refreshed by it. The weight of winter lingered, the air still leaden and oppressive, and it seemed of a piece with his interior landscape. Oppressed was how he had been feeling, in an amorphous way, and he was counting on the sing to lift him out of it.

Heading out to the lake was also remedial. He caught the seed of freedom that came with a breezy drive out Route 63 and he was looking forward to another shot of Jack's good-natured gloom. One side of the road going out was already greening while the other side, less penetrated by the sun, had dollops of snow on the wooded hillsides. The dregs of winter would not be entirely dislodged this early, but Jack would be. The ice had spoken.

"You did it," Ian said, on greeting the older man. "Lived through another winter." This in reference to Jack's standard rejoinder to any bright prospect, *Sure, if I live that long.*

"I am alive. But then, isn't everyone alive an hour before they're dead?"

"Profundity at the crack of dawn!"

"One minute before they're dead. One split second. All those organs inside you, going along unseen, functioning decade after decade. What's to keep one of them from malfunctioning the very next second? Like an old truck running smooth as ever, then suddenly throwing a rod and becoming junk."

"They must have taken something away from you since my last visit."

"Well, the ice, obviously. I do love the ice, you know. The winter. Guess I'm different from most."

"No doubt about that. Maybe you should relocate to the North Pole. The ice up there might last a few years longer, if the Democrats can get back in power."

"No politics, *por favor.* Let's start loading this stuff before one of my vital organs fails."

"Or one of mine. I actually did have one fail, you might remember, whereas you just grouse about the prospect."

They had the move down to a science after doing it together ten years running. When Jack broke it down, organized the elements of his life on the lake (annually citing Hopkins' "gear, tackle, and trim"), the results were layered as programmatically as the folds of the flag at a war veteran's burial. What had been a fully equipped residence fit neatly into the bed of Jack's truck and the trunk of Ian's car.

It was just as programmatic at their ritual stop in Dinsmore Falls— "Breakfast All Day" for Ian, the meatloaf sandwich on soft soggy white bread for Jack. "Nothing artisanal," he specified sarcastically. Whether or not Dick and Perry had ordered the meatloaf for their last meal, it would surely be Jack Sutcliffe's choice. As this was occurring to him, Ian realized it was the first time in hours he had thought about Anita or the "situation" he had shelved.

"I thought they took coffee away from you," he said, as Jack signaled the waitress for a refill.

"Apparently, the sons of bitches couldn't keep it away."

They did settle into genuine conversation for half an hour. Politics after all, and family. Jack had two "kids" as well, both by now in their middle fifties. "What do you do when your youngest child has white hair?" he said.

"Give the gift of Grecian Formula for Christmas?"

"Should have done that before the snow fell on his head. Too late now, everyone's seen it."

"Polly has just started to show a little gray."

"Polly's sixty-something, Ian, she's a grownup."

"Fifty-five isn't?"

"You know what I mean. By Christ, I have got a thirty-year-old *grandchild*."

The ride south was quiet, a comradely quiet. Jack was tired, Ian distracted. His issues were lurking, popping up in thought bubbles here and there. Last night's awkwardness with Polly was foremost. Today's events would help Ian but they were of no value to Polly; the two of them would be right back where they were. He almost hoped they would miss connections, that she would not yet be home when he left for the sing.

Ian was mildly anxious about the sing. He had not spoken with Karin in a month—Ian talking to her machine, Karin talking to his—and had not seen Harv or Ward or anyone else from the band. Winter was like that, people hunkered down, watched a lot of DVDs. He wondered if their gossipy disapproval had softened, or lapsed. There were factions within the band (Faith, Lexa, Sandy) whose moral universe did not always accommodate man's imperfections.

But it went well from the start. The ride over was mostly chatty catching-up, along with a few reminders about Karin's choices for the night's program.

They were to drop the harmony parts from the first two lines of each verse on "Gift to be Simple" and let Faith's soprano carry it. They would bring back "Stand by Me" even though a majority wanted to give it a rest.

Then they were there, at the Wellman home in Barlow, making their smooth entrance, staggered voices coming in on "Jordan River" as they moved into the room single file. Ian had forgotten how music could thrill him, take him several steps higher on the emotional ladder. There was a time when basketball did that. Coming down the ramp to the gym floor, hearing the drumming of basketballs and the kibitzing voices, he could feel his heart "soar." A cliché, absolutely, yet it was real, visceral, flooding the brain or the heart with endorphins. Music could do it. Their rendition of "What A Friend We Have in Jesus" was so deeply felt as a spiritual that for several minutes Ian felt the tug of the church, drawing him back.

He had considered quitting the Angel Band, leaving the group rather than go on feeling scrutinized, or ostracized. In the midst of tonight's radical bonding, all that seemed like paranoia, plain and simple. A good thing too, with everyone from Dear Abby to his daughter Carrie urging him to sign on for those *activities*, get going on that elusive hobby. He needed to be joining things, not quitting them.

"We missed you, Ian." Karin said this in the huddle, before they piled back into the van. "You too, Harvey," she added. "The truth is, we haven't seen a lot of folks lately. There just haven't been many sings."

"Business has been bad," said Harv, their standard jest.

"And that's always good," came the standard rejoinder.

"You forget, dear Karin, that occasionally people do suffer and die without asking us to serenade them."

"You know what, dear Harvey? Maybe I haven't missed you so much after all."

The pervasive uplift of the sing carried over to the ride back to Blaine and finally to The Draught House (The Draft Horse, as the locals called it) where Ian, Harv, and Ward repaired for a round or two of Guinness. Halfway down the second pint the endorphins were overflowing, with friendships cemented, April at last within range, and any petty concerns swept aside on the tide of alcohol. Apart from the question of whether it was a neap tide or a spring tide they were riding, they agreed on everything.

There was a price to be paid for this bonhomie and it was not Ian's share of The Draft Horse's modest invoice. It was extracted as he walked into his own dark house and realized he had missed Polly clean. Not only had she already gone to bed, she had shut down the first floor as if he did not exist, was not expected home at all. Worse, he realized that he might have missed her on purpose, to avoid another confrontation over Anita or the sister. At the least, he knew he was pushing their clock by staying out so late.

For months he had been confronting the prospect of losing Anita, whether because he abandoned her to assuage Polly or because the accursed glioblastoma took her. What jolted him now, as he groped for the light switches room by room, was losing Polly. Not literally, of course, that was impossible. But losing their connection. They, the two of them, were what they had left—a life together, resting on a foundation formed and maintained over the decades. They needed to begin shoring up that foundation right away. Or he did.

Impossible? Ian presumed as much without even needing to actively presume. After nearly forty years spent building a life together, raising children, buying three houses and selling two of them, shaping the rooms inside those houses and the landscapes surrounding them? Jettison the whole package?

Yet here was Polly, delivering it like a telegram, as brisk as a postcard scribble from friends traveling in Tuscany, yet the message read *I am leaving*. Wearing her cloak of bone-dry objectivity, all traces of emotion sheared away. The postscript, slightly less chilling, read *no need to fuss, no reason this should not be friendly*.

Friendly? "Four decades!" he exclaimed, when she finally sat still long enough to go beyond the postcard. How could she be saying such a thing, this was their life, the *children*—

"The children have their own lives, Ian. You must have noticed that. They have their own children, or Carl does. It simply isn't relevant."

They had been a good team, getting the kids to school and soccer and gymnastics and camp, mustering three meals a day for them plus appropriate snacks. Ian had such a clear picture of Poll holding the snowsuit while he lowered Carrie into it, inserted her—Carrie squalling, the two of them laughing. It was enough to blur his eyes, blur her face in the process; he must be crying. He felt something clog his chest, felt a lead sinker there, but then there was Polly's hand on his neck, softly, and as his vision cleared he saw she was closer, her expression softer. She was rescinding it. She would say, We'll talk, we'll work this thing through . . .

What she did say was good-natured, almost affectionate, albeit in a tone laden with rue. "My poor dear Ian. You can hardly argue we should stay together for the sake of the children."

Why couldn't he argue that? If she actually did this, up and left, Carl would be deeply concerned for each of them: aging alone, getting sick, becoming a burden sooner than anticipated. Carl would not worry as a child, he would worry as an adult. That counted. Anyway, he could argue they should stay together for their own sakes, not for the children, for the two of them. Because of the bond.

"What is this about, Poll?" Calm and clear. Locked down, going with calm and common sense. "Where is this coming from?"

"You always think everything can be explained."

"I do think I deserve an explanation of something as big and weird as this. I am half of it, you know."

"No, Ian, that's the thing. You are 100 percent of you and I am 100 percent of me. But all right, if you need something that could be taken as a *reason*, I will offer you this: you quit."

"What does that mean, I quit."

"Life. You quit doing it."

"Don't tell me you are going to give me that hooey about embracing death just because—"

"No, this is not about your hospice business, or your little hospice friend. Although I will say the notion of pursuing the *sister* did tip matters a bit."

Little friend? Ian resisted the urge to make Anita life-size, make her the five-foot-five or whatever she was, taller in fact than Polly. He resisted the temptation to characterize his "notion" regarding the sister as an embracement of life and therefore the polar opposite from quitting it. Instead he countered with capitulation, guessing capitulation had a better shot.

"I will quit if you like. Not life. I'll quit the sings. I'll quit trying to help Ms. Richardson, if it matters that much. I'll happily allow the sister to remain in the dark—neither of them knows I had the idea anyway. I'll quit quitting, whatever that means to you."

"It doesn't work that way," she said.

"There has to be more to this, more than a blank wall. Another man—"

He could not summon even a weak belief in it, until he realized he had thoroughly lost track of Polly, what she did, where she went, for months, possibly for a year. More and more frequently she had been working—if she was working—into the night. They had been drifting in different directions. Which didn't mean that with new awareness and a bit of effort they couldn't drift back.

"We can fix this, Poll. You're a board certified professional at fixing such problems. Fix us."

"We don't fix anything, we only help people understand what's going on with them. We try to guide them toward clarity."

Clarity? As if! But Polly could close a door as firmly as anyone. She could deliver the worst messages with a face as fixed as a dry dusty two-dimensional portrait. All those years tossed into the rubbish bin while she sorted through drawers, packing right before his eyes.

"Nothing is being thrown away," she said. "We lived it. Enjoyed it. It isn't in a trash bin, it's in our personal bank accounts. Now it's a time for some fresh deposits, that's all."

"Oh, is that all! Fresh deposits. For you, maybe."

He hated himself for going along with her metaphor, the bank accounts. It smacked of such cheap shrinkery-pokery. At least he didn't come back at her with some concomitant bullshit about a joint bank account. Though it occurred to him they did have joint accounts, joint holdings. There were practical aspects to her casual exit.

"For you as well, Ian—"

He stopped her there. Certain she was all set to say something nasty about his "little friend," even suggest he was free to take up with her *if he hadn't already*, he stopped her with a palm, like a crossing guard. "Enough. Please."

"Things do change," she said. "You retired—that was a big change. And as you know better than most, people die. Marriages can die too. Expire."

"That's—"

"Absurd? Is that what you were about to say? You do always say that when we disagree."

"I was going to say they do not expire, they grow. They mature, like bonds," he threw in, to show he could do a fiduciary metaphor too. But he felt silly saying it. He was beginning to regret sounding calm and clear, bandying semantics while discussing a disaster.

"They can do that," she conceded. "Sometimes they do."

Would it help to start shouting at her, firing off all the arguments ricocheting around his brain, all the unspoken anger at being hit with this? Because it *was* absurd. It was crazy. It was also impractical: "Polly, we cannot begin to afford two houses. Practically speaking, we have no choice but to live together."

"I will stipulate that you get to keep the house. And the children. And the dog! How's that?"

Was this humor? Humor from Polly Nelson at a time like this? Either she was so on top of this, so comfortable with it that she was flat out happy, or she was the one in crisis. Not quite herself. Temporarily off the rails. But there was nowhere to go with it, not right now, nowhere except out the door, away from the sound and echo of her bloodless declaration of independence.

It might have been the longest walk they had ever undertaken—to the river, down the river all the way to Hoyt Village and back, then over to the park and thrice around the perimeter. Eight miles? Ian was too rattled to reckon it strictly and because he never wore a watch, he had no idea how long it had been until he saw the kitchen clock.

Polly was invisible, under a duvet in the guest room. She had written him a note: *Really, you will come to know it is for the best.* Did she even have a plan, a destination? She must have, this could not be a momentary impulse. Polly did not do momentary impulse, neither of them did. He tried to begin believing in this sudden new reality but it had stranded him in a dreamlike state, dreamwalking around the city, struggling to focus on the past, present, and future all at once. The past which he had misjudged, the present that had stunned him, the future which felt impossible.

Whatever Polly had for a plan, Ian's only plan—their conjoined lives going along in the same lane until they hit the big stop sign in the sky— had gone glimmering. Now the future was a complete blank. He could die without conceiving a new plan. Die alone. Thank goodness (he said ruefully, drenching himself in bitter irony) it was *all for the best*!

"Mom called."

This was his son Carl on the phone. Mom called Carl so Carl called Dad. It was not anyone's birthday, so Polly must have made it official by "telling the children." It had not taken her long.

"Called, and said?"

"You know. Said you guys were having problems. My parents! Were . . . maybe separating?"

"I see."

"I told her it came as a real shocker and she told me to get my head around it."

"Yes, she said the same thing to me, more or less."

"What the hell, Dad. I asked for an explanation, did not get one—unless you count 'these things happen.' Maybe you can give me a sense of what sort of thing happened?"

"I'm afraid I can't. I mean, nothing *happened*. Your mother had a nice phrase for the Millers when they split up, said they had been skating different ponds for a while. I suppose that has been true of us, but not in any adversarial way. Nothing contentious. As you know, she is still working and I am, well—"

"Retired, Dad, you are retired. You sound almost embarrassed about it."

She had voted no at the time, but it could not be that simple. Polly saying he "quit" because he hadn't enough to do? Citing his failure to find a hobby or sign up for a few activities? Even if that gave grounds for concern, surely it did not give grounds for abandonment.

"My life does seem to have gotten smaller," he said to Carl.

"What exactly does that mean?"

"Nothing exactly. It's definitely inexact. I suppose stopping work did leave a pretty big hole. I thought we would travel, but we've hardly left Greater Blaine in the last few years. Some friends have moved south, some friends have died. You knew the Renfrews. And Ben Lehman? It's smaller, what's left."

"Greater Blaine, that's a good one, Dad. But the rest of it sounds sort of normal, no? As one grows older?"

"It doesn't feel normal."

"There you go. I'll bet that's also normal, that you would have trouble fielding the changes."

"Maybe you could talk to her. You are her one son, her bright shining son. She does listen to you, Carl."

"Mom listens to everyone. Listening is her M.O. Have you ever heard her finish listening and say, Oh, you're right, I hadn't thought of *that*?"

Ian tried to think of such a time.

"Anyway, I did talk to her. And then I called you, seeking enlightenment."

"Maybe try the Buddha next time. I got nothing for you, as someone famously said."

"Mickey Mantle?"

"Could have been the Mick. You're the expert. But I got nothing for you, Carlo, I am sitting in the dark over here."

When the phone rang right back, Ian flipped quickly through the possibilities. Carl often called right back with an addendum. Carrie was possible if her mother had disseminated the news evenhandedly. It could be Polly herself, if not to announce a course correction, then at least to reassure him she was all right. After all, he had no idea where she had gone.

It was none of the above. The name displayed on the tiny telltale screen (hence *screening* calls, he realized, after living for decades with this technology) was A. Richardson. It was Anita, compounding the fracture. He should let it ring.

"Hi," she said.

He had only picked up because she could be in crisis, but she did not sound distressed. She sounded *bouncy*, that was the word that came to him. Playful. He would have responded to a crisis, he would not rush over to play. Blaine was not the sort of place where comings and goings went unnoticed, Ian already had proof of that. A visit to Brierly so close on the heels of Polly's departure would yield speculation that there was cause and effect at work. It could boil up to a small-bore scandal, give rise to gossip damaging to all three of them.

"You're okay? You sound okay."

"I'm fine, thanks. Can I tell you my idea? Which does involve a sort of favor—"

"You need a ride to the hospital."

"A ride, yes. The hospital, no. I'd like to go to the fairgrounds."

"Really? I mean, there's bound to be slush and mud out there, and I'm pretty sure it's closed. The gates will be chained."

He was responding as if her whimsical announcement was something ordinary or expected, which it surely was not. Mud was hardly foremost among the reasons for demurring.

"When I moved here last year? Feeling horrible about Sally but not yet feeling horrible about myself dying? I went out there one morning and had a sort of magical moment. Where everything somehow felt okay. And beautiful, actually."

"I have had a few of those. Moments."

"I wondered if it could work again. I was thinking about tomorrow. It's a huge imposition, I know, and of course it doesn't have to be tomorrow. I might still be alive on Friday or Saturday."

"You sound very much alive."

Here he was, doing it again, bantering when he should have left the damn phone alone. Or said tomorrow would not work. Or said this was a terrible idea, period.

"I'm good at that. I look awful and I feel awful, sounding is all I've got. What do you say?"

"Tomorrow, this would be?"

"Tomorrow is the pick-of-the-week on Newsline Nine. Sunny and close

to fifty degrees. It seemed like the right day if there was any chance you
would consider it."

"Sure," he heard himself saying.

Having uttered the word, he could not take it back. Then it struck him
that he had uttered it because he wished to. Wished to say yes, wished to
see her. Just how small was he prepared to let his life get? Wasn't he too
far along in age to concern himself with what other people chose to think,
especially if they were wrong to think it? Wasn't he too mature to worry
about appearances?

"Sure," he reiterated, "happy to do it. What time works for you?"

Ian had not been to the Holdenborough Fair in decades, not since the last
time they took the kids. They loved it: the tractor pull and the Clydesdale
pull, pony rides and fried dough. One summer they came home from the
Fair with a rabbit. Carrie begged—she had already *named* the soft creature—and neither Ian nor Polly could think fast enough to stop the child's
momentum.

O'Riley the Rabbit came home with them and lived happily-ever-after
for all of three months before he vanished. Down the rabbit hole? Into the
mouth of a coyote? There was not a shred of evidence left behind, not so
much as a tuft of fur, so the mystery went unsolved. A cold case. Carl joked
that O'Riley was at large ("He's alive in the foothills"), like the fellow who
parachuted from the plane he hijacked. D.B. Cooper?

He had driven past the Fair dozens of times over the years since then,
and he could have driven right past it now since he had no reason to be
there, not after Anita called it off. All his surmises proved true, broad acres
of mud bordered by a shrinking fringe of soft snow, the gates chained and
padlocked. He was alone there until a sweat-suit dude came to run his dog,
a husky with piercing blue eyes. The fellow had heard the locks were off,
refused to believe his eyes, circled the perimeter searching for signage that
could prove him right and therefore wronged. He went around muttering
and cursing before he gave up and got them back in his truck. Mush, you
husky?

Anita had called it off not long after she had proposed it, less than an hour later. "Miss Anita regrets," she said with mock formality, referencing, to his surprise, the lyrics of a song from his parents' time, "she is confined to quarters on doctor's orders."

"You saw the doctor? Since we spoke?"

It seemed so unlikely that she would have, or could have, managed this. But she still sounded playful, laughing it off: "No, I just read his mind."

Foolishly or not, Ian had come around, was looking forward to this outing, but he would not question the wisdom. There could be no doubt she had read the doctor's mind accurately. "Maybe another time?" she said.

"Sure thing," he said. "And maybe I'll go anyway. To the Fair, in your honor."

"Honor?" she laughed, again. "Ian, you are a very nice man."

A nice man or a man with nothing else on his calendar. Maybe he had come out to the fairgrounds simply because that was the plan and he had no alternative plan with which to replace it. It was as good a place to go as any.

Especially when—as it turned out, and as places can—it yielded up these pleasant memories. Ian had not considered O'Riley the Rabbit in years, had not stopped to reclaim enough of the now-distant happy childhood he and Polly had so assiduously provided the children. Keenly aware of Polly's tendency to label him a sentimentalist, he sometimes steered away from the old family stories they used to swat back and forth—Carl falling from the maple tree, Carrie's graveyard for gerbils.

To Polly, the past was valuable mainly as a source of trauma. No one came to a shrink to work through their happy memories. But that ought not require Ian to forego his. Unapologetically sentimental at the moment, he called it out aloud across the rumpled mud and shaggy grass, "I am a sentimental man!" He had no urge to reopen an inquiry into the fate of O'Riley, he was simply reclaiming Carrie's joy in holding him, Carl's comic displeasure whenever a fresh trail of tiny turds came to light in the hallway.

There was an arc to life, to lives, an arc along which each person becomes several people in succession. The adult Carrie was firmly connected to the child Carrie, yet she was not the same person. It was not possible to relate to her in the same way, with lullabies and silly jokes and hugs. He could not toss her in the air anymore. She had to be met and processed anew, as she had at fifteen, at thirty, as she would later be at forty-five. Tina Destino had shocked him when she admitted, quite casually, that although she had adored her children, she had a difficult time even liking them now.

Polly labeled him morbid for liking to read the obituaries. *Morbid* stood alongside sentimental among the indictments. He marveled at the ones with side-by-side photographs, one showing the deceased as a handsome dark-haired oarsman, the other as a hairless shrivel-faced resident of Old Folks Acres. Was it the same person? Yes and no.

Was the young woman with bright lively eyes the same person as the eighty-eight-year-old granny with epicanthic folds and turkey neck? To what extent did she feel herself to be the same person? Ian's mother at sixty-five would dance her way from the driveway to the door, dance the grandchildren around the living room. In her own mind, she was clearly in close touch with her much younger incarnation. She had been and still was the belle of the ball. What the world saw was never how you saw yourself.

Ian felt firmly trapped inside the current version of himself: he was Ian Nelson, roaming the fairgrounds alone for no reason. In the end, the warm spring wind and the warm memories it evoked only served to bring on a melancholy. And there it was, the trifecta: sentimental, morbid, and melancholic. A field day for Polly.

At least he was hungry. Five Guys was on the way home, lunch was something to do. Five Guys burger-and-fries, what the hell! Make it a large fry, for that matter. He was hungry and he was too old to die young.

The first few nights without Polly, he found leftovers he could work with in the fridge. The freezer, with its less-well-defined holdings, was daunting. While he did presume they held potential as meals, the opaque knobs and fists of food, with their frozen plastic-wrap creases, were more alarming than appetizing. Nonetheless he dislodged them, identified them, thawed them, ate them.

After that it was pizza. One consolation with Polly out of the picture was that he need not specify artichokes on half the pie. "Yes, the whole pie with broccoli and extra cheese," he repeated, Dino sounding doubtful, perhaps raising an eyebrow as he took the rogue order.

For days, he went back and forth on calling Anita. Did he owe her space following the cancellation or did he owe it to her to check in? Whenever it was too early to call, or too late, he felt relieved of the decision. Never too late for Carl, though, and here was an urgent message from him. "Do not ignore this call, Dad. Call me back, however late it is." So, however late it was, he called.

"I took you at your word. Is everything okay there?"

"Here? Sure. I needed to make sure things were okay *there*."

"Why wouldn't they be?" he said, somewhat foolishly under the circumstances, although Ian had never stopped being a father and always wished to be a solution, not a problem, for his children. "Because I was out earlier? Hey, maybe I went to the movies. I do have a life."

"A small one, as I recall you saying. What did you see?"

"I didn't go to the movies, I was just reminding you not to worry if I don't happen to answer the phone."

"Was it one of your singing nights, then?"

"No, it wasn't. Why do I get the feeling you are investigating my movements?"

"Mom told me you were Being Nice to one of the stricken. Especially nice, like beyond the call of duty. I thought maybe . . ."

"I didn't know that being nice was something to be made fun of."

"With Mom it's more like Being Nice is an activity. She can be a little cynical."

"I don't know what's going on, but lately I keep getting accused of being nice. Intended as a compliment, I think."

"I'm sure it is. And hey, it's nice that people see you that way."

"It also starts to feel weird. Feels like a veiled way of saying you're a loser. Didn't someone famously say that all nice guys are losers?"

"Nice guys finish last, is the citation. Leo Durocher."

"I should have known it would be baseball. And you with the whole baseball encyclopedia at your fingertips."

"And in my speech patterns, apparently. Once a judge cautioned me. She said, 'Attorney Nelson, that is your third baseball analogy in fifteen minutes. This court sets a limit on those.'"

"Sounds as though she had a sense of humor."

"Maybe. She ruled against me the next day."

"Three strikes and you're out!"

"Good one, Dad. You sound better already."

"Better?"

He did feel better. Before Carl, Ian had spoken to just one human being all day—Dino—when again he phoned for a pizza and when he went to pick it up. Dino asking, as he invariably did, how the kids were doing.

"You know what I mean. That is, I didn't mean anything, though you do sound better. And Dad? You do sound like a very nice man."

He had missed her at first. Their patterns, their nightly regimen. He walked Fred, she finished up in the kitchen, they watched a show, then read their books side by side in bed. There were understandings, there was togetherness.

Or was there stasis? Staleness. Maybe Polly had turned against the very sameness which gave Ian comfort. He had been sleeping poorly, or more poorly than usual. Earlier nights he had slept poorly for missing her, lately it was for worrying he did not miss her, that he was only missing the very predictability she deplored.

Polly never believed his sleep tally. To her his wakefulness was exaggerated, if not imaginary: he had no idea how much he slept and was temperamentally inclined to underestimate. While he hoped she was right, he did not see how she could know more about it while sleeping than he could while wide awake.

She had a colleague who specialized in sleep deprivation, someone willing to hook him up to a machine, run a nightly tab. This was not a machine to help him sleep, it was one to measure how much he did and didn't. The way Polly put it, the results might reassure him; the way Ian saw it, the machine was to prove Polly right. Which would have been fine, except he knew the very nature of this intervention—the machine, the wires, the presumption—would guarantee its failure. How could you sleep while being tested for sleep?

Fred was restless too these days. Spring was in the air and Fred was an animal. Ian doubted the dog was missing Polly. Polly reported that whenever Ian was away Fred would alternate between pacing and pressing against the front door. Would brighten at the sound of his engine approaching. "I'll bet she doesn't do that when I'm away," said Polly, and it was true, she did not. Even now, with Polly "away" for a length of time, Fred rarely strayed far from Ian's feet, dogging his steps as though to explain how the phrase came to be.

Thinking back, Ian had to ask if she had really cared about their dogs, any of them. Not the way he had—that was asking too much—but still, when Sinbad died, she was against getting the kids a replacement. And then after Carlsbad, she argued against tying themselves down. With the kids gone, they would be free to travel more. Had it not been for his heart attack and the stern marching orders the surgery generated, he would have been hard pressed to sell her on adopting Fred.

When he and Fred would come back from their after-dinner ramble, Polly would always listen to his scraps of narrative, the sights they might have encountered. Fred's peccadillos and adventures were a topic. Ian could never resist giving Poll an account of the latest episode of Dancing with Squirrels. But her listening could feel so *pro forma* that to test her one night, see if she was really listening, Ian reported that he and Fred had both walked on their hands for the last mile.

"In that case," she said, "be sure and wash up before you set the table."

Part Two

Black Holes

HOWEVER MANY HOURS he had slept or failed to sleep, Ian rose decisive.

And there was yet another trait Polly liked to brand him with: *indecisive*. He kept stumbling onto this vocabulary of disapproval from her, a tendency he had excused as nothing more than a manner of speaking, or again the *lingua franca* of her profession. The judgments were delivered so flatly that they never sounded harsh, could pass almost unnoticed, especially if there was nothing to be gained by noticing. It was such a casual onslaught that Ian rarely felt under attack.

However decisive she wished him to be, Polly would not have endorsed his decision to find the sister. He had found out where Sally Shumway was living and knew this would be an all-day affair, Blaine to Maine and back, so he left a note for Polly, in case she chose this day to return. Letting her know he might not be home by dinner time.

Lunch he packed: egg salad sandwiches and a thermos of coffee for himself, mixed biscuits for Fred, and a bag of chips for the two of them to share. The undertaking was borderline crazy and likely futile, given that Sally Shumway would neither answer the phone nor respond to messages and emails, so that he did not have an arrangement with her or any assurance she would be at the address. And if she had listened to his messages, she might very well choose to disappear for the day to avoid him. On top of all that, it was a weekday, so she probably went to a job. All he could do was cast it as fun, sell it to Fred as the fun road trip he had devised for himself and Polly. "We'll bond," he said.

So it was pure luck—beating the long odds—when he found the house, rang the bell, watched the door swing open, and saw a woman who must be Sally Shumway eyeing him suspiciously. "You're not Carol," she said. "I was expecting Carol."

"Not Carol. But maybe you were expecting me too? I'm the guy who called."

"If you're looking for Richard, I can tell you where to look. And it is not here."

"Richard, your husband."

"Richard my soon-to-be-ex-husband."

"Actually, I was looking for you, Mrs. Shumway."

"Not buying, whatever it is you're selling."

"I'm not Carol and I'm not selling anything. I'm here with sad news about your sister."

"My ex-sister. Who are you, anyway? You can't be her boyfriend."

"No, I'm not that either."

"All these things you're not. So what are you?"

"I am the bearer of this news. Bad news, about her health. Maybe we could go inside?"

"Yeah right. What if you're not a messenger, you're an axe murderer. Don't say it, I know, not an axe murderer."

"We could go somewhere neutral if you're concerned. A café?"

"It's that long a message? I mean, Carol will be here any minute. But what the hell, come on in, if she finds my dead body it will make her day."

Superficially, Sally Shumway was cut from different cloth than her sister. Her hair styled and highlighted, eyeshadow and lipstick, conventional old school outfit of skirt-and-sweater. A pin. But her voice, the pace and timbre of her speech along with the tripwire wit, felt familiar. Then it turned out she drank the same herbal tea, had put out a plate of the same Canadian biscuits. For all he knew, she was nursing an as-yet-undiscovered glioblastoma in her brain.

"I'm sorry to hear about your marriage," he said, stupidly, as they settled.

"Don't know why you should care in the slightest, but thanks, I suppose. Maybe you can get to the point. Is Anita using you as a flag-bearer, a peace offering of some sort?"

"No, Mrs. Shumway, she doesn't know I came here. She is very sick. Dying. And I thought you should know."

"What are you, her doctor?"

"Not her doctor. A friend is all. And I do understand why you are angry at her."

"Is that so. Angry, am I?"

"Upset, then."

"Angry is okay. Angry and upset. Shocked, disappointed, appalled, grossed out. *Betrayed*. My sister and my husband? Ex, in each case."

"They are just people. Human beings—"

"That's what you say. And I don't know why I am even talking to you."

At a loss for any response that might slow her negative momentum, Ian extracted a biscuit, the way one might do while playing pick-up sticks, preserving the integrity of the pile. Sally was harboring toxins and he had released them into the air.

"By the way, she doesn't know that you and your husband are estranged."

"No? Did that girl think I would live with that boy after the little party they had? Would you, mister, if someone did that to you?"

"I might try thinking they didn't do it *to me*."

"You'd be right. They did it to me."

"I can't argue with you there."

"You surely cannot! I mean, who the hell are you? I don't even know your name. And by the way, I do not for one second believe that girl is dying. Why would she do that? It's a trick, that's all, like every other trick she's pulled. Send some nice old man to say she is about to fucking croak."

"She really is dying, Mrs. Shumway. From a brain tumor."

"Oh, a brain tumor is it. That might explain a lot of things!"

"You will need to be on top of some stuff. The practical mess that comes with death. As next of kin, you will be the one."

"This is all a big lie. The girl lies."

"Doesn't everybody lie about something like that? What she did."

It might have been the only conscious lying Ian had done in his long marriage, lying for months about Ella Morehouse. You could only do it if you were lying.

"I'll tell you a story, Mr. Nice Guy. Your sweet Anita is seventeen, I am eighteen, Gary is nineteen and he likes me a lot. He is coming to pick me up for a date. Anita answers the door, tells Gary I'm not around, and kindly offers to serve as a replacement. Off they go to the movie together. Later she will claim she had no idea I was upstairs. She will apologize. But she becomes Gary's girlfriend for the next six months, waving to one and all from the back of his beloved Harley. Got the picture?"

Ian liked Sally. The more exercised she became, the more attractive she became. He liked her spirit, the way she could almost enjoy her misfortunes, transform them into a source of strength.

"I don't think it's worth giving up a marriage over one slipup," he said, as her every feature registered disbelief at his presumption. "I understand, this was a particularly bad slipup—okay, worst case. Still, it's only half an hour out of a long life. Thirty minutes."

"Is that what you believe, the thirty minutes? Not that it matters. Thirty *seconds* of those two in *congress* is plenty sufficient. And that's without mentioning a few other half hours, because sweet Anita was not the first. There were a few Bonitas and Chiquitas to blaze the trail for her."

"I am sorry to hear that."

"Are you a married man? I'm not seeing a ring."

"No ring—we never did the jewelry—but yes, I am." He hesitated (*why tell her?*) and there was such palpable significance in his hesitation that she waited him out with something resembling interest. "Or, I think I am. It seems my wife may be leaving me."

"Don't tell me. Did it just happen to be that girl who caused your wife to leave?"

"I am sixty-six years old, Mrs. Shumway, as you noticed. I honestly don't know why she is leaving, but your sister and I are just friends."

When the doorbell chimed, they pivoted together like synchronistic gymnasts. Before Sally got to the door, a tall woman came through it bearing a white waxed bag redolent of Indian spices and smiling inquisitively at the sight of Ian. Sensing awkwardness, she waited only briefly for an introduction before moving through to the kitchen with her victuals.

"Couple of really quick questions before I go," said Ian. "Where is Richard now? And where do I find Gary?"

"Gary! What has he to do with the price of apples—like twenty years after biting into one! And if you for one second believe Richard the Dick Shumway is about to step in as Sir Deeply Concerned, I've got some oceanfront property in flyover country to show you."

She must have feared he would simply stand there in the portal refusing to leave, so she did surrender a number for Richard the Dick ("He won't answer and he won't call back") before all but stamping her feet as she spit out "Do not be phoning *me* again."

Her best guess ("for what it's worth") was that Gary Higganbotham would not have gotten far, would likely be somewhere in the Portland area. "Selling vacuum cleaners or used bikes. Probably fat and prematurely bald." She had no number for him, just a few possible contacts, places he might frequent and might not. "For all I know, the sorry bugger could be dead."

The price of apples notwithstanding, this Gary was the only other human Ian knew of who could tell him anything about Anita Richardson. He might be worth a conversation for that reason alone, whatever he looked like. Bald and fat, though? Purely on spec? It seemed that Sister Sally had not forgiven that little transgression either. The original sin.

Coming into Portland, just over the bridge, Ian had driven past Becky's Diner. He was surprised to find it still going, a thousand years after they had stopped for lunch there, the four of them, on their way to Bar Harbor. Whatever happened with Sally Shumway, he knew he would be going back to Becky's for lunch afterward. The egg salad sandwiches he had packed hours earlier had never appealed much and by now had no appeal at all. Fred, who loved egg salad, was the happy beneficiary of the revised menu.

Ian ordered coffee, a hamburger with grilled onions, and French fries well done. As he ate, he leafed absently through a free local paper, mostly ads.

Because he sat on a stool at the counter, he was face to face with the lineup of pies beneath their plastic domes and he knew he would yield to the temptation. He was about to go with the banana cream when the waitress told him that only the apple was homemade, told him it was best warmed up with a scoop of vanilla on top, and that he would want more coffee to go with it.

Her smile implied such happiness as only pie a la mode can bring a man, so he did it her way. The happiness was real, it just didn't last. It was a sugar high which soon gave way to a weary sense of futility. Maybe he was simply weary after the long drive and the stressful interview. He felt as though he was encountering resistance everywhere, swimming against so many strong currents. Ian was comfortable with resistance, had worked with it for decades, fielding angsty *teenagers* for goodness' sake. He was all in on Jack Sutcliffe, who Polly called "a help-rejecting complainer." It was the women who had him walled off. They were all women, weren't they?

The phrase "disillusioned with women" came to him, was literally inscribed on the screen of his mind. The notion seemed phony, culled from a bad movie (he could see a Woody Allen gnome whining about it to his New York shrink) but at the same time it rang true. Women had been letting him down, one after another.

Starting with Polly. Poll, so critical of everyone—except herself. Poll who had no compunctions about upping sticks without the ghost of an explanation, after a lifetime together. Talk about letting him down, she had lowered him down a mine shaft!

Then there was Carrie. Why did she have to be so distant and difficult, dead-set against hearing what anyone else had to say? He could tell her the weather report and she would contradict it; show it to her on the computer screen and she would say his computer was *archaic*. Offer to show her the sky and she would not come outside to look. This was only a slight exaggeration.

He had only himself to blame for Sally Shumway. He asked for it, so to speak. Still, why did she have to be so sour when his sole purpose in coming there was to help her? And why was he there to help her anyway, after her sister had taken him for granted, scheduling and cancelling him without compunction. Anita was fine with setting him up, equally fine setting him down.

He shut his eyes and pressed lightly on his eyelids, forgetting where he was, elbows on the lunch counter. When he looked up, the waitress was topping up his coffee. "Either you caffeine up or go in the back room and get some sleep," she said with a smile that doubled her tip. Ian told her he was not really tired, that this was a trick for relaxing, she should try it sometime.

"Some of that mindfulness bullshit, is it?" she said, laughing, making him laugh in spite of himself, probably tripling her tip.

The waitress' kindness had cheered him—here was a woman on his side!—and he was already regaining his balance on the drive west from Portland. She made him take even more caffeine to go, enough to inspire a vision. It appeared to him, bold as a billboard: *Begin by trying to see it from their point of view.* Ian was being directed back to the teachings, to Morris' textbook, *Methods and Ethics*, and the guiding principle of guidance counselling. No wonder it could "appear to him," when this billboard image was nothing more than a blown-up reproduction of the motto posted over his desk for years at the high school: *Begin by trying to see it from their point of view.*

He went back over it, plaint by plaint, starting with Polly. From her point of view, Polly was merely being honest. Identifies her situation, tells him the truth, acts on it. Unless marriage is seen as sacred, non-refundable—which it cannot be—Polly could be in the clear. As she said, the fact that Ian was the center of his own universe did not make him the center of hers.

Carrie. From her point of view, Carrie was a strong independent woman, possessed of the rare self-knowledge that she had never wanted children. From her point of view, they should just shut up about it. She was not a child, she was nearly forty years old. Maybe if he stopped being her parent, stopped trying to raise her, she would stop resisting.

Likewise reconsidered, Sister Sally became a woman betrayed by her husband and her sister, therefore appropriately soured yet not so much so that she lacked a sense of humor. Points for that, no? A woman who does not know him and has no desire to know him—why expect her to decant the milk of human kindness?

And it was thanks to Sally that he came around on Anita. It was the teenage boyfriend-stealing business with Gary that did it. Ian would never have guessed something of that sort attached to her, but then what made him think he was equipped for any such guessing? What he did not know about Anita Richardson occupied a wide range, from how did she get her groceries to had she ever been married. She had let him glimpse a small portion of herself, a presence so lovely and lively that it felt fuller than it was. Any biographical details were offered in shorthand, when not edited out entirely.

She owed him nothing. Yes, he had been good to her, but goodness ought not be a mode of exchange. You did not give in order to receive. Ian had mistaken his sense of their connection for hers, expected more than he should have from her. A woman facing what Anita Richardson was facing had license to do anything she damn well pleased. It was absurd for him to feel slighted by any aspect of her behavior.

And that was that. Professor Morris and his motto had allowed him to absolve the women, all of them. The bitterness was gone before he was back in Blaine. The problem was, the sinking feeling stayed with him. If he wanted to shake it, he would have to crack open a different fortune cookie.

Lately every day seemed like Sunday. Even when it came to Polly's departure, that cataclysmic event, he could not reckon the time span, much less the date. Had it been a week? Three weeks? He turned to their joint desk calendar, which Polly had left behind, for assistance. Polly never failed to cram something in her small legible lettering into each day's box. She always had something on, or they did, as a pair. But he saw that the trail went cold over a month ago, the grid blocking out week after week of white space, every box a blank.

The meaning of this dawned on him slowly. She was recording no reminders because she needed no reminding; she had laid her plan to disembark long ago and this calendar had long since ceased being *their* calendar. Polly's life here and their life together called only for this blank slate. He had given her credit for radical honesty, exonerated her on those grounds, yet here was evidence she had in fact been dishonest for some time.

It was in deference to Polly that he had held back from seeing Anita. He had pushed the whole situation aside. True, he was drawn into making an exception when Anita called with her whimsical suggestion about the fairgrounds. But when she bailed on that, he decided that going forward he would respond to, not initiate, any next contact with Anita. Leave it in her court.

Now that changed. Now the deference he had granted Polly gave way to dismay at what the calendar told him. He would not slide past Brierly in the morning, he would march over there purposefully, check in on Anita properly. Sooner or later she would find herself in dire straits, in need of help, while he dithered about what Polly wanted or what "society" might think.

Professor Morris notwithstanding, Ian did not live by homilies, but he did harbor a few. He had even devised one at work: while you won't be able to end war or famine, you might be able to do something for the troubled kid sitting across the desk from you, the one who has come there asking for your help. In this case, Anita Richardson had done the asking—though he did have to admit she had not asked lately.

A few lozenges of snow lay on the shaded flagstones leading to the side door. Everywhere else was clear, pale grass emerging, the tall tangle of forsythia coming into bud.

Ian had not phoned ahead for fear of waking her. He had no sense of how her mornings went. Now, standing outside, he had no choice but to press the buzzer. When he got no response for over a minute, the more dire possibilities seemed more possible. He was considering the wisdom of busting in (versus calling 911 and letting the authorities bust in) when the neighbor tapped him on the back.

Nice old guy, maybe an Irish name, with a whispered hello that startled the hell out of Ian. The man was as stealthy as an Iroquois in soft moccasins; either that or Ian was so inward he would not have noticed a helicopter touching down on the lawn behind him.

"She left," the fellow was saying.

"She must have left quite early," said Ian, miming a glance at a watch he never wore.

"Oh no, she left quite some time ago. I'm surprised you didn't know."

"You don't mean left as in—"

"Moved away. Yes."

"But how could she . . . manage that? And the house. Is she selling the house?"

They might have been discussing a different person, not Anita, someone healthy, with options, perhaps a new job that called for relocation. It was strange anyway, for here was good news—Anita was not in distress, not dead—that felt like bad news to Ian.

"Oh no, she was just renting the place," the neighbor said. "The Hutchinsons still own it."

"Wow," was Ian's first response. Then: "What did she say? About where she was going."

"Oh, I don't know. That is, she didn't say anything to us. I suppose she must have said something to Doris or Harold."

"Doris?"

"Doris Hutchinson, the owner. She was our neighbor until she moved into Spring House. The place was empty for quite some time after that, before her son Harold decided to rent it out. For the income, you know, and the upkeep too, I suppose. Always good to have someone in there with an eye on things."

Ian was reduced to treading water through this flood of information, before surfacing with more questions. "You don't know how she left. I mean, not in an ambulance or—"

"Oh no, nothing like that. She went off with the young man, on his motorcycle."

"Young man? Someone you knew, or met?"

"Only to wave to, like yourself. A visitor. When the weather improved, it did seem he was around more often, two or three times. They could get outdoors more easily then."

"You mean, like sit in the yard?"

"Oh no," the neighbor laughed. "Farther than that. Though who knows where. At first I thought it was a terrible idea for her to ride on the back of a motorcycle, so jarring and all, but Ida pointed out that whatever was going on inside her head, the girl was not exactly frail. If it was fun for her, then why not. She had been sick for such a long time."

"Was she sick?" Confronted with this new narrative—the young man, the motorcycle, the leaving—Ian was forced to confront yet again Polly's charge that Anita was some sort of fraud. At the very least, things were not adding up.

"Oh yes, surely you knew that."

"What I mean is, she must have gotten better. Must have improved. To go off like that."

"Maybe. She didn't let us in on her plans, she was just gone one day. All I can say is that she looked—well, lovely as ever, last time I saw her. But then she always did, if you know what I mean. Look lovely."

The old guy, past eighty for sure, had not lost his eye for the ladies! Ian could not quite withhold a conspiratorial smile: they were males and they registered that this was one very attractive female.

"She must have left a note. A forwarding address."

"No, nothing. Again, you might check with the Hutchinsons on that. But she never got much mail. Ida noticed that, always said how strange it was. She did keep up with her bills, I know—Harold was very pleased not having to worry about the gas and electric—but being young as she was, she may have used one of those phones to pay her bills. Isn't that what they do now?"

"You're probably right. And I appreciate your coming over. As you see, I am a bit surprised—"

"Oh, so were we. But then—" And here the neighbor shrugged, and Ian nodded. Anita Richardson, they could silently agree, was nothing if not surprising.

"You said a motorcycle. You didn't by any chance notice what make it was?"

"Sure I did. It was a big Harley, 650 cc, with all those new bells and whistles on it. And a pretty serious dual exhaust. Had the big double thrum going."

Ian looked at the neighbor with fresh eyes, the octogenarian wistful as he revealed he used to ride, though his was "just" 350 cc. Ian flashed on those obituaries, the ones with side-by-side shots of the deceased, then and now. This senior citizen had once been a biker! In the "now" photo he retained a sparse fringe of white hair on the sides, in the "then" he might have sported greasy black hair and a Rollie Fingers moustache.

They shook hands and walked in different directions. Ian paused at the gate, certain he must have more questions, there must be more answers. But he didn't, and apparently there weren't. Not now, in any case. *Ahern.* The name came to him as he watched the neighbor reach his door, saw wife Ida framed in the opening, no doubt eager to debrief him. Mr. Oh-No was Mr. Ahern.

Meanwhile, Ms. Richardson was, somehow, gone and the somehow sounded suspiciously like the same Gary who ditched Sister Sally for Anita eons ago. A Harley? It might even be the same damned motorcycle.

Many years ago, after reading his way through a dozen classic mysteries—the hardboileds like Chandler and Hammett, clever Brits like Symons and Gilbert—Ian decided to write a detective novel of his own. For fun. Somewhere in the garage, in a file inside a carton, were the dozen or so pages he had managed before acknowledging there was more to it than clearing space on a desk. All he recalled now about the "book" was a note he had scribbled in the margin, urging himself to come up with a better name than Harry Walker for his sleuth.

He also recalled being told by a colleague of Polly's at a Christmas party around that time, that yes yes, chuckle chuckle, sooner or later everyone tried their hand at writing a mystery. *Not a writer*, he could hear himself telling Sally Shumway with a grin.

Not a detective either, of course—he was not about to embark on a career in crime solving—but as with his short-lived literary impulse, just for fun, he decided to put on some imaginary gumshoes and try to find this Gary person. It might be a wild goose chase. He might even catch the goose and gain no insight into the riddles surrounding Anita. Gary was a longshot, though Ian preferred to style it a hunch. Anita was gone and only a man with a motorcycle knew where she went. At the least, the project would occupy him for a day or two, possibly amuse him.

He tried two phone numbers that were "no longer in service," and unearthed from the White Pages of the Web a few addresses which were not necessarily current. He did have one serious lead, as he was calling it half in jest. Or all in jest. Although, recalling Sally Shumway's initial reluctance to yield up information, Ian wondered if he might possess a knack for extracting clues from recalcitrant witnesses. Might be good at this.

The lead was a workplace address in Portland, a motorcycle repair shop on Telander Avenue, where Gary Higganbotham had worked and possibly still did. But no one there ever answered the phone and although the answering machine promised a swift response ("This is the hot line, dude, back at you in a shake"), it seemed their notion of swift was never. So, to follow his lead he would have to go back to Portland, which was patently ridiculous. Clearly, that would be taking it too far.

But something had come over him, something that went beyond silly to maybe a little crazy. He felt the trajectory of it sweeping him along that night and the next morning, felt it as he and Fred set off for Maine around eleven, and now here he was at 242 Telander Ave. in Portland, happy to see that the virtual apparition of Rick's Bike Fix had a bricks-and-mortar counterpart, or more accurately a sketchy edifice of sagging plastic and battered aluminum. And inside Rick's Fix, there was an eponymous Rick, with his feet up on a chipped veneer desk, jabbering away on the phone, perhaps in swift response to one of Ian's messages.

He responded to Ian's entrance by holding up an index finger (meaning wait? meaning one minute?) and during the several minutes Rick continued with his call Ian looked around casually, not revealing by his movements or facial expressions that he was doing detective work. There was a large Plexiglas window separating the office from the repair area, where he could see a single motorcycle and a rolling rack of tool drawers in a space large enough to park half a dozen school buses. The detective in him, straining to see, could detect very few oil stains on the pale gray concrete floor and entertained the possibility that Rick's was a front. Drugs, maybe. If it was money laundering, there was only so much money this place could plausibly launder.

"Help you?" said Rick, swiveling at last in his chair.

"Hope so," said Ian, electing to match him syllable for syllable, match his tone. "I'm trying to locate Gary Higganbotham."

"*Locate* him," said Rick. "Good luck with that."

"Oh?"

"Dude can be damned elusive. What's he wanted for this time?" Then, registering Ian's surprise, Rick quickly amended. "Just kidding, dude. Our Gary's cool."

"He doesn't work here anymore?"

"That's correct. As the cops say on TV. Ever notice that?"

"Any idea where he does work now, or where he lives?"

"Working—not if he can help it. Pretty sure he does continue living. He moves in with his gal pal from time to time."

"He must move back out from time to time, too, then," said Ian. Though the remark contained a mathematical truth, both he and Rick, who froze in a double take, wondered why he made it. "You wouldn't have her number handy, by any chance?"

"Know what? I believe it's time to ask what this is concerning. Cop? Nah. Bill collector, tax man, what's the beef?"

"Nothing like that, nothing he would mind. I want to check in with him about a mutual friend, someone I've lost track of."

"And he hasn't? A friend that is mutual to you and to Gary Higganbotham, somehow."

"That's correct," said Ian with a sly smile that earned him a wider one back from Rick and that may have positioned him one step closer to Gary. Now that Ian knew what the cops always said on TV, he was all right with Rick.

"Hang on a second, let me see what I can do for you." Rick with his feet back up on the desk, punching in a number, landing the girlfriend. "Aggie baby, yeah, me. I'm not committing you to anything here, you are anonymous and free, there's a guy wants to say hello. Feel free to hang up on him, he's nothing to me."

Ian accepted the handset (pleased to smell gas and oil on it after all) and asked the girl named Aggie if the boy named Gary was anywhere about. Aggie went all Sally on him, however, with the same weary man-wary irony in her voice. "No, but should you see him, do tell him to fuck himself for me, yeah?"

"Yeah, sure," said Ian, agreeably.

"Or no, that's harsh. Tell him I hope he runs his fucking Harley into a really solid tree."

"I'll tell him, if you tell me where he is."

"Under a rock somewhere? Mind you, I'm just guessing."

"Any other guesses, Aggie?"

"The pool room?"

Rick mimed a knowing nod in corroboration of the tip. "Aggie knows best," he added. "Shooting for fives is Gary's idea of work."

Ian laid a twenty-dollar bill on the desk where Rick's hobnailed boots had worn a pale portion. "An advance," said Ian. "On my next tune-up."

Starting with the missing letters in their neon sign, The Felt Palace looked slightly down-at-heels for a palace. It looked right for a pool hall, though, and Ian had a good feeling about his plan until he stepped inside. He had anticipated encountering suspicious, even hostile stares—an outsider, an unlikely fit—and then earning acceptance by running a rack. Because pool was his game, or it had been, by chance. Teenage Ian spent a lot of afternoons at the Presbyterian Church, where he "volunteered" under parental duress, and many of those hours had been devoted to the pool table in the basement. The Youth Rec Center featured Ping Pong, pool, and a vending machine that never worked. In homage to Fast Eddie Felson in the Newman movie, high school pals dubbed him Fast Ian Nelson. His one claim to cool: he was a shooter.

Right away he saw his plan was foiled—not a soul was there to hit him with the hostile stare. He should have guessed that three p.m. would be a dead hour. The only greeting he got was neither hostile nor friendly, just a neutral nod from the fellow stocking a short fridge behind the four-stool bar with bottled beers: Bud and Bud Light, Michelob for the snobs. This was not a venue for the new wave in beer, where the stuff had fruity noses and oaky notes, like wine.

"I was hoping to find a game," said Ian. "Maybe talk a bit."

"Talk about what?" said the palace guard. He looked a lot like Rick, same hairstyle (was it called a mullet, that clump in back?), same medicine ball cantilevered over his belt. *Wally* was embroidered in cursive on his shirt.

"Gary Higganbotham?" said Ian, coming right to the point.

"It's five for the first rack," said Wally, "three after that. Table two is open, cues are right over there."

Tables one and three were also open but, going with the flow, Ian selected a stick, settled a rack, and broke strong, leaving himself a nice wide-open field. He potted the 2 and the 7 casually, strolled around to line up the 10.

"You wouldn't care to join me?"

"That's all right. Knock yourself out."

"So Gary," Ian said, trying again on the strength of banking the 10 cleanly. "Has he been in lately?"

"You going to tell me you have some prize money for him? Or a time share he is eligible for down in Boca? What's your deal?"

"I'm hoping he has news of a mutual friend, someone I've lost touch with. I heard she was sick, guessing he might know more."

"And who would that friend be?"

"Her name's Anita," said Ian, finessing a tricky angle on the 5, tough enough it might have gained him traction. He looked up and saw that it hadn't, but a long diagonal jolt on the 4 registered.

"Don't know an Anita. Gary's out of town. Or was. Heard he might be back, haven't seen his handsome mug as yet. Try his cell?"

"I have an old number is all," Ian shrugged.

"I guess you can't arrest him over the phone," said Wally, writing something on the back of an empty envelope. It might be a phony, seven digits selected at random; it might be too smeary to read; it might be Gary Higganbotham's phone number. A breeze of pure confidence washed over Ian as he banged in the 9, laid a twenty-dollar bill on the dot—a terrific bargain in his TV understanding of what detectives paid for information—and left the 8-ball poised on the lip of a corner pocket. Walking away from a gimme always turned heads. He sauntered toward the street, no other way of putting it. Had to restrain himself from saying it ("Knock yourself out"), said "Thank you, my good man" over his shoulder instead, feeling pretty good about his progress.

Also feeling dumbstruck by the luck of it, these good old boys opening up to him, until he did remember that Gary Higganbotham was not a criminal.

That there was no sound reason for concealment. Still, in this world Ian was an outsider and Gary was an insider; it must have taken some sleuthing moves, the gumshoe touch, to get this far. Even if the phone number failed to fetch Gary, it was a safe bet he would float up at The Felt Palace sooner or later. If such startling progress didn't rate a late lunch at Becky's, the chowder and maybe another go at the pies, what the hell did?

The bike repair shop was empty, the pool hall was empty, now the diner was empty too. Ian worried about Portland. Here was this beautiful city and he was its only paying customer? By comparison, tame, tiny Blaine was a teeming bazaar. The waitress assured him it was all good, things were just a little dead at half past three.

The fish chowder was a little dead at this hour too, reheated one time too many. He had not lost confidence in the pies. He hesitated more because of Rick and Wally, with their beachball bellies. Could you get like that drinking "lite" beer? Or had they fought the good fight against pie and lost? They were forty, though—forty-five, tops—and Ian was sixty-six. He reasoned he had more room to expand and less time to deteriorate—he would be dead before he got that fat—and in the end gave himself permission to tap the plastic dome over the lemon meringue.

He considered staying over in Portland or somewhere nearby. He was convinced that Gary was the key and the word had Gary back in town. He might turn up at the pool hall tomorrow. From neighbor Ahern's account of her sudden impulsive exit, it seemed possible that Anita had gone off on some sort of glorified assisted suicide mission. Go out in a fiery motorcycle crash or fly off the edge of someplace like the Grand Canyon. She would beat the Grim Reaper to the punch, with Gary as her corner man.

He also had reasons for going home. The motels were all expensive and the one that was happy to welcome Fred was even more expensive. And Polly might have come home, this could have been the day for it. Ian had been expecting her ever since the night Carl told him she seemed "at loose ends." Really, he had been expecting her ever since she bolted.

In truth, Ian went home to be home. He was a homing pigeon, a tame animal who retreated to his lair at night. But he arrived there blear-eyed and hungry again, and the pickings were slim. He fried his last two eggs, toasted and buttered the last two halves of an English muffin, and wedged some kale from the freezer for his vegetable course. He was glad the kale was tasteless because he hated the taste of kale almost as much as he hated the texture. Bottom line, he was being a good boy, eating his greens.

Only after escorting Fred around the park did he face the mail and messages, each of which contained unexploded ordnance: in among the robocalls was a message from Polly and, nestled in the reams of junk mail, was a letter from A.R. When he opened the letter and read it, his first thought was that it was a good thing Polly had not chosen this day to come home. Had she seen this letter, she would have turned around and gone right back to her loose ends. Not that the message was incriminating, it only appeared to be such. It was terribly misleading that way, because the wording implied that he and Anita had discussed running off together.

I seem to be doing all right—can't say for sure, no doctors were involved in the making of this movie—and did want you to know that. Sorry about bailing on our fairgrounds plan—I wanted to throw out an idea to you, a little trip, see what you said. What happened was an old friend showed up and was good to go, so we went. Westward ho! Anyway, thanks, Ian, for everything.

With love, Anita

Ian had already connected most of the dots. Gary was the old friend who showed up, and it was Gary she went off with. West? Maybe it really was the Grand Canyon she had in mind for a grand finale. He wanted to disbelieve the assisted suicide scenario, wanted to believe she really was "doing all right," having fun, and that somehow he might even see her again. That she cared enough to write the letter gave him some ease, as did knowing Polly would not see this harmless communication and misconstrue it. They had enough misunderstandings as matters stood.

When he braced himself and pressed the button on the message machine, he had no idea what to expect from Polly. There could be a brand-new misunderstanding. But for better or worse, it was strictly business. She had received a text message (this the price of her having a smart phone, Ian trailing the revolution) from Doctor Wiggins' office, and she recited it for him verbatim in a flat, almost robotic tone: *We are looking for Mr. Nelson. He has a three o'clock appointment and now it's gone four. Please let us know.*

Listening to Polly's recitation, Ian could hear the voice of Robin, Doc Wiggins' sweetheart of a receptionist, her solicitousness tunneling through Polly's chilly timbre. *Please let us know* translated to *Please reassure us about his heart.* Robin wondering if he'd missed his appointment because he was lying in the gutter somewhere, clutching his chest, gasping for air.

He took out the blank calendar and in tomorrow's blank white box wrote "Call Robin." He scribbled a note to the same effect and left it under the coffee pot so he could not possibly miss it. He would call the minute they opened and tell Robin how sorry he was.

"I have been distracted lately. Forgetful, obviously. Not that there is any excuse. I totally expect to be billed for the appointment."

He knew Robin would forgive him and waive the charge. He also knew that she would insist he come in today. Doc Wiggins took the milestone checkups seriously, every six months, and this was a six-monther. Ian would have thought the six-monthers were in the rearview mirror by now, that he must be in the clear a decade after the "event," but he was not about to argue with Robin and drove downtown right after breakfast.

"So," said Doc Wiggins, in his kindly way, likely unaware there was anything to forgive. He might well have benefitted from Ian's lapse, since he was always an hour behind by three p.m., the price a doctor paid for providing proper medical care in the twenty-first century. "How is our heart doing these days?"

"I thought you'd be telling me that," said Ian.

"We will run a few tests, for sure. How are we feeling, though? Have we had any unusual fatigue? Weakness? Pain?"

Pain? Did Polly's ditching him count, or Anita's vanishing act? What about his existential loneliness—not that he had ever understood what the word existential meant. He told the Doc there was no pain, he was ticking right along.

"Good work, then. Let's poke around and get that verified. I always say, if we have a functioning heart and brain, we're halfway to Oz."

"Ray Bolger," said Ian. "Bert Lahr."

"Pass. Heart and brain, intact. Good work, Ian."

He was back at the house by ten and already weighing a quick return to Maine when he noticed the red message light blinking on the answering machine. It proved to be another reminder, this one just in time—a sing tonight in Dexterville. If Ian blew it off, Karin would drop him to the third string, unless she dropped him from the roster altogether. She was partial to that business about showing up being 90 percent of the battle, though she was not above saying there was no point showing up if you were going to sing like *that*.

So he stayed put. Took a nap, walked the requisite five miles, shopped up a skeletal larder at Market Basket (frozen pizza, frozen meatballs, frozen broccoli, milk, bread, eggs), and ploughed through a cloud of blackflies to the Yew Yew parking lot at six sharp. His first sing in a while, first in the better weather. It was still light out when they went in, might still be warm when they came out.

They were singing to the father, Barton Jencks, though they would agree in the post-game huddle that they were really singing for his daughter Abby. She was a singer herself, a regular in the Congo church choir, and confessed she was hard pressed to remain silent on the soaring chorus of "Angel Band." But their voices, she gushed, were so tightly blended, there was no room for another voice.

"It was too perfect," she said. Her father smiled at this, more likely expressing pride in his gracious daughter than acknowledging the perfection of the band's rendition. He had smiled once or twice before, and nodded, but had not spoken a word the whole time.

"We do get to rehearse that one a lot," said Karin. "Pretty much everyone we visit to has to put up with the Angel Band singing 'Angel Band.'"

Though it had never happened before, it happened spontaneously this time, a reprise of "Angel Band" as they filed out. Abby's praise may have inspired it, but it felt so right that they talked in the huddle about incorporating it on a regular basis, go out singing. Why hadn't anyone suggested it long ago? A man coming down the block, coming home, took them for itinerant minstrels, and started fishing in his pocket for a dollar. He laughed when Karin explained, then asked for her card. "You never know," he said.

"The blackflies have gone to bed," Ward observed as they climbed down from the van back at the church. "And that's exactly where I'm headed myself."

"Ward, come on, it's eight o'clock," said Ian, eager for some company. "Plenty of time for a nightcap. If I buy?"

"Thanks anyway, Ian, you guys go ahead. I'll get you next time."

Three was easier than two. With three, the banter rolled harmlessly along; with two it could threaten to become a conversation. Men did not do this well. And the acoustics at The Draft Horse were terrible, everyone leaning forward to hear above the din, so Ian was surprised to find himself trusting Harv with the news that Polly had taken off for parts unknown. That this could become a problem. It became almost real to him in the telling, so he was not sorry to have his friend close it off as solidly as a brick wall at the end of a narrow alley. "How far can she go," Harvey shrugged, "when her work is here?"

Ian had not considered this aspect. Had Polly quit her work at the same time as she quit him? Or taken a leave of absence of some sort? He had pictured her in Boston, or Pittsburgh, where she had lifelong friends, not staying with mutual friends in the area or at one of the Copper River B&Bs. "Her work, yes," he said, "but there is work elsewhere. She is a free agent."

"So is Bryce Harper," said Harv, and happily they were right back to sports and weather.

Ian may have said too much, but he was glad of the occasion. The companionship helped and the Guinness did its job, rendering him mellow. At home, getting ready for bed, he could count the day as a good one. Good to have his heart ratified in the morning, good to reestablish with the band and with friends. When the phone rang, he was reluctant to even look, risk tampering with the day's results.

"Hope I didn't wake you, Dad."

"No, Carl, I'm still up."

"Tell the truth."

"I'm up. Though in another five minutes you wouldn't have been able to wake me if you started jackhammering in the kitchen."

"I'll be brief. I thought you should know your brilliant granddaughter got in. She will be going to Stanford in the fall."

"That's wonderful. Such a good school. Is she there? I'd love to congratulate her."

"Here? Be serious, Dad. Phoebe is eighteen years old. She is not here, at her former home, currently in use as an occasional crash pad."

It was utterly mysterious that Phoebe could suddenly be old enough to attend college. In Ian's mind she was still a sprite, a pretty blonde child, and now the child was going to Stanford University, embarking on a California adventure, probably meeting her first husband there. Old joke. But Ian was the only first husband in their circle who had not been unseated by a second husband or, in Matthew Blanchard's case, a third.

Ian was delighted to abandon for once his belief that the phone brought only bad news and unsolicited sales pitches. (And how did that phrase ever gain credence? Who ever *solicited* a sales pitch?) It was nice of Carl to call, nicer still that he came bearing glad tidings. Polly only called when Ian forgot a doctor's appointment. He made a note to send Phoebe a check in the morning, ever so slightly lamenting that these days you had to send a hundred bucks. Anything less was chicken feed to the newly rich young.

The plan had been to try Gary's cell in the morning. Ian might learn all there was to learn in a two-minute telephone conversation. He had a couple of questions to ask, and Gary might be able to answer them. And wherever he was on the map of America—east, west, or in between—Gary's phone would be right there with him.

There were implications to the wherever part. When Gary's phone sounded its, no doubt, supercool signal—Ian guessed it would be the sound of a motorcycle engine revving—he could still be "west" and eating breakfast in bed with Anita. They could be sharing a laugh at Ian's expense,

Gary snickering, *Who is this guy chasing after you?* But that would have to count as good news, wouldn't it, Anita alive and having some fun? Because if Gary was back east, she might have ended it all.

At this point the phone number was all he had. Aggie the angry girlfriend, Rick the repairman with nothing much to repair, Wally in his shabby palace—all the effort and all the luck boiled down to ten digits. Ian had gathered the available data. Dialing those digits was not only the logical next step, it was the only one.

Instead, illogically, he got in the car, gassed up at T-Bird Convenience, stopped for scones at The Bakery (named, by Tillie, after the fashion of her "all-time favorite band," The Band), and started for Portland. Alongside the usual disclaimers—nothing better to do, nothing wrong with a drive through the sunny springtime landscape—he had formed a conviction that he had a feel for detection, a talent, and he would get better results face to face with his witnesses. They were more likely to talk to him in person than confide in a plastic device.

Ian had met an actual detective once, or a "private operative," as the fellow styled himself. A Baltic-sounding last name—Prokoschka?—though he was just Charlie and spoke with a Boston accent. Charlie was third baseman at a charity softball game where Ian was stationed at shortstop, and over the course of seven excruciatingly slow innings, Charlie removed all romance from the detecting profession.

His most recent case involved a divorcée who felt invaded by her neighbor's relentless sexual suggestions. Charlie, a big guy, knocked on the man's door, flashed a phony badge, and laid down a grave warning—did Casanova know he could spend ten years upstate if he did that sort of thing again? "It worked," said Charlie, "and I got three hundred bucks for five minutes on the job. But hey, we charge for results!"

Mainly he trailed and photographed motel cheaters or located missing family members by tracking their credit card purchases. Which sounded easy, a possible starting point for locating Polly, so long as you had a way of tracking credit card purchases. Asked how exactly he managed that, Charlie referenced *connections*, then made a shushing gesture, his index finger waggled near his nose. Ian was dubious. Hard to imagine that those ladies who spoke to you from distant switchboards in Lagos or Calcutta, the ones who said could they help you and then didn't, were about to share with you what a third party had just spent at a restaurant in Miami.

No, it was better to be lucky than connected, especially when luck was all you had going for you. And Ian had it going yet again when the man astride a big Harley (and sharing a laugh with Rick at Rick's Bike Fix) turned out to be none other. "He just showed up, twenty minutes ago," said Rick, as if to dispel the implication he had been caught hiding Ian's star witness. "This is the dude I told you about, G.B."

"G.B.?" said Ian.

"Gary Barry Higganbotham," said G.B., extending a hand. "Branded at birth by parents who thought they had a sense of humor. Then branded forever in junior high."

"Ian Nelson. How about I buy you lunch?"

"She said she was calling it in," said Gary, with a sheepish what's-a-guy-to-do expression.

He had a technique for the French fries, extracting them from the pile one by one and dragging the tip of each bite through the pool of ketchup established at the rim of his plate. This operation was almost scientific in its precision, each application roughly ten seconds apart. Metronomic. Ian was sure a stopwatch would confirm that the intervals were uniform.

A pact had been made, Gary explained, "back when we were younger idiots than we are now." He would take Anita to Big Sur. "She always wanted to go there—this was something that sprung from a book she read. And here it was twenty years later on and she could have gone but she never did. So . . ."

"You went on that motorcycle?"

"Dude, I would have taken the Bentley, but . . ." Another shrug, a joke, no Bentley. "It was just crazy enough to get me there. Plus this is Anita we're talking about—know what I mean?"

"She is a very attractive woman."

"On the phone, she gave me all this talk about wasting away and shit? Like don't look at me, just imagine me still at twenty and let's hit the road. But I am telling you, the girl looked better than twenty. Anita Richardson, man. Ditched me long ago and now here she was."

"The way I heard it, you ditched her sister. What goes around comes around, I guess. Ditch and get ditched?"

"Ever been there, man? Two sisters? Sally is great, you like her a ton, but then *boom*, you see the other sister and suddenly it is like extremely clear which one is going to eat your lunch. No point trying to kid yourself."

Ian had, in fact, been there. Barb and Nan, the Holley twins. Indistinguishable to most kids in high school, a constant theme how you could never be sure which was which, even their gal pals hesitating to go out on a limb, yet to Ian it was obvious. He had the crush on Nan. Barb was nice-looking, Nan was beautiful; Barb was appealing, Nan irresistible. And they were identical twins.

"You in there, man? G.B. speaking. Come in, old dude."

"Sorry," said Ian, and told Gary about the Holleys. Told him about his career, the perils and pleasures of counselling high schoolers. Shooting the breeze over BLTs, him and G.B. The detective establishing rapport, laying down a comfort level before turning to the business at hand. Call it technique.

Gary was a pretty good egg, harmless and even pleasant. The necklace, sure, and the tattoo farm. Ian always tried to keep an open mind about generational stuff. He was not an education snob, either, though he could not help grading Gary higher after learning about the two years of college. He felt compassion hearing how G.B. lost the other two years: "Had to drop out when they took away my scholarship. Far as they were concerned, my hardship ended after two years. For me, it kept going a while longer."

Water under the bridge. He had his electrician's license and that was a hell of a lot more useful than a sociology degree, no? He had just "welcomed some serious coin"—financed the trip west with it, in fact—by wiring the new pool hall. No, not The Palace, the new one, The Velvet Cushion. "I'm good for now," said Gary, patting his wallet. "Not that I object to you buying lunch. I like to coast between jobs, not get ground down, you know."

Ian agreed Gary was wise not to let himself get ground down. He assured the waitress Gary would have the lemon meringue, Gary giving him wide-eye and how-did-you-know.

"Big Sur," said Ian. "That's where she is now? Big Sur, in California?"

"She might be there. I don't know. She fired my ass, man. We parted company in old New Mexico."

"That's interesting," said Ian, for God knew it was that.

"Here's the gist of what came to pass between us. She started in soft, like it was all just conversational, hypothetical, but would I be okay with helping a friend die. Would I be freaked out, or maybe get all legalistic about it. I said freaked out absolutely, because I was already in rapid retreat from her so-called hypothetical. I mean, who thinks about anything like that?"

"So she let it drop."

"She did not let it drop, she pushed it. Said, 'Imagine it's your mom and she is a hundred years old. She can't move a muscle, can't feed herself, she's on intravenous, in constant agony. Would you help her swallow one tiny pill if she begged you?'"

"Hard not to say yes to that."

"Maybe. Except it's a gateway sort of yes. I went light with it, said 'Oh, *that's all*, one tiny little pill.' Lighten it up with some irony, you know? Because this was getting heavy and I was not into heavy. Dude, I thought we were going for a fucking *ride*."

Ian could not have hoped for more. Finding Gary, getting him to open up? *Results*, man, as Charlie Babushka might have put it. And whatever Anita had in mind, it was good to learn she was alive and still looking "choice" at last sighting. "This was not someone about to swallow some sort of pharma death," Gary testified. "I was trying not to bounce her brain—on the bike, you know?—and she was like *faster faster*."

Anita and Gary had parted company "amicably." Ian did not ask about and Gary did not address the terms of their travel with respect to intimacy before they parted ways in Gallup, New Mexico. Gary bought her a turquoise necklace there (which looked "primo" on her) and she bought him a pair of cowboy boots, one of which he raised and displayed for Ian, with a rearing bronco embossed on each leather instep. Then he rode home. Her plan was still California, but then again, "she had this mantra, you know, this line how it's the journey and not the arrival that matters. Like a quote from somewhere?"

California was a big state and there were big spaces in between New Mexico and California. Anita's "journey" could have taken her anywhere in that vastness (taken her and left her, dead or alive) and Ian could think of nothing even a real detective could do to find her. Then he remembered Charlie and his sketchy credit card connections. Mel Bromberg had organized that charity ballgame, must know the guy and be able to find him on the list of donors. It was for the firefighters, raising money toward a new water truck for the Blaine Fire Department. So there was that, Charlie, and his contacts in Africa and Asia.

Either that or just go to Big Sur and look for her there. When he Googled it, Ian learned it was a small, tight community, a few hundred people all of whom knew each other, and though tourists came, there were very few places to stay or eat. He could stake it out.

He was beset by contradictions through another wakeful night. He hated thinking Anita might be a fraud; on the other hand, if she was a fraud she wasn't dying. He wished Polly would come home and hoped that she wouldn't, not yet anyway. If she came home now, what would he tell her—knowing all too well what she would tell *him* with regard to any fact finding mission out west. She would say it was juvenile, embarrassing, and crazy, and worse, she would be right.

All of which only complicated the central contradiction, namely that he felt a powerful urge to go at the same time as he saw the impossibility of doing so.

When Ian ran through all the arguments against going west, Fred was foremost. Dogs could fly, he knew, but you had to either sign up for the farce that your pet was necessary to your emotional well-being or consign her to the cargo hold of the plane, where Fred would go nuts. Once they hit the ground in New Mexico and began traveling out from there, he would constantly face the question of Fred's intestines and face each night the need to find a hostelry willing to host her. Ian would be put upon much of the time and Fred would be miserable.

On the other hand, if he left Fred behind, put her in a kennel, he would be guilt-ridden and she would be just as miserable. It seemed there was no good way out until Ian got talking with Ann Darlington at the library. One always did get talking with Ann, it was always a treat to soak up a little of her vitality and her knowledge. There was a word—Ian could not think of it—for people who knew something about everything; Ann was someone who knew a lot about everything. Harv said it best: "If normal people could be stars, Ann would be the star of stars."

Ian had gone in looking for a book, *Travels with Charley*, John Steinbeck's tale of going on the road with his dog. Steinbeck probably sugarcoated it, but Ian figured he could read between the lines and come away edified, one way or the other, encouraged or discouraged, depending on how things had gone.

"Nope," said Ann. "Looks like we don't have it."

"But it's a classic."

"I didn't say it was not a classic, Ian, I said we don't have it. I'm sure I can get it for you in a few days on inter-library loan."

"You know what, why don't I try the bookshop first. Wiley might have a copy."

"No harm trying, but I see it's out of print. *Grapes of Wrath* is a classic, *East of Eden* is a classic, and I'd be surprised if Wiley stocks them. *Travels with Charley*—and now I am saying it—is not a classic. It's sort of an okay throwaway with a few good scenes."

"You've read it."

"Long time passing."

"When it came out."

"I was not born when it came out, Ian. I read the book sometime after I was born."

"I was wondering what he had to say about traveling with a dog. That's what it's about, no?"

"Sufficiently so for Steinbeck to give it the title he gave it. I'm trying to think if there are other books that might help. Thomas Mann has a wonderful story about a man and his dog."

"I was more curious about the traveling part."

"There was one patch where the dog got sick and had to be abandoned. Left with a vet for a week. So that was one complication. You would have to anticipate complications, maybe more of them now. Back then it was not such a big deal where a dog pooped."

By this time, Fred had worked her way around the library desk and joined Ann in the inner sanctum. She knew where Ann stored the biscuits, but also knew enough to be polite about it. She simply gazed up and submitted the brown-eyed entreaty. "Just one," said Ann, shortly before coughing up a second biscuit.

"When are you going off on this trip?" said Ann. "And where to?"

"Undecided. All of it. When I'm going, *if* I'm going, whether Fred is coming . . ."

"Do I take it Polly is staying home?"

"Actually, she is away for a while herself, so either I take Fred with me or I don't go."

"Listen, Ian, if you want to go off on your own, keep things simple, see the world or whatever?—I'd be happy to take Fred. You know I love Fred."

"You would? But this would be for several days, maybe even a week."

"For as long as it took I'd take her. If you never came back I would miss you, but maybe Polly would let me keep Fred."

Travels with Charley was not the only book Ian came in looking for that morning. He had called Gary the night before and Gary had called him back. Ian was surprised to find himself liking Gary, surprised to feel strangely close to him. Ian had called with one simple question and though Gary could not answer it, they spoke for half an hour. Before they were finished, Ian heard himself inviting Gary to come with him to California, like the two guys in the book.

Gary had mentioned it in passing, a book that might explain Anita's impulse to see Big Sur, something she read in high school. That was Ian's question, but Gary could not come up with the author or the title. He had never, he said, been much of a reader. So Ian was merely guessing it was the Kerouac novel, *On the Road*. Everyone read that book in high school: two guys traveling cross-country, having colorful adventures along the way in flophouses and bars and hobo jungles. Even at a callow seventeen, Ian took it for a crock, a blur of frenetic nonsense written by a guy trying to invent life so he could crow about living it. And even at seventeen, like everyone else, Ian wanted to be that guy, taking that trip.

"That's very cool," said Gary. "You're bound for the coast of Californ."

"Maybe. Would you be interested?"

"In hearing all about it?"

"In coming."

"Dude, what have you been smoking!"

That was food for thought—maybe he ought to be smoking something. Was there a variety of medical marijuana that addressed indecisiveness? If you came unmoored from your life—or your life came unmoored from you—could you puff your way back to safe anchor with life-crisis-marijuana? Ian was absolutely ready to try new things. Or not, for he was relieved Gary turned down the blurted invitation and remained wary all night of Gary changing his mind, calling back to sign on.

"That one we do have," said Ann. "Though I see it hasn't gone out in years. Ten years, to be exact! Not exactly cutting edge, Ian."

"It was."

"So was *Mein Kampf* at one time, and not only in Germany. Here's a thought. Why don't I keep Fred tonight, or for the weekend. A trial run, see how we do."

"Ann, I don't even know I'll be taking this trip."

"Sure you do," said Ann.

Could Ann Darlington read his mind, even when he could not read it himself? Polly could, Fred could, why not Ann? Apparently, he was going. The problem of Fred was solved that morning at the library and the problem of Polly was solved that evening when she called. Or when he came home from Fred's nightly tribute to the Squirrel Oak and listened to the message she left.

New voice mail. When confronted with this prompt, Ian's impulse was the most typical one: there is a message, let's see who wants what. This time, wary of the content, he found his attention deflected to the nonsense question of how a voice could be mailed. And if a voice could not be mailed, which seemed obvious, then what phrase would better describe this form of communication. It was a habit of Ian's to notice a usage, examine it, sometimes even research the etymology. But this was delay, pure and simple, and he could only delay for so long.

It's Polly. Please don't leave me any more messages, okay? There will come a time for talking but right now it won't help you and it won't help me. So please?

Steve Harper. Why had this not occurred to him before? If Anita Richardson could look up Gary Higganbotham, why couldn't Polly Nelson look up Steve Harper? This was the age of late-in-life Internet lookups and hookups, where lots of people were suddenly seized by a sentimental urge to rekindle long-gone love or missed chances at it. Bob Baskin was not the only one who left his wife for a high school sweetheart (of fifty-nine) who he'd found and corresponded with on Facebook. It was becoming as common as dust. Nothing to keep Polly from exhuming Steve Harper from the pages of her past, Steve who wept over *Love Story*. Had a younger Polly charged *him* with sentimentality?

The notion that good old Steve could be revived led him directly to Ella Morehouse. Ella wasn't on Uranus or Neptune, she was in California and she too could be found on the Internet. He had taken Ella's new job in Oakland as a sign from above, a way out of their impasse. They were planning to wait until they *wanted* to end it, then the decision was taken out of their hands—a blessing, really. Still, in a way it was an ending that meant it had not ended, that it was ongoing on some level, in keeping with the precept that matter could neither be created nor destroyed. Their affection for each other had simply gone underground. And if he was about to travel west (and he was, because Ann Darlington had spoken) then he and Ella would both be in California.

These were all black holes—Polly, Steve, Ella—and none blacker than Anita. At this point she was that other cliché, an enigma wrapped inside a riddle wrapped inside a muddle. Something like that. Who she was, where she was, even whether she was. Whether he could find her and what either of them would make of it if he did.

He would have to figure out travel, figure out the house. He would have to put in his request for a sabbatical from Karin. Organize Fred and organize Ann, Fred-wise. Show her their routes along the Copper River and where they always paused for a biscuit on the Ruggles Bridge, identify for her which of the countless oak trees in Watchman Park was the Squirrel Oak, though he might be able to leave that detail to Fred. And Jack. He would have to make sure Jack was doing all right.

His brain was busy with all of this, but it was Polly's message that kept him from sleeping. It stuck in his craw, and there was another cliché to linger over. He didn't even know what his craw was, but the reason it stuck was clear. He had decided on his own against calling Polly anymore. After half a dozen requests for an audience with her, he was ready to cut bait. (Were there *only* clichés?) Now here he was, resenting the fact she had beat him to the punch. He found himself wrestling with the urge to call her solely to assert himself by overruling her request that he not do so.

He knew he would not do so and still, he wrestled. And it did stick in his craw.

"Why don't I call back when Karin is home," he said.

"Suit yourself," said Philip, "though I can probably supply the same information. In fact, I am seated at her desk as we speak. Our desk, I should say, albeit covered with her detritus. She grants me the coffin corner for any independent concerns I may have."

"I know the feeling," said Ian, sitting at the desk that he and Polly shared. In Polly's wake, it had taken a few days before he noticed there was room for him, that with her had gone the sprawl of files and loose paper he was cautioned never to rearrange. Or touch. Now the desk was all his, although this inheritance, like most inheritances, came well past the time he had much use for it.

"One thing I can tell you—and this may be exactly what you are after—is that we are in a lull. People have decided to enjoy the burgeoning spring weather in lieu of dying."

"Or maybe one or two decided to die without having us croon to them first?"

"Die in peace? Surely. But isn't that what we aim to provide? A peaceful exit?"

"Understood, Phil, but isn't it possible that one man's peace is another man's white noise?"

"Or one woman's, to be correct politically. In any event, Ian, I see no sings on the calendar and no rehearsals either. Karin is framing that as a mercy she bestoweth, though the truth is we are going to the Cape for ten days."

"Hey, me too. That's the reason for my call—not the Cape, but I am off on a little trip and wondered about taking a sabbatical."

"Save your acorns. Don't even inquire of her ladyship and I will not alert her that you called. That way, you retain the option of a sabbatical request sometime hence."

Sometime hence. Ian did enjoy Philip's turn as Professor Kline parlaying the King's English every bit as much as he enjoyed when Philip became Phil and spoke the colloquial American language. He especially liked it when Phil cursed, something that occurred almost as infrequently as the lunar eclipse. Philip was good people. Still, it seemed doubtful he would neglect to tell Karin about the call. Those two were a tight team, addressing one another with their eyes at rehearsals, or whispering, lips pressed to an ear. Apparently, they had love, or a partnership based on a foundation of love. They could count on that steady trickle of gestures and expressions and light glancing touches that barely registered as physical yet were.

Ian missed having that. He could not say when it had lapsed, or when he began missing it. It might even have been this very minute as he and Philip signed off and he imagined Philip scratching a note to Karin, *Ian called, ask me for details* at the same time as Ian was scratching *Karin/sabbatical?* off his master list for leaving. At least there was that, another detail falling into place, further proof that the trip was ordained as opposed to arbitrary or misguided. The master list was shrinking fast and still all the lights were flashing green for Go.

Western Swing

HE WOULD FLY. Driving across the country would take too long and Ian didn't have that kind of time to spend. Actually, he did have it but would be uncomfortable spending it—and spending the money. The *per diem,* as Ann put it. Ann did not travel but she liked to read all the travel blogs and advised allowing $150 a day minimum for gas, food, and lodging. "Double that if you like to go high end."

Ian Nelson would not know high end if he fell into a bright blue pool of it. What he needed to do was seek out the low end, or maybe the middle, to have any chance of Polly forgiving the indulgence. Then again, how did he know Polly was not indulging herself this very week, cavorting in Gay Paree. He might be the one called upon for forgiveness.

Unlikely, though. Polly had never been eager for ambitious trips. They both favored day trips, out and back, to sleep in their own bed free of charge. They did push themselves south for a week each year in mitigation of the endless New England winter, trying various places that friends had ballyhooed in Mexico or the Caribbean. Last year they had not gone at all and now Ian was unsure if they had gone the year before. The years ran together, his memory of them clotted. He pored over the desk calendars, going back nearly four years before he turned up a week they'd spent in the Dominican.

As usual, Polly had organized that trip, a birthday gift, tickets to see a couple of Red Sox up-and-comers who were playing winter ball down there. Polly thoughtful, self-sacrificing, baseball of no more interest to her than bocce. Why hadn't they gone anywhere since? Though the globe was warming fast, it had yet to make the Copper River winters cozy. Vermont not yet Virginia, Maine not yet Maryland. So far, global warming was making the winters worse by producing borderline events like ice storms and "freezing drizzle"—new terms were called for. What once fell as fluffy Disney snowflakes now fell as, or landed as, or soon became ice. People fell constantly. Not just old people, everyone fell. It was just that old people could not always get back up.

Polly had always handled the travel arrangements, done the work of planning, which left Ian unaware it *was* work until he undertook it now. She never made it seem like a big deal, just got it done. Patched it together online, printed it out, put it in a folder, and told him what time they needed to leave for the airport. Ian would joke he was not lazy, merely incompetent, or (proudly) far less competent than his wife. Tonight it was clear how extreme that gap was. It was easy enough to gather information, pure frustration to act on it, or rather, to make the computer act on it. Every time he got within an inch of booking a plane, the reservation slipped away. The price jumped sideways, timetables and availability shifted, flights disappeared that had been there seconds earlier.

He Googled the Ten Best Hotels in an area, focusing on a couple of them only to discover there were no hotels in the area. Blaring a Ten-Best listicle was someone's idea of marketing, but marketing what, exactly? How was it a good business plan, even in the ether, to place an advertisement offering nothing for sale?

The rental cars did seem to exist and the prices looked reasonable until you agreed to rent one. The more serious you let your fingers get, the harder some canny algorithm drove the bargain. Everything either dissolved or ballooned. Ann Darlington was right, frugality was out the window, so much so that, after an hour of stressful failure, Ian got up and walked away from Googleville thoroughly discouraged. He remembered how fragile his motivation for going was in the first place, remembered that he did not have to go at all, decided he might not go after all.

He and Fred took in fresh air, lots of it, over an hour's worth. It was dark and he could smell more than he could see, but the smells were wonderful: damp earth, river water, early bushes coming into bud. He returned to the computer refreshed and, with a drop of whiskey for courage and a little sympathy from the Google gods, he was reasonably confident he had secured seat 34A on a flight that left from Boston and flew to Houston, where he would occupy seat 19B on a connecting flight to Albuquerque, New Mexico.

While it seemed you had to book a flight over the Internet, you could rent a car from a human voice over the phone. You called and they answered! The pleasant lady with a singsong Southern voice was patient with him even though he kept telling her their weekly rate could not possibly be more expensive than seven times their daily rate. And she kept patiently explaining, "If you rent the car for a week, sir, you get the weekly rate," as though it was a perk to pay more. Still, he appreciated that she was not an algorithm and by the end was pretty sure they would give him a car in Albuquerque.

The plan was to get himself to Gallup, New Mexico, the town where G.B. had last seen Anita. They had said their goodbyes at a western-themed hotel called the El Rancho, so Ian visited their website with an eye to making a reservation, until he saw the prices. The Hotel El Rancho veered very close to high-end and breakfast was not included. At all the cheaper chain motels it was coffee in the room and a free continental breakfast.

"No," said Harvey, explaining that the free continental breakfast would be a banana and a stale pastry. "Here's what you do. You go over to a Marriot, walk in like you belong. Go up in the elevator, then come back down holding any old plastic room key. Then head for the buffet. Anyone asks, you are Room 201. It's a terrific breakfast."

"I could never do that," said Ian. "Stricken by honesty at an early age."

"You're not saying incurable?"

"I'm afraid so, Harvey. The next thing I steal will be the first. I know, it's pathetic. Even when we were kids, and everyone else was pinching baseball cards and candy bars."

"This wouldn't constitute stealing, though. Studies show that one in every four Marriot lodgers leaves without eating the breakfast. If you act as a surrogate for one of those lodgers, you won't put a dent in the obscene corporate profits."

Fun with Harv. It could be a TV show, half an hour every Thursday at eight, Harvey's dreams and schemes for repairing an America gone wrong even before the fools put a gold-plated fool in the White House. Harv liked to cite Arnold Toynbee on the fall of civilizations any time he graduated beyond the fall of his beloved New York Knicks. To him, Trump was merely the grotesque final chapter of a nation that had always glorified ignorance.

Whenever Ian considered the unreal reality called Trump, he did not think of the Fall of America, he thought of Carrie's boyfriend Warren. He and Polly despised Warren, though they had never met or even spoken to him, because they were informed that Warren had voted for Trump and was either unembarrassed about it or so thoroughly embarrassed that he couldn't admit he had been played. Best he could manage, according to Carrie, was "Even a horse's ass can face the sun."

The best they could manage for solace was to remind themselves that Warren was probably temporary. Others before him had been temporary, six months seemed to be the standard term of office for Carrie's candidates. The trouble was, Warren had been installed in office some years ago, his incumbency had begun to solidify. "He must be terribly good looking," Polly guessed, though neither of them had seen Warren or heard his voice. Carrie's phone took pictures, of course, and she posted a lot of those pictures on a Facebook page Polly could harvest. The harvest yielded a hundred images of animals and mountain streams and Carrie's female posse, but never a one of Warren.

At least she had escaped Utah without converting to Mormonism, as Polly feared. Ian considered this highly unlikely, Polly thought it inevitable. "What else would she be doing in *Utah*?" She could be married to a Mormon banker, be one of the Mormon banker's seventeen wives, the one required to make all seventeen beds every day. *Utah*, for goodness' sake. They were both relieved of Polly's anxiety when Carrie relocated to Colorado.

All this confused speculation about his daughter somehow resulted in a call to his son. The reason was shamefully simple: calls to Carrie rarely went well, calls to Carl were reliably pleasant. Carl was normal. One wife, two kids, two houses, two cars, and a job. That was Ian's sense of a life. He was comfortable with his son's radical normalcy. Ian did not hitchhike across Europe after college, he went to grad school. He didn't have sex with two women at once, or with a man, or with a Q, so far as he knew. Instead, he had sex with one woman at a time and at times with less than one. He could not even say he regretted that this was so.

Alfie answered the phone, said "Oh hi, Grandpa, I'll get him," and vanished before Ian could say another word. Ian and Polly had been relevant when Alf was small. Alf the Elf. Ian had changed a lot of diapers, sung songs, reveled in his robust, redheaded grandson. At four, five, six, the boy would come to them for country weekends—sledding on Gallows Hill and skating on the pond in Watchman Park in winter, swimming at the lake and going for ice cream at Zazie's on summer afternoons. Now the boy was eleven and Ian had lost track of him. Lost the connection, gained a portion of guilt.

Each time he spoke with Carl these past weeks, he meant to ask after Alfie. There had been something about an upcoming competition, Tai Kwan Do or one of those, with a chance at the blue ribbon. There was something at school, Alfie either excelling or struggling . . . No, the thing there was that he would be starting at a new school, leaving friends behind, and riding a bus that took forty-five minutes. But Ian would forget to ask, fail to express interest—or have any. All he had was the rush of guilt that came afterwards.

This time he began with Alfie, how was the new school going, but Carl laughed, reminded Ian that the new school would not start until September, then wondered what Ian had really called about. Ian told him about the trip. "It's a good idea, don't you think?"

"Unless it's just a strategic move to make Mom jealous."

"She wouldn't be jealous. For starters, she is never jealous—came out against it a lifetime ago."

"Is that so?" said Carl, pausing for emphasis, silently reminding both of them how Carl had interpreted "the fuss" his mother described. Carl had seen the shape of the trouble and identified it, rightly or wrongly, as jealousy.

"It's true she didn't care for that business, but there was absolutely no cause for her to be jealous about it."

"Isn't that for the other person to decide? Whether jealousy is felt? But whatever. Tell me about this trip. I hope this isn't some of that bucket list nonsense."

"I didn't even think of that. Actually, it's fairly specific . . ."

Ian trailed off. It was perfectly specific, but the specificity was better left unspoken. Why hand Carl what would surely be taken as evidence there were grounds for jealousy? Ian couldn't help that it might look that way, could not begin to express how the goal of finding Anita, highly unlikely in any case, would end with the finding, and finding out how she was. That there was nothing beyond that planned or even possible. The trip was an escape, an escapade designed to dislodge Ian from stasis. From quitting. From boring *himself*. He was beginning to realize that he was going simply to be going.

Earlier, when he set out to compile a list of everyone who needed to know he was going, Ian was struck by how few were on the list. His children, because they were his children. Karin, for practical reasons. Jack, for humanitarian reasons. He had let Harv know, but that was just for fun. He had not even thought about having someone keep an eye on the house until Harv offered.

"Specific," said Carl. "This isn't about a job offer, is it?"

"Sightseeing. Some specific sights. The Four Corners is one—everyone raves about that area, the canyons, the red rocks, and so forth. They say how different the light is. Your mother and I talked about going there."

It was true, they discussed it, though that was seven or eight years ago. Also true that someone, probably the Renfrews, in extolling the landscape, spoke of how delightfully *empty* it was. Ian recalled thinking the Chamber of Commerce would fire any such yelpers in a New Mexican minute if that was their idea of promoting tourism. Empty?

"Everyone says I should be more active, maybe travel counts as an activity."

Ian had felt the temptation to entertain Carl with a play-by-play of his detective work, thumbnail sketches of Rick and Wally and G.B. He was sure those episodes would not be boring, even if he was the one to relate them. He held back, though. That was the price you paid for discretion. To introduce those characters was to introduce Anita, or "the fuss," as a topic. As *the* topic, the gold he was rushing to.

"Send me a postcard of these red rocks. Maybe Livvy and I will put them on our bucket list. Or our pre-bucket list."

"Done. But right now I want to hear more about Alfie. I'd like to hear all about his latest adventures, if you have another minute."

"A minute? I can try to compress, but better settle in, Dad, by the time I get to the broken nose it could take half an hour."

Ian refused to be irritated, this was just Jack being Jack. What on God's glorious hell-on-earth, Jack flared at him, made Ian think for one second he might have a stroke or heart attack and call someone in *New Mexico* for help? Just go! Have a nice time.

"Have you ever heard of something called friendship?" said Ian.

"Friendship, sure. But that's no excuse for treating the thousand-year-old man like a child. Maybe you need someone to take care of. Suffering a case of empty-nest-what-have-you."

"Jack, my nest emptied out about twenty years ago. I have been used to it for nineteen."

"Used to it doesn't mean you've come to terms with it."

"I like that. I mean, what in creation have *you* come to *terms* with?"

"Aging. Solitude. Dying."

"Sounds like a recipe for misery. Just add a pinch of salt in those wounds."

Jack's laughter registered genuine. "It does sound that way," he said, "so I should give assurance I am far from miserable. For one thing, they have yet to take away bourbon or beer. For another—and this is top secret, Ian, not to be bandied or made too much of—I have got a gal."

"What, you bought a puppy and it's female. Is that the joke?"

"Remember Sarah Connaughton, taught both French and Spanish at Blaine East?"

"I remember the union made a stink when they let her go. And their charming defense was that they were dropping languages altogether."

"Part of the noble effort to kill education in America, nothing wrong with that! And you have to concede it is working. Anyway, Sarah was at The Draft

Horse with some pals, a cluster of old gals drinking wine at a table, you know, and I was at the bar with my Friday fish and chips . . ."

"And she jumped your ancient bones."

"She came over to say hello. Gave me a line from a movie, hate to see an old friend drinking alone. So we drank together for a minute."

"Go on."

"Well, we've been getting together. At the Horse a couple of times, then twice she cooked me dinner at her house. Braised leg of lamb last night, with roasted potatoes and buttered beans."

"I won't ask what was for dessert. Or whether they restored orgasm."

"Mind your manners now, young fella."

"Sorry, not meant as a serious question, just a joking reference to your complaint—one of your many complaints—last winter at the lake."

"Whatever, as they say. Bottom line is I am looked after a bit. Someone else has applied for the mother hen role, so you can travel in peace. Sarah's got my back."

"So much for solitude, you old goat. Wedding bells ringing in the chapel?"

"When pigs fly. Send me a postcard, yes?"

"That's what everyone says."

"All kidding aside, Ian, you should know I appreciate your concern, all your help. There can't be too many former employees worrying over their nasty former bosses after the both of them are out to pasture. You are a damned good man."

This was a version of the sentiment Ian had become accustomed to hearing: he was a nice man. It was a stunner, though, coming from Jack Sutcliffe. Kidding aside? When did Jack ever wish to accomplish that? He was a grim, gallows humor version of Harvey—Jack's lightweight jabber was just a few shades darker. Now Sarah Connaughton had reeled him in and all bets were off. It sounded as though they were somewhere on the spectrum between companionship and love in bloom. Ian could only marvel at the inverse analogue: Jack going from radical solitude to coupling, while Ian had gone from the most extreme form of coupling, the bloody forever-marriage, to isolation.

Isolation was a strong word, a hard word to confront, yet if he was not isolated then where were the dozen close souls he needed to contact? Where were the half dozen? No wonder he had decided to chase after a phantom. That phantom had become, or seemed to become, someone who cared. Who wanted his company. He was aware it could be illusory, aware there might be no point pursuing it, but he preferred to believe it was not (illusory) and that there was (a point). Exactly what that point was, he could hope to discover on his journey.

Maybe that was all he needed to do, stop calling it a quest and call it a journey. That's what journeys were for, what they did, allowed you to discover truths about yourself. Hadn't he fed that line to countless confused juniors and seniors at the high school? Hadn't it worked more than a few times?

The last time Ian had traveled across the country? Never. This land had not been his land. He got as far as Chicago once, when Jack shipped him out to a weekend conference, and as far west as the Mississippi River in Minneapolis, where the river was not yet majestic, for a wedding. Even if the trail grew cold in New Mexico, this would mark a new westerly best for him.

The plane, or rather the planes, and the time spent in between them or motionless inside them, afforded ample time for Ian to "have a ponder." That was a favorite phrase of his father's, one that came to him often when he and Fred were out walking. Along with dutiful compliance with the surgeon's urgings, that was the point of walking, therefore the point of having a dog. Their strolls were companionable and their visits to the natural world instructive, but above all they were whiteboards for sorting situations, composing lists, testing ideas.

He could only wish he were out ambling with Fred during the hour they devoted to the activity called "waiting for pushback," but it did give him plenty of time to sort matters out. Even after they pushed back and started on the first leg to Houston, it felt as if sky time was diluted, four hours serving as a concentrate that you added to make forty. Kerouac spent months hashing over life's vagaries *On the Road*, Ian spent what only felt like months hashing things over *In the Air*.

He pondered the gossip. He knew that all his friends would view this trip as Ian chasing after Anita, a futile chase by an old man after a young woman. A young woman, moreover, who blew town—and, just incidentally, was dying. They would see it as pure folly. Which left Ian no choice but to embrace the folly. He needed a break, he was taking a break, let them call it what they will. He wrote that down, something to keep in mind. Embrace the folly.

His train of thought gave way to the arrival of the drinks cart and the tiny packages of tiny pretzels, at which point his seatmate became as chatty after downing two quick nips as he had been silent prior. The man unleashed a treatise on ice hockey that ran the gamut from Cheevers to Rask and Ian was too polite to check him. Bursting with pride over having paid "five thousand bucks" to play a round of golf with Bobby Orr ("And let me tell you," the fellow said, embracing *his* folly, "it was worth every penny"), the superfan confided he had the Boston Bruins' logo tattooed somewhere on his "lower body." Ian ignored clear signals to ask for the coordinates.

Midflight, when everyone else on the plane had slipped inside the aura of their tablets and laptops and a third drink had put the Bruins booster to sleep, Ian was able to re-enter the bubble of his ponder. He resumed by asking himself a question: when you do not do something that on pure instinct you would do, when you choose against action, what lies behind the choice? Cowardice? When Ian fell under Ella's spell, when his instinctive drive was to get closer to her, he held back. He waited and let her take action. Only then was he, even tentatively, on board. So, cowardice, for sure.

But also morality. He was a married man, morality got in the way. In his case, morality would be an easier sell had he not gone on to have the affair, though he did suffer terrible pangs. If he was fishing for goody points in the big game of life, he might argue there were no other blemishes on his record. Maybe he could get partial credit for attempted morality, for guilt and regret on account of it.

What is morality anyway; why does it matter; where does it come from? Back in the day, it would be family teachings—especially his family—and the church. Peer pressure, if your life centered around the church. And

God, of course, or the idea of God. But Ian Nelson, seen as so proper, so devout, had not believed in God in a very long time. Fourteen years old? Not much later, certainly. By college, God was more easily explained away than explained.

In a philosophy course, junior year, they were given a quotation from Robert Walser, whoever he was, to "discuss" for three pages. Ian remembered Robert Walser's words to this day: *The universal panacea of belief is a paltry condition of the soul, by which one achieves nothing at all. One just sits there and believes, like a person mechanically knitting a sock.* He also remembered sitting there mechanically struggling to write three paltry sentences, while Hetty Hargraves was dashing off her three pages around the clever argument that there was no higher calling than the knitting of socks. Hetty got an A, Ian got a C-minus and felt lucky to pass.

Easy enough to see why the primitive peoples posited gods. They had no explanation for thunder and lightning, floods, lava, even the wind, and because they could plainly see the earth—see no governing menace upon it—the ruling forces must therefore be above or below, out of sight, whether gods or devils. Yet these superstitions persisted in a world where, even as a child, Ian could look through a ten-dollar telescope and view the planets. Now, through the Hubbell, astronomers peer into infinity, cataloguing an endless realm of shards and stars and planets so far "beyond the sky" as to certify Heaven a pleasant metaphor.

Still, for millions it persists as reality, the image of a paradise above the clouds. At a cruising altitude of thirty-five thousand feet, Ian was above the clouds right now, looking down on them, yet he had seen a study estimating that 80 percent of his fellow passengers firmly believed that somewhere up here they could expect to find billions of dead people picnicking in the sun. On emerald green grass, by peaceful waters.

Can that really be what deterred him all his life? The promise of Heaven and the concomitant fear of hell fires tended by the devil? Admittedly, the seed was planted deep and for years it did grow high; at the least it cast a shadow on his choices. A superstition so strong that, even lodged in his subconscious, it could be stronger than he was. Until now.

Or until he met Anita Richardson. He had been behaving differently since that first night, behaving badly, making choices that were not even on offer previously, much less choices he would previously have made. To fully embrace the folly, Ian would not only have to ignore the urge to explain or apologize, but the impulse to even care. He had come unmoored and landed on this airplane, lured by something more forceful than anything blocking his ascent. And that included Polly. For there would be a cost to be paid for his rashness.

The hockey fan stirred and shifted, the drinks cart was mounting another charge, but Ian continued bearing down. There would not be a cost with Polly until Polly came home and learned of his detective work, his unaccountable quest. The immediate cost? She might turn right around and go back to wherever she went before. And right there was the rub: where the hell had she gone? Hadn't she taken it upon herself to be unaccountable? To act without a scintilla of concern for what anyone—husband, children, brothers, friends—might make of her choices? In fact, she had taken the very step Ian was now taking, was every bit as blameworthy as he was.

He had left a note by the toaster, her first stop always. Poll would burst in the door, put the kettle on, and pop an English muffin in the toaster before she saw to any other concern. He'd left the note in a sealed envelope, lest Harv should find and read it when he stopped by to bring in the mail. It was for Polly's eyes only. The note that in an early draft had started out blaming her would end up (on its final revision) thanking her for clarifying what it is to be an individual. For understanding in advance why he has *gone west to grow up with the country*. Ian always did love that song.

He had also provided the number for the cell phone he bought, the same minimal unit he had foisted on Jack Sutcliffe, ten bucks for the phone, thirty cents a minute if by remote chance he ever used a minute. Though this phone was not smart, neither was it expensive or invasive. Harv paid a hundred dollars a month for his phone, justifying the cost by constant use. It was his dictionary, encyclopedia, clock, calendar, newspaper. He even watched movies on it, very small movies. So much for the big screen, a term once employed as the reason to go to the movie theater instead of watching TeeVee. Now they watched TeenyVee.

Polly could call him, he wrote, and he would drop everything, fly right back home to hash out their differences. He had felt a rush of affection as he signed the note ("All my love, Ian") followed by a twinge of something less devoted as he pinned the envelope on the counter with her beloved cast-iron rhino paperweight.

His last night at home had not featured sleep. It featured all the last-minute stuff, preparations for leaving and preparations for being gone, colored throughout by intermittent flurries of anxiety. The trip itself—car, train, plane one, plane two, shuttle—took eleven hours before he found his way to the bank of car rentals in Albuquerque. Consequently, he was fried, unsure if he could take the anticipated glitch—they had no such reservation, they did have one car left but it was a gazillion dollars a day—but the glitch did not happen. They gave him a car at a price not significantly higher than the price they had quoted. Only after he had driven over the one-way spikes did he hear Polly's voice reminding him to always get a second key. While he did not always lock it inside the car, they both knew he would lose the key for a little while each day.

Men, famously, refused to ask directions. Not Ian Nelson. Especially now, when he was without Polly's sureness with maps, her uncanny sense of direction. He asked first at the car rental desk, in hopes he could at least get himself out of the airport, and stopped to ask twice more before making his way to a strip where chain motels lined the highway. He pulled in to the first one he saw.

The marquee read $59 and Ian could only be delighted when it topped out at $73 after the "room tax" was added. The friendly girl at the reservations desk offered to upgrade him to a king-size bed for the same price, her smile confiding the belief that everyone wanted everything to be bigger, everyone liked a bargain. When he asked, out of mere curiosity, why a room that was after all *only* a room should incur an additional room tax, she cheerfully explained that it was "so they could put fifty-nine dollars on the sign out front. It sounds cheaper that way."

Indeed! But the price was fine, the room was fine, and he collapsed happily onto the king-sized bed he had tried unsuccessfully to decline. Supine at last, eyes blessedly closed, Ian felt gratitude wash over him and sleep close in.

Having feasted on two cups of airline coffee and three packages of tiny pretzels since the Houston stopover, he was hungry, just not hungry enough to stay awake. His last thought as he sank into sleep was that Polly would have planned better, packed sandwiches and bags of healthy nuts and berries. Polly would not have let him starve.

The world was changing while he rested. The wide sky had dimmed and the roar of the roadway softened. He heard a hive of late arrivals jostling in the motel parking lot and a few of those short sharp horn blasts that sound when cars are being locked remotely. Listening to the weary, hassled voices of his fellow travelers, he tried to remember whether he and Polly tended to bicker when they reached a far destination after a long day.

Several glowing-red digital readouts—night-table radio, television set, microwave—were in agreement that the time was 9:05. He opened the door and saw that above a file of stalk-like light standards, the sky was black. The ruckus of random noise had ceased and the new quiet emphasized the obvious: he was alone. He had come all the way here, to nowhere special, U.S.A., for no good reason. Find Anita Richardson? Highly unlikely. And if he did manage to locate her, wouldn't her very first words be, "My God, Ian, what are you doing here?" In that instant, his efforts at detection, not to mention his ill-defined affection, would be rendered flat out foolish. He had embraced the folly but at that moment he felt the folly far more than the embrace.

He felt old. Not in relation to Anita (that was not relevant, romance was not on the table even if *cherchez la femme* was the misleading pretext), simply too old to be doing this, whatever it was. Venturing forth, seeking adventure—whatever constituted the opposite of quitting. "We have to press the Refresh button now and again," Ann Darlington had advised. But Kerouac was in his twenties, at an age for foolishness, when he went On the Road; Ian was sixty-six when he went In the Air and as he stepped out into the warm New Mexico evening he felt every bit of sixty-six.

But a lot of it was fatigue and the cobwebs of fatigue were dissolving. The soft dry air was an immediate pleasure and he took his time sorting through the eateries along the hotel strip. He mistrusted one that might be good—it was crowded at a late hour, presumably popular—because it had one of those suspect menus offering every cuisine from tacos to pasta to blini. He felt safer going with a breakfast-all-day place and was rewarded with thin, tasty pancakes and peppery sausages. The clientele was diverse: a wordless couple each reading a book, a pair of truckers nearly as silent, four teenaged girls filling the airwaves like a flock of birds, and two Hispanic men in uniforms emblazoned with the name of a landscape company. Diverse but united in ignoring him. Here he had no sense of being an outsider. Even dining alone, he fit in without fitting in. He found there was comfort in anonymity.

That was something else Ann had said when he dropped Fred at her house, barely twenty-four hours ago, though it felt like a month. "They say one neat thing about traveling alone is that you become sort of a ghost. No one sees you, you're invisible and unaccountable. I bet you'll love that."

"I guess I can hope so," said Ian, aware that lately he had felt like a ghost in his own house.

Expecting to find a banana and a stale pastry at the continental breakfast bar, Ian came down to a spread more like the one Harvey had urged him to steal from a Marriott™. One stainless steel tub contained hundreds of small sausages, another a mountain of scrambled eggs. There was one of those rotating waffle makers, plus muffins, yogurt, hot or cold cereal, middle-of-the-road coffee. Barely finding room to open the roadmap in the midst of the cornucopia he piled onto a tray, Ian would soon be well set up to hit the road.

He saw that one could race to Gallup on the new highway or amble a bit on old Route 66, a throwback road made appealing in song and story. It didn't seem to be radically roundabout or slower, so he opted for song and story. Without Polly, he fully expected to grope his way west, getting lost at least twice a day, but soon found it was hard to get lost here. The day was clear and bright, the traffic sparse, the signage constantly reaffirming. They kept letting you know you were on Historic Route 66, with its passing landscape alternately moribund and kitschy.

The road had been paved with good intentions that had gone bad some time ago. Of all the picturesque businesses proliferated—bars, diners, gas-ups, motels—most were long since shuttered. Some were so severely sun-faded they almost disappeared into the flat, even light. The motels that remained open were so cheap he was tempted to check in and stay awhile. $26.95? Why not stop for a nap and smell the sagebrush?

He did make a pit stop in Grants, one of the bolder dots on the map. Take a break from driving, poke around on foot for an hour. At a café just off the highway there, he bought coffee and a doughnut and asked for a recommendation, what was the one sight not to miss in Grants. "Most folks go to the arch," said the proprietor. "Isn't that right, Dolly?"

"That is what they do," Dolly affirmed. "Or maybe the mining museum. But they like to take their selfies under the arch."

This proved to be the case, though the arch was not, as Ian had pictured it, a natural rock formation of interest. It was manmade and any charm it held must have taken hold at night when the neon outline showed up. Still, there were selfies being taken. Ian was dislodged from a bench and commissioned to take a non-selfie of an older couple who joked about having left their selfie stick back home. ("Didn't we, Laura. Left it home.") Ian told them he didn't have one either, didn't even own a phone with a camera, agreed they were all three of them dinosaurs. This was travel. You went to designated places of interest and took a picture of yourself on site. Made new friendships that lasted a few minutes.

"I liked the looks of your doughnut," said the jocular gentleman.

"That was the problem. I did too."

For years at Blaine High, the esteemed principal Jack Sutcliffe had spiced up Fridays by stowing two dozen doughnuts from Meg's in the teachers' room. Free coffee and free doughnuts, a benign offering which earned Jack endless complaints from the healthy-food-police. His ready rejoinder ("No one is forcing you to eat them") was met with further carping about the limits of willpower. How was a beleaguered teacher, freshly escaped from a horde of unruly teens for fifteen blessed minutes, supposed to resist a free glazed doughnut? So there was precedent: Ian had never resisted then and he did not resist now.

Back in the car, back on Historic 66, he came through the town of Thoreau, where the joke was in the pronunciation. Ian naturally took it for the author of *Walden*, but here for some reason the name was pronounced Through. If you stopped for gas, the attendant guessed you were "just passing through Through." Ian guessed he must guess as much a dozen times a day.

By now he was so busy traveling (making a point of experiencing his passage as "travel" after pleasant human transactions in Grants and Thoreau) that Gallup snuck up on him. He had almost forgotten he had a destination and now, suddenly, he had reached it. Historic 66 took him straight into the center of the town, which bloomed in lively and colorful contrast to the flat and pallid approach. A freight train was coming at him on tracks parallel to the bustling main drag, and it kept coming after he parked. Clattering and hooting and endless, the train mesmerized him, a single black locomotive pulling at least a hundred linked cars. There were parts of the country where you could forget trains still ran; here, clearly, people lived in close contact with them.

As he started walking down the commercial strip, the strangeness of his being in Gallup gave way to the strangeness of Gallup itself. The ways it was different. It was a small sample—center of the town for less than ten minutes—but it seemed that the Indians outnumbered the cowboys, so to speak. Which made sense if you knew, as Ian soon would, that Gallup was at the heart of the Navajo Reservation and that several other tribes were based nearby. It was good to get out of the house now and then! With all the chatter about the sameness of life in the U.S., the homogeneity, he had entered a very different world here. He crossed paths with a young girl, slim and pretty with long shining black hair, in high leather boots and a bright flowing dress with lavish rows of beads. You did not see such a person on the streets of Blaine.

Nor would you see the proliferation of pawn shops. Or pawn and jewelry shops—they seemed to combine the two routinely. A sign caught his eye: *Check for your dead pawn.* Would he feel too stupid asking what this meant? Did he mind feeling stupid? His daughter Carrie had always been bold that way around strangers, justifying her boldness by pointing out "They'll never see me again." He thought of Carrie's insouciance and of Ann's incognito: why be embarrassed when you were invisible?

He had his land legs, glad to be out of the car again, when abruptly he found himself directly in front of the Hotel El Rancho, the place where Gary Higganbotham had last seen Anita Richardson. This hotel, an edifice both grand and funky, upscale and downscale all at once with its array of pillars and balconies and neon, was his first destination. If Anita was last seen here, there was a chance she might still be here. Ian realized he had no plan for that eventuality, then realized he had no plan at all.

The hotel lobby was generous in all dimensions and emphatically western in its appointments. Twin staircases with handrails fashioned of tree limbs curved up impressively to an open second-floor balcony where the balustrade continued the style. There were antlers mounted on two stout posts, Navajo blankets on the walls, Navajo rugs on the floor. The furniture, wooden benches and chairs and tables, looked handmade and aggressively western.

The desk clerk, a thin man with an angular face, wore a dark blue suit, a bright yellow shirt, and a lavender string tie. Behind him on the panel of keys was a photograph of a beautiful Native American woman. "Your wife?" said Ian, using the photo as an opening gambit. He was not a tourist seeking a room, he was a detective seeking information.

"In my dreams! That's Onawa Lacy, man."

"Someone famous around here?"

"You bet. As in Miss New Mexico. Should have been Miss Universe, but you know the deal. And I knew her when."

Ian was sure he was about to hear a twice-told tale, which was fine, let this pleasant gentleman tell it, let him get rolling. "Knew her back before she was Miss Anything? I'm Ian, by the way."

"I'm named Sam." Was this an odd usage, a local thing? He wasn't Sam, he was only named Sam?

"Okay, Sam, spill the beans. About you and Miss New Mexico."

"We were in the same homeroom in high school. I sat two dunces down from her. Nothing—and I mean nothing—would get them to trade seats, neither of them."

"I guess they weren't such dunces," said Ian, drawing a smile, even if their whole patter felt rehearsed and familiar.

"Onie was taller than me. Taller than most of us, but she was always nice."

"Tall people aren't generally nice?"

"I didn't mean that. Anyways, it's been so quiet the last hour I got to talking too much. I should be asking, you have a reservation with us?"

"Not yet. I'm not quite sure I'll be staying over in Gallup tonight, sort of playing it by ear."

"Ear is good. We won't fill up until around six anyways."

"I've heard such great things about this place. It's really quite unique."

"Can't be. It's unique or it's not unique, the word accepts no modifier."

Ian laughed out loud, delighted to have the grammar police show up in string tie and cowboy boots. He thought the grammarians had all stayed in New England, going back to the days of Cotton Mather.

"True enough," he said, only to be caught again.

"Hey, something is either true or it's not true—can't be true *enough*."

"In a minute you'll have me afraid to utter another word," said Ian, happy to go along with the game. The detective building trust.

"Silence is good. We do have the restaurant, over here behind me—even if you don't stay overnight with us."

"You know, my daughter stayed with you recently. She's the one," Ian lied with shocking ease, "who recommended you. Not sure when she left, exactly—her name is Anita Richardson."

"I remember Anita. She was with us a week or more. Testified she was on a rest cure. See that big old chair by the Tiffany? That's her spot. Warm afternoons she would sit under the fan there for hours, reading her book."

"I'll bet you even noticed which book it was. You seem to have a pretty sharp eye."

"Have to stay sharp when you are the gatekeeper, my friend. Lots of books is the answer, she trucked right through them."

"She always loved to read, even as a child. After a week you must have thought she would take up residence here."

"No sir, because I knew her plan. Had to go west, had a date in California. An *appointment*, she called it. I gave her the wink and said it was okay to call it a date."

"Big Sur, right?"

"Oh, so Papa knows the lucky fella."

"I know of him. Never met," said Ian, who knew no such thing and by now might have more trouble locating the truth than adding to the string of fabrications. But his own reading had informed him that to be a detective was to invent any framework that could extract information. Tease, exaggerate, fabricate—whatever it took.

Polly once had a client who suffered from terrible shyness, was withdrawn in public until he rented a gorilla suit one Halloween. Ended up keeping it, or buying one of his own, because from inside that costume he could joke with store clerks, shout at basketball games, ask girls to dance at parties. He asked Polly if she thought he should wear it to a job interview. This gumshoe role-playing was Ian's gorilla suit; from inside the persona he could lie with abandon.

"I figured she was keeping it under her hat," said Sam. "The *appointment*. Because she came here with a different fella, big guy on a big old Harley."

"Gary."

"Ah, so you do know Mister Gary."

A family of five came through the door and Ian saw Sam's attention shift over. Paying customers, most likely, where he most likely was not. He was relieved when they detoured toward the restaurant to study the menu, so the conversation could resume.

"They're old friends, Anita and Gary," Ian said. "Nothing romantic. Not like, you know . . ."

"The rondy-voo on Pacific shores!" said Sam. "I was almost jealous of these fellas, Gary and the mystery man, 'cause that daughter of yours is a charmer. We had a little connection, see, we would kid around a bit every day."

"Anita was always so open, even as a child."

Sam was pretty open himself and might have gabbed all day had not a stream of customers begun appearing, as though a gate was thrown open and they came rushing through. It was mostly the restaurant, local businesspeople by the tenor of the back-and-forth, and tourists with their quite different tenor. Then several guests, descending the curving staircases. It was lunch time, although one fellow had come down to report a clogged toilet. All in all, Sam was spoken for.

At the same time, Sam had spoken: Ian had his clue. She had come and she had gone and Ian was pretty sure he knew where she was going. He leaned forward to drop a twenty-dollar bill, the detective's ready-money, on Sam's dais. "No need," said Sam, as he tucked the bill into his breast pocket, as smoothly as a close-up magician.

"No need," agreed Ian. "Just call it the tip I would have left if I'd stayed."

"Don't confuse me now," said Sam, who seemed anything but confused as he cleanly fielded both the twenty and the commercial traffic, a sudden flurry of requests coming at him.

Back on the street with the sun blasting down from directly overhead, Ian came up with the question he should have asked Sam. In fact, it was one that Sam could likely answer. No matter. Ian the detective and Ian the traveler had reached consensus, it was worth the expense to stay over here, spend one night at the El Rancho. He could ask Sam his question later on.

Ian only knew pawn shops as a feature in old black-and-white B movies, where all the men wore hats. He had never been inside one. Here on the main street of Gallup, where they were so prevalent, it struck him as something one did routinely. The shop he chose was clean and orderly, and almost psychedelically colorful compared to any of those dingy establishments visited by Humphrey Bogart. This one was stocked with crafts and jewelry made by tribal artisans, Navajo and Zuni.

"Everything authentic," said a hawk-nosed gray-haired lady from behind a counter so high, she had gone unnoticed until she spoke. "I can tell you the name of the artist responsible for each and every piece."

"I gather you encounter a few skeptics?" said Ian, aware for the first time, perhaps under the influence of Sam the Grammarian, that "prove" was the first part of provenance.

"A few," she smiled.

He believed her claim of authenticity, even though he now knew how easy it was to lie, that anyone could say anything. We now had a president who lied two dozen times a day, on average. But the bracelet Ian settled on, silver with a small turquoise stone inset, was lovely whether it had been made by a Navajo or a cattle rustler. It would make a perfect gift—for

Anita, or Polly, or for Ann, who had so graciously and open-endedly taken Fred.

Or Carrie. She had not occurred to him in the first raft of candidates, but this bracelet would suit her perfectly. Carrie never wore makeup, decorating herself instead with necklaces and earrings and bracelets and (he merely suspected, whereas Polly was certain) tattoos. Finding himself so close to Carrie's neighborhood—a neighborhood he defined loosely as "the west"—Ian was positioned to hand deliver it to her and maybe he would do exactly that. He had never glimpsed her in her new habitat, which after six years was not so new anymore.

Yes, for sure he would do it. He would follow through on this impulse and find his daughter in Colorado, just up the road. He picked out a second bracelet, much like the first. Works of art, the tiny lady assured him, each one "very unique." He did not correct her, or refer her case to Sam the Gram, he was simply pleased to have these gifts in hand, one for his daughter and one as a sort of wild card to play.

As the sales lady was writing out a receipt, a large man pushed through the curtain of beads at the rear of the shop, like an actor responding to his cue to come onstage. He was tall and mostly thin, except for the incongruous overhanging belly that threatened to pop the lower buttons of his shirt. It was he who wrapped each bracelet in white tissue paper and then placed them in delicate boxes that folded like origami. It was he to whom Ian directed his inquiry about the sign, two doors down, *Ask about your dead pawn.*

"We get that a lot! Mostly from tourists like yourself."

Ian waited for it, dead pawn explicated for tourists like himself, but the shopkeeper moved on to a different question, one that had not been asked. "The other one we get? Where to eat. And that one's easy. You head out to Virgie's, not far at all, and you order the enchiladas verdes. You will not be sorry."

Outside the town, Virgie's Café was surprisingly situated in a sort of lowkey red light district, sandwiched as it was between a massage parlor and a strip club, and Ian wondered if the pawnbroker had steered him to lunch or to his brother-in-law's brothel.

Or maybe the idea was to patronize these three establishments in sequence, strippers for an appetizer, then the enchiladas, and a massage for dessert. Two ladies who could be described as shapely, who were dressed in any event in a way that both shaped and displayed them, sat at one table. In case they were strippers or massagers, Ian resolved not to blush if they looked his way. Which they did not, nor did the waitress, riveted to her phone. She was in no hurry and after a few minutes he realized he wasn't either. Realized that in a way he was killing time.

Was it Sam's influence again or just the space left in an idle mind that made him parse the phrase *killing time*? You did kill it, never got it back, though that was just as true if you used every second trying to cure cancer. They killed a fair bit of it in the kitchen too, but when the enchiladas finally arrived they were as good as promised and left his tongue pleasantly seared. He countered this with a scoop of ginger ice cream before heading back in to the center of Gallup.

As he turned into the circular approach to the El Rancho's entrance, he spotted Sam coming out. Ian rolled down the window to say hello, Sam recognized him and saluted. "You're late for lunch and early for dinner," he said puckishly.

"But hopefully in time to book a room?"

"You bet. Mr. Earl is at the desk now, he'll take care of you."

"You're off?"

"Shift change. Sammy out!"

"If you have a minute, there is something I meant to ask. About my daughter. See, she doesn't drive, or hasn't lately, so I wondered if you noticed how she—you know—how she went on to California."

"She took the Chief, chief," Sam shrugged. "Many do."

"That's what, a train?"

"Southwest Chief, catch it right down the street, take you straight to Hollywood. Just as Hollywood once came here. *Sea of Grass* is still my favorite."

"Favorite book?"

"Favorite of all the movies they made here, back in the day. Tracy and Hepburn, man. Make yourself see it sometime, you might catch a glimpse of my grand-uncle. He was an extra in a bunch of scenes. That worth another twenty?"

"What about Mr. Earl, at the desk?"

"Split one even-steven. Ten for Earl, ten for me."

Ian handed him a twenty and went inside to book a room.

He was finding his way as a traveler, seeing sights, enjoying one brief encounter after another. Everyone was friendly to a traveler, who might also be, he did understand, a paying customer. He was renting rooms, buying meals and trinkets, even buying information.

And the information continued to come so easily. The skein of clues he had extracted, one by one, from Sally and Gary and Rick and Wally, now extended to Savvy Sam in his string tie. Venue did not seem to matter. Ian would come for a clue and get one, just like Philip Marlowe, and he managed it without getting coshed on the head like Marlowe, or arrested on trumped-up charges like Jim Rockford.

As he watched Mr. Earl fill out a card, he remembered again what made his "investigation" so easy. None of those people were part of a complicated plot. No crime had been committed, no one was hiding, no one was holding secrets close. The mystery was all in his head. Meanwhile, Mr. Earl, as silent as Sam was voluble, nodded him toward the stairs.

The hotel's rooms were arrayed around the second-floor mezzanine and each room bore the name of a movie star who had allegedly slept there, like Kilroy. Ian's was the Tyrone Power Room. He experienced the oddity of this more so than the honor. Nonetheless, standing under a hot Tyrone Power shower, he did test himself, rummaging among his remaining brain cells for some of Power's big film titles. Once upon a time, Ian had been a whiz at Trivial Pursuit, though that time had passed, his information chain broken somewhere in the 1980s.

It was not until he stretched out on the bed—clean, dry, shaved, naked—that he came up with one. Power had played the trickster husband of Marlene Dietrich's far trickier defendant in *Witness for the Prosecution*. Unless that had been Alan Ladd? Someone short and good-looking from the period. It was distressing to have such details, once ironclad, turn fuzzy on him.

Possibly because the bed was extremely large for one person, Ian found himself speculating on the likelihood that if Power had stretched out on this very bed there would likely have been, stretched out alongside him, an ambitious twenty-two-year-old starlet. That's how the game was played, back then and probably now, everyone knew that was one of the perks of film stardom. While he could see it that way, as a perk or even a male fantasy fulfilled, just now Ian was happy having this whole cool bed to himself. It was sleep, not sex, tugging at him once more.

He dreamed of ice fishing, no doubt because of Jack, though Jack was not in the dream, which was so convincingly realistic that Ian woke disoriented, expecting to find himself on the frozen pond in a parka. Neither Gallup nor Tyrone Power entered his mind until he noticed the spinning blades of the ceiling fan and felt the heat of the day that those fan blades were mitigating and saw his urtext of *Travels with Charley*, on the nightstand.

He was delighted to be in Gallup, be elsewhere, uplifted by the simple act of traveling, by the brief encounters with his fellow Americans and the unexpected things one learned from them. Onawa Lacy! How else would he have ever known of her existence? And when he went down to dinner (amused by the John Wayne Burger, ordering the Jay Silverheels instead) he learned from his waiter that there were more horses than people in the state of New Mexico. "You can check it on Google," said the waiter.

"I'd rather take your word for it," said Ian. He liked this factoid; did not want to take a chance the Google might contradict it. More horses than people, maybe so!

After breakfast the next morning (huevos rancheros and decent hotel coffee, with no bragging about the beans), Sam the Gram was back at his post with some Tyrone Power trivia. Though it sounded as phony as any Hollywood moniker, Tyrone Power's real name was ("Wait for it," said Sam) *Tyrone Power*. And Power, Sam testified enthusiastically, "took to wife, *one* of his wives, you understand, the beautiful Mexican lady Linda Christian."

"She does sound beautiful," said Ian, "but she doesn't sound very Mexican."

"Dude. Not her real name. Born Bianca Rosa," Sam supplied, trilling the r impressively. Sam himself was "half Zuni, half Mexican, and half Irish-American."

"Three halfs are better than one," said Ian.

"Halves," said Sam, choosing grammar over humor. "He died young, heart attack. Not in your bed, though, no worries. None of the greats died here, they all left Gallup alive."

As with any matters of demography—horses versus people, Indians versus cowboys—Ian could easily gather Sam's data if he so desired, but the details were meaningless. They acquired a modicum of meaning only because they came from Sam. Had he looked it up, Power's marriage to Linda Christian, nee Bianca Rosa, would have vanished from his mind instantly. Gleaned from Sam's mental Rolodex, the delightfully useless knowledge might stay with him to the grave.

Ian was having a good time, he was having *fun*, something he had forgotten grownups could have. Travel for travel's sake, you go and you're gone, just like Jack Kerouac. It occurred to him for the first time that he might savor the miles to Big Sur rather than hurry across them, be more the traveler than the detective. At the same time, he knew the connecting thread between here and Big Sur was not the highway, it was the quest. Anita Richardson was still the Golden Fleece.

Unless she wasn't. Because he could decide to drop the whole thing, the so-called quest. Hadn't it already served the purpose? Pressed the "Refresh" button and jarred him loose from the doldrums? In fact, he felt so thoroughly refreshed that it hardly seemed possible he had left Blaine a scant forty-eight hours ago. The problem was that, refreshed or not, going back was such an unappealing prospect that at least for now it clinched the case for continuing west. Ian was unsure what he would do when he got back, whereas it mattered not a whit what he "did" out here because the doing was all in the going.

Or in the being gone. Wasn't that the whole deal with Kerouac? Keep moving, take what comes, call it life? You never needed to know what came next because you never needed to *know* anything. And you could do whatever you chose to do next; just so, an hour after breakfast at the hotel, Ian was in a café ordering a second breakfast.

He ironed the road map with his palms as another long freight train approached from the west. When the by-now-familiar racket rattled the café's plate glass window, the counterman smiled and shrugged as if to say this was his soundtrack. Ian saw that the Arizona border was barely a quarter-inch up the road. One inch equals whatever—he could not read the miniscule legend—but all of Arizona was just two inches across. The Grand Canyon, trite and touristy yet also astonishing, literally a natural wonder, was a mere three inches to the north. If he changed course and went that way, abandoning the quest but not the journey, he could easily continue on to Boulder and make good on delivering Carrie's bracelet.

Carrie would be there next month, though, and next year. If not there, she would be somewhere, whereas Anita had short expiration dates on both her location and life. The sooner he reached Big Sur, the better his chances of finding her, helping her, helping himself in some obscure fashion. So by the time the last boxcar had disappeared down the line, headed east, Ian was ready to continue heading west. He would go the quarter-inch to the Arizona border, then cross most of Arizona before stopping overnight a quarter-inch from the California border. Symmetry.

Right now, he would stroll back to the El Rancho and check out, bidding farewell to Sam and to the phenomenal reams of trivia at Sam's fingertips. Tyrone Power's wives were clearly the tip of a very large iceberg.

Old 66 was fertile ground for kitschy novelties. At the Jackrabbit Trading Post, there were seemingly sane people posing with a gigantic plastic jack-rabbit. There was a row of classic cars embedded nose-down in the earth, Leaning Tower replicas, the World's Largest Cross. Some of these Ian saw, others came via photographs his fellow travelers were kind enough to share, selfies taken alongside these fabulous sights. It was all in fun, they invariably assured him and truly, what else could it be?

Kingman, a quarter-inch shy of the California border and for that reason alone the arbitrary choice for Ian's next destination, would soon give rise to larger questions of fate and free will. Previously unaware that this unprepossessing town in Arizona existed, Ian could never have guessed he would find himself there, nor imagine that something memorable would occur during his brief stay. Arbitrary?

It began with a tough pork chop at dinnertime, the Pork Chop from Hell as he would always remember it. He had not even noticed the name of the place, just read the menu posted in the window and went inside to order. The pork chop special looked like a good choice, but he was so hungry the whole menu looked good. Hungry enough to eat all the stale bread in the basket, devour the shoestring potatoes, and drain two cups of coffee so flavorless it reminded him how Ella Morehouse would drink a mug of hot water in the teacher's room while everyone else was drinking strong coffee from East Coast Roast and eating Jack's free doughnuts. What they served here was hot water they chose to call coffee.

He dispatched all of that but could not make inroads into the chop. What could they have done to render it so wrinkled and salty and stern, so adamantly resistant to knife and tooth alike? Ian doubted even Fred could reduce and digest this specimen. Clearing his plate away with a friendly grin, the waitress chastised him: "People are starving in America."

"I thought that was China," he said. Said he wasn't all that hungry.

"Tell that to your shoestrings," she said, an offer of proof that he was. She was doing her waitress thing, making small talk, connecting with the customer, but Ian was fine with it. Chalked it up as one more of those glancing connections, five-minute friendships he found warming to the soul. Returning with his bill, she winked and said, "I know, genuine leather. But some do seem to like it."

"I might have liked it," said Ian, noticing her more closely as she smiled, the dimple on one side. She had a throwback look, a sort of 1960s peasant dress with a vest over it, a mass of brown hair twisted up into a busy nest atop her head, blue eyes set deep above tapering cheekbones. "I just didn't want to sacrifice any teeth finding out."

"Yeah well, we do get customers in here with more toes than teeth. You mind if I smoke?"

Without waiting for a response, she settled casually into the other chair at his small round table. Ian was intrigued by her nonchalance, her extreme calm.

"What if I do mind?" he said.

"No matter, I don't smoke. Not cigarettes, anyway. That question was just part of a survey."

It was here that Ian registered the hour, saw that the room had emptied out. Things shut down early in a cow town—was that a line from a movie or something someone said to him? Was Kingman a cow town?

"So, you're passing through."

"I am. You're staying?"

She laughed, to Ian's delight, in what seemed a completely natural way. Her slanted, pokerfaced banter was infectious.

"Yes, staying, till further notice. It seems I live here for some reason. Where in the kingdom of Kingman are you staying tonight?"

"Nowhere special. Nowhere at all as yet, though I saw a Motel 6 with the vacancy sign lit up. I'm open to recommendations if there are better places?"

Ian expected her to recommend one of the other motels in town, one that offered more for less or, more cynically, one owned and operated by her aunt and uncle. Then she said, "For big savings, you can't beat my place." She raised her eyebrows and shrugged, turned her palms up, all as if to say here was an offer too good to refuse. Ian thought of the rug salesman in Blaine who made a similar gesture after knocking 20 percent off the price.

It stopped him cold. Not the association with Mo's Carpets, which came and went in a flash. She could not mean what she clearly meant, could she? And if she did mean it, what the hell was he to do? Only Ian Nelson, he mused, would concern himself with hurting her feelings right now. Not that she looked the least bit vulnerable. She was hardly some sad case. She was younger than he was and more attractive, not least because she seemed to possess such a radical comfort with herself. It was as though she'd suggested to a friend that they see a movie or grab a bite downtown.

"What do you say? Good idea, bad idea?"

"I say I am pretty sure this isn't happening."

"Hey, you might be right, only time will tell. As to that—time?—I'm here another half hour. If you're here that long, too, it could be happening."

"Why me?" Ian managed to ask, as she stood.

"Why not you? Something I should know?"

"Age? My age. You could start there."

"Age is definitely a bitch. I just hit fifty."

"You look great for fifty."

"You look all right for what, sixty? So that makes us a helluva good-looking pair."

As she—Keely was the name on a badge pinned to her vest—slipped into the kitchen, Ian faced the fact. This was not one of his mildly interesting five-minute friendships, this was an open invitation. Ms. Keely had invited him to have sex, and that was both appealing and alarming. He had surprised himself by offering age as a deterrent, when the fact that it was daft—that it came out of the blue, stranger to stranger—was the most obvious deterrent. She might do this sort of thing; Ian did not.

Disease occurred to him. A penchant on her part for such casual sex could have involved any number of transmittable infections, something Ian, as a monogamist, had not needed to consider. It was also something he could not see himself asking her about.

The longer he sat, the more expectant she would be, and the harder it would be to disappoint her. He chastised himself for entertaining this pressure, counseled himself to resist it, for here he went again, concerned about a complete stranger's feelings when he needed to be concerned about his own. He heard cautionary voices, disapproving voices: his mother, his wife, Pastor Andrews, who he had not seen in forty years. They blended and became his own voice, his own conscience as marinated in all that moralistic noise. And now Keely was back with a bottle of beer for him. "Saw you waiting, thought you might be getting thirsty," she said.

She was still working, "doing the close-up a while longer," but she looked fresher, scrubbed up, maybe awakened from the boredom of her job. The blue of her eyes had brightened, her smile was wide and inviting. She had been attractive, now she was more attractive. It had been her surprising offer that tempted him, now it was Keely herself. And luckily or not, Ella Morehouse now joined the chorus of voices, albeit with a very different slant, Ella insisting they were two willing adults, why forego the riches of life . . .

"I would be happy," he said, "to keep you company when you finish here."

"Company? That's good." She paused, leaned closer, mock-whispered: "I have heard that it's bad to go too long without. That it's unhealthy."

"How long is too long? A week? A month?"

"Oh darlin', a month? How about somewhere between zero and Haley's Comet. Now if you don't do a runner on me, I'll be out in a few. Beer's on the house, by the way."

The tasteful informality of Keely's apartment relaxed him. It could have been the home of a graduate student, with bookshelves, Navajo rugs, familiar prints by Hopper and Gaugin. Ian felt diminished for expecting less.

The bedsheets were smooth and cool, as was her skin. She was not young but her skin was, slick as silk from top to bottom, almost slippery as his hands traversed it. Her touch was light and disturbingly expert. Still saddled with too much awareness, Ian had to push his hesitancies away: why shouldn't she be expert at the age of fifty? And why shouldn't he let himself be the beneficiary, not a victim, of her experience? Increasingly, perhaps inevitably, this became the case, as their tentative moments gained momentum.

Credit to Keely for that. Recognizing his timidity, she put him on top at first and let him get going before she spun him onto his back, still connected, laughing as she did it. Ian found himself laughing too, forgetting himself as he approached the far edge of restraint, at which point she disconnected and lay back alongside him. "Listen to us breathing for a minute," she said. "Look up." When he did, he saw there were stars pasted on the stucco ceiling and arranged into glowing constellations. She had called a timeout, three minutes, with an advertisement for the stars.

They were both smiling when she spun once more, onto her knees, and presented, as it were, her silky bottom upraised. "You still there?" she said, reaching around behind her. "Apologies for any cellulite you see."

Ian, who could see no cellulite and no stars anymore, was still there. Keely was soft and slick outside and in, too much so for him to hold back any longer yet sufficiently so that he could go again right away. None of this was plausible, least of all that a fifty-year-old woman, a complete stranger at that, could make him twenty-five again.

He thought of Jack Sutcliffe, for some reason, maybe because he was grateful they had not yet taken orgasm away.

Keely slept. A streetlight picked up honey-colored streaks in her brown hair. Her face was hidden in a pillow, her hair fanned out on the pillow informally, everything about her so informal. Wide awake, regarding her, Ian felt ashamed for having suspected, or at least considered the possibility that her offer might be transactional rather than blithe. That he was simply too naïve to recognize the nature of her overture, too dull to understand he was expected to pay for her favors. When she brought his bill to the table earlier, the question of tipping became impossibly complex. Ian was a ridiculously generous tipper. Was he expected to make this tip more than generous? And if not, if nothing so complicated was involved in her invitation, might she not feel mildly prostituted by a ten- dollar tip on a fifteen-dollar check?

And now, more shameful yet, he calculated—or at least became aware— that as he lay in this sweet woman's bed he was saving money. She had given him something of much greater value, something of herself, and here he was, happy to have pocketed the cost of the Motel 6. Though it was Keely who had joked about it, saving money at the Hotel Keely versus the Motel 6. He recalled that Ella, who kept cropping up out here in the world, had a firm principle, never allow money to dictate anything you did. Though Ian protested that then no one would work for a living, he understood perfectly well what she meant, agreed with her, and always intended to meet that standard.

Fortunately, these belated and belabored fiduciary tangles had assailed Ian without entangling Keely. She slept soundly while the whole unlikely night continued to ricochet around Ian's brain. The Pork Chop from Hell, was that where this began? Keely had said as much, joked that the pork chop may have been tough but it had yielded some tender benefits. It was true, he would be alone at a chain motel if he had cleaned his plate like a good boy.

He was married. Why didn't he feel guilt or regret for letting a night like this happen when, yes, he was a married man? Assuming it ended here—an aberration, a shooting star, here and quickly gone—should it remain a secret or would he need to confess it to his wife? In truth, at least for the moment, Ian felt more pleased than repentant and it occurred to him that he might even tell the tale proudly, albeit selectively. Tell it to Harv, let him chew on it, Harvey who made fun of Ian's recalcitrance yet was only more adventurous verbally. When it came to action, Harv was stuck in the same middle-class mud.

Eventually all his fruitless musings came down to that which would soon be real: the coming morning. There they would be, together, possibly reigniting, possibly showering together like younger lovers, this lovely stranger and him. They would stand in the light of a new day. *Then* what?

Then, at least for the now of then, his hyperactive brain relented and released him into sleep.

He woke to the aroma of coffee and toast, familiar and enticing. The musty smell of sex lingered in the sheets. Keely was sitting at a square wooden table under a window that bled sunshine through a lacy yellow curtain. She was wearing a blue work shirt, unbuttoned, nothing else. It was strange, without a doubt, that Ian felt right at home.

"Morning, cowboy," she said, turning.

"What can I say?"

"That's easy. 'Good morning to yourself as well, fair maiden.'"

"Yes. Absolutely."

Ian went to her, touched her shoulder, leaned over thinking he should kiss her. The right thing to do. She turned her head enough that the kiss was deflected onto her cheek.

"Unwelcome?" he said, seeking guidance.

"Kissing, you know. It gets personal, don't you find?"

"No doubt it does," he said, dropping fathoms deep in his well of expectations. He had no firm idea what he expected, but not this. Not a distance. He had failed to grant significance to the fact, or even notice it at the time, that they had made love last night without once kissing. So this was chapter one of *then what*.

"Scrambled eggs sound all right?" she said.

"You mind if I ask a question?" he said, gesturing yes to the eggs.

"You just did—as they say."

"When did you decide on . . . doing this? With me. How did you?"

"One: no one sees a fifty-year-old woman. You saw me. I saw you seeing me."

"I didn't. Honestly," he said, but recalled Anita saying something quite similar, how she had focused on him because he focused on her. "And you look thirty, not fifty."

"Forget that. Anyway, a girl knows more about these things. Looking and not looking."

"Okay, I saw you. I'm sure a lot of people see you, Keely."

"Two: you seemed real, and very nice."

"I don't know how you concluded as much from my suffering that pork chop, but you are not the first to charge me with the crime of being *nice*."

"Hey, they could tell you worse."

"You said one and two. Is there a three? I'm still wondering."

"Intangibles," she said, topping up his coffee. The waitress in her?

Or the wife. Maybe she had gone through a few husbands, a Western gal taking life on the fly, playing it fast and loose until it left her stranded. "It's hard for me to believe people can live so—I don't know—unpredictably? I'd say existentially if I knew what the word meant."

"Sometimes people have no choice," she shrugged, "sometimes they might choose it. What about you? You didn't say no way, lady, this ain't true love and all that."

"Maybe, except I had just made a commitment—"

"Oh God no!"

"Sorry, didn't mean to scare you. This was a commitment to . . . to *not quitting*."

"That's cool."

"Is it? That's a word no one ever attributed to anything about me. Nice, yes. Cool, no."

"I could retract it?"

"No, don't do that."

"Maybe you're so uncool that it's cool. That is possible. Anyway, I like the not-quitting. Keep on trucking, keep grabbing life by the tail."

"Something like that. More the keeping-on than the grabbing."

"Hey, cowboy, you grabbed me by the tail last night, didn't you? We had some fun. By the way, that word? No one knows what that word means, starting with the little French dude who invented it."

"Existential?"

"That one, yes."

She was standing at a dresser now, dragging out items of clothing. Watching her step into tiny black panties Ian was tempted to grab her by the tail again, but she had tacitly conveyed that such grabbing ought not carry over. Last night was last night, this morning was this morning.

It was like magic, sleight of shirt, the way she shucked the one she had on and replaced it first with a lacy camisole and then a pullover without ever seeming naked. The blue jeans went on slower, involved some serious tugging before her bottom settled all the way in. If not grab, maybe he could pat?

"So, what now?" He said this as neutrally as possible, having no idea what his own answer might be, much less hers.

"A new day dawns. Life proceeds. Thought I might get in an hour at the gym."

"I meant—"

"I figure a guy planning a night at the Motel 6 is on his way somewhere. So, off you go!"

"What about you?"

"Me, I'm good. I'm staying—remember?"

There was no hesitation, no note of regret or sadness. Quite apparently, their "date" was never about getting together in any sense recognizable to Ian. *Getting to know you / Getting to know all about you*—the melody and lyric popped a thought bubble as he watched her stuff a gym bag with gear. It was not about connection, or a relationship, or even sex really; it was about what floated up to do. It was Keely's version of the five-minute friendship, just a tad more expansive.

For her it was about just doing it, whatever it was; for Ian it was about not *not* doing it. Wrong to say it was over between them, more accurate to say it simply wasn't. Like a pretty passing cloud, or those colorful boxcars streaming through Gallup, here and gone. The irony, for Ian, was that he expected to retain salient details from the last twelve hours for the rest of his life.

She did allow this: "You know where I live, as they say." Still, he heard more of a caution than an invitation. She did hug him lightly into his car. When he shook his head and laughed, she took his laughter for agreement: they had done something well together. It had gone all right. "See ya," she said as he pulled away.

See ya meaning I won't see ya. She even declined a ride to the gym, walking there was part of the day's regimen. "Don't need a Fitbit to know when I've taken my ten thousand steps." Quoting Chairman Mao or some two-bit fitness guru?

Ian rolled out to the highway and turned west. His only plan was to go a few miles, pull over, study the map, and *make* a plan. Catch his breath, really.

He drove for ten minutes before steering into a gravel turnout with a view of a chain of mountains he was too distracted to try and identify though he had the map in his hands. He stared at the map briefly and blankly before lighting instead on the notion that women could easily rule the world. Because they have been given veto power, they have also been given its opposite, the power to act. They call the shots. Even in high school the girl decided, red light or green light. So maybe it is not power but powerlessness that makes men so aggressive, drives them to sexual assaults and rapes at the far extreme. Men bossy in the workplace, dictatorial in the home, all out of frustration? If rejection isn't present, it always looms. Maybe it is why cultures that can get away with it repress women so severely. Give them an inch and they will rule the world.

A state trooper pulled in alongside Ian's car, rolled down his window and asked if there was a problem. Apparently, Ian had been there not the five minutes he intended, more like half an hour. Flourishing the map to explain himself, he thanked the young man for his concern, was told to have a good day, and went back to processing his vagrant thoughts. He had just spent the night with a sharp-spoken independent woman who, as far as he could recall, did not even know his name. Had it not been for a nameplate on her vest at the diner, he would not know hers either. He might have dreamed the whole thing.

Keely did not need to know his name, not the way she had framed the night and the day after. On one level Ian felt he should go back to Kingman simply because of what they had done in the course of that night. Sex. Sex was intimate, personal, and for him rare. Rare as in never with anyone but his wife in a very long time. Rare enough to be strange and wonderful, touching new skin, being touched in new ways, in a new bed. Keely made it simple, made it seem ordinary, while for Ian it was neither of those things. He was not arranged to consider sex insignificant.

Of course he couldn't go back, not when he had been flat out dismissed. Keely chose to end by never beginning, blink and you'd miss it. The girl decides, red light or green light.

Picking at his scrambled eggs an hour earlier, Ian had probed a little. "What would happen if I came back here in a week. Or a month. I'm just curious."

"Who knows?"

"You don't? Have any idea?"

"Right now I sure don't. You know it when you see it. It's all about the moment."

Back to existentialism? These clichés—*in the moment, living in the Now*—were shorthand, but he knew what she meant and wondered about her history. Had she been burned by someone, scorched so badly that she was extremely averse to being burned a second time? Had resolved to forever keep men at arm's length? He asked if she had ever been married and got a derisive snort in response: "Marriage is a scene most definitely *not* about the moment."

"Is that a no?"

"Had a close brush once. And true love, once or twice. Though I suppose if it's twice it must mean it was not true love."

It was not as though he wished to return, undertake a relationship with Keely. He could not picture it going forward. He got that it was a popup love affair, like a popup restaurant, solid as stone one night, non-existent come morning. He did not even believe the sex could work again, that it was a trick she managed. He found it convincing at the time, unconvincing in retrospect. The whole night may not have been a dream, but it had the shape and characteristics of a dream. It was a full moon phenomenon, the psychological equivalent of a tongue twister. Polly probably had a name for it.

Meanwhile, he was finding the map did not really matter. He was still so tangled up with what had just occurred that he did not care what came next. He wasn't ready for the *what next*. He would simply resume pointing the car west, cross the state line, and coast along the highway for an hour with no special intent. Coasting for coasting's sake, stopping anywhere that caught his eye. Let free will and determination battle it out on their own terms.

A tourist brochure he had taken at the gas-up promised he was embarking on a fifty-mile ribbon of "Old 66 with all its quirky charm." How could you instead choose Route 40, where eighteen-wheelers merrily sandwiched you or careened downhill behind you with evil glee, as though granted license to send you hurtling to kingdom come? But the brochure withheld any news of the slow, tricky progress through mountains and desert. There were places where boulders as big as pianos had recently rolled down onto the road.

Or maybe not so recently, maybe they had just gone unattended, for he also came to narrow ledges where cars could easily roll down onto rock-bed far below. A blue sedan that had done so looked as though it had been there for months. Led to such precipices with no signage alerting you to the danger, you were clearly on your own in the Wild West. Whether you lived or died was all the same to whoever—if anyone—was in charge.

He did encounter quirky charm in the town of Oatman. Mined out long ago, Oatman had apparently become a ghost town, until they'd refurbished all its ghostly edifices and added a few authentic fakes to lure the tourists. But Ian *was* a tourist, so he dutifully stopped to stretch and spend some money. In one respect Oatman was thriving, in another it was sinking, and he felt obliged to help keep the enterprise afloat. Sure, it was fake, a bit of a theme park, but the people selling souvenirs behind its facades were real.

Postcards. When you traveled, you were supposed to send postcards and at a dollar apiece. The Oatman cards would fill the bill nicely. If he spent twelve dollars on cards, six dollars on coffee and a cherry Danish (no cherries harmed in the making), Ian could say he'd held up his part of the bargain. He even grabbed a bag of chips and a Snickers to go.

He tried to recall the last time he had mailed anything other than checks. Letters written in ink had pretty much gone extinct in the age of email and Ian, who did not text or tweet, had been informed that email itself was now extinct. But postcards, the pretty picture and the wish-you-were-here, were still in style, and a funny card would help him re-establish contact with his grandson. It was possible Alfie had never received a piece of physical mail, an object he could hold in his hands.

Ian worked up a list: Jack, Harv, Carl, *Carrie*. A postcard could alert Carrie to the fact he was touring the Golden West and would soon be dropping by for a visit. Ann Darlington, thanking her and at the same time providing Fred with something to sniff, his master's DNA no doubt detectible. And one to Polly, at the house, in case she docked there in his absence. *Home soon, hope all's well*, he scribbled.

The card he chose for Alfie was Oatman-themed, or donkey-centric. It depicted a cluster of donkeys in the street. That was the other schtick here, after the ghost town and the played-out mines: free-range donkeys. They had been given the key to the town and, more problematically, the key to the highway—there were more donkeys than cars on the streets of Oatman, one more item for his catalogue of surprising proportions. Anticipating Alfie's logical question ("*Why*, Grandpa?"), Ian tried to draw out the answer from local entrepreneurs. The responses were various, if not edifying. He got: "Good question!" "It sells tickets?" "Shit happens."

But they owned the streets of Oatman and, being donkeys, they were disinclined to share them. They were immovable subjects, as sacred apparently as the cows in India, nudge one at your peril. Ian thought of the wild turkeys who often clogged the back roads of the Copper River villages, large flocks of them, though Ian knew the word was "rafter." Not a flock—a rafter of turkeys. Alfie had asked about that too; he was a curious kid, no stone unturned. The turkeys, though, were nimble in their awkward, bobbing fashion, always willing to yield the right of way. "Don't hit them, Grandpa, don't hit them!" Alfie exclaimed the first time he saw the road dammed off by a wall of turkeys, not knowing they would scuttle to safety on their own.

Ian wrote on Alfie's postcard: *These guys don't behave as well as our turkeys do. They think they are statues and act accordingly.*

He thought he was exaggerating for effect when he wrote those words. Shortly afterward, he discovered he was not. Leaving town, or trying to, he approached them gingerly, tapped the horn softly—toot toot—rolling up close enough to see their manes move in a light breeze. When they did move, they did so like a Korean drill team choreographed never to leave an opening a car might squeeze through. Ian pitched the remains of his Danish out the window onto the boardwalk of a fake saloon, to no avail. A dozen donkeys, a whole rafter of them, turned their poker-faces sideways in unison and ignored him.

Fred, for whom only selected vegetables were inedible, would have sprinted and pounced at the very suggestion of a crumb. Either these donkeys knew better than to ingest any baked goods from the Oatman General Store, or they were employed by the Oatman Chamber of Commerce to keep the suckers in town a while longer.

Cape Disappointment

FINALLY HE WAS in California, though this was not the Edenic California he had always pictured, verdant fields and orchards flooded with sunshine. This was desert, vacant not verdant. A lake shown on the map was a bone-dry bowl, the lakebed baked and fissured. Those Oakies must have had quite a shock, having fled the Dust Bowl for this flat platter of cousinly dust.

They kept going, though, and so did Ian. They made their way to Bakersfield, oil country now but not far from Steinbeck's own complex Eden, Salinas. Bakersfield had become Ian's destination for the day until the heat and fatigue dragged him down outside the town of Barstow. Willing to change his plan on the fly, *flexible* as travelers must be, he took the second Barstow exit.

Economy was the theme in this town. Econo Lodge sat directly across the street from the Economy Motel, both of them a stone's throw from the Budget Inn. The chain stores all advertised big sales. Steering through the residential streets, Ian saw more utility poles than trees and, cooked or not, headed straight back out to the highway, Interstate 40 now, where the traffic was brutal and there was no quirky charm.

And there were easily more trucks than cars.

Bakersfield still seemed too far. Another hour was all he had in him, so he recalibrated for Tehachapi. Tehachapi held some appeal, had its place in the culture. There was the name—Ian always a sucker for place names—and there was that song "Willin'," a classic trucker song which Ian had always liked and which now, surrounded by eighteen-wheelers on all sides, he understood better. Place names must have appealed to Lowell George, too, as he scribbled the line *"from Tombstone to Tucumcari, Tehachapi to Tonopah."* He must have known at once that he had come up with one of those lyrics that can lay a lasting claim on listeners.

There was also the prison. Hollywood again. Ian tried to recall if there had been a Humphrey Bogart Room around the mezzanine at El Rancho, but he knew without consulting Sam that when Bogey said "I got to send you over" to Mary Astor, he had sent her to the prison in Tehachapi. If it was still there, either as a working jail or a tourist attraction, he might check it out in the morning.

For now he would be content with the GASFOODLODGING of highway signage everywhere and Tehachapi had it all. The Santa Fe Motel ($49) stood side by side with Kelcy's Café ($9.99 for the chicken-fried steak) and both were appealingly down-at-heels. He could hear Polly disapproving of the food at Kelcy's, suspicious of the sheets at the Santa Fe. Not that she would have been wrong, just a lot fussier than Ian could afford to be at this point in his day. Like Heaven, Bakersfield could wait.

No chance tonight's waitress had her eye on him. Impatient, impervious to humor, she was either an unpleasant person or having a bad day. She did not wear her name on her lapel or her heart on her sleeve and she seemed to take offense when Ian asked if could have a glass for his beer. "And will we need a fresh glass?" she sneered when it came time to plunk down a second bottle.

He had already paid up as he sat nursing the second bottle—decanted into the same glass—and maybe it was seeing the 30 percent tip that caused her to leave him in peace with his thoughts. Aware that soon, possibly tomorrow, he would reach Big Sur, Ian admitted to himself that he had slowed the pace, delayed the endgame of this odd journey. He had delayed it partly to "smell the roses" and partly out of fear. Fear of not finding Anita, fear of finding her, in more or less equal measure.

He ought to be driven by the goal, the grail, at the very least by the spirit of adventure he had admired in Keely. There she was, living in the moment while Ian, forever hesitant, was living in his head. This was a sad truth, you are who you are. At the same time, he had to believe you could tweak that a little. After all, here he was in Tehachapi. That had to count for something.

After a day when the thermometer touched ninety-five, the night air was cooling quickly as he walked through the twilit neighborhoods, imagining the possible plot twists tomorrow might bring. The most farcical of them, and far from unlikely, would be a blowout on the road. His day could end right then and there, anywhere. Tires had exploded every half mile in the desert and no one bothered to gather the shrapnel. Out here they cared no more about dead tires than they did about dead cars—or possibly dead bodies. He doubted they came to collect those either.

Inspired by Sam's devotion to a romanticized past of Hollywood royalty, Ian played a game in which he envisioned how the movie version of his quest would end. The most likely outcome in the movie, he decided, was the least likely in real life: man finds woman and together they find true love. Wasn't that what happened as reliably as buttered popcorn and Junior Mints? Though there was a variation: man does find woman, they do find love, but she dies in his arms. *Love Story*.

Or, more personally, *Love Story* with hospice: man finds woman, they spend days talking heart-to-heart as her health is failing, he sings to her (the Tennyson at last, "Crossing the Bar") as she dies in his arms with a beatific smile on her lips. In soft focus. This was pretty good—the singing was an obvious touch—but instantly he was ashamed he could imagine it. Ashamed that playing a game led to his trivializing her death when it was meant to trivialize his "quest."

Coming back to the present, Ian realized he was lost. He had made his way carelessly through a grid of streets that all looked the same, with names he had not troubled to notice. The town seemed so small he had rambled aimlessly; now in the dark it was larger, and there was no one he could ask for directions unless he knocked on a darkened door. And this was gun country. If he knocked on the wrong door (and in gun country they could all be wrong) he might well be shot dead on the stoop. Shoot first and ask questions never.

And no one would come to collect his body.

More than once, Ian had gone off hiking in the hill towns back home and gotten lost. The forest trails were blazed, so you didn't worry. Then would come a stretch where no blazes were visible, all the trees looked like all the other trees, and the sun, directly overhead, could not serve as a compass. Tonight in Tehachapi, the darkness could not serve and he continued to wander and probe, increasingly unnerved through an hour of false starts and reversals, before he finally found his way back to the Great White Way, such as it was, back to GASFOODLODGING. Sometimes the sight of crass commerce could be a comfort.

Late that night, past midnight, he was browsing through Steinbeck's pilgrimage, mining it for the interesting anecdotes and incidents the same way he had done with the Kerouac book. There was nothing remotely as interesting as his own "incident" in Kingman, or not until he got to The Cheerleaders. Steinbeck's account of naked race hatred stood out starkly from the rest of the book, which was lightweight and lighthearted.

Steinbeck was on his way home when he came across these creatures in Louisiana, a coven of grown women who banded together to terrorize a handful of small children integrating a New Orleans school. With a rabid blood lust and insane rage, they appeared "on stage" outside the schoolhouse each morning, and crowds came to egg them on and enjoy the ugly spectacle. Steinbeck stood riveted and appalled as these harridans taunted the Black children and, for fun, threw in calls to "hang the New York Jews."

Between learning of the awful people in 1960 Louisiana and knowing that similarly awful people still wanted to hang the Blacks and Jews over half a century later, Ian set the book down—reading had lost its appeal—and switched off the light. Directly above him, a smoke detector flashed a tiny red light at intervals, reminding him of the constellations on Keely's ceiling. What a difference between last night and tonight!

And what a difference between tonight and tomorrow? Ian's journey was nothing like either of the journeys detailed in the books he carried, nor was the ending apt to resemble the denouement of a movie. It was just a short strange pause in his life, which would not conclude after two hundred pages like Steinbeck's travels, or after two hours, like *Love Story*. With luck it would last two decades. Ian would turn sixty-seven next month and if you did not die young, you died at eighty-seven. Both his parents and both of Polly's, all four of them, gone at eighty-seven. Even if you were lucky enough to reach it, eighty-seven was the finish line.

Which granted him twenty years. And the prospect led him to the question he had been ducking for a month or more. Chasing after Anita was, in a way, a diversion from coming to terms with Polly, or Polly's leaving. He could have gone in search of Polly, not Anita. The simpleminded detective in him could have opened Poll's credit card bill—like the private eye/third baseman Charlie Baltic—and traced her movements. The card registered purchases online before the monthly bill came, so he could have known where she was on any given day. Why was he willing to intrude on Anita Richardson and not on his wife?

It seemed that *timing* was always the benign answer. In 1960s-speak (and Poll did speak it) she was "doing her thing," she needed her space. She was fine for now. Whereas Anita might be doing her thing too, but only because she was running out of time for doing anything at all. With her, it was an emergency, a now-or-never from the moment Ian met her. Even conceding this rationale was also a rationalization, it had considerable validity. So, there was timing.

Ian could concede there was also something else: he was doing what he wanted to do. He wanted to find Anita and, at least for now, did not want to find Polly. He had glossed over some of the rough things she said to him. "Marriages sometimes come to an end" had struck him as such an obvious generalization that he scarcely took it in. "A marriage can die unnoticed" sounded as if it came directly from a session with one of her clients. It did not occur to him she could be talking about her own marriage. *Their* marriage.

Marriage was all about habits, patterns, and clearly their pattern had allowed them to exist in parallel more than in tandem. You could see it in hindsight or by checking Dear Abby in the paper—a marriage *can* die unnoticed. But Polly noticed. It would hardly matter where her credit card placed her on the grid if she had pronounced their marriage dead. There was no real point to finding Anita; maybe there was no point finding Polly either.

Finding Yourself. It was such a terrible cliché that Ian cringed at the phrase, recoiled from the Simple Simon banality of it, yet he was sure he had uttered just such touchy-feely-mealy words to more than a few derailed, distracted high school students who had "lost their way." He sometimes gave them an exercise, try to think of something that had made them happy in the past. Giving himself the exercise now, he pictured Carl and Carrie when they were small, carrying one in each arm at playgrounds and lakefronts. He pictured Myra, his college girlfriend, early on when they were new, sex was new, the world was new. Walking with Myra in May to the canoe rental kiosk on Lake Jericho, a bottle of wine in the blue and white bag she carried everywhere.

Those images came from the distant past. Was Keely in the past? If the past began anew each passing minute, she was. He pictured the moment when her nakedness began disappearing into clothes, her bottom snugging into blue jeans as he smiled with absent-minded idiot joy. He was happy just last night! Though maybe happiness was always in the past . . .

John Steinbeck had gone in search of America, but hadn't he also gone in search of himself? Not unlike Ian, Steinbeck found himself at a dead end and came up with travel as an exit strategy. Since so much of what he found looked to him like a rich past sullied by a botched, corrupted present, he may have concluded that finding himself was not such a hot idea. So far, Ian had been luckier. He had found Sam the Gram and some live pawn; found Keely. Whether it was America or himself he was finding, it had begun to matter less whether or not he found Anita Richardson.

He had thought his way in and out of so many corners that his head hurt and his eyes stung, even when he shut them. His circuits were overloaded. It was time to stop thinking so much, about the past, the present, or the future. Time to let it be. He had set the book aside an hour ago, now he needed to set his brain aside. The clock told him it was quarter to three and Ian recollected vaguely that someone famous had once said, "In the dark night of the soul, it is always three a.m." Or something to that effect. He turned out the light quickly, while there was still time!

Harvey liked to tell about the time he drove ten hours just to have dinner with a girl. "I felt I was losing her, needed to stake my claim." He lost her anyway, but she was nineteen, it was college, and in the end it did not matter to either of them. "The dinner was a loser too. We ate in her dining hall out there, beef stew hold-the-beef and soggy carrots swimming in gluey brown stuff." It may have been a loser, but clearly that meal was memorable.

Was Ian driving six hours now "just to have dinner with a girl"? Probably not. Probably he was driving six hours because it was the next thing to do after having driven the previous six hours. Bakersfield had been "up the road a piece," a small enough piece that he wished he had kept going and gotten there last night as, after Bakersfield, he would still have nearly three hundred miles to cover, including a famously slow crawl up the coastal highway to Big Sur. Apparently, it was not an easy place to reach.

He stopped once for gas and once for a chicken salad sandwich, did not stop for any of the attractions, which turned out to be a sinful omission. When he settled up for his sandwich at the register in Cambria, the young lady ventured that he "must be going up to the Castle." And when Ian demurred on the Castle ("Why would I do that?"), she turned on him. "People do, is all," she snapped, with the unmistakable implication that Ian was therefore not "people."

The Hearst Castle, like so many western venues, did carry a suggestion of past Hollywood glory, even if it was only that William Randolph Hearst had more or less imprisoned a minor actress in his mansion on the hill. Maybe Hearst got the idea from a movie, or a book made into a movie more than once, *Jane Eyre*. Sam, back in Gallup, would know the names of every actress who played the woman in Mr. Rochester's attic and every biographical tidbit about the minor actress in Hearst's mansion. Ian was sufficiently pleased he knew what the surly girl at the checkout was talking about when she mentioned "the Castle."

Dramatic panoramas came and went. Each time he pulled over to gaze, Ian tried calling ahead to Deetjun's Inn, the place Gary Higganbotham had understood to be Anita's destination. When his phone did not work—no reception from one wild outcropping to the next—Ian was not displeased. This small defeat for technology outweighed his need for a room reservation. If others beat him to the punch, if they had better phones with better service, he would sleep in the car and call it an adventure.

Trying to stay awake, he wondered how it was that some people got three names. No one ever said William Hearst, it was always William Randolph Hearst. Oliver Wendell Holmes always got three, while Larry Holmes got just two. There were those who did not even get two (Madonna, Prince, Beyoncé) but they chose for themselves. Who determined that a person rated three?

There were these idle thoughts. There was the radio, if you liked static, and there was the changing landscape. He had yet to see the blue Pacific of fantasyland, that must have been Hawaii or Tahiti. Here he saw steep dense forest on one side of the highway, alarming cliffs on the other, and far below the cliffs a steel-gray sea shattering furiously two hundred yards offshore as though outraged at the very suggestion that land might interrupt its violent stride. It was an environment that would have its constituency— the Romantic poets would have found inspiration here—while others may have been more frightened than inspired.

The inn, which he reached late afternoon, might have been created to allay those fears. It was reassuringly rustic, with a lodge, cabins tucked into the wooded hillside, and a larger wood-frame building that was like a jigsaw puzzle of tight hallways, narrow stairs, and small quirky rooms. Asked at the desk how long he would be staying, Ian said "It depends" and was delighted when the fellow did not ask on what it depended. Live and let live at Deetjun's.

After dropping his bag on the bed in a tiny triangular room, he ducked back into the lodge, glanced at the restaurant menu, and said hello to a shaggy fellow, beard as big as a holly bush, who was poking logs in a quiet fire. The fire made no sense until he crossed the road to the cliffside, where the air was "bracing" when the wind stopped, icy when it blew. The turbulent gray-green sea below looked even colder.

Anita had read about this place and may have come seeking something magical about it. Ian feared she may have come to jump. He had pictured it as an escarpment, a straight drop, one of those places like the Golden Gate Bridge that attract suicides, people who while feeling hopeless derive some uplift from the notion of a grand release, a satisfying exit from the strain of living. It was not a straight drop, though. The terrain made for a rough, irregular passage down the incline that would feature broken bones and hospitalization with no guarantee of a beautiful death.

She had tested Gary on assisted suicide, sounded him out. Gary testified that she seemed upbeat when they parted, though it might have been an act. Said she was grateful for his help in getting as far as Gallup, needed to be footloose on her own going forward. Hopefully, she was still keeping The Blob at bay. Hopefully, Ian would see her in the lodge at dinner time rather than find her broken on the shoals below.

After an initial reconnaissance of the surroundings, up and down the road, up and down the cliff, he went back to his room to rest before dinner. Read a bit more, enough to get Steinbeck out of benighted Louisiana. Steinbeck knew this coast well. A native Californian, he revisited his old haunts in the course of his *Travels with Charley* and was dismayed at how much had changed. Without doubt, much more had changed in the decades since. Though very little went unscathed in half a century in America, it was possible to believe that Big Sur and Deetjun's Inn had resisted change better than most.

This place had its very own climate. The fire in the lodge was burning when Ian arrived, burning later that night, burning the next morning. The day's supply of wood was stacked neatly on the side hearth. His waitress—same one at dinner and breakfast—could be overheard repeating pleasant rote sentences about the weather, and Ian could already discern the locals from the tourists by the slant of her patter. The tourists were "freezing" in the same air the locals counted as a warm spell. They all found grounds for laughter in it, possibly owing to Kate.

She had been nameless at dinner, became Kate at breakfast when she had more time on her hands. There were fewer patrons and she recognized all of them. "Nowhere else to eat, I guess," was her line for him.

"Or maybe nowhere better?" he smiled back. He was smiling mainly at the realization that waitresses now constituted his entire social life, not to mention his love life! Was this inevitably the case for a solo traveler? Waiters and waitresses, innkeepers and bartenders? Those five-minute friendships had tapered off after Route 66, where the boosterized Attractions, both wondrous and silly, did foster bonds between fellow travelers.

"So, you're with us for a while?" she asked.

"It depends," he said, the same answer he gave to the desk clerk the day before, and again it was permitted to rest there. Let it depend, let it be.

He took his lunch in a backpack, fruit and cheese and a bottle of beer, hiked up the road a few miles, sat on a flat rock resting and eating. Here, all of nature's elements smelled wonderful: the tangy salty air, savory emanations from pine and fir, the musty aroma rising from the earth. Here, inhaling might count as an Activity.

At dinner that night he revised his response, told Kate he loved it here and might stay forever, not just "for a while."

"So what it depended on was love," she smiled. "A lot of people find they love it here. Fortunately, they don't all stay forever."

He would gather Kate's story in fragments, meal by meal. A schoolteacher (early childhood ed., fifteen years of it), a relationship that started well and inspired her to leave her job, only to get ditched in Mexico. "*Boyfriends*," she said, rolling her eyes before starting in on the current one. Ian listened (the current boyfriend was Henry, a forester, she liked his smell, which was "foresty") and wondered if someone Kate's age could be classified as a girlfriend. She was late-forty-something, gray eyes with slight hollows beneath them, straight brown hair parted in the middle, young enough in appearance yet with a faint suggestion of gray at her temples, perhaps too old to be girlfriend to a boyfriend. There must be better words for lovers in that age group.

He had already learned more about Anita. Had insinuated himself into the office, concocted a version of the daughter story, gathered that Anita had indeed been here but checked out six days ago. Between that knowledge and the groundwork of camaraderie established between them, Ian felt okay about broaching it with Kate. They would have talked.

"My daughter was the real reason for my coming here. We had a sort of plan to meet up if our schedules worked out. Plans got complicated when my phone stopped working."

"Mountains," Kate nodded, knowingly. "Unless you're like me and forgot to charge it?"

"I'm afraid she gave up on me. Thought I wasn't answering."

"Hey, you're welcome to use my phone if you'd like."

"That's a lovely offer, Kate, but I'm afraid she's long gone by now, and I'll be needing to get back home before I can catch up to her."

He lingered as the tables emptied. Took an Irish coffee to the hearth and sat there reading. Sat there so long, he joked he should help the staff clean up at closing time. Conversation with Kate was necessarily sporadic, but he managed to keep it going. "I'll bet Anita sat right here," he said, accepting a top-up, more whiskey than coffee, "with a book in her hands."

"She really did, especially on rainy days. And she made, like, *notes*. Is she a writer?"

"A little poetry," he fabricated. It could be true. Rummaging for scraps of truth in his own patter, Ian could almost forget Anita was not actually his daughter. "We have family in San Francisco," he fabricated, "and she did study poetry there years ago. In fact, I'll bet that's where she is headed next."

This was a new Ian Nelson, wild lies rolling off his tongue like sleds flying down icy hills. Family in San Francisco! But, if there was any chance Anita was going to be a jumper, he had to eliminate the Golden Gate Bridge.

Kate hesitated. Either he had somehow given away the game or she was hearkening to a voice coming from the kitchen. He was relieved when she got past whatever it was and picked up the thread. "I don't know about San Fran. The only place she mentioned was Cape Disappointment and I'm pretty sure that was just a riff. You know, not like she was serious about going there, more like she got a kick out of the name?"

"Family trait," he pressed on. "Seems we're all drawn to places for no better reason than their names. Back east, in Maine, they have all these towns named for cities—Naples, Paris, Rome, Mexico . . ."

"Mexico is a country."

"True."

"Those others are cities. Just saying."

"No, you're right. Funny they did that. But wait—there's also Poland. And Norway."

"Countries," she allowed. "I guess they have both."

Kate would have gotten along well with Sam the Gram, teamed up with him to correct everyone's misstatements of fact. Ian would feel guilty manipulating such welcoming souls had they not so clearly enjoyed engaging. Sam was happy to bestow a few Hollywood factoids on anyone who stood there long enough to hear him out and Ian was far from the sole recipient of Kate's open nature. Every table she served soon enough began to feel like a small private party, with cheerful banter and laughter.

It was true, he could have stayed longer. If breathing was an activity, this was one place God made for it. Plus, by day three he was friends not only with Kate, but with Carlos the groundsman and with the Ellerbees, Jim and Lynn, who invited him to their table at breakfast. At first he assumed they took pity on him eating alone, but it didn't feel that way. They called to mind a kind of couple Polly described, a strong twosome who derived some of their strength from taking on a third wheel, always finding someone else to include. It was as if he completed the Ellerbees' connection, which ran back and forth through him like electrical current.

If not forever, he could stay as long as it took to decide where to head next. Unless he was so far gone as to treat Cape Disappointment as a clue, he had no more leads, nothing to steer him. He had spent his informational capital and all he had purchased with it was this extraordinary air. He had successfully detected his way to a dead end, a literal one, at the very end of the continent. This was his Cape Disappointment.

Not that he left off trying. Still probing for clues, he asked Kate by what means Anita had come to Deetjun's and how she had left. (She doesn't drive, yada yada . . .)

"That was the amazing thing, she came in a Lyft! And I was, like, to *here*? Nobody does that. We all wondered how many millions it must have cost her, but didn't dare ask."

She departed on Kate's day off, so it was pure speculation whether she had done the same thing, "Left in a Lyft!" as Ian joked, embarrassed to think the same line must be uttered a thousand times a day in a new world where young people summoned drivers with their thumbs. Ian made the odd connection to hitchhiking back in the day, young people soliciting rides with their thumbs then too, one thumb pointed up instead of two pointing down.

"She may have done," said Kate. "She wasn't rich or anything—I suppose you would know—but she told me she was trying to spend every penny she had. Like it was some sort of project. I thought it was weird but kind of admirable. In a purist way, you know?"

Ian nodded as "sagely" as he could manage, going for fatherly. To Kate this was banter, something she did to pass the time, to him it was the subtle extraction of every drop of information there was to extract. Now the vein was mined out.

"See you at breakfast?" he said, standing to leave, and Kate touched his shoulder sympathetically, squinching her face to express her disappointment about Cape Disappointment, or possibly her hope for the Cape of Good Hope. Yes, she said, turning the squinch into a companionable smile, she would see him at breakfast.

On his fifth full day at Deetjun's, Ian spent the entire morning roaming the steep defile that hung above the sea, following any suggestion of a path, assessing the danger of every outcropping. He saw the way this place was both knowable and unknowable, heavily touristed yet still mysterious. "Our main crop around here," Carlos had told him, "is eccentric self-appointed would-be artists. Not much else will grow."

All along, each day, he had been searching for her body. Kate had not seen her that last day; she might never have Lyfted off at all. He searched, knowing no one else would, knowing he might very well find other bodies, unrecognizable if animals had found them first. The fact that he did not expect to find her did not keep him from experiencing relief each minute he did not. Working to banish the notion she had died, he would summon her up alive and marvel at her energy, her will. Admire her impulsiveness, boldly asking him to take her to the Fair and then just as boldly going west with Gary instead, what the hell.

People could do what they wanted to do—a radical thought for Ian Nelson—but only if they let themselves do it. If they gave themselves choices, then all it took was the courage to choose. Had anyone asked him—last month, last year—Ian would have been quick to assure them he loved his life, never doubting it was so. Looking back at Blaine from Gallup, from Tehachapi, and from this place at the end of the open road, he saw something drearier. And that was looking back at life in Blaine before Polly packed a bag, adding disruption and disorder to the equation.

Good for her, though. She gave herself a choice and chose.

He was well down the slope when it started raining and a sharp wind that felt like cold tin hitting his face hardened the chill. By the time he clawed his way back to the road, he was soaked and shivering. In the bathroom mirror he glimpsed an unfamiliar old man with graying disarrayed hair and thought of Lear in the storm, betrayed by daughters, just as he had thought of Lear at that sing where the good daughter vied with the bad for control. Then, standing under a steamy shower for as long as the hot water lasted, he thought of his own daughter and all at once he knew where he was going *next*. He would check out in the morning and head for Colorado.

When he got set to make some calls that night, touch some bases, he elected not to call Carrie. Not alert her. What if she told him not to come!

Instead he started with Ann Darlington, the responsible thing to do. How long had he been gone? How long had he told Ann he *would* be gone? If he had booked a return flight, Ian had lost both the ticket and any memory of arranging it. Apparently, he had planned the going, not the coming back, even though he had left Fred on her hands.

But Ann was completely sanguine. "Fred can tell it's you," she said cheerily. "She's going crazy here."

"Not in general, I hope."

"In general, she has been just the loveliest companion. I should probably tell you I've decided to keep her. I've even had Harry coming to visit because of her!"

Harry, Ann's son, was a few years out of college and unemployed, living with a friend in Boston. Adrift, he was loyal to his mother yet altogether absent from her days.

"Harry is a dog lover?"

"Oh yes. I lured him with pictures and now he has come up twice for dinner."

Hearing Ann's voice (and Fred's background vocals, the soft, familiar plaintive woofing), Ian felt an infusion of uplift about home, a brief sweep of emotion and recollection to counter his earlier, bleaker sense of Blaine. By now the blackflies would have tapered off, peach and apple blossoms would be afloat on ten thousand trees, and as the Copper River snaked its way through Hoyt Village its banks would soon be teeming with mountain laurel. After the thrashing of spring floods and before the low water doldrums of late summer, the river reached a sort of perfection. These minor keys—of nature, of beauty—might be enough to restore his equilibrium.

He thanked Ann, thanked the stars for her generous nature, and again went along with her joke about custody of Fred. ("I'll barricade the door," she said, "if you try to take her back.")

Once more he spread out the map, cased the states he would be crossing—Nevada, Utah—on his route to Colorado. Then he walked over to the lodge and took a whiskey to the fireside, where he joined a young man who resembled Dennis Hopper, the actor, but was far less excitable. The man smiled but did not speak, passing up the chance for a five-minute friendship. Ian wondered if this was Kate's foresty boyfriend until a young woman resembling Amy Adams appeared and swept him away.

Back in his room, he called Harvey. It was late back east, too late for most calls, yet well under the wire for Harv the night owl. He was the only person Ian knew who watched *The Daily Show* when it aired.

"All quiet on the eastern front," reported Harv.

"Any calls?"

"Sorry, man, not even a robocall. No one wants you."

"Well, everyone knows I'm away. And robos don't leave messages."

"There you go, then."

"Right. So, all's well with you? Beth? The band?"

"All of the above. In fact, the band had a good one on Saturday, a pretty Colonial on Longleaf. They had the old guy set up on a daybed out on the screen porch, so it was sort of an outdoor concert, very cool. So cool that neighbors began drifting over, like pilgrims. It was a scene from a feel-good movie on the Hallmark channel."

"You're making me miss it. I didn't, until you painted your pretty picture. You're making me want to sing."

"So, sing. Sing in the shower, it's good for you."

"You know what I mean."

"There is one morsel of sad news to report, Ian. I'm afraid your true love has crossed over."

"Come again?"

"You know, the pretty woman who captured your heart? Couple of gigs we did on Brierly?"

Ian made a sound, a noise he had never made before, did not recognize. He drew in air deliberately, as though a bus had bowled him over and he was laboring to stand, regain his breath.

"I'm really sorry, man," said Harvey, sensing the hit, filling the dead air. "Karin did one of her—what does she call them?—*bed checks*. And the poor lass was gone. For Rent sign stuck on the front lawn."

"Wait. That's it?"

"What do you mean?"

"She wasn't there. The woman."

"Right. She wasn't there."

"As in she *just* wasn't there. She was somewhere else."

"Well, yeah, *but . . .*"

"Got it," said Ian, considerably restored. Karin had made an assumption, as had Harvey, but as the cops on TV say, they didn't have a body. They didn't and he didn't. He already knew Anita was "somewhere else," this was not news at all, much less sad news or a death notice in the *Blaine Plain Dealer.* The bus that hit him drove away and he found his injuries were minor.

"And how is our Karin?" he said as jauntily as he could, eager to pretend he had not been run over at all. "It feels like I've been away for months."

Ian was relieved, reinvigorated, if at the same time chastened. *Your true love. The woman who captured your heart.* Harvey kidding around, as always, though Ian expected it was the party line through the group. They had been making fun of him from the start, early winter, and from the start he had dismissed it as offhandedly as he could. Sure he found her attractive—who wouldn't?—and yes there were moments when their connection had come to feel a bit special. That was a far cry from love. He held that truth to be self-evident—until Harvey drove the bus over him. If that blow hit him in the heart, it can only have pointed to a matter of the heart.

He had ruled it out preemptively, the notion that he could love someone so young and so little knowable. Love someone so superficially. Now he recalled how his gaze would lock onto her face, how once the fleeting image of her bare backside had burned him bright red, how he looked forward to seeing her and how slowly the days went when he was not seeing her. To call that love was as unrealistic as "loving" a film beauty. It was as hopeless as his high school crush on Nan Holley. He barely confessed those feelings to himself, would never have confessed them to Nan.

You ruled it out, but then what? Pretend, if you can, and try to ignore it. Define it away as a passing infatuation. Fantasize about it, if that helped. Polly would know the clinical names of all the coping mechanisms. The main thing you did was survive it. After all, didn't the mass of men lead lives of quiet desperation?

You could wait it out. At his fortieth high school reunion, the only one he attended, Ian had introduced Polly to her. "*That's* the legendary Nan?" said Polly, having encountered not a sleek irresistible teenaged beauty but rather a blowsy, heavily made-up woman who everyone agreed must have "had work done." Ian could not deny he too felt a burden lift when he glimpsed the finished product.

Even if it came to that, quiet desperation figured to be a lot more manageable at sixty-six than at eighteen. He had not embarrassed himself with Anita and he would not. The odd thing was that he felt anything but desperate. The admission (not that he might love her, just that it was possible, regardless of age differences or star-crossings or hopeless outcomes) was as much a relief as had been the late reckoning with the mature Nan Holley. What he had really seen that day was not Nan's degraded good looks, it was what an extreme mismatch they would have made once he got past what lay on the surface. For they had talked.

He felt lighter, whether for good reasons or for no reason at all, he simply did. He had been traveling toward Anita Richardson, or the idea of her, and now he would be traveling in a different direction, and this was somehow, magically, okay. Anita was "somewhere else." Not dead in Blaine, not dead in Gallup or Big Sur. She was alive *somewhere else*, or so he felt freed to believe, and she could remain alive in his mind as he started traveling east to Colorado.

He put the phone on the charger, brought everything in from the car, dumped out the duffel, and took stock. It was not a straightforward job, categorizing laundry as clean versus dirty, everything was ambiguous; not easy digging out the toothbrush and the hairbrush. Chaos had been pursuing him on the sly. In the next day or two, in the next state or two, he would need to locate a laundromat.

Which should not be a problem. Had Barack Obama ever put in a good word for laundromats, Trump would have tried to ban them by now and the Deplorables who enjoyed kissing the hem of his garment would have shouted "Yessiree, them laundries are Socialistic." The United States were not united about very much these days, but so far washing your clothes was still acceptable to everyone. Nevada would have laundromats, Utah would have them.

Ian was buoyant about it, taken with the very idea of a coin laundry. He had not washed his clothes in a coin-op since graduate school and was tickled by the prospect of doing so in Nevada or Utah. Doping out the soap packet dispenser, drowning in a flood of quarters from the change machine, leafing through a tattered, year-old magazine? What better way to start life over? He might feel young again.

How, exactly, had he become convinced that Kerouac and Steinbeck were the primary sources for Anita's fascination with Big Sur? Poring back over both books, Ian could find no mention of the place. His urtexts had both proved somewhat disappointing—the Kerouac catchy but silly, the Steinbeck pleasant but pedestrian—and now it appeared that neither could have served as the inspiration for Anita to make Big Sur her destination. Still, it *was* her destination. Gary Higganbotham had been right about that.

But why, when Steinbeck's haphazard narrative proved irrelevant, was Ian making Salinas his first stop on the road to Boulder? Well, something had to be his first stop and Salinas was a scant hour out of the way. It was also the cradle of American agriculture, the long fertile valley where someone ("illegals" from Mexico?) grew and harvested a lot of the nation's food. In earlier books, a younger Steinbeck had rendered the valley with poignance and beauty. So it was an attraction without being an Attraction.

Salinas had a population of three thousand when Steinbeck was growing up, thirty thousand when he last visited. Now it had one hundred fifty thousand. Would he even recognize it? So much was already unrecognizable when he set off on his *Travels with Charley*: "The four-lane concrete highway slashed with speeding cars I remember as a narrow, twisting road where the wood teams moved, drawn by steady mules." He went back to Monterrey, to his roots, only to flee the place in distress. "They fish for tourists now, not pilchards," he wrote, sixty years ago. Fortunate he did not live to see them fish for tourists everywhere that had something to offer and many places that did not. Ian expected that he too would flee, but first he had to get there.

On getaway day, he sat down to finalize his route at breakfast, in consultation with Kate. That woman brought more to the table than scrambled eggs and fried potatoes, she brought enlightenment. Kate was one more example of why Ian was prepared to let waitresses run the country.

Vegas had been high on his shortlist, a place you "had to see," and here was his best chance to see it. The Reifsnyders went there every year for an entire week, and their enthusiasm for it never flagged. Then again, the Reifs liked to gamble and they liked gaudy shows. They also went frequently— with a charming absence of embarrassment, long after their children had grown—to Disneyland. In any event, the shortlist notwithstanding, Kate nixed Vegas.

"No way," she said. "Trust me, I've done the research for you. We were there one Christmas, believe it or not, my ex and my daughter. I admit, the verdict was not unanimous—Bart liked the showgirls, their tits and tushies—but Raney and I voted him down. In fact, we voted him out of office a month later, though that's neither here nor there."

"You hated it—because?"

"Of everything about it? But, okay, check this out. We are in a big glitzy department store, and we are like *shopping*, because, you know, it's Christmas. Up we go in a glass elevator, inside a glass tower, until we're looking down on this totally mad scene, thousands of mice scurrying around—"

"Mice?"

"People, looking very small. Scurrying. But with armloads of shit, cartloads of shit. And Raney takes one look and, sensible lass that she is, says 'You can do what you want, Mom, but I am out of here,' and right back down in that snow globe we go. That was our Vegas."

"So Tonopah. I do need to see Tonopah, don't I?"

"Got the reference. Tehachapi to Tonopah. Love the song. The place, not so much."

"You've been there?"

"I have."

Enough said, apparently. Ian had also shortlisted the Grand Canyon. Photos of it are invariably stupendous and invariably people say the reality is far beyond what can be captured in a photograph. Another once-in-a-lifetime shot at seeing it, until Kate crossed it off. Literally leaned over the table, took the pencil from behind her ear, and crossed it off the written page.

"School's out, my friend. You can look it up: *two million visitors are expected this month*. You want to make it two million and one?"

"But wait, I saw in yesterday's paper that someone plunged to her death taking a selfie at the rim. Won't that cut down on the crowds for a while?"

"You made that up, right? Anyway, if it did happen, it would more likely bring 'em on the run. *Millions rush to take selfies at the Selfie Death Site. Services can't keep pace, toilets overflowing!*"

"You are quite the cynic, young lady."

"I believe realist may be the word you are searching for."

Ian did not dare introduce the Great Salt Lake. It was all he had left on the shortlist, could not afford to have her shoot it down. Of course, there would be plenty to see along the way, rivers to cross, main streets and mountain passes, dozens of small *a* attractions. Still, he clung in silence to the Great Salt Lake, hoping Kate had not noticed it on the list.

He thanked her for five days of friendship and food, asked if she would be offended by a hundred-dollar tip. "By what reasoning would I?" she said. He gave her the tip, assured her she had his vote in the next presidential election, and half an hour later was driving north on the coast road, bound for Salinas.

The one-hour ride took nearly three hours, reminding Ian of Ward Longstreet's formula for reckoning the cost of repairs at Hal's Automotive: take Hal's figure, double it, then add the vigorish. That way you could be pleased if it came in a scrape lower. The same rule applied to the coast highway in June, when road work was general and traffic coagulated: Flagman Ahead, Prepare to Stop, mile after mile.

Then, the Salinas he eventually reached bore little resemblance to the one had Steinbeck described in 1939, or 1952, or even 1960. His books were still read in high school, could still form bucolic technicolor pictures, but those were bygone times—except at The Steinbeck Center, a museum after all, where living in the past was the whole point. Ian planned to duck inside, take a quick peek, buy a few more postcards. Somehow, before he could do any of that, he found himself drawn into a discussion of literature with Charles.

Charles, a docent, might well engage in the same conversation with every patron, or at least with everyone who had read enough to know what he was talking about. He pounced on Ian in a hallway plastered with plaques and oblations testifying to John Steinbeck's genius. "Which one is your favorite?" said Charles, having sidled up silently. "I'm always curious."

Sensing he was being tested, Ian hedged: "I'd hate to commit."

"I know *exactly* what you mean!" said Charles. "It would be like choosing a favorite child, wouldn't it?"

"I read them so long ago," said Ian.

"But you are a fan. I can tell that much."

"I have watched some of the movies more recently," said Ian. "*East of Eden*? Made me want to go back and read the book."

"And did you?"

"Oh, and *Viva Zapata*. Am I right that he had something to do with that film?"

"Indeed, you are. Indeed, he did. He had everything to do with it."

Ian had a sudden impulse to confess. He had never read *East of Eden*, he was pretty sure Marlon Brando was the best thing about *Viva Zapata*, and having recently experienced disappointment with *Travels* he could not say he was a fan. That yes, he was here at the museum, but he had no good explanation for his presence. He heard a bell ringing from somewhere close by, a church bell or a town clock, and wanted to be out on the streets.

"Here's the gist of it. Faulkner was so difficult, so downright confusing to read, they had no choice but to call him great. Am I right? Hemingway was at the other end, so damn simple-headed they had to call him great too. Whereas John simply *was* great. You read him with pleasure and at the same time you learn so much about real people. About *life*."

"What about Fitzgerald?" said Ian, inexplicably taking the bait. Professor Loeffler, in the survey course Ian had taken sophomore year, asserted unreservedly that *The Great Gatsby* was the perfect novel. Beyond that claim, Ian did not remember a thing about it.

"Ah, it seems we have an English major with us today," exclaimed Charles.

"Soc Psy, actually."

"Sock Sigh? I don't know what that is—an Indian word? Native-American, I should say. As for Fitzgerald, yes, he wrote a good one, but just the one. Think of it. And Wolfe—I hope you weren't about to propose Wolfe?—was a blowhard-in-print. Words words words. If words were dollar bills, he would have been the first Godzillionaire. And then, you no doubt know the Max Perkins aspect. Whereas John was his own man, all the way."

"You seem very partial to Mr. Steinbeck," observed Ian.

"I suppose I am. After all, the sign outside doesn't say Fitzgerald Center, does it? But look here. John penned four great big novels and four great smaller ones, plus a whole lot more. And just for the heck of it, he also wrote the greatest travelogue in American literary history."

"I'm sure he did."

"*Travels with Charley*. Charley was his dog. You can look it up. For that matter, you can purchase it in the museum shop."

"Actually, I have a copy. With me. In the car."

"There you go. So you are traveling with *Travels*, we do see that here."

All of John's volumes were "available for purchase" in the museum shop and, looking over them, Ian did wonder which were the four great bigs and which the four great smalls. He had just picked up a nicely designed new edition of *Travels* when he was ambushed by a second expert: "Don't bother with that one," said the man with a wink, and a wide smile which emerged from walrus-droop mustaches.

"I was just told it was the greatest travelogue in—"

"Yes, I overheard him. Steinbeck can be good, but that particular book is a fraud. He made up half of it and disguised the rest."

"He didn't have his dog with him?"

"The dog was real. But all that 'Roughing It' stuff? He had his wife with him much of the time and they stayed in fancy hotels. Book's a fraud."

"Wow. The Cheerleaders? That whole scene was made up?"

"A good question. Because that really happened, and he describes it well, which was a valuable thing at the time. Very few people north of the Mason-Dixon could imagine the extent of the bigotry down south—how vile, and how violent. What is not clear is whether he saw it firsthand. After all, the book is a fraud."

Thanking the professor for the heads-up, Ian purchased two leather Steinbeck bookmarks and half a dozen postcards of old Salinas before hurrying back outside into the warm June air. The feeling he got from escaping the experts reminded him of the rush he would feel after the sour-smelling three-hour lab for Chem 88, his science requirement, when fifteen students would burst through the door, relieved to find the natural world still existed in all its glory.

He had planned a second stop, at Steinbeck's childhood home, a handsome old Queen Anne structure redolent of turn-of-the-century Salinas. Well and good, but what if there was another dogmatic docent inside? Moreover, he read in a brochure from the museum that the waitresses would be decked out in period garb, parading in mobcaps and calico, possibly disqualifying them from cabinet positions in Kate's White House. The breeze was too sweet, freedom too precious. He strolled past the childhood home for a quick look, picked up a newspaper and a coffee, and spent the hour sitting in a small sunny park, reading and sipping. And breathing.

Back in the Geo an hour later, leaving town, he soon saw heartening evidence of the other Salinas, a vast fertile expanse that was still there, fields
planted as far as the mountains. He shot right past a roadside taco truck
with *Hablo Ingles* painted on the flank and regretted not having stopped; it
had to be good. Barely a quarter-mile down the highway, he thought *I am
hungry, I am not in a hurry, what the hell*, and turned around. He laughed
out loud when he saw that *We Speak Mexican* was painted on the truck's
opposite flank.

"Mexican is a language?" said Ian, after ordering two chicken tacos.

"It's, like, a political statement, dude. Get it?"

"Got it," said Ian, doing a two-thumbs-up while thinking how a political
statement that was cool-to-go in California might get the fellow burned out
overnight in flyover country.

It was not that he mistrusted Kate's judgment (presidential timber, after all),
it was just a matter of right time/right place—and a handy laundromat—
that found Ian in Tonopah at the end of his day.

For the next twelve hours, the Mizpah Hotel would be his home base. The
old hotel provided most of the town's local color in the lobby, where in the
first ten minutes Ian saw old photos of its silver mining history, had the Old
West feel validated by a Wyatt Earp anecdote from the desk clerk, and then
the Hollywood connection established via a Howard Hughes anecdote from
the braided and bearded barista. The Mizpah also had what Harv would
call a *mitzvah*—air-conditioned rooms—because the wide flat streets were
baking and the high desert air was as hot as the inside of the dryer.

The handy laundromat failed to live up to his malfunction fantasy. There
were no gossiping ladies folding sheets, there was no oddball pacing and
muttering to himself. There was only Ian and his clothes, spinning wet then
spinning dry. The change machine coughed up correct change, the soap
dispenser dispensed soap, the washers did not stop in the middle of a soggy
wash, the dryers dried efficiently. Everything worked. Sometime in the
intervening decades between grad school and old age, they had ironed out
the kinks.

Now looking out through the plate glass window at a vacant street (not a soul in sight and no cars except his renter and a decrepit red pickup that looked like it had been immobile for years), Ian felt the strangeness of the place. Or the strangeness of his being in this place. True, it was on the way to where he was going, yet he had a distinct sense of being stranded here. The blank prospect echoed a blankness within himself, a momentary loss of focus. The barren landscape was mesmeric, the spinning machines hypnotic.

He worked at getting back to basics, the journey and the arrival, and the question: was he journeying toward something (Anita previously, Carrie now) or away from a reckoning with the future? Between the return ticket he had not booked and his thorough indifference to destinations, it was as though he had abandoned his old life, abdicated his old self. But in favor of what? Toward what end?

At times he was running down the road, hustling, at other times he was deliberately slowing the pace, delaying. This tug was with him constantly. Whenever he stopped—to stretch, to pee, to eat, to admire a roadside scene—he felt an immediate pressure to resume, get going. When he did resume, rushing away, he remembered he had no cause for hurry. No one was waiting for him. No one cared that he was washing his clothes in Tonopah, or that he was beginning to need a haircut. He was completely on his own.

Getting organized to leave in the morning, Ian calculated he was roughly equidistant from Salt Lake, looking ahead, and from Kingman, looking back. It seemed that whenever he hauled out the map, Kingman jumped out at him. There it was. The hours he had spent there with Keely were so fleeting and unreal, the whole episode such a dramatic intrusion into his undramatic life, he still had not processed it. Though events often came into focus for Ian after the fact, this one remained a blur.

He wanted to understand Keely's part in it; he also wanted to understand his own. If he headed south to Kingman now, he might get some answers. Would he feel something for Keely, be attracted to her? Would she even recognize him if he walked into that restaurant? Her love life was somewhere between zero and Halley's Comet, she had laughed dismissively. At the time, Ian took it to mean their assignation was a rarity, perhaps not special—how could it be?—yet not ordinary either. By now he could see a lot of territory between zero and Halley's Comet, could see a thousand nights where single men sat down at her tables.

It was tempting. Rerouting to Kingman would have a purpose, where his other choices were arbitrary, if not absurd—Price and Rifle, chosen for no other reason than their names. No one mentioned Price, Utah, or Rifle, Colorado, on a brochure, they were just there. "Because it was there" may have been the reason Sir Edmund Hillary famously gave for climbing Mount Everest, but Rifle was hardly Mount Everest.

In the end, the Geo—by moving fifty miles in the direction it was pointed— made the decision for him while he maundered. You could overthink something to the point where it disappeared. Ian would never know if Keely would be pleased to see him, or he her. He would not know how Anita would have received him either. He suspected that these unknowns might tug at him for the rest of his days. Only then did he remember Polly and take note that he *would* come to know where he stood with her. He had given more consideration to these nothingburger towns on a road map than to his wife of four decades, the wife who might by now be glad to see him or glad never to see him again. Alarmingly, Polly was an afterthought.

Had she quit him for good? Would Anita have been pleased to see him? Was he one-in-a-hundred to Keely when she was a miracle to him? In a way, these questions were all the same overriding question: *did he matter to anyone.* He wanted to count somewhere, to be connected to someone or something. Racing across this relentlessly indifferent western landscape, he felt disconnected from everything, treading air in a Limbo province.

They had never visited Carrie after she crossed the Mississippi and became a westerner. California, Utah, Colorado—she always managed to elude or co-opt them. If they announced they were planning a trip, she would blurt out that she had *just bought* a ticket home. After she shut off her landline in L.A. and went to smartphones exclusively, they could never be sure where she was beaming in from, even where she lived.

They were on the verge of booking a flight to see her setup in L.A. when she announced the move to Utah, so that was not a good time. Then Utah became Denver, which in turn became Boulder. And it was always a studio—no room at the inn—even when she added Warren into the equation. She made light of it; they were squashed into four hundred square feet, half of which were taken up by Warren's two big feet.

Twice a year she came east, stayed a few days. More than a few of those occasions went south before Carrie went back west. It made Carrie nervous when things went smoothly, made her crazy when they didn't. Sooner or later, she and Polly would end up screaming at each other, after which she and Ian would go for hikes, for the most part in comradely silence. Any family issues or conflicts, any matters of the heart, were set aside as they admired the way Jenny's Creek spilled down the granite slope in Dexterville or noted the declining health of the sugar maples in Barlow Forest.

Now here he was descending on her, no better way to put it. He would be arriving unannounced, leaving no tunnels through which she could escape. That did not figure to please her, not after the many creative evasions had signaled her desire to shake free of them, stand apart. Polly had once remarked (after a bad shouting match that was, frighteningly, "about nothing") that at times it felt as though Carrie would be delighted never to see her parents again this side of Heaven. That was a bit dramatic, Ian had offered. But no less true, Polly responded.

Bottom line, Carrie was not exactly the ideal partner in Ian's quest for connection, someone to whom he would *matter*. More than likely he would cause her distress. But he was her father, he reminded himself as he forged bravely on. Boulder or Bust.

First came Salt Lake. He would spend one night, re-up as a tourist in the morning. See the Great Salt Lake and the Golden Spike, then make a hard push to Boulder.

He had imagined Salt Lake City as a peaceable kingdom, had pictured a few subdued Mormons walking the streets in wide-brimmed hats. The only Mormons he actually knew, a couple of pleasant fellows who were in his dorm freshman year, were subdued in the morning because they were not allowed coffee or tea, subdued at night because they were not allowed to imbibe spirits. And they were older, more serious, having spent two years proselytizing Ugandans. They wore suits. In college!

Now here he was in bumper-to-bumper traffic, and some of the drivers—pointlessly blaring their horns, leaning out the window to yell at anyone who did not immediately advance the available five yards—did not seem the least bit subdued. After advancing half a mile in half an hour, Ian bailed out, pulling off at a random GASFOODLODGING exit and checking into a motel whose marquee read *Sleep Cheap at $69.*

Given the congestion, Ian believed the proud claim made by Lester at the motel desk that "SLC" was the fastest growing city in the nation. Lest Ian get the wrong idea and fail to relocate here, Lester went on to explain that the dense traffic had to do with a basketball game tipping off in an hour: "We're growing, but we surely are not Chicago."

Ian slept cheap, rose early, and walked to the Copper Kettle for scrambled eggs and sausages. In keeping with his habit of trust and respect, he asked the waitress for a few pointers, what to see, how to go about it. "I assume the Great Salt Lake really is great?"

"We say it is," she offered ambiguously. Not so great? She was older, his age, which made her furry, doughnut-sized earrings surprising.

"But it definitely is salty?" said Ian, extending his goofy joke.

"That it is. What they don't tell you is that the flies will swarm you something awful. Or that it stinks. Rotten eggs? Whatever you do, don't *stand* in it. People like to do that, wade out a ways? That'll stir up an *awful* stink."

He had prevented Kate from crossing "SLC" off the shortlist, yet here was the next candidate for high office doing the honors for her. "Is it really that bad?"

"Well, you do get terrific views from there. The mountains. And they have," she said, with a boatload of irony in her puckish smile, "a wonderful souvenir shop."

Ian was prepared to confirm his endorsement, Kate for President, and nominate this old gal for Secretary of Laconic Wit. The Great Salt Lake smelled like rotten eggs and it seemed the Golden Spike was not here, it was an hour away—two hours if there was a basketball game in the offing!

His whole list had gone a-glimmering. The only places circled on the map now were Price, which made no claims for itself (You get what you pay for in Price?) and Rifle, where their main claim was proximity to Boulder. Plus, of course, the name.

Rifle was not named by or for the N.R.A., it was named for Rifle Creek, from which flowed the nomenclature of the pretty Rifle Bridge, which oddly did not bridge the eponymous creek, spanning instead a narrow neck of the Colorado River. There was a mesmerizing tripartite waterfall at nearby Rifle Gap. Ian was absolutely on board for these features, this small-bore tourism, and soon after checking in at the Gateway (sleeping even cheaper at $59) he was standing on the pathway below the falls, watching and listening as thick ropes of white water kept twisting and thundering down.

Fearful that a waitress might cross Price off the list, he ate in the motel room, two hamburgers in a paper sack and a bottle of Coors, which used to be good. He took a hot shower, watched CNN while he dried and dressed, then set about organizing his approach to Boulder. *The Denver Post* told him this was a Tuesday, so Carrie ought to be at work during the day tomorrow, ought to be findable after work. Now was the time to call her, give her fair warning, the decent thing to do. You did not just land on someone out of the blue, not even your daughter. But then, Carrie was Carrie.

And wasn't Warren some sort of tradesman, early to bed and early to rise? Best not to chance disturbing his rest. It made more sense to get himself there and do a reconnaissance, scope out the address, call after he got his bearings. Call around noon tomorrow. That would give her some advance notice, if admittedly not a lot. He would sell it, a nice dinner at the restaurant of your choice. Bring Warren or not, your choice. No big deal, we will just "catch up on stuff."

Stuff was one of her favorite words. What was she doing, just some stuff; what was there to discuss, just some stuff. He clung to biology. This was Carrie, whose diapers he had changed, who he had walked to school a thousand times, bearing lunches he had often composed. This was the child he had loved her entire life.

While all this was true, there was no point being unrealistic. It occurred to him that she might not really live in Boulder, Colorado. Carrie had been a moving target for years, maybe only the smartphone hackers and trackers could really say where she was. She could be living in Coeur D'Alene or Cleveland. But then the detective in him raised up, that lamp still faintly glowing: *she got her mail.* The birthday cards, the checks, occasionally paperwork they were charged with forwarding to the Boulder address. She got all that *stuff* and acknowledged it in a timely fashion.

He needed to walk. He had taken up the habit of walking after dinner wherever he found himself. It was almost a revelation that he could do this, even though he did it every day back home. Exploring so many new places, he would sometimes feel a stirring toward his old haunts, his standby routes in Blaine. It could feel strange walking without Fred, not carrying on all the one-sided conversations he had with her. He suspected he may have conducted a few of those conversations anyway. Without Fred. Talking to himself.

He did miss Fred, especially when he was out walking, and wondered if Fred missed him. Maybe he had ceased to matter even to his dog.

The walking soothed him. The risen moon, huge and flame-colored at first, was now high and white and full. Standing on the Rifle Bridge a second time, he tried to empty his head of everything except the moonlight edging the iron frame and the water sliding below the span. A young couple came onto the bridge, greeted him pleasantly, and kept going. Ian was afraid they had intended to stop on the bridge only to have his presence wreck it, but soon the steady hushed cadence of the river helped empty his mind of that concern too.

The river keeps going, he thought, but it never is gone.

A piece of snail mail had come to the house that day. It was not a bill or a plea for money, or an ad. None of the above, Harvey insisted, it appeared to be that throwback thing called a letter. "And I am holding it in my hand as we speak. Shall I read it to you?"

"You opened it?"

"Certainly not. All I am saying is that I can open it if you so desire."

"Who is it from? Are you sure it's not one of those with the fake-real handwriting?"

"Handwriting appears to have been formed by a human hand. No return address."

It had to be from Polly. She would not put a return address, not after shrouding herself in witness-protection-level mystery. And it could not be good news, not in a letter. He told Harvey it could wait, he would be home soon enough. "In fact, you could let Karin know I'll be available next week. I did sing in the shower, as you suggested, but the urge remains. I'd really love to get back on track."

"The lady in question will be notified of your wishes. Good thing you'll be home soon, old chap, because your yard is getting out of control. June, you know. Grass is ankle high and gaining."

"Mow it?"

"Me? There could be a million ticks. There could be a dozen rats. Besides, people *sweat* when they cut grass."

"I was just kidding, Harv, about the grass. I am very grateful for all you've been doing."

"It's pretty easy watching a house when nothing goes wrong."

Ian agreed. Everything is pretty easy when nothing goes wrong.

Part Three

The Education of Ian Nelson

CONCERNED ALL ALONG that Carrie would be shocked to see him, Ian never expected to be shocked at seeing her. He was braced for some sort of blowback—Carrie aghast, Carrie ungracious—and he was braced for Warren to be revealed as a creature dwelling outside the bounds of polite society. He was not prepared for what he got.

He was slowrolling harmlessly through her neighborhood, enjoying the bright midsummer midmorning, when he came to the corner of 26th and Iris. He turned down Iris, squinting at house numbers, looking for 104b, a one-bedroom apartment carved out of a one-family house . . . then there it was. And there *she* was, his daughter. Not at work—though that was the least of it.

What he saw from within the invisibility of his renter car capsule took him a moment to grasp. There was Carrie chatting amiably with a tall young woman, both of them sporting the new uniform of formfitting black leggings . . . and then they kissed. Their hands came together and then their lips and the tall young woman patted Carrie on the bottom as they turned away laughing. They slid into two different cars, drove off in different directions.

Even now, Ian's first response was *What would poor Warren think of this.* Then it settled into place, declared itself unambiguously. The things a parent could not know! Or didn't. Could this alone account for their daughter's evasiveness, her distance? If so, it meant she took them, Ian and Polly, for Cro-Magnons. Did she so fear they would disapprove (or pretend to approve in order to be politically correct) that she would feed them years of lies?

They had a gay daughter. He was startled by this revelation but not the least bit distressed. Did he even care? He found his way to a Starbucks and sat with a cup of coffee and a croissant while his initial confusion sorted itself. Soon he found himself smiling, delighted. He *did* care and his caring fell on the joyful side. Carrie's companion looked lovely, their connection seemed quite sweet; it looked like a dose of true love on a green and golden morning. Instantly, it reduced the hypothetically egregious Warren to an apparition. Better still, it made it possible that Carrie's need for distance was grounded in fear of her parents' reaction rather than any deep estrangement from them, any absence of affection for them.

Or for him. Because it was possible that Ian alone was deemed the Cro-Magnon, that Polly knew all along, however far back "all along" stretched. Even that did not matter to him, not now, when he would soon be able to show his daughter he was . . . *evolved*? Was that the word for it? Whatever the word was, he qualified. Relieved to see Carrie at the very address they had for her, overjoyed to see her looking happy and healthy, untroubled by her *sexual preference*. If those were the words.

Though he did think of Alfie. That Alfie might well be the last grandchild they would ever have. When Alfie was born, when Livvy said "I won't be doing *that* again," they all assumed she did not mean it. That it was a sentiment uttered at a moment when every woman must feel that way to some extent. But it turned out she did mean it, and now Carrie was foreclosed.

Ward had six grandchildren, the Reifsnyders had five and talked of little else. Should Ian feel impoverished with only one in hand? Phoebe had somehow become eighteen years of age, was off to Stanford in the fall, no longer counted. Grandparent-wise, she had ceased to count around the age of thirteen. They had gone off her screen. So there was only Alfie.

Then, almost at once, the evolved Ian, the *woke* Ian, recalled that the times had been a-changing. Single women had babies. Same sex couples did too, in all sorts of ways. Carrie and the tall young lady might present them with a grandchild after all, who knew. Given Carrie's history of extreme secrecy, it was plausible she had been guarding a nest, that such a love child already existed. Within the walls of 104b Iris, he might find a beautiful toddler in the tender care of a young Swedish nanny!

Regardless, the prospect that had riddled him with anxiety for days became a penny dropped into a well of good fortune. Radically uplifted, Ian not only ceased to regret the chocolate croissant he had already eaten, he ordered another, and a second cup of joe to wash it down. Though the bright day beckoned, he felt no need to rush.

It was Carrie's turn to be dismayed and try to pretend otherwise. "I won't get out of work until very late, Dad," she dissembled. "Came in way late this morning."

"Whenever," he said, mellow to the max. "I'll find you when you're ready to be found. We can get a late dinner."

Seeing her exit ramps blocked, Carrie elected to level. Her voice went soft, softer than he had heard in years. "Dad, there is something I guess you are going to have to know about me."

"Yes, sweetie. I do know. And I look forward to knowing as much more as you wish to share."

"What do you mean? What do you know?"

"I know you have a lovely friend. A companion?"

"But how—Oh my God, don't tell me you've been spying on me. That you guys hired a *detective* or something."

"No no, sweetie, I did not hire anyone and any detecting was purely accidental. You know how bad I am at directions—and without your mother? So I tried finding the street earlier. But this was long after I imagined you would be there, long after you would have left for work."

"You could have called. A week ago. Or *yesterday*, at the least."

"I know. But I have been—I don't know, spontaneous?—on this little trip."

"You, spontaneous? Hey, I've got some oceanfront property for sale in Arizona."

And just that abruptly, Carrie's tone had shifted from aggrieved to cheerful, as if a thousand-pound gorilla had dismounted from her back and lumbered away, leaving her unharmed.

"I'll take it," said Ian, thrilled with the transaction. "You can name your figure."

Sold! Not the Arizona real estate or the cobbled-together excuses, his and hers. The connection: they had both bought it. Even with a sketchy suggestion of the truth out in the open, they were already in the clear. Ian could look forward to an interesting evening, not a scary one.

"I can't believe this," said Carrie.

"And I can't believe you just ordered something called fried pickles."

"You'd like them, Dad. And by the way, dinner is on me. I chose this place and it's way too expensive for you."

"Is that a dig? Sounds like a dig."

"More like I am honoring your lifelong commitment to frugality."

"I'm the parent, Car, and the parent always pays. Even if he is mistakenly regarded as a cheapskate."

"Except that the children caretake the parents in their golden years."

"We can discuss that when that time approaches."

Ian could not believe the fried pickles, that much was true, though it was just a metaphor for what he truly could not believe, this sweet and easy rapport he and Carrie had not enjoyed since she was fourteen years old. They were having fun, simple as that, going back and forth about nothing. Oak, the "fancy-schmancy" restaurant she had chosen, was indeed expensive and Ian could not have cared less. He would have paid a thousand dollars for this dinner, it was a pearl without price.

"What I can't believe," said Carrie, "apart from the fact that here you are and all, that you dropped out of the clouds, is that suddenly it's old home week all around. You're here and Mom says she may be coming next week. And neither of you has ever been here before."

"We weren't invited," Ian managed to say, as he struggled to absorb this news flash about Polly and remain deadpan.

"You weren't *invited* now either," Carrie pointed out. Teasing, though. Not sorry he had come uninvited.

"I had no idea your mother was planning to come—in case you think I'm trying to one-up her or something. Honestly, her whereabouts are a bit of a mystery to me."

"She definitely wasn't definite about it. It was, like, she might drop in? As though *dropping in* was a thing she did every now and then?"

They ordered a second round; a quirky local microbrew (something with "strong notes" of something) for Ian and a quirky local cocktail with about fourteen ingredients for Carrie.

"Said she might bring a friend. Roseanne? You must know her?"

"I do not," said Ian, still going for deadpan as the revelations kept coming. "Probably a colleague. Your mother doesn't share a lot of that side of things."

"She's not all that much of a sharer, is she? Generally."

"Look who's talking!" Ian burst out, as by now the microbrews were asserting themselves, promoting laxity. But Carrie was not into taking offense tonight, she was into dinner-with-Dad of all things. As with so many turns of the screw on this journey, Ian experienced it as a sort of waking dream: was this really *happening*? "So tell me, what do make of this business, your mother and Roxanne?"

"Roseanne, I thought. Dunno. But hey, is something going on I should know about? Between you and Mom?"

Was it possible Polly had spilled the beans to her son and left her daughter in the dark? It sounded that way, unless Carrie was feigning ignorance, probing for what *he* knew. Who was testing whom? And who knew what?

"Maybe so," he said. "But you are assuming that the something-going-on is something *I* know about. Which it isn't."

"Seriously, are you guys all right? I mean, you don't seem to be, like, exactly communicating."

Carrie had pressed a rhetorical finger directly on the inflamed nerve. Communicating was exactly what they were not doing and had not, it seemed, been doing for quite some time.

"Dad?"

"I'm thinking."

"Tell me the truth. Am I about to become a child from a broken home? Is this why you guys are suddenly descending on Boulder, to deliver this news?"

"Not I. I had other reasons, spurious reasons, for being in the west. And being in the west, I was struck by the absolute rightness of visiting. You."

"In my natural habitat."

"Yes. Over fried pickles and these highly original western beverages. And maybe later, as I say, I will have a chance to meet—"

"Baz. Barbara Ann Zimmer, age thirty-six, professor of modern European history at C. U. Boulder—"

"See you bolder?" said Ian, recalling the Steinbeck salesman and his Sock Sigh.

"Right, the Boulder campus of Colorado U. She hails, originally, from upstate New York, where her parents are both also teachers, though she has been the child of a broken home since the age of nine. She runs—many miles a day, and she *fishes*. The girl knows her fishes. Oh, and I might add, she is really nice and totally beautiful."

"I hope all this data isn't offered in place of my getting to meet her."

"No, just a little scouting report for you. Plus, I do tend to brag about her."

"She sounds pretty darn good. A damn sight better than Warren ever sounded."

"Let's leave Warren aside for now. And if you're really going to insist on paying, you should know I want dessert. Specifically, I want the chocolate bread pudding. It's big enough we can split."

"No, you eat it all, Car. You look thin to me."

"Not thin, lean. I'm the exact same hundred-eighteen pounds I have weighed since college."

"Eat the pudding and then we'll weigh you, see if you can't hit one-twenty."

Ian would not meet Barbara Ann Zimmer until noon the next day, when Carrie dispatched the two of them, Baz and Ian, to Illegal Pete's for lunch. "If I came with you, Baz and I would do our magpie act and you wouldn't get to know her. Better this way."

Observing her briefly from the car the day before, Ian had mainly noticed her height. Carrie was fairly tall and Baz had seemed taller. But a lot of that must have been in the boots, because today, in low black sneakers, Baz was far more noticeable for her eyes, almond-shaped and tear-dropped at the corners, greenish-gray behind light brown lashes. And expressive. She really was what his mother would have called a "looker." And with those eyes bright and smiling she declared herself "ready for the interview."

"Better to call it a conversation, I think."

"No interrogation? No intervention?"

"None of the above, Barbara. Should it be Barbara?"

"I answer better to Baz. When I hear Barbara, I assume they must be talking to someone else."

"Baz, I am very happy to meet you. Especially as it seems I just met my daughter last night. Or the updated version of her."

"Did you like her?" said Baz, the green eyes glittering with light comic challenge.

"I absolutely loved her."

"So, that makes two of us."

"I guess that answers the only question I might have had if I had any. Which I don't."

"Sure you do. How long have we been together. Are we thinking of marriage, or of children. Are we planning to stay in Boulder, maybe buy a house. Do I have any burdens from the shadowy past, a rogue early husband, a stray abandoned child—"

"Baz, can I say that I wouldn't care if you did? Have a few shadows?"

"Together twenty-nine months, may or may not choose to marry, no-thank-you to children (cross-footnote Philip Larkin, for the literate), house for sure but not in Boulder, unless we win the Lucky for Life, which is unlikely since we never get around to buying a ticket."

"Actually, I do have one question. Sorry, it just now came to me. What does Carrie think about her mother's recent . . . peregrinations."

"Wow, like, *Use this word in a sentence.* Afraid I don't have the inside scoop on anyone's peregrinations. I did hear that her mom—your wife!—may be coming to visit, and I know Car's reaction to that was, like, *Huh?* And to worry, I suppose, since we are this deep-dark secret."

"You *were*."

"Not to any of our fifty best friends, some male some female some straight some bent."

"Not to your mom and dad? Just Carrie's?"

"My mom knows. She's mainly upset by the no-grandbabies part. My father could care less, about me or anything else. He is outside the frame."

"I'm sorry."

"You wouldn't be if you knew him."

Baz looked brittle as she said this, behind the bravado. An old bruise flaring, one she was in the habit of pretending to disregard. Ian did not doubt the man had failed her, he only doubted that his failure had left Baz unfazed. They were wandering into Polly's territory, though. He would leave the psychological component to her.

Walking back toward her campus, they could see from the center of this modern and substantial city, a string of mountain ridges rising and falling like a graph.

"Hey," said Baz. "Now we're outed, maybe we can come east together sometime. I won't tell you how thoroughly I've been educated about the wonders of New England in October."

"It's a different landscape from what you have here," said Ian, gesturing. "Though not so different from upstate New York."

"We could still visit."

"I hope you will. If permitted, I would insist on it."

He was not sure, when they parted company, who initiated the familial hug.

At liberty for a few hours, Ian felt something like joy, as though the warm mountain breeze was flowing right through him. Polly liked to say that happiness was a silly word, a fool's calculus for the human condition. Ian, to whom psychology was a less precise science, felt precisely happy.

He had felt this way (or was moving toward feeling this way, he now reckoned) ever since his dalliance with Keely. He searched for the word, found and approved it: *dalliance.* The very fact he was capable of a dalliance gave him the initial jolt. Next month, Ian would turn sixty-seven. The 3rd of

July was his birthday, one day shy of Independence Day. Did that mean he was destined to come up short every year, denied independence annually, or did it mean he was closing in, about to gain it? This morning he felt he was closing in, released, even if he could not say from what. From everything, maybe. From himself, possibly; released from all the training and traits that had held him back. While it seemed unlikely that the dalliance alone could have brought about such a sea change, it did ratify the notion that *anything can happen if you let it*. He had, for a change, let it.

He had pressed Ann Darlington's Refresh button, taken her suggestion to heart, filled her prescription. Before Keely there'd been Sam the Gram in Gallup, and after Keely came Kate in Big Sur, and along the way there were a dozen others, casual connections that both derived from and contributed to this freeing-up. Strangers all, though. It was possible he could be free only with people who did not matter, in situations that were not part of his actual life fabric, like Polly's client inside his gorilla suit.

Except that here was Carrie. Carrie was as essential to the weave of his life fabric as anyone, which meant the change, peaking here in Boulder, was real. It might prove temporary. Back east, in Blaine, he might revert and become an Ian Nelson he liked far less than this road-tested fellow who had words for everyone he encountered, a blooming vocabulary of words and notions and *humor.* He had taken to joking with everyone, up to and including his daughter. The other Ian Nelson only joked with Jack and Harv, and with those guys, jokes were wild.

He went so far as to coin a phrase for the change—he had undergone a *personality transplant* and the operation was a complete success! No doubt his team of doctors would advise him to take things slow, keep an eye out for side effects, warn that the benefits were sometimes short term. They would insist he take his rehab seriously, keep hitting the gym, even if the gym in this case was only his own conscious mind.

The newly liberated Ian ducked into an inviting bookshop (more books than shelves!) where the clerk, with nothing else to do, engaged him in a practiced riff, bookshops as a haven from the nation's raging chaos, from the relentless horror that was Trump. How was it, said the goateed, granny-glassed savant, that everyone knew what a monster Trump was and yet no one stepped in to arrest him? "Well," said Ian, "he is living in the White House. That could be a deterrent."

The savant suggested, reasonably enough, that he could be carried out of the White House and transported to the Big House.

The new Ian bought a book—a Steinbeck novel, fat enough to be one of the four great ones—and took it to a park named for an Irishman, curiously, as all the other parks were named for creeks and bears and boulders. He settled himself on a bench under the broad canopy of a big blue spruce and started reading. The sun on the back of his neck felt wonderful. Now and then he looked up from the labor squabbles of the Depression years and watched the parade of walkers, runners, and bike riders. A man jogged past with a child strapped to his chest, a black squirrel hammered away at a nut on the pathway. Ian recalled the old Chuck Berry song "No Particular Place to Go."

There had been an agenda. Anita. It began there. But in the end, the impossibility of finding her liberated him from the quest. He had entertained the notion of looking up Ella Morehouse, but that notion evaporated the day it became possible, with Oakland just a stone's throw away. Carrie had loomed as a problem to solve and he had solved it, though in truth it had gone and solved itself. Hanging out in this hushed and leafy park with the Irish name he had slipped the shackles of their complicated past. They were good, father and daughter.

Polly had a homily that was a close cousin to Ann Darlington's Refresh button: people needed to make "fresh deposits in the bank of life." Was Keely his fresh deposit? What if someone else had brought his pork chop to the table that night? For that matter, what if he had managed to eat the damned thing? Or if Keely had not been the free spirit that invited him to her home? What if—naïve Ian had never until now considered the possibility—she only brought him home so a violent boyfriend could emerge from the closet, club him, and take his wallet?

Had he been consigned instead to a few pages of Steinbeck and a spate of political drivel on CNN that night, would this personality transplant have come about?

He decided it would have, or better, that it already had—before Keely, before Sam the Gram. That it began when he chased down Sally Shumway and Gary Higganbotham. Or earlier still, when he had gone out of bounds with Anita. He had broken the rules, right from the start. Had ignored Karin's discipline, absorbed the inevitable jesting from Wade and Harv and Philip, deflected Polly's ironic jibes. Keely had merely shaken him up, it was Anita who had shaken him loose.

Now he was at liberty, and strangely at peace.

Carrie could talk across a table, she had that skill, but she still talked most freely when moving. Which was why the morning's across-the-table talk began with Ian's asking if there was a good place nearby where they might hike. "Seriously?" she said. "Dad, there are only about a hundred places that would qualify."

Throughout the Copper River region, town by town, one found mountains to climb and rivers to travel by kayak or canoe. But the mountains were just two thousand feet high and many of the rivers were more like brooks, no wider than a driveway. Charming as they were, those natural bounties did not approach the scale of the western mountainscapes. Ian cautioned his daughter that he was not in shape to take on Kilimanjaro.

"Then we'll take on Mt. Sanitas. If we take the Loop, we can avoid the mamas with strollers and the fancy dogs walking their fancy owners."

"Hey, kid, you are talking to a dogwalker."

"Trust me, Dad, dogs like Fred need not apply here. Fred is a different breed of dog and you are a different breed of walker."

The Loop was a gentle trail and the conversation stayed tuned to what they encountered along the way. Occasionally, where it was steeper and rockier, the talking gave way to audible breathing, which Ian was able to identify as his own. Lately he had been walking over flat ground in the cool evenings. This was different on both counts, and he found himself lathered. Carrie, who was not the least bit warm or taxed, thoughtfully pretended she was and suggested they rest for a minute. From the bench she chose, they had a straight shot through a notch to a distant peak that wore the forest like a monk's tonsure, a thick fringe circumscribing its barren top.

"You know, when Mom said she might come here? I wasn't convinced she would actually come. It was more like she was telling me something. Did I say this already? That maybe something was wrong at home."

"Telling you without telling you."

"Well, yeah, sure. *Mom*."

"She calls and may not show up. Whereas I fail to call but do show up. Which is worse?"

"It's a tie. Because neither of you are telling me."

"I thought I did tell you. That we seem to be in trouble . . ."

"Is it about the girlfriend?"

"Roxanne?"

"No, Dad, your girlfriend. The one Mom said turned you into an adolescent head case."

"Let's stop right there. Have I ever lied to you, Car?"

"I can only assume so."

"No. The correct answer is no, I never have. So listen up: there is no girlfriend, there has been no infidelity—not on my side anyway. On my side, there has been confusion and uncertainty. About lots of things, most of all your mother's actions."

"She has taken actions? Such as what? What are you withholding?"

"I told you, didn't I? She has decamped. Why, and to where, and for how long—all that is a mystery to me."

"Are you saying she moved out of the house?"

"She said very little and took very little, so moved out may be too strong. On the other hand," he shrugged, "it may not."

"She did this and so you lit out for the West. Like Davy Crockett."

"You remember! *He lit out a-grinnin' to follow the sun . . . Davy, Davy Crockett—*"

"—King of the wild frontier. Yeah, I remember. I remember a lot of my childhood, Dad. You weren't, like, wasting your time."

"And here I thought you were nursing grievances."

"Actually," said Carrie, pausing to consider, "just one grievance, and even that one I let go years back. We're pretty good as far as grievances go."

"Hold on. What was this one big grievance? What did I do wrong?"

"It wasn't even that wrong."

"Fine, but what was it?"

"Guess."

"No idea."

"Didn't think so. See, to you it was open-and-shut and you shut it, like totally. I knew that."

"Tell it."

"The Glass Bottom Boat."

"I don't remember us ever going on a glass bottom boat."

"That's because we didn't go. You blew off the trip and then, clearly, forgot all about it."

"How could I forget something we didn't do?"

"You forget how much I wanted to do it and how much I hated you for saying no."

"It was probably a joint decision, me and Mom. A considered decision made by two wise and caring parents."

"It was a cheapout decision made by one superfrugal parent. It was all about money. Though you pretended otherwise. Insisted the trip was too long, everyone on the boat would be puking, yada yada. And I said I didn't care, I wanted to see the bottom of the sea."

Going to Florida was a rare extravagance for them in those days. They took that vacation knowing it would cause them to scramble financially for months. And people did throw up on those boats—hell, they passed out barf bags as you came up the gangplank. It would have been nuts to pay for the privilege.

"There was a long line. We got out of the line, everyone else in the line got on the boat. You bought us a bag of peanuts and we sat on 'a nice shady bench,' eating the peanuts. And here we are now, Dad, on another nice shady bench!"

"Minus the peanuts. Does your brother hate me too?"

"Carl was—still is—a softie. He never hated you."

"Just you, then. Okay, so we fix it. We'll go, you and I—we'll *bond*. Or if you like, Baz can come too and the three of us will bond. We'll do it this winter, the glass bottom boat trip."

"I love it, Dad. I do. But we don't have to go."

"I *want* to go."

"For me, though, it's not a thing anymore. I actually . . . I went. Warren and I did it."

"Wait. Warren? There really is a Warren?"

"Was a Warren. And he was sort of real—or so I did, for a time, believe."

"You and Warren went on the glass bottom boat."

"We did. And Dad, you were so right. It was ridiculously expensive, way too long, and we didn't throw up but we both spent the whole time trying not to. He looked green, I felt green. And whenever I dared to open my eyes and look down—because the tour girl would shout 'Look, Look, window seven to starboard, there's our baby shark!' and 'Look, window four everybody! That's our whatchacallit fish!' And 'Oh, a barracuda!' But she was the only one who saw any of these creatures. So yeah. No."

It was useful that Carrie went on at length about this, because Ian was still processing Warren, trying to get his footing now that the Warren had become (sort of) real after all. Meaning? Carrie was one way then and now she was another? She was both? He understood the matter was increasingly blurred, knew there were new acronyms for this phenomenon—it had begun while he was still at the high school and needed to know the new wrinkles—but his understanding was limited. He could say LGBTQ, he just never did figure out what the Q was for.

"All right," he said, "we'll go somewhere else, somewhere super expensive, and I'll hand over my credit card without asking what anything costs."

"Dad, it's not like that. I get it, very little is worth what it costs. It turns out I'm cheap too."

"Weren't we going with 'frugal'?"

"Sensible. We gladly pay for the things that are worth paying for."

"Beer. Coffee. Music."

"Cat food. Weed."

"Of course," he said, smiling, as-if.

The Loop was a loop but they hiked back the way they had come, over the same terrain, which was somehow unfamiliar, as though he had not seen it two hours earlier. They were seeing it from a fresh angle, a different perspective. Ian thought of a quotation from somewhere, "everything looks different from two paces west." Last year they installed a new stop sign on the corner of Liberty and Henley and for months Ian did not notice it. Heading out, he and Fred would always walk past the dull gray back of the sign, the B-side so to speak, largely curtained by drooping pines. Then they would return by way of the Spring Road, so they never did face the bold red-and-white STOP on the front.

"It's all downhill from here," said Carrie, taking his silent ponder for fatigue.

"That's good—except when it's bad," he said, and went on to channel Sam the Gram. "All downhill can mean things get easier, but it can also mean the exact opposite, like saying it's all downhill once you reach a certain age."

"I guess you haven't reached it. You seem good, Dad. You seem very, I don't know, *sprightly*?"

"Do I? Do I seem different to you, Car? Almost like a different person?"

"Strange question. Do you feel different?"

"I do. But it's hard seeing yourself accurately from the inside out."

"Well, from the outside, you look like the same person. I definitely could pick you out of a lineup."

"You know, I would never have asked you that sort of thing before. But I guess it's time I need to focus on the fact that you're thirty-eight years old!"

"Thirty-nine, actually. Happy birthday to me! You, too, by the way, in a few weeks. And you know what, maybe you do seem different. You seem happier. Which is a little weird. I mean, there's trouble at home with Mom, and you seem happier?"

"I didn't forget your birthday, sweetie," said Ian. "Of course, I should have called. But I did bring a present for you."

"Sure you did."

"I did, and it's pretty nice. I think you'll like it. But do you remember your mom's cousin, Walter Scanlon? We used to see a lot of Walter and Sylvia when you were kids. They had a slew of kids, seven or eight of them, and you were pals with the oldest boy, Peter. Well, one day Peter complained to Walter, accused him of not knowing his birthday, not remembering any of their birthdays. And Walter said, 'Your *birthdays*? Kid, you're lucky I remember your names.'"

"Those kids were like a plague of locusts. Carl and I would always try to hide from them. And that Peter guy was *not* my pal."

"Your mom felt the same way sometimes, even though they were her people. She would have been happy to run and hide when they came. But I thought Walter could be very funny."

"Did she ever do that? Run and hide. Or is that a new thing for her, now?"

"Aren't you the sassy one," he said, laughing at this girl who had been running and hiding for years. "Car, I am so glad I got myself here. It might be the case that it is the reason—you are the reason—I seem happy."

It was and it wasn't. And it didn't matter, causation didn't. Ian was perfectly content with the results, which were new, and strange, and very welcome. He had taken for granted that he was a happy fellow living the right sort of life. Measured now against his mood since Kingman, the postulated happiness of the past was revealed as a pale ghost of the real thing.

Which was? Trying to understand it, define it, Ian came up with the word *lightness*. A sense that everything was consequential because it was inconsequential. This was a letting-go, one that had been sixty-six years in the making. Either that or six months.

At dinner that night, Ian presented Carrie with one of the silver bracelets from the pawn shop in Gallup. He had bought it for her; maybe subconsciously he really did buy it for her birthday. Consciously, displaced onto the road, he had indeed lost track of the date, and every other date as well. When it came to gifts, Ian was normally afflicted with doubts—was it appropriate, would they like it—but he knew this one was right, knew Carrie would love it. He attributed the absence of doubt to his newfound lightness.

"It's gorgeous," said Baz. "I want one too."

Baz had cooked the dinner in the tiny kitchen in their tiny apartment. Roast chicken, roasted potatoes, and pan-fried Napa cabbage enhanced by thin-sliced pan-toasted almonds. She and Carrie were working their way through a bottle of cheap merlot Ian picked up on his way over, along with a growler of the local craft beer he was assured stood "head and shoulders" above the rest. Though he could not help thinking of dandruff, Ian went along with the recommendation.

"As it happens, Baz, I do have one for you," he said on an impulse, and they all laughed—obviously, it could not be true. Yet it was, or could be made true once Ian reassigned the second bracelet, the one he might have given to Anita, had he found her, and would not be giving to Polly because of, he realized, an increasingly acknowledged antipathy toward her. Polly did not deserve a present.

"I'm serious," he said, bathing in a mist of paterfamilias generosity. "It's not identical, but it's similar and just as nice, I think."

"I wasn't. The least bit serious. I mean, you didn't know I existed. All I meant was that the bracelet is lovely."

Ian tapped his temple and claimed clairvoyance. "I not only sensed your existence, I knew your taste in jewelry," he said, wondering if all three of them felt the same wave of recognition, that these bracelets might come to be worn like wedding rings, or be better than matching rings in that they were mated and at the same time individualized. The old Ian would never have entertained such a notion. He would more likely have wondered if the bracelets would be stowed in a deep drawer and never worn once he left Boulder. Or pawned.

The gooseberry fool Baz prepared for dessert was one more gem to decorate the evening. Ian did not even try resisting the scoop of vanilla ice cream she deposited on top. He did say "I didn't order that" and Baz was quick to reply "But I knew you wanted it. You're not the only one who is clairvoyant."

"It seems," said Carrie, "I'm the only one around here who is normal."

Plans? In asking this, Carrie took it for granted he *had* plans. A schedule, a plane ticket. He had decided it was time to get home, resume his life, test the newfound lightness against reality. But he did not have a plan as such, or a schedule, or a ticket. Appearances aside, Carrie teased, maybe he really was a different person.

There were logistics to wrangle, and costs. After all, the new Ian was no wealthier than the old one. Carrie did the research and told him it would cost an extra $358 to drop the Geo off in either Boulder, where there were planes that went some places, or Denver, where the planes went to places you might wish to go.

Ian had stopped keeping track of money, stopped caring, and now was beginning to be alarmed by the overall cost of his little spiritual journey. Though the checking account was joint, he and Polly got separate-but-equal credit card bills, so he could hope the full extent of the damage might go unnoticed. Then, too, wasn't Polly likely compiling a big bill of her own? For all he knew, she could be gallivanting around Paris, with Roseanne on the cuff.

The only way he could save the $358 was by retracing his steps, driving the car back to Albuquerque. If he did that, he could weigh the prospect of revisiting Keely on the way. He pictured himself conducting a test: walk in, sit at the same table, order the Pork Chop from Hell, see if she even recognized him. Was he of some significance to her, or was he just a leaf blowing past her on the street? He asked Carrie to research Kingman for him, was told the distance was eight hundred miles, the drive time sixteen hours.

"Why Kingman? You're not getting hooked into some internet scam, I hope. Free condo, if you come for a two-day presentation! A thousand shares in a thriving silver mine if you wire us twenty thousand dollars in the next hour!"

"Nothing like that, sweetie. I am still of sound mind."

"What, then?"

"It's kind of hard to explain. Call it one small corner of my spiritual journey."

"Kingman?"

She did not push it—neither of them would allow this visit to go off the rails—but knowing that air conditioning was against her father's religion, she pointed out that both California and Arizona were going to hit ninety-nine degrees all week, which would mean three days in the car with the AC on and two nights in motels with the AC on. She calculated that between GASFOOD and LODGING, he would spend a lot more than the $358 he was trying to save.

"The Kingman option isn't looking good, Dad. As an investment?"

It occurred to him that he could *write* to Keely. Enclose a photo to jog her memory. Say how are you doing? Say hey, if you're ever out east, I'll treat you to a side of shoestring potatoes. He did have an address for her.

Or he could just let go of it.

He was under no obligation to Polly, he had convinced himself of that. The guilt should be hers, not his. No obligation to anyone, really, now that Jack Sutcliffe had a girlfriend to keep tabs on him. Ian's only obligation was to give Thrifty back their little car.

There were favors to acknowledge. Another call to Ann Darlington revealed she had incurred expenses for Frontline ("It is tick season, you know") and a fifty-pound sack of kibble. Not that she was dunning him, just updating. He had expected to be away for a handful of days, now he was into his third week. He did not regret presenting Baz with the second silver bracelet, he only regretted not buying three of them. Had he been truly clairvoyant, he would still have one for Ann.

"I will be glad to see you, Ian," said Ann, "but by now Fred may have abandonment issues. Don't be surprised if she gives you the cold shoulder."

Maybe they would sell bracelets at the airport in Denver, or Navajo blankets—some sort of Western swag he could bring back for Ann. He would have to come up with something nice for her, the universe would have to support his search. No need to call upon the universe when shopping for Harvey, though. They would have a bottle of Grand Marnier at the duty-free, and it would be mission accomplished.

He had licensed Harv to make himself at home at the house, fix himself a drink while he was overseeing things, so he was not surprised to hear it come back now as a joke: "Sorry, my friend, your liquor cabinet is bare, not a drop left on premises."

"Did you find the hidden bottles too?" said Ian, who did not have a liquor cabinet, or any hidden bottles.

"I know I said there wasn't any mail, but that wasn't counting the catalogues. You guys must be some shoppers to judge from the pile of that stuff."

"Pitch 'em all." It was true, Polly was gone, Ian never looked at those glossy solicitations. "What about real mail?"

"Are bills real? I didn't count those either. But still just that one letter—the one with the apparently real handwriting? That you forbade me to open? And one real phone message, with a recorded message that you did not forbid me to audit."

"You audited it?"

"Your wife called. Your apparently real wife, who said, quote unquote, 'Just letting you know I'm okay, hope you are too.'"

"Got it."

"Forget 'got it.' What's that about, the I'm-okay-you're-okay."

"It's a long story."

"Harvey has time."

"Well, but it's a long story and I don't know it."

"Then how do you know it's long?"

"All right, the hell with it. She upped sticks, Polly did. She sort of, I don't know—maybe bolted."

"Upped sticks? Bolted? Are you telling me—or is the BBC telling me—she has left you?"

"I already told you this. That something was going on with her. But listen, I'm coming back and I'm taking you out to dinner on Friday. We'll sit down for a nice meal and I'll tell you everything I know then."

"Not necessary, old chap, old shoe. The free meal, that is. It's the story I want."

Later on, in bed at the hotel, Ian fretted over the letter. His best guess, it was a lawyer letter. Polly probably hired a lawyer. He could have asked Harvey to open it and read it over the phone, but who knew what charges Polly would level against him? She might be legally obliged to make him look bad, charge him with abuse or neglect. Their problems, however she characterized them, were still personal. He would be there soon enough to read it himself.

He pictured himself there, at the house, first wading through the knee-high tick-rich grass, getting the standard look of disapproval from Mrs. Ferry next door, seeing a sprawl of six-color catalogues on the dining table, feeling the silence. He had forgotten to open windows, so there would be a musty odor, there could be mildew. Good idea taking Harv to dinner that first full day back, wise to have something like that planned against the emptiness, and the silence, and the smell.

And why not take Ann to dinner on the second day, if she was free. That way he would have a second something planned and by the third day, with the universe supporting him, he would be adjusted. Maybe the universe would mow his lawn. On Sundays all across Blaine you would hear the harsh music of lawnmowers, weedwhackers, leafblowers. It was a first-world cartoon, or a *New Yorker* cover, Pleasantville at its most predictable. By the third day, Ian would be acclimatized, ready to remove any remaining mice from the guts of the lawnmower and yank the rope to start it.

"You could stay a bit longer, you know," said Carrie. She felt safe suggesting it now that Ian did have a plan and a plane. "It's almost your birthday, I could bake a cake, or better yet, Baz could. As you know, she's the master baker."

"She is that, for sure," he said, having just consumed a large portion of leftover apple crisp for breakfast. "But you know the old saying, fish and visitors."

"But you are neither, fish nor visitor, you are the dear old dad."

"So glad to know it, Car."

"You really are different, you know. The dear old dad—first edition?— would never have pissed away a few hundred bucks. Drop a rental car at a *remote location*? Never."

"It's only money."

"That was also true at the glass bottom boat."

"You seem different too, Car. Ever since you sent old Warren packing."

This was as close as he would come to asking directly—what happened and what did it mean—and it was not close enough to draw out a response. Carrie just laughed, whether at Ian's joke or at the very idea of Warren. Ancient history? My life as a heterosexual?

"Or maybe," he said into the brief silence, "it's Baz's cooking" and this time they both laughed, Carrie keeping her own counsel and Ian suppressing another old saw, the way to a man's heart (or a woman's?) is through his stomach. Did the new generations—X, Y, Z, and whatever—even know the old saws? They had developed a whole new language celebrating the shallow truisms of the digital age in acronyms and emojis.

Live and learn, another old saw. Years ago, at Jack Sutcliffe's urging, Ian read *The Education of Henry Adams*, and though the book was brilliant it had made him wonder how such a witty insightful mind could have such terrible lapses, the anti-Semitism and all. The title came back at him during this last day with Carrie, for this whole visit was nothing less than *The Education of Ian Nelson* or perhaps, in light of everything he had experienced since touching down in Albuquerque, *The Further Education*. Live and learn.

"Leave some room in your suitcase," Carrie had said. "Not a lot. As much as you would leave for a book, roughly, though it will weigh a lot less than a book."

"It."

"Yes. It."

He was under orders not to open the It until he got home and by the end of that brutal passage (losing hours connecting, losing more hours to time zones, then the drive from Boston to Blaine) he had forgotten to be curious. The package came out of the duffel with a clump of socks, in a plain brown wrapper labeled *Plain Brown Wrapper*. The card read *Do Not Open Until 67 Years of Age* but he opened it anyway and found a flourless chocolate cake baked by Baz and decorated by Carrie with sixty-eight tiny candles in keeping with the family tradition of adding "one to grow on."

At the stroke of midnight, he tucked into the cake and devoured a quarter of it, craving a glass of milk the whole time. The cake was not too sweet, but the transformed daughter was sweet as could be and so was her companion. Gender be damned, the choice between Warren and Baz was a test even the old dad might have passed.

Life tossed a lot of curve balls at you, for sure, kept you off stride much of the time, yet sometimes you squared one up and drove it out of the park. A metaphor worthy of Carl, he mused, as he went on to paraphrase yet another old saw: What will it profit a man if he loses a wife yet gains a daughter?

Ian had no idea how thoroughly exhausted he was, not until he woke at two in the afternoon. He had slept twelve hours and felt he could easily sleep twelve more.

He splashed gallons of cold water on his face, stood under a long hot shower, brewed and consumed a pot of coffee, and stepped outside for some fresh air. Glorifying the west, he had almost forgotten how the air here always came freshly filtered through pine-forested mountains. He had almost forgotten Mrs. Ferry, too, but there she was, lying in wait with that sour closed-off expression, her standard greeting, disapproval writ small. He waved and smiled, she did not wave or smile back, par for the course. He was too jetslugged—or too liberated?—to care.

He needed to call Ann and relieve her of the dog. Needed to thank her profusely, gift her decently. Though the universe had not supported him at the airport in Denver, the Internet had. He bought a gift certificate for $100 worth of AbeBooks, knowing that Ann loved Abe as much as she hated Amazon. $100 would get her a dozen books she could choose for herself. She might have some fun with the rest of the present, too. Ann was the most engaged of librarians, constantly recruiting, enlisting, arranging. He bought her a notebook—the airport had provided that—in which to record her selections and promised to read them when she did, read and discuss them with her. Ann would love the idea.

All set to bring her the gifts and take away the dog, he was derailed by unlikely news from Ann's message machine: *We are away until Sunday, will return your call then. Thanks!*

Away? Ann never went away. And if "we" was Ann and Fred, it meant Fred was also away, on the day Ian had said he would be coming to fetch her. *Travels with Fred* after all, yet without Ian?

The day opened up, five hours until he was due to meet Harvey, and he knew what he should do with those hours. Confront the slightly threatening phone message, face the mysterious lawyer letter, call Carrie, who had insisted on getting the all-clear safe-home . . . But he was not eager to do any of those things. He was eager to delay doing them. Better to start attacking the yard.

The yard might prove challenging—a hungry cow might have better luck

than the rattling old mower—but there was the fringe benefit of driving
Mrs. Ferry indoors, removing her pinched gaze from view. For ten years
Ian had been smiling her way, greeting her cheerfully, offering help—and
getting only the sourest of pusses in return. No wonder *Mister* Ferry was
long gone and hard to find all those years! Well, the new Ian Nelson was
done with smiling, he was ready to bring the noise, bring it right up to her
ridiculous ankle-high plastic picket barrier from Big Lots. He might even
forego his usual consideration and spray a few clippings over the picket line.

Calvin Coolidge had provided the wise advice: *You can't do everything at
once but you can do* something *at once.* Ian would cut the grass.

Harvey had played a trick on him. He must have worked fast too, given
the timetable, gotten it done overnight. As they pulled into the parking lot
behind Thorne House—Ian was good with dinner at the fancy venue, a deal
was a deal—Harv tossed off a teasing line, how he had never seen so many
cars in the lot. How Thorne House must be doing well. Ian, as blank of brain
as a fish, idly surmised it could be a private party, they hosted those sometimes.

"I suppose it's possible," said Harv, with a straight face.

Even as they strolled past a light seating in the main dining area and
continued through the doors to the Hallowell Room, the large space
reserved for "functions," he was caught off guard by the sight those sliding
doors unveiled. Harvey had done something both wonderful and horrible.
He had somehow gathered three dozen friends to celebrate Ian's birthday.

"You fucker," Ian whispered, his smile both pinched and genuine. He was
horrified and gratified in equal parts in the presence of so much friendship.
Everyone was there, including Fred, who was not "away," any more than
Ann was, and not afflicted by abandonment issues either, as she scrambled
into Ian's arms whimpering with emotion. He turned to Ann and this time
whispered, *"Et tu,* Darlington!" Ann shrugged and pointed the finger of
blame at Harv.

Jack Sutcliffe came forward, extending his famously bone-crushing,
cartilage-compressing handshake and Ian, with a "Hello, you old rascal,"
endured it. Jack's other hand never strayed from Sarah Connaughton's hip,

except when it drifted down to her bottom, causing Sarah to pry it free and tell him, audibly, "John, we're in public." Rascal, indeed!

He and Jack would later have a moment outside, a cigar break without the cigars, where Ian accused him of having taken out a new lease on life. Or congratulated him on it. Jack, of course, demurred: "I'm still preparing for the alternative. Signed away my organs, in fact, as if anyone would want them. Still, Sarah . . ."

"That was her thing? She persuaded you?"

"Hell, why not make the nice lady smile. It's not like I'll be needing any of them."

"The nice lady has clearly made you smile, John Marr Sutcliffe."

"We're sort of engaged," said Jack, looking for once in his bold-spoken life at his shoe tops.

"You? Who vowed never again? Who for years declared himself perfectly content to visit that lady of the night in Willow Falls—Vanessa?—every now and then?"

"This lady wanted a ring, what the hell."

"She must be some cook," said Ian, once again trotting out the oldest of metaphors. He would wager that Sarah Connaughton had given orgasm back to Jack Sutcliffe. The shadowy "they" had taken it away, a particular *she* must have brought it back.

"There's more to it than that," said Jack, at the same time responding to the metaphor and pretending it wasn't what it was. Orgasm confirmed, as far as Ian was concerned, especially when Jack was for once the one to blush.

"Hey," said Ian, "maybe I'll donate my organs too."

He had left the house expecting to buy Harv a steak and a couple of drinks, only to find out he was off the hook, the dirty dozens were funding this bash. When he tried to mount a protest—it wasn't even a benchmark birthday, sixty-seven was a random, middling, crooked number—it was Karin who put it bluntly: "Just shut up, Ian, and take your punishment." When everyone laughed, Ian had to laugh with them. Karin stayed, stood there, waiting for him to blush.

To the question the Angel Band routinely asked ("How Can I Keep From Singing"), the obvious answer was Karin Kline. She could start him or bench him, according to whim. Ian had a theory, that from junior high school to the NBA, every basketball coach cuts one player who should have made the team and benches one player who should be starting. "I'm ready," he told Karin. "Just so you know. Ready and eager. So if you happened to be thinking of a birthday gift—"

"Done," she said. "You're on for next Wednesday, check your email tomorrow for details." Was this Karin Kline or was it the universe supporting him? No matter, either way he was in the starting lineup.

Ian should have cottoned on to the surprise the instant they pulled into the parking lot. He should have registered that Karin's car, her Outback with the ANGEL plate, was here and he might have recognized a dozen other cars as well. He was bad at cars, though, they were all just cars to him, so many of them that drab gray-silver color. Still, there was Karin's ANGEL plate and there was WARDOFF on Ward Longstreet's car. He could only blame the jetlag for his failure to connect the dots, or even observe them.

Now they were back in the parking lot, all of them, but the festivities were not quite concluded. They had one more treat in store for him. His song, the one he had for years pressed Karin to include on the setlist (and which, because she had refused to do, they had never once sung or rehearsed), was somehow performed in something like 33-part harmony even though Harv and Karin had to have organized this whole megillah in a matter of hours. Regardless, "Crossing the Bar" was a smash hit. Several Angels made a point of telling him how right he had been. "*May there be no moaning at the bar when I put out to sea*," recited Ward. "Who wouldn't be happy to die after hearing that?"

"It's a birthday party, Ward, not a funeral." Ian was overwhelmed; the joke was to cover his embarrassment, which only intensified when Alexis took his hand to say, "Your song absolutely decorated the night."

Two by two, they drifted to their cars and rolled out to the road. Harvey announced he would catch a ride home with Bill Crichton. He did not wish to listen to Ian rag on him for what was in fact a "brilliant deception and, incidentally, a show of affection. Under the circumstances," said Harv, "complaint would be inappropriate."

Ian assured him he would utter no complaints, might even utter a word or two of thanks, but Harv was gone, trailing a backwards palm of farewell out the passenger side window of Bill's . . . CRV? A large gray-silver car with a symbol that no doubt provided a clue to its identity.

He had only to sort Ann and Fred. Late as it was, he offered to swing by her house and gather Fred's gear—the bed, the food, the chew toys. "I have it all in my car," she said, as though stating the obvious. "You didn't know I'd be here, Ian, but of course I knew you would. And I knew you would want to reunite with Freddie, even if we are going to be sharing custody in the future."

"Freddie?"

The dog was sharing herself at the moment, midway between them as they stood beneath the ornate calligraphy of the Thorne House signpost, parsing out their goodnights. Once more, Ian elected to roll with the custody joke: "I guess I'll have my lawyers talk to your lawyers."

"Either that, or we can hash it out between ourselves and save on attorneys' fees. You can't be settled yet, why don't you come to dinner tomorrow night." Did this make it too late to announce his dinner-out-my-treat plan? Make it seem like an afterthought, a counteroffer rather than a clear intention? For a few seconds he was the old Ian and stood blushing while Ann went on: "I need a guinea pig for this new chicken dish I want to try."

Then it struck him that she knew. Inviting him, just him, to dinner? She had to know. And if Ann Darlington knew, everyone must know. Harvey had spilled the beans. Come to that, Polly herself might have confided in someone, weeks ago. There could be people here who knew more than Ian himself did! Suddenly his birthday bash was revealed to be something quite different, a sympathy thing, which cast a different light on all of it, including Ann's dinner invitation.

"We can't properly deal with the custody issue until our divorce is final," said Ann, smiling. "And we can't divorce until first we marry."

Unable to handle the possibility that her going on like this was anything but a joke, Ian continued to field it as such. "I'm afraid I'm too jetlagged to figure out our marital status, Ann. But I did want to return my late library books and take you out to dinner. Not the other way around, I mean. Not after all you've done."

"A date."

"Maybe more a debt than a date. I owe you bigtime and I wanted to do something to return your incredible kindnesses. And I do have a present for you."

"Why don't we flip a coin. Heads I cook, tails you treat. And sure, we can defer the conference on custody to some future date when your head is clear."

"You know about us, don't you. Me and Polly."

"I did hear, yes. Sad news."

"What, exactly, did you hear?"

"Enough to conclude that it is way too early, but that you will soon be seen as the most eligible man in town."

This was more of her kindness. If not for Fred, someone would soon enough be offering him an emotional support dog. "Me? Eligible? That's an awfully nice way of describing someone freshly discarded!"

"Yes, you, Ian. Nice, smart, handsome, funny you."

"I doubt anyone sees me quite that way."

"You'd be surprised. Well, I gather you *are* surprised. People do tend to be polite, you know. Women don't go around flattering married men. If they did that, they would be as bad as men."

The new Ian was confronting a new Ann Darlington. Bold, flirtatious, almost rapacious. But, recalling the many bottles of wine, empties soldiered up on every table, and the vodka tonics, he guessed Ann was either saying things she would by morning regret or forget having said. Alcohol was doing the talking here.

Still, right now he needed to take Ann at face value and round off this exchange. He could sort the rest of it later. His naïveté diluted of late, he could believe that Ann—at least the Ann fueled by booze—was coming on to him, something that was apparently possible even when a man was sixty-seven and a woman was somewhere in her fifties. Instead of pigeonholing Ann as his friendly librarian, he was being asked to notice that she was a charming, attractive woman of (it occurred to him) about the same age as

Keely. Had he stumbled blindly onto a sweet spot, whereby he was somehow appealing to women in that age group? He could sort that later too unless, best case, it simply went away, Ann with no memory of the exchange.

"I'm going to insist," he said, sure of the one thing, that the neutral ground of a restaurant was safer than Ann's house would be. "We will go someplace nice tomorrow night. Or not nice if you prefer. Your choice."

Ann leaned in and kissed his cheek, her hand traveling down his arm as she straightened, and they began transferring that which was Fred's from her Honda to his. He could recognize a car when it was the same as his own, especially if it came in the same color. With their identical green cars arranged side by side for the transfer, Ann made the old quip about great minds thinking alike and Ian came up with the standard riposte—weak minds trickle in the same gutter—though neither was applicable since it was Polly who had shopped for the car.

Home late yet oddly energized, Ian was as rattled as he was pleased by the party. Hoping to clear away the loose fragments left behind by time changes, plane changes, possible life changes, and such booze as he had himself absorbed, he went out walking well after midnight. Fred was beside herself and pranced all the way to the Watchman Park portal, then sprinted the length of the serpentine pathway to the stately Squirrel Oak.

Watching Fred pee on the base of the tree, Ian felt almost grounded. Fred was again the still point of the turning world, a sign that order could be restored. A new order, perhaps, but as Jack would say, what the hell. And after all, wasn't he the new Ian?

Reckonings

WAKING THE MORNING after his birthday bash, Ian knew he was in for some reckonings. With Ann he expected it to be minor, with Polly it would be as major as reckonings get. He did not anticipate there would come a moment of reckoning with Anita Richardson but there would be, as he was about to learn. His craving for an uneventful Saturday morning, a few sunny hours of tranquility, would vanish before his coffee got cold.

Not that it was all bad. The phone message from Polly was only bad if the goal was to preserve their marriage and it seemed that was not the goal anymore. Certainly not for Polly, who was all for clarity and concision: *We will need to talk, of course, but I will write out some of it beforehand so the talk can be as short as possible. And Ian? As unsentimental?*

There was no chance of Polly getting sentimental, or of coming back, obviously. As he sat on the porch with a second cup of coffee, he recalled Ward Longstreet saying "divorce can come from left field." Some serious irony there, given that Ward's divorce stemmed from adultery, *his* adultery, which placed it closer to home plate than left field. Though Ian did not suspect adultery here, the kicker was that it did not matter to him one way or another. He had traveled a distance and he had gained some distance; it dawned on him, had been dawning for a while, that he did not miss Polly. In an analogy he knew would date him, that insight had emerged like a photograph emerging into focus from an acid bath.

Thirty years ago, Nan Sutcliffe left Jack for greener pastures that soon went sere. When she came back six months later, carrying the same suitcase she had taken when she left, wearing the same dress she had worn, she went straight upstairs and began unpacking. Came back down and started cleaning the refrigerator. Jack admitted the fridge was in serious need but said "If she had asked, I'd have told her no. But she didn't ask. Walked in acting like nothing had happened, like she'd gone down to the store for milk, and I was too dumbstruck to give her the boot."

Nan would remain at Jack's side another five years before "God kicked her to the curb." Jack knew it was God because she had just put on "that same damned dress" when the stroke took her.

Ian very much doubted Poll would reappear in six months and start unpacking. Poll was a straightliner. "Don't look back" was her mantra—another bit of irony, since looking back was the essence of her life's work as a therapist. It was fine to look back at a client's doubts and fears, just not her own. Ian wasn't sure he would be able to give her the boot if she did have a change of heart, he was only sure it would be the best thing to do. Somehow it really was over. He would be fine with minimizing the conversation, a conversation that so recently felt essential and before that impossible to imagine. By now, Ian was angry enough at Polly that he might *write some things down* himself, though in truth he did not care a fig who got the couch or the paintings.

The letter, the one in apparently human handwriting and bearing no return address, was not from Polly's lawyer as he had assumed, it was from Anita. At first this brought only surprise and confusion. Then, as he read and re-read the letter, he found he was angry at Anita too and wondered if he was simply out of sorts emotionally, jetslugged and surly. Because the news that Anita was alive was cause for rejoicing, yet Ian did not rejoice. He did not care for her tone, so breezy and cavalier.

Dear Ian,
I wanted to let you know I'm back—just guessing you remember I was away! I will bet a billion you can't guess where I am

*now. Answer, at Sally's! Wonders never cease, not when I have
the miracle of ongoing life and when my sweet-and-sour sister
proves willing to take me in. Of course, both of these wonders
figure to be temporary. Anyway, hope to see you sometime soon.
Love, Anita*

Anger was all wrong, he knew that. He reminded himself that Anita had
been just as cavalier when she vanished in the first place, yet as he searched
the Big Sur cliffside for her he felt only concern. Had she turned up by the
fire at Deetjun's Inn, he would have felt relief and affection. What was the
difference? She had cancelled an informal outing, nothing to be bothered
about there, especially after she sent a note apologizing for the change of
plans. She had kept in touch.

But the bad vibe did not leave easily. It simmered. He had Sally Shumway's
address. He knew her phone number. He could call or drive there right now.
He knew he would do neither, call or go, and he knew that made no sense.
Anita was alive, in apparent good spirits, and the news *annoyed* him? Still,
it did. This friendly airy little note of hers was not enough. She would have
to do more—he could not say or imagine what that might be—if they were
to rekindle their friendship. He could criticize, even abhor his own reaction,
could not endorse it from any angle. Nor, however, could he dismiss it.

He went to the kitchen—he was on a zip line, back and forth between
kitchen and porch all morning—and made a fresh pot of coffee. When
Fred submitted a request for exercise, the famous brown-eyed entreaty, he
shushed her impatiently; he was even angry at the dog. But the dog was
having none of it and persisted. Silently, she filed charges. You want to talk
about cavalier? About abandonment? Dude, you owe me *fifty* walks, and
long ones at that.

Ian sighed. Apologized. Finally, something dark and gnarly left him, like
a breath held too long. Fred was right. The morning was glorious, it was
wildflower season, yellow sorrel and Indian paintbrush cropping up "in gay
profusion" everywhere, and Ian wished to believe he was sane enough to
gainsay this giftwrapped world even had Fred not been there to nag him. He
wished to believe that swimming through the singing sailing air, he would

shed his useless surliness like a snake shedding its skin and heedlessly leave it behind.

"I want to hear all about your trip."

Maybe not *all* about it, Ian smiled inwardly. Though who knew? If Ann enjoyed living vicariously—poring over travel literature in lieu of traveling— she might enjoy hearing about his astounding encounter in Kingman. Then again, she might not. He elected to emphasize the rest of it: the donkeys, the docent, the dramatic Big Sur landscape, and above all his healing visit with Carrie and Baz. "They seem to be," he said cautiously, "something of a couple."

"That's wonderful, Ian. I got to know her a bit when she was a senior in high school. Smart as a whip, and maybe with a bit of a whip in her arsenal?"

Did that mean something sexual, S and M (for a moment he couldn't remember what the letters stood for, only what they implied) or did it signify a strong woman? The whip was one thing, the arsenal another. All Ian said was, "She has settled down considerably. Really calm and sweet. It was a revelation, a real joy."

"Did that Steinbeck man really lecture you or was that just you embellishing?"

"Oh no, he was a true believer. He did inspire me to read another book— you know, after the one about Driving with My Dog. I read a hundred pages of *In Dubious Battle* on the plane coming back and so far I'm impressed."

"But you said you came back *de*pressed."

"Not depressed. More like disoriented. And surly."

"You?"

"I'm glad you haven't noticed."

Though The Draught House offered only two desserts—essentially it was a bar, with bar food—both were deemed necessary. They ordered both the peach upside-down cake and the banana extravaganza, with a plan to split them even-steven. "Practicing teamwork," said Ann, with a hint of implication, while Ian tried to keep it in neutral, going on about the second Steinbeck man, the one who labeled the dog book a fraud. Ann shrugged. For her, Steinbeck was done as a topic.

She looked good. She was pretty in such an understated way, you could easily not notice. Her brown-lashed brown eyes registered first as *friendly* and the soft confiding smile almost sisterly. She wore a cotton dress that Doris Day might have worn in a 1959 movie—Sam the Gram would know all the titles—and used minimal makeup. Ian would have said no makeup at all, except Polly was always telling him he was fooled about that, how so-and-so wore *tons* of makeup, he just couldn't tell. Well, he couldn't tell now either, and he liked Ann's Doris Day dress. He realized he had never considered her "looks" one way or the other. She was Ann. Harvey ogled women for fun; Ian, for better or worse, did not. Sometimes he worried that he must be suppressing, and maybe so, for here he was assessing.

"I don't like the idea," she said as they stood at her front door, "that you are working off some sort of debt. Can't we just think of this as a lovely social occasion?"

"Sure we can, why not. It is that."

"And we could do it again, without calling it a date. The word seemed to alarm you."

"Only because I just turned sixty-seven. Date?"

However either of them characterized it, it did behave like a date. No question the world had spun a few times on its axis since Ian had learned his lexicon and his boy-girl lessons. Staid Ian Nelson had a *one-night stand*, no better way to put it, and now here he was, x-ed out by his wife and seemingly x-ed in by the likable librarian. It was flattering in a way, yet he was so freshly connected to the pleasures of his own company, to seeing liberation where he might have seen loneliness, that he shied from Ann's eagerness.

She must have sensed as much. "I want you to know that I am not some, I don't know, desperate creature—"

"Ann, I never—"

"—who places ads in the personals shopping for company. Lonely librarian seeks bookworm who enjoys long walks in pretty places? I'm just mature enough that, if I see a chance to get to know someone I like a little better, I might come out and say so."

"It's fine. I like you too, needless to say—always have. That's not in question."

"Long walks in pretty places is a standard, you know. Occurs in 87 percent of all ads placed by women over the age of fifty-five."

"You're over fifty-five?"

"No. And as I told you, I don't place such ads."

"You read them, apparently." He grinned as he felt the moment easing, any threat deflating. She made him take the substantial remains of both desserts, neatly packaged in unnecessarily attractive, beribboned boxes, and declared she would not god-forbid-kiss-him-goodnight. He did kiss her, delicately, on the cheek, and declared he would be happy to take long walks in pretty places with her, as long as she promised not to tell him what a nice fellow he was for doing so.

It was too soon, she said it again. Nevertheless, she was planning to do the Riverwalk after dinner, one of the routes Ian had designated and which Ann had obligingly taken with Fred half a dozen times. If Ian wasn't game, maybe she could borrow the dog for a couple of hours?

Ian had been planning the same walk, looking forward to it. Teeming invasive species would have taken over by the moribund paper mill, a thick wall of Japanese knotweed on one side and sumac spilling down the hillside opposite. If these plants were so hellbent on invading, it was fortunate they were as beautiful as they were.

He could bail on his plan. Could lie to Ann and say he had company, or chores, but then she would come to the house for Fred—he could hardly say no to that generous request. So he went, or they did. Ann nonchalant, Ian somewhat self-conscious, knowing the way people read the surface of things and form conclusions. He told himself he should not care, that with his newly transplanted personality he was free to act as he pleased, except being back home in Blaine cut into that resolve. The old home teased out the old Ian and left him stranded halfway, at times unsure how to act.

They walked and they talked, harmlessly, until Ann said, "Do you ever wonder what someone would be like in bed?" She said it casually, as though it was just another conversational strain of their standard, harmless Copper River fare—the weather, the landscape, the unfathomable moral lapse of the Republicans. "Someone forbidden or out of reach, of course, maybe even a movie star."

"No, actually," said Ian, and this was the truth, he had not wondered. Everyone was forbidden, after all, which rendered wondering fruitless or worse, frustrating. Had he ever considered the matter consciously, he would have placed wondering in the same basket as ogling. Why ogle? If there were benefits, he was blind to them.

"I'll bet you're the only one who hasn't. Not in a prurient way, more like who would be funny, see it as a fun thing to do rather than a test, or a job of work. Who is like the person you see on the street and who becomes an entirely different person. No?"

Ian made a neutral sound and left it at that, while musing to himself that probably everyone was different. How could they not be when in the first instance they were fully dressed and chatting on Court Street and in the second they were buck naked and intimate someplace private? Whatever had gotten into Ann Darlington, going on like this? Ian would never have been eager to weigh in on sexual nuances, even if he had something to offer on the subject.

"It's fine, Ian, if you don't find me attractive—you know, in that way. Walking in pretty places might be just the ticket for us."

"I never said that," Ian responded, taking the bait, accepting the necessity of contradicting her verdict. "You are perfectly attractive."

"You don't have to say that. You don't have to always be so—"

"Nice?"

"Polite. But let's drop it, shall we? My self-esteem will survive and I assume yours is just fine."

"I guess it is. I mean, considering my wife just ditched me."

"When I ditched Samuel, he took his self-esteem directly to Missy Frommer, no problem! But enough of self and esteem, we're here for Freddie and I sense she is getting annoyed with us."

They dropped it. For the most part dropped conversation altogether and gradually left any residual discomfort behind. There was nothing but comfort to be had from the sunset over Bible Hill, the mackerel clouds shading from salmon to slate gray, and the granite palisade above the river from gray to a soft watermelon red. This sort of display, the ineluctable beauty of it, came closest to reactivating Ian's belief in God; one could almost leave reason behind, surrender to it and call it holy. When he and Ann were in bed a scant hour later, he wondered if the sunset had played a factor, promoting romance, though the Creator he had been encouraged to know would never have endorsed such wanton behavior.

Ian had not intended for this to happen. Quite the opposite, he had stood resolute against it happening. He had been back such a short time that any turn toward new intimacy was unthinkable. He had signed on for a rich solitude, welcoming the time to *take* his time, about everything. Had he imagined even the possibility of intimacy, with anyone, he would have warded it off. Nor had he imagined it, yet here they were.

And at once he was faced with an example of just how different people could be in bed. Ann Darlington in a dowdy dress was one thing, Ann with her ample breasts bared and her lean, muscled legs was another. Shy she was not. Her hair let loose from its standard bun transformed the librarian into a much younger woman, who treated sex as a game they were playing and whose playfulness made it easy to join in. When she had mused about people being fun in bed, not sententious or self-conscious or competitive, she was in fact describing herself. She could laugh at herself, laugh that they could know each other for twenty-two years and not know *this*.

What was this? "You know," she said, "the part where we are skin instead of cloth."

It was not until it came time to talk about it—define, explain, *account* for it—that Ian's reluctance returned. What if Ann took this for something it wasn't, something other than an accident caused by the sunset? What if she presumed, naturally enough, that they would do it again the next day, or the next. Define it as a relationship, or even God forbid a love affair. What if she went so far as to suggest they schedule a joint wedding with Jack Sutcliffe and Sarah Connaughton! The way Ann was behaving, none of this seemed entirely farfetched.

With his mind racing in all these directions, Ian was more than slightly abrupt in leaving. He leapt into his clothes like Wallace or Gromit— whichever one wore clothes—and all but sprinted away. Ann was still laughing as he retreated, as if he were a frightened little boy whose fears did not upset her in the least. Halfway home, it struck him that Ann, far from contemplating marriage, may have been vetting him. Toying with him and in fact welcoming his flight because it relieved her of the burden of kicking him out.

He labored for balance. It was equally misbegotten taking Ann for granted—imagining her shopping for wedding dresses!—as it was imagining such a serious person could be acting cynically or frivolously. Ann was indeed different in the nude, but she was not an entirely different human being. As he sorted it, this way and that, he was ashamed at how fervently he hoped no one had spotted them on the Riverwalk or guessed how the evening proceeded. He chided himself even as he formulated it: *Where was the new Ian when you needed him?*

He was baffled by the swiftness and carelessness with which he had abandoned his own firm intentions. He needed to take a step back and Ann's email the morning after ("Take some time, dear friend") definitely helped. Setting Polly aside was easy enough, since she had set *him* aside so unambiguously. No point overthinking that whole mess until she let him in on what in hell she wanted to do.

Anita was tougher. He did not cling to his initial recoil for long. He knew it was petty and immature. Why was he establishing ground rules or making demands of Anita, when he had never before felt he had any such right? Anita Richardson was a brave young woman who welcomed his company when it fit into her difficult days. He was a sympathetic friend offering support when it was appropriate. Anything else was a figment and a waste of time. He should call her.

Yet there, for now, it rested.

So he had set everything aside. That night he slept seven solid hours and woke refreshed, with a plan to do nothing all day—the sort of nothing that included yardwork, window washing, walks with Fred. He paid the bills. He read with pleasure a mystery that made no sense.

Fred was radically energized by a quirk of weather, a one-day taste of autumn. The combination of sunshine and sharpened air set her dashing through the park like a steeplechaser, leaping some obstacles and dodging others at speed. She was the Barry Sanders of canines! Ian was not vaulting or making sharp cuts, but he felt some of the same energy as Fred, a surge from the snap in the air. Later, when he drove over to meet the band, he felt more alert than he had in ages, more alive. Had he been living inside a sneaky minor depression, or was he just the beneficiary of a decent night's sleep?

It had not exactly occurred to him that he might have been unhappy and was now, for whatever reasons, happy. When Polly had declared happiness to be "a ridiculous calculus for coming to grips with the vagaries of life," she was no doubt right. It was too shallow, it was abstract, subjective. And yet Ian felt himself drifting toward the ridiculous calculus, however shallow or subjective—didn't know what happiness was, just knew it when he saw it, like art. And here it was, the old uplift, that visceral lifting of the biological heart as the singers converged like pilgrims on Karin's van. It was *on* and he was part of it.

A large part. Karin had assigned him the solo on the Tennyson, since it was "your baby," and the others had rehearsed the harmonies. He had rehearsed too, in the shower. There would be nothing transcendent about the evening's sing; they were welcomed, fed tea and cookies, then sang what they called their Greatest Hits, with the single exception of "Crossing the Bar," Ian's star turn. For him, it registered as a pleasant return to normalcy.

The client, Harold Wilkerson, was sturdy enough to strive for courtesy. He gave the impression of a decent man who reckoned he was dying at a decent age, hence without the bitterness that can carve away good manners. "Please, call me Harry—I have always hated Harold," he said. When Faith told him what a lovely smile he had, Harry fessed up, his "choppers" were new and what's more he was running out of time to get used to them. He had a way of making his weaknesses seem like strengths. Harry struck Ian as a man who had always taken it upon himself to please, to entertain, and who would stay that course to the end.

Ian mainly reveled in the togetherness. This was felt despite the absence of Ward or Harv, and the presence of a woman Ian had never met. He forgot her name while she was still saying it. It was not about names or the shifting personnel, it was that they all *got* it. They came ready to work together in harmony and, by doing so, wove a cocoon of kindness, provided a safe harbor not only for poor Harry but also for themselves. Ian, who had lately been celebrating (if not always practicing) the benefits of solitude, found himself overwhelmed by the riches of community.

He almost flinched admitting it. He felt the whip of Polly's scorn, the old charge of sentimentality, and maybe it was corny or intellectually flabby. The very word "community" could so easily be thrown back on itself as a joke—the *songbird community* standing in opposition to the *logging community*, the antique car community showing up at town meeting to demand a place in the holiday parade. The word had been hijacked by ironists. Still, it might be the best thing we have after love, and the best after love has failed.

He thought about Jack's Hollow Lake posse, a bunch of loners who kept resolutely to themselves yet were always aware they were members of the same tribe. Their annual pig roast in October was a marvel, revealing the bond between a dozen reprobates otherwise arrayed around the lake, nodding hello from a distance until the tribal drums beat. Watching them at the roast, you would have guessed they got together all the time, not just once a year or when someone needed help with a shanty. They came together infrequently but they knew it was there, the community. They could trust it to be there.

He thought of the Blaine EMTs, who came from such different walks, brought odd slants. Ed the plumber, Sid who ran the hardware, Sandy who taught third grade, three volunteer firemen volunteering for this too. They came as a tight unit that had trained together and functioned smoothly in every crisis. Smoothly and joyfully. By definition, they came only to emergencies—stove burns, heart attacks, old people who had fallen—where their camaraderie and pride did much to mute disaster, mitigate pain.

There was a German word, *gaborgenheit*, that Jack had told him was famously untranslatable into English. ("Famously?" Ian had said, guessing Jack was the only U.S. citizen who had ever encountered this famous word.) No single word, said Jack, corresponded, in part because like many German words, *gaborgenheit* bodies forth a concept or a phenomenon. This one describes the way in which something—often long-held family traditions—

can embody a center that *will* hold, a sort of cultural embrace. Possibly in America, land of the rugged individual, the country where chaos is king and so many families are fractured, it isn't the word that is missing, it's the phenomenon behind the word. The reliable warm embrace.

Ian did not argue the point with Jack. It sounded good, it was interesting, enough said. But tonight he saw plenty of ways in which people come together to provide what *gaborgenheit* provides those Germans who possess the famous word. It could be a basketball team, pulling together through a long season. Or a unit, like the EMTs, or Jack's posse at the lake. Polly might call it a support system, citing AA meetings, or the parents of murdered children coming together once a month because only they could understand.

It could be a choir.

Why do they sing in church? They don't have to sing, no one mandated it, yet they all do. Whether a lugubrious Jewish chant or a soaring Baptist hymn, they all sing, they all include music. For many, the music is at the heart of it, the distilled essence of their faith.

Earlier that day in the park, Ian detected something special in the wind, as that cone of cold air came tunneling through the warm sunlight. It seemed to him a version of perfection. And his response to it was song. Ian was reserved, the meadow was a public place, so at first he hummed. Then, drifting behind the empty grandstand, he let it out simply because he could not hold it in. Whatever was holy in that warm chill squeezed the music out of him. If someone heard him and labeled him crazy, so be it. Their problem, not his.

They dispersed after the sing, went their separate ways. No one in this newly formed crew suggested a round of drinks. Ian went straight home. He had nothing to drink at home either yet he felt a lingering thrill, a pleasing dizziness, as though he was tipsy and abuzz. It was the music. And community. It was *gaborgenheit!*

What must Anita think? That he was a serial Samaritan who granted her a portion of his sympathy, lost interest, and was now off nursing some new terminal case? That this was what he did, who he was? He feared as much until he got a second note from her, worrying that her flighty cancellation had alienated him, jokingly requesting a second chance at their fairgrounds visit. She didn't say if she planned to take an Uber from Maine to Blaine to make good on the offer.

Her light touch was perfect, and the note made clear that she did value him. It did not matter how or how much she valued him. He had no need to define or quantify it, not at a time when he could hardly begin to quantify his own feelings, toward anyone.

He tried framing a note of his own in response, made several false starts before he finally picked up the phone. Hoping to get Sally's message machine, he got the live version instead and it sounded as though Sister Sal had been honing her knives. "Well well, if it isn't the just-a-friend friend. The guy who isn't this and isn't that. Please hold while I summon the queen for you."

"This is the queen speaking," said Anita, coming on the line a moment later. "Imprisoned here in the tower of guilt! Ian, I'm so glad to hear from you. I was sure you were shunning me. Are you? Shunning me?"

"Hello, Anita. No, of course not, I was away is all. Off on a little trip and just recently caught up with your note."

"That's so nice you were off on a vacation. Much better than if you were shunning me."

"Not exactly a vacation. The main event was a visit with my daughter," he said, picking his way through a minefield of distortions and omissions. "Though I did get to explore the great American West a bit."

"You're kidding. I did exactly the same thing!"

He let her go on about her own trip west, let her telling drain away the significance of his own going. The truth about that would not change or help anything. He almost goofed and brought up Cape Disappointment, but she saved him by veering onto the subject of her guilt, "which only begins with the tower of guilt where Sally has imprisoned me."

Sally was only being nice in order to ratchet up the guilt "from before." (Clearly, the word Richard was not to be spoken.) "But that's not the end of my endless guilt. I'm afraid I need to confess to you again."

"But why?" he said, for she had already confessed, back at Blaine General Hospital, when the word Richard *was* spoken. He assured her he had no problem with her bailing on the fairgrounds that day. Told her that he had gone there anyway ("Without me?" she dared to sass him) and was glad he did; how being there helped him reclaim a few fond memories. He filled her in on the life and hard times of O'Riley the Rabbit, making dinner party conversation over the phone.

Her guilt was not about the fairgrounds, it was bigger than that. Did he recall her hospitalization? Recall bringing her home from the hospital? "I lied to you about everything. Before, during, and after. I lied lied lied."

"But I was there," he said. "I know you were in the hospital."

"No, about *why* I was in. See, I changed my mind about getting treatment. I did let them fry my brain. And instead of telling you the truth, I kept on pretending."

"I still don't get it. Not that I had a vote, but I would have been all for anything they thought might help."

"Embarrassment? Shame? I mean, after putting up this brave front, I end up being a scaredy-cat? I folded and I didn't want you to know it—know I was two-faced, and cowardly, and totally dishonest."

"You're telling me you were dishonest in order to avoid *appearing* dishonest?"

"I was such a weakling," she said, but her tone was already softer, almost merry. She was relieved by his kindness, grateful for his non-judgmental take.

"You changed your mind, that's all. You saw the light."

"That's sort of true, actually. I read about this guy who had been living with a Blob for seven years. I mean, he was one in a hundred, but there were others who lasted three years, five years. I did the math. Five years out of forty is an eighth of my life, it's a big chunk. Say you were a kid, five years old. The next five you learn to read, you learn to play a musical instrument, maybe you become a soccer star . . ."

"Absolutely. Your reasoning is impeccable."

"Impeccable!" interjected Sally. "What a girl it is, with her impeccable reasoning!"

"Sorry," said Anita, "she grabbed the phone. Anyway, that scared me too, trying to stay alive, but I guess it scared me less than the dying so I let them fry my brain. Then I just blew town. Went out to the west coast and wrestled with the devil out there. It was kind of crazy—or I was. I'd have a nice morning and then decide to kill myself in the afternoon. But it's a long story . . ."

That weekend Ian drove to Portland to hear Anita's long story, which would serve to confirm that his fears in Big Sur were well founded. She had indeed gone to those cliffs in a very dark state of mind. He had not found a body because, fortunately, she decided not to leave one. Some days the vote was 51–49, other days 49–51.

"The truth is, I planned to jump. This was a place where the cliffs are high up over the ocean—a super romantic way to go, right? I went on trial runs, scouting locations, picking the ideal runway for my takeoff. One night, I wrote the note I would leave behind when I jumped the next morning, into the beautiful fog."

"Then," said Sister Sally, emerging from the kitchen with a platter of cheese and crackers, "*then* she came to her fucking senses."

"It was cold and nasty out there and jumping looked a lot harder than I'd bargained for. I had pictured those guys who sail off the cliffs in Acapulco— graceful forms cleaving the air, cleaving the water. That was not going to happen where I was."

"Way too much cleaving," said Sally.

"What *was* going to happen was a broken neck, two broken legs, and lying there helpless until the wild animals ate me. Plus, it dawned on me that those cliff divers weren't committing suicide, they were committing capitalism, diving for dollars. I couldn't see charging the tourists to watch me get eaten by animals, so I went back to this lovely inn where I was staying and ordered a bowl of hot chili."

"She chose to live," said Sally, without the needle, touching her sister's elbow tenderly.

"Well, not to die that way. I didn't choose to live until Sal forgave me."

"Not forgave," said Sally, less tenderly. "Some other word."

"She took you in," said Ian. "They say that's the definition of family— when you show up, they have to take you in."

"Well," said Sally, "I do have plenty of room with Rick the Dick now housed in beautiful downtown Lewiston. And what the hell, this girl and I shared a room for eight years, I guess we can share a bloody eight-room house."

"I am paying," said Anita.

"Money, she means. The emotional debt she can never repay." But this was delivered tongue-in-cheek, Sally's tone light and her lips puckered.

"Money does help, though," said Anita. "Besides, on the emotional debt, so-called? You told me I did you a big favor."

"Right. By accident. Intention-wise, you were an incredibly careless shit and if I ever do forgive you I'll not know the reason why."

"Love?" said Anita.

"Blood is thicker than water?" offered Ian.

"So is bullshit," said Sally

"I made a mess, is what I did. Of so many things," said Anita, looking first at Sally, then back at Ian. "Even making you come all the way to Portland today. I mean, you were walking distance in Blaine. I didn't even think about the imposition. I should have come there or, I don't know, at least met you halfway."

"Halfway?" said Sally. "That's rich. The girl doesn't drive! Even though—hello?—it is the 21st century. And I am damned if I will be her chauffeur. Landlord is bad enough."

"You drove me to the doctor yesterday."

"Would you believe it?" said Sally, turning to Ian. "The girl was going to take an Uber. Ten bucks to go two miles!"

Or a hundred bucks to go a hundred miles, if he took her up on a second shot at their fairgrounds plan. Moving on from guilt and Ubers and from having to pretend the Big Sur landscape was news to him, Ian remembered he had brought a bottle of wine and a pint of Irish whiskey. He lifted the bottles from the canvas bag he had left by the door with his shoes and then produced one more gift, a copy of *East of Eden*. He was definitely boosting John Steinbeck's sales.

"I should be giving you gifts," said Anita. "Still, I am hoping we can make you sing for your supper. That was where it all began, was it not?"

"All?" said Sally. "Began? Something I don't know?"

"Trust me, we don't know it either," said Anita. "Just a figure of speech. Though we did meet when Ian came to my house in Blaine to sing."

"No one ever came to my house to sing," said Sally.

"You have to be on the shortlist for the morgue, sis, so be glad they didn't."

It was a good meal—homemade lasagna and "Sal's kitchen-sink salad, vegetables in it you never even heard of"—and a good time. They got along easily and well. Sally told Ian he was welcome to stay over, make the long drive back in the morning. She might even cook him breakfast if she woke on the sunny side. "Do you sing in the a.m.?"

Ian had left Fred at home. Sally's super tidy house was not one to welcome pets and it would have been a long dark time for Fred in the car. He might have been able to enlist Ann, except bestowing the dog on her would give rise to the question of where he was going. While there was no reason not to provide an answer, there was an undefined yet weighty reluctance.

There was no need to make an excuse here, either—easy enough to say a simple no-thanks to Sally's hospitality—it was just Ian's reflex to provide one. He could not stay over because he had never in their nine years together left Fred alone in the house all night.

"Oh," said Anita. "I just assumed that your wife—"

"Yes, well . . ." said Ian, "that's also kind of a long story."

"This needn't be a dirge, you know. If you like, we could think of it as a milestone. We could even celebrate it later, as a sort of anniversary."

Polly had come to write the ending to *their* long story and she offered this bit of creative framing under the presumption Ian was still in denial. That indecisive, sentimental Ian would cling to the idea of marriage, through sickness and health and *sturm* and *drang*. In fact, his only hesitation lay in the issue he raised at her first declaration of independence, back in March.

"I can count, Ian. I know very well we can't afford two houses. Fortunately, we don't need another house. As I told you then, the house and the dog are yours to keep."

"I took that for a joke."

"It could be, I suppose, in an Oscar Wilde comedy. In any case, Rosie has a house."

"Rosie—is?" He said this, though he knew Rosie must be Roseanne, formerly Roxanne.

"A dear friend."

"With a house."

"An old farmhouse, actually, with wonderful gardens. Someday—if we do decide to celebrate the anniversary of our divorce the way people do their weddings?—you may want to visit."

"Oh, thanks awfully," he said, Britishing her for some reason. Because she had "bolted"? Upped sticks? Such British touches seemed right for the sarcasm of separation. Still targeting his wife with sarcasm, he surmised he might take a pass on visits to Rosie's country estate. To himself he confessed there was something of consolation in the Rosie development. If Polly was leaving him for "another," it was somehow less of a blow that the other was female. It just was.

Not that he could quite believe it. Polly?

"Does this mean you have gone over to the other side? Is that the phrase for it, playing for the other team?"

"I am an individual, Ian, not a teammate."

"Rosie notwithstanding?"

"Roseanne and I are very close. Very comfortable sharing the house and the world around it. Beyond that, all I'll say is that you should bear in mind that not everything is about sex."

"That isn't what your man Freud says." Ian was virtually strutting, enjoying the argument, if that's what this was. More of a snipefest than a proper argument.

"Freud For Dummies? The gentleman in question wrote forty thousand pages and I have read enough of those pages to know his thinking cannot be reduced to a popular cliché. Besides which, I'll remind you that 'I am not now and never have been' a Freudian."

"Neither am I, Poll. I'm just a layman trying to figure out what the hell happened."

"I'll say this for your edification: it is the 21st century. If two women were to form an alliance that encompassed their sexuality, it would not be a revelation to much of the civilized world."

If two women. Polly was not going to say it and maybe it was not the case. It did seem that women in their circle had been banding together in various ways—afternoon teas, mahjong nights, book groups, casino outings. Ian knew women who had opted for same-sex relationships after ending long-term marriages to men. But his mind was wandering away from the snipefest with Polly and toward broader issues the snipefest hinted at. He was distracted by the fact that the same people who hated gay marriage also hated abortion, even though same-sex marriages would greatly reduce the need for abortion. But no, that was pragmatic and they were purists. As far as many of the purists were concerned, the Supreme Court's reactionaries could endorse eating their young, so long as those babies were first allowed to be born.

Freshly advised by two women, one young and one old, that this was now the 21st century, Ian definitely wished to disassociate himself from the knuckle-dragging community. He could accomplish this simply by telling Polly about his visit to Boulder. He was in the clear, had won his spurs on the issue through Carrie and Baz. Faced with absorbing that rather dramatic shift in the family landscape, he not only emerged morally unscathed, he liked what he saw. Liked Baz and liked how Carrie was in Baz's orbit. There was a rightness to it that so clearly transcended gender.

The problem was that Polly might not know. She probably did, and she would in time, but for now Ian could not risk betraying a confidence. He couldn't use it.

"Seriously, Poll, I am not as hidebound as you seem to think. I honestly don't disapprove of anyone's choices. But it can't be that farfetched for a husband of forty years to be curious how his wife abruptly ceased to be his wife—or even his friend."

He almost stopped himself at the word "abruptly." Maybe it had not been so abrupt.

"I sincerely hope we can get back to that—*be* friends—after the dust settles."

"The dust. Roxanne."

"Roseanne."

"Can I call her Rosie?" he said, slipping back into sniping.

"You see, this is why. Why it will take time. This is you sounding bitter."

"I should sound bitter. I should *be* bitter, but no, that was me sounding frivolous. Searching for shreds of humor here and there."

"You can't see me living with another woman and I can't see you being frivolous, Ian Nelson. And this after forty years in the closest proximity. Honestly, I sometimes think there is precious little to be gained from trying to unlock the chambers of the human mind."

"Little to be gained beyond two hundred bucks an hour. Not to be frivolous."

"My word. Frivolous and *cynical*."

"I thought you could use some new adjectives for labeling me," said Ian. "Besides morbid, and melancholy, and sentimental, and *stupid . . .*"

"I never said stupid. Nor thought it, by the way."

It was over, he knew that, but Ian could not believe *how* over it was, nor could he fathom how lightly the loss of it touched him. Polly had come in like a cold wind, but it was the same wind he had been feeling for months and he had already caught the chill and recovered. Somehow, there was nothing left, nothing worth saving.

He recalled Ella Morehouse saying she and Frank were apart for three years before the final paperwork came and she had to read it, sign it. She genuinely did not care and yet her stomach sank and churned as she affirmed the end in ink. The same thing might happen to him. Polly had driven off, back to Rosie's farm & garden, without speaking the word divorce. Her notion of kindness? Letting the dust settle? He would watch for a lawyer letter in the mail, or perhaps "papers" to be served by a constable at his front door. It was when third parties came into the picture—counselors and lawyers and judges—that the stomach might yet sink and churn.

The curious thing about reaching finality with Polly was that it did remove one serious obstacle to accepting Anita's latest dinner invitation. And the curious thing about that was that he was happier declining, in favor of the charity horseshoe toss on the village green. That would be fun and worthwhile, and he could walk to it.

He had enjoyed seeing Anita but something of the allure, if that was the word, had gone missing. He remembered the compulsion to see her, whether she was a quarter of a mile away or thousands of miles; remembered when *not* seeing her felt like real deprivation. He had not forgotten the feeling, he just no longer felt it. It seemed farther in the past than it was in fact. Anita was the same, just as beautiful, still charming, and needy in a way that made Ian feel needed. It wasn't Anita who had changed, it was Ian.

Declining the dinner in Portland freed him not only for the horseshoe toss—money for the library fund—it also freed him to accept a dinner with the librarian. Again, it was so much easier to go one mile on foot than to go 100 miles in the car. That was a factor. More than that, though, a few weeks had slipped away and Saturdays were Saturdays with all that a Saturday implied; he was reluctant to disappoint Ann.

Was this the call of duty? Not exactly—it was subtler than that. It was the taking-on of responsibility at a time when he wished to be free of all responsibility. A hit song came to him from out of the past, "Ricochet Romance," along with one line from the lyrics, *I don't want no ricochet romance, oh no not me.* Because despite her protestations and reassurances, Ann wanted something she could count on. She was ready for a relationship and why shouldn't she be?

Ian had let this happen. He had been passive, a passive participant with Keely and now with Ann. Another song lyric came to him—they often did, he was a singer after all, probably knew a thousand songs—this one with the line *I've taken up my share of your sweet invitations.* But the sentiment didn't fit. Ian was hardly the rake and rambling boy who knew how to accept sexual favors while keeping apron strings out of the equation. The problem was not that Ian was reborn a libertine, the problem was the sweet invitations. Coming out of the blue, they had simply wrongfooted him. He told himself he would be ready if a third invitation should crop up. He would stand his ground.

He did locate the courage to convey his mixed feelings to Ann, liking her so much yet at the same time determined to steer clear of "entangling alliances." The phrase, both formal and comical in the context, made Ann laugh. She complimented him on his knowledge of history, asked if that familiar bit came from the Declaration or the Constitution.

"Neither. Entangling alliances is in Jefferson's first inaugural."

"How can you know a thing like that?"

"Documents in American History, junior year in college. Two thick volumes of bills and treaties and speeches we were supposed to know one from another. Problem was, the more inaugural addresses you read, the more they blurred. I have no idea why that one stayed with me."

"Look, Ian," she tacked back, "there's no need to quote any speeches or sign any treaties. Or decide anything. And if it helps you, we can keep whatever we're doing a deep dark secret."

It was already clear they could have good times together. Meals, movies, and yes, long walks in pretty places. Sex. Sex was welcome. Ian welcomed it back into his life with but one qualm—that even in the 21st century it carried with it a promise of seriousness. He was not a rake and rambling boy, and Ann was not a product of Generation X, Y, or Z. It was indeed the 21st century, but he and Ann were both children of the 20th century by experience, and sometimes the 19th by inclination.

One side effect of sex—it was private, yet it altered the public aspect, nipped at the margins. Questions arose. To what extent would they go forth as a couple? Would they be invited as a couple to Jack Sutcliffe's wedding next May Day? Would they hold hands in public? Ian was never a hand-holder and had Polly disdained it unequivocally, but Ann was revealed as hardcore: when she said "Look at this," it meant "Take my hand and come look at this."

So, it was too sudden and too soon. Ann kept saying she understood "all that." She understood there was an imbalance, that her hopes were the flip side of Ian's fears. She had been so blithe the first time they were in bed; the second time she was self-conscious, felt she was being judged, apologized for her imperfections. Ian did not expect a fifty-five-year-old woman to be perfect, physically. He had never been perfect, and at sixty-seven felt unworthy even of the word imperfect, since it carried the implication that one came close! *Flawed* would be a better choice. Ian was far from rendering any critical judgments of Ann. If anything, it was his attraction to Ann that was imperfect.

Manageable was the word. Their connection was manageable, where ideally one wants a relationship to feel inevitable. The more Ann expressed her understanding, the more Ian feared she was really expressing her awareness of how imperfect was his ability to reciprocate. Each time she assured him she knew it was *too soon*, she was asking for license to let it ripen. That was the subtext: yes it was too soon, but it was also right, and would ripen in time.

For Ian it would be too soon for any relationship, even one he perceived as ideal. Travel had cleansed the palate, so to speak. It had opened a window, let in some light and air. Each time he saw Ann he enjoyed himself, no question. He never stayed overnight, though, and on each of those occasions he was elated to find himself waking alone to the light and air of a new morning streaming through the windows.

His head was spinning, he told his son. So many changes, coming at him so fast and from tricky angles. Carl, who knew nothing of his father's connection to Ann or Anita (or to Keely, which he simply would not have believed), had to presume any such confusion had to stem from his parents' baffling separation.

"Oddly," said Ian, "it isn't that, though I'm not up to explaining it all. The truth is I couldn't explain it if I tried."

"So things change. That's good."

"Is it? I mean, *yes*, it certainly can be good."

"You adjust. One day you move your catcher to first base, next day you might DH him."

"Right. I adjust. I knew you would translate it into baseball terms for me. So yeah, I guess I'll DH for a while, give the field a rest."

"There you go, Dad."

It was true, confirmed, he was no longer under Anita's spell. Not that she had ever cast a spell, much less extended him any of those sweet invitations. Whatever attraction he had felt toward her had always been at most hypothetical. Rigorously dismissed by the Old Ian as inappropriate, now suitably muted for the New.

What clarified this, oddly enough, was Anita's "sweet and sour sister." Sally, in her unnecessary makeup and unflattering suburban outfits, was equally capable of capturing his attention. In the dimly lit room where they sat that night in November, it was Sally's energy that burned the brightest; her acerbic humor was the salt and pepper on their conversations.

"You know that seven-year guy?" she'd said, referring to the one-in-a-hundred Blob survivor. "That's what really terrifies me. What a hassle it would be to have the girl in my hair for seven years!"

They were laughing at death with this sort of talk, whether at the approach or the retreat of it. "We did enjoy a pleasant little chat about cremation," said Sally. "A cozy little chat about where to relocate the girl. In a different form, you understand. Ashes to ashes?"

"If Richard comes back," said Anita, "she will kick me out. For sure. And unceremoniously."

"Hey girl, news flash. If I ever let that dude come back, I will kick *me* out. Or wait, here's a better idea—get a gun and shoot him at the front door." She raised her right hand and swore: "Just standing my ground, Your Honor. Keeping America great."

"I should jump before I'm pushed," said Anita. "I have thought about moving back to Blaine. I liked it there. But then I realized I'd have to be dead first. Don't you think, Ian? I'd feel too guilty to go back there alive."

"Guilty about being alive? I don't think so."

"I do. You guys sang to me on the assumption I was a goner."

"I'd say that ninety-nine-to-one odds probably qualify you for a serenade or two. You wouldn't even be our first miracle. That honor went to Carter Hodge. He beat the odds."

Ian did not add that Carter beat the odds but did not, in the long run, beat the Reaper. Then again, in the long run nobody did.

"Seven bloody years!" Sally erupted, reprising her putative worst case for harboring her sister. Sally was a pistol. That he could be in the same room with both sisters and respond in kind to each was part of what muted Anita's magnetism. Though it did occur to Ian that another factor (*yo, stupid!*) was that he had so recently "slept with" two other women, real women and not figments, and that such reality might serve to blunt even a subconscious fantasy.

Ann was a sweetie, she was the personification of the benign Copper River culture. Anita was sweet with a definite edge. But there was nothing sweet about Sally, she was out there swinging for the fences. Sal did not care a fig for what anyone thought of her unfashionable utterances. If she had cared before The Big Bang (her phrase for the betrayal by her sister, "my own flesh and blood, mostly flesh"), she did not care anymore. Ian, still inclined toward polite consideration, admired her heedlessness. Still, he would not envy Sally Shumway's next boyfriend. That poor soul was going to reap the whirlwind.

The Last Concert

ANITA HAD COMPLETED another round of treatments and the oncologist told her it was "looking good." He also told her to expect severe headaches and bouts of dizziness, irregular and unpredictable. He put her on a drug called Temodar and told her it would make her nauseous, constipated and, somehow at the same time, diarrheic. "So you see," she said to Ian, "it's looking good!"

It sounded so hard to stay alive that she remained open to a mercy exit, or "Mexit" as she called it. She would go down to Acapulco, pound a few tequilas, and really do the cliff dive. What fun it would be before she landed and died. But then after six weeks on the drug, Anita had yet to suffer any of the pernicious side effects. "Some of our patients do handle the medication better than others," the oncologist told her.

Perhaps infected by her sister's devil-may-care sarcasm, Anita declared herself proud to be providing food and shelter for a Blob, not everyone could say as much. Making it to her birthday in December, her fortieth, was looking like a gimme. Placing her bets, she enrolled in two courses at the community college, Southern Maine, one on the history of 19th century European art, one on documentary photography.

Sally was puzzled. Why learn "all that stuff" if you were going to croak? It was Ian who explained that all the knowledge you gathered in a lifetime would be going with you to the dustbin, whether acquired at age two or ninety-two. Enriching your mind was part of enriching the days of your life. "That's the truth, Sally. The trick is to believe it."

"I guess that's my problem right there," said Sally. "Never did master that trick."

"Besides," said Anita, "you flat out can't die when you have a term paper due. It's like when I asked you to tell me stories. Remember, Ian?"

"Stories?" said Sally, winking at Ian. "Exactly what kind of stories?"

This was kin to Ian's fortune-cookie philosophy of life, the last concert no less valuable than the first. If the last one was futile, then so were all the others, mere useless crumbs along the pathway to Jordan River. Just as The Blob was a reminder that disaster was always lurking, the last concert was a reminder that everything mattered. Like oil and water, life and death existed in colloidal suspension.

Death lurked. Every time the phone rang—through October, November, the first snowfall of December—Ian feared the end had come before Anita handed in her term paper for Art 201. It came as a great relief each time the caller was a robot or a scammer, or led to a pleasant chat with a politician's plebe dialing for dollars. "You have no idea," he said to an idealistic young Bernie sister, "how glad I am it's you."

This stopped her in her tracks, forestalling the stale sales pitch before she even teed it up. "You are?" she marveled. "You're my first positive all morning!"

He felt so relieved and so sorry for her—believing in the good causes, working the phones to such little avail—that he pledged $27. He remembered the figure from the last campaign, all of Bernie's famously small donors (were they all four foot high at the shoulder?) who chipped in what they had in the cookie jar while Hillary was getting here a million, there a million. "I am not necessarily *for* Bernie," he felt obliged to confess, because the money was for the phone-banker, for Rebecca, who sounded too young to vote herself.

Sometimes there were real calls. Harvey checked in, needled him about Ann, tried ridging "the two of you" out to a restaurant. "Not ready to do couple-life," Ian insisted, whatever Harv thought was going on with the two of them. He did go to the restaurant with Harvey and "the wife," and similarly went singly to a few larger dinner parties at friends' houses.

Carl called to tell him Alfie was "rounding third" on his big amphibians project, called again to invite him for Thanksgiving. That would prove to be a high-spirited occasion at which Ian discovered that Alfie had become tall as a Watusi overnight—or possibly during the eight months since Ian had last glimpsed his nephew in the flesh.

Carrie called. They were not going to voyage out on a glass bottom boat but they would be going to Iceland for four days in April. Warm springs, glaciers and geysers, schnapps and vodka. Baz demurred; the trip would be strictly father and daughter. He and Carrie discussed it, refining the plan each time they spoke, and Ian felt sure they would really do it.

Karin did not call—instead she made Ian learn to text. He could do it on his burner, she said, insisting against all evidence that human fingers could pick out the tiny letters on the tiny keyboard. He tried and he learned because he needed to sing. How could he keep from singing when he felt so much better at sixty-seven than he had at fifty-seven?

Anita called, not to report her demise but to report a couple of significant numbers. She racked up a 95 on the Art 201 final, though the ordeal took so much out of her that she "napped" for ten hours afterward. ("Hell of a nap," snapped Sally in the background, her voice cutting in like a whistling firework.) More importantly, the number forty. She had made it, and she wanted Ian to join her and Sally for birthday cake. Ian could perform the official rendition of "Happy Birthday."

That night in Portland, half birthday and half Christmas, "Happy Birthday" was just the opening act. Anita and Sally played piano side by side, sharing the stool, as the three of them sang "Oh Come All Ye Faithful" and "Oft in the Stilly Night" in surprising harmony, the sisters' voices blending into one.

"Beautiful," said Sally. "I mean it really was. This was us singing you right up to Heaven."

"Hardly," Anita protested. "Just up to cake and coffee."

"So this isn't that last concert you two keep going on about?"

Ian and Anita looked at each other and smiled. "Hopefully not," said Anita.

"Not," said Ian. And they let their smiles break into laughter. Sally stood up sighing, said "I'll start the coffee," and left the room.

"Happy Birthday," said Ian.

"Thank you, sir. I am so glad you're here to celebrate with me. So grateful to you, Ian."

"Does that mean I'll be invited to your fiftieth?"

"As if," she said.

And he wondered—because you never did know—which of them was less likely to make it ten years down the road. For his part, Ian was "a young sixty-seven," everyone said so, and for hers The Blob was presently the size of a grape, so at least they were both off to a good start.

Sally returned with a tray, cups and plates, coffee, and slices of cake, and gave Ian one of her winks. Was it a meaningless facial tic, or a confiding gesture? He never could tell with her, so he covered both bases by nodding and winking back. It was one of life's surprises, and there were so many for Ian these days, that the three of them could feel almost like a family, a variant. He recalled the couple in Big Sur who'd kept asking him to join them—for breakfast, for drinks—as if they were assigned to illustrate Polly's third-wheel theory. Ian wondered if he was serving as a useful third wheel here, whether Sally and Anita could be this harmonious only when he, or someone, occupied the third chair. Whatever the case, it did seem to work.

For him, for now, there was this, Portland every now and then, and there was the Angel Band roughly once a month. There was Ann, with Fred. They too were a variant, a threesome that took form more frequently, at least once a week. Then there were the days, the majority of days, when Ian was just an old man with a dog, walking in the park or along one of the Copper River trails. And that was fine, that was a thing, as Carrie would say.

"Why," he said, about to sample the birthday cake, though it bore a frightening proportion of pink icing, "am I so fortunate as to find myself *hanging out* with two lovely young ladies? How did that happen? What did I do to deserve it?"

"Now that is a really good question," said Sally, and they left it at that.

Acknowledgments

FOR HER WILLINGNESS to brave the Vermont snows in order to so generously share her expertise and experiences on hospice singing, special thanks go to Kathy Leo of the Hallowell Singers. Ms. Leo bears no responsibility for any of the author's imaginings, nor is she the source for any of the individual sings described in the story.

About the Author

LARRY DUBERSTEIN WAS born in Brooklyn, New York. He graduated with honors from Wesleyan University and was a Harvard Prize Fellow at Harvard Graduate School of Arts and Sciences. Since leaving academia, he has held parallel careers as an author and a builder, having published ten volumes of fiction and dozens of essays and short stories, and having built and remodeled hundreds of houses. Among other distinctions, Mr. Duberstein's novels have twice been chosen New York Times Notable Books, and his overall body of work earned him the 2020 Ewing Arts Award in Literature. He lives and works in rural New Hampshire with his companion-in-life Lee Brown.